BLOOD CHAIN

J.J. FRANCESCO

Scene and chapter designs by Obsidian Dawn
www.obsidiandawn.com

Background cover photo from CathyK of freeimages
www.freeimages.com/gallery/CathyK

Appo Paint font courtesy of DaFont user, Grafito Design
www.dafont.com/appo-paint.font

Hands cover photo by Kaitlyn Neill

Cover models: Natalie Neill and Lucas Neill

Blood Chain
Rivershore Books
Copyright © 2014 Jonathan Francesco
All rights reserved.
ISBN: 978-0692271186
ISBN-10: 069227118X

FOR YOU

So God created humankind in his image,
in the image of God he created them;
male and female he created them. (Genesis 1:27)

CHAPTER 1

At just past three o'clock on a blistering July afternoon, Seaside Point beach was roped off as a crime scene.
The lifeguards of the popular South Jersey shore point
gave swift reaction to Eric Holden's grim discovery. They
dragged the body on to the sand. A jagged bullet hole
to the forehead was visible. Lack of other visible injuries
intensified the contrast between the wound and the boy's
pale skin. No knee scrapes, no tan. Didn't he even play?

Eric couldn't take his eyes off of the dead boy, despite
fighting the urge to vomit. He wanted to leave but the
corpse captivated him. He knew the boy. Was certain of
it.

At school maybe? Something told him to stay.

"Eric, you shouldn't see this. I'm taking you home."

His father tugged at him but Eric refused to move.
Did not even look up.

"Eric, I know this is scary. But they're going to take

care of him. You don't have to stay here."

"I'm fine." He moved his father's hand off him. "I wanna sit here." He sniffled. "Just a few minutes. Please."

His dad took a few steps back with Eric's five-year-old little sister, Susie.

She hid behind their daddy's muscular leg. Her thin form could almost disappear behind it. She peeked out at Eric.

He could see her knees shaking.

He returned his gaze to the scene. He couldn't even see the body anymore. Everyone else blocked his view.

The beachgoers continued to discuss the situation among themselves. Maybe the victim was a kidnapped victim molested by a sexual predator, then executed and dumped in the ocean. Alternatively, a parent may have abused him and things got out of hand. Perhaps he was being held for ransom, a ransom that was never paid and the penalty for such a thing carried through. Whatever his story was, he became an instant spectacle.

There was not one person who didn't try to get a look at the body and commit it to memory for later description. It looked like they were almost enjoying this.

Luckily, the lifeguards and the yellow tape kept people at a distance, guarding the victim as much as possible from being further robbed of dignity.

Eric felt Susie's fair-skinned arms wrap around him. They rubbed against the dried sand on his skin.

Eric felt his father at his side. He hadn't even seen him come back.

He rubbed Eric's head like he always did. "It's going to be okay, son. You'll be okay."

Eric nodded just a little. A tear rolled down the side of his face but his dad wiped it away and pulled him closer.

Police officers began making their way onto the scene. Within minutes they cleared out the beach and declared it an official crime scene. Anybody who was not a direct witness to the discovery of the body was sent home. Direct witnesses were all asked to give statements.

A shorthaired, African American man walked onto the beach. He didn't have a uniform on like the other cops, but he held out his badge to ensure people knew he was a detective. The man spoke to a lifeguard. The lifeguard pointed right at Eric and the detective began to walk towards him.

Eric's dad shot up. He stood between Eric and the detective. "My son has been traumatized. The only reason we're even still here is because he's too scared to move."

The detective raised his hand to speak.

His father inched closer, staring the detective in the eyes. "You're not going to put him through an interrogation."

The detective adjusted his tie. "I'm Detective Clark and I just want to get a few things straight before we let you leave." His voice carried a compassionate veneer. "I understand your son discovered the body?"

His father made a fist. "Yeah. My name's Burke Holden. I just want to get him home as soon as he lets me. I don't need a bunch of cops swarming him with questions."

"I understand completely." He pointed to the dead boy. "But a child was killed. Surely you understand why we want to get as much information as we can. As quickly as possible. This is someone's son. Somebody's going to want answers."

"Exactly. Things like this are horrible." A beautiful blonde detective approached the two of them. She was dressed in a suit and had her badge clipped to the waist-band of her pants to identify herself. "I'm Detective Julie Martel. And I understand your frustration. I've been at scenes like this too many times." She looked him in the eye. "But if your son can tell us anything helpful at all, we have to know. I'm just going to ask him a few questions. Then you can leave."

His father took a hesitant step to the side. "Just don't push him too hard." He folded his arms. "Eric's been through too much in his life. And this is just adding a whole new load of sh..." He looked over at Eric and saw him looking his way. "Crap...to it."

Julie nodded. "Of course. We won't be long."

Clark scowled at the woman. He blocked her path to Eric and whispered something to her that Eric couldn't make out.

Julie whispered back to him. Eric could hear some-thing about her son Patrick being a little older than him and that he might feel safer talking to her. Everything else was too muffled to understand.

Clark stood frozen a moment. He hesitated but he moved aside. He was clearly annoyed but didn't make a scene about it.

Julie approached Eric with a motherly smile.

Susie ran into her dad's arms. She seemed a little scared of the police officers and hid her face from Julie.

Eric's father took a seat on the sand in front of them. He was watching closely.

Eric looked at Julie. "You wanna know what I saw, right?"

Julie nodded. "My name is Julie Martel, but you can call me Julie." She smiled at him. "I know you probably want to go home. I just need your help for a few minutes.

Is that okay?"

Eric closed his eyes and nodded.

"Can you tell me how long you'd been in the ocean before you found the body?" Her voice sounded like Caroline, his Religion tutor. They had those same caring eyes.

Eric turned to her, still trembling. "I can't remember. Only a little bit."

She gazed into his eyes with concern. "Can you tell me what happened before you found him?"

Eric looked down. "I got smacked down by a big wave. Then I felt something weird under my feet. I was so scared. I've never seen a kid dead before." He fought a sob.

She turned more serious. "Did you see anything weird or strange before you saw him?"

Eric shook his head. "Everything was fine. The ocean was really fun. We were supposed to be having fun. I just wanted to swim. I didn't want somebody to get hurt."

Julie placed her hand on Eric's cheek. "I just want you to know, none of this is your fault. Somebody hurt the boy before you even showed up at the beach."

The body was carried off the beach in a long black bag.

Julie tried to block his view. "You shouldn't have had to see that. We don't have to do this here."

Tears streamed down his face. "I wanted to stay here. So he'd know that he wasn't alone. All the other kids went home. It's scarier when it's all grown-ups standing over you. And I know that's stupid 'cause he's dead and he doesn't care."

"It's not stupid at all. That was very kind of you."

"Does he go to that place where everyone's covered

with sheets, like on TV?"

Julie took his hand. "Yes. I know the coroner there well. She will try to tell us things about his death that can help us find out who did it."

Eric thought of the dark gray rooms he'd seen on TV. He began to feel cold. He coughed up a clump of mucus onto the sand.

Julie patted him on the back and helped him catch his breath. "Deep breaths."

"I'm sorry I didn't see anything that helps." He wiped away drool from his mouth and gasped for air until he settled down a bit. "If I saw something you could find who did it better." He turned away in shame.

She shook her head. "You couldn't have seen anything more than you did."

Eric looked at the empty crime scene. "Can I ask something?"

She smiled reassuringly. "Of course you can."

"What's the boy's name?" He stared solemnly into her eyes.

"We don't know yet. There's no way to tell who he is right now." Seeing his disappointment, she said, "But when I find out, I'll tell you."

Eric was slightly relieved. "Good, 'cause I want to say a prayer for him, and I want to make sure God gives the prayers to the right person."

She placed her hand on his shoulder. "I think God will know who you mean, even without a name."

Eric raised his head again. "Will you catch the guy who hurt him?"

"You bet I will." She sounded motivated. "I'll put the bad guy where he belongs."

Her promise allowed Eric a small smile.

"I think it's time for you to go home." She pushed herself up from the sand. "I have no more questions right now and the boy's not here. There's no need to keep you here anymore."

She took out a sheet of paper and wrote down a phone number on it. "Look, I don't know if you're going to want to talk about this with anybody right now. But I want you to know that you can call me. Just to talk. I've known kids who have seen too many bad things happen to them and their friends and..." A tear formed in her eye. "Maybe you can call me. I'd like to help." She handed the paper to his father. "If you want to, that is."

Eric looked away. "Thanks."

Julie turned to go.

Eric's father went after her. "I appreciate you offering to help more. It means a lot. I'm sorry about what I said to your partner before."

Julie nodded. "It's fine. Take your son home. I think he'll let you now."

She walked over to Clark. "We're done here for right now."

Clark shook his head. "You realize I would've asked the boy the same questions you did, right?"

She turned to him and said, "It's not always about what you ask, Clark."

Clark shook his head. He grumbled under his breath and watched as Julie walked off the beach.

Eric's father helped him to his feet. "Let's get you home."

Clark was waiting at the edge of the beach. "Sorry about keeping you here so long. If we need anything more from you, we'll let you know."

"No offense, but I hope we don't have to see you

again." He ruffled Eric's thick, blond hair. "Eric's going to be scarred by this, and the sooner we can put it behind us, the faster he can heal."

<hr>

It was dark out now. The rest of the day seemed a blur to Eric since he left the beach. He didn't even remember the ride home.

He stared out his window. Nobody was around. It was quiet aside from the sounds of his father supervising Susie's bath time in the next room. She sounded so happy. He wondered if he ever sounded that happy. Or if he ever could again.

The quiet was interrupted by the blare of a motorcycle outside. He watched one of his neighbors ride down the street, turning a corner.

He imagined the dead boy on a bicycle. Had he ridden by the house before?

Eric had seen that face before. Church. School. The mall. Somewhere. He just couldn't remember. Or maybe it was all in his head.

He turned to his dresser and noticed a picture of himself two years younger in his baseball uniform, gleefully holding his bat on the field. He looked so happy then. He picked up the picture and ran his hands across it. He couldn't believe that was really him. He looked up at his reflection in the mirror. The boy he saw staring back was only a few inches taller than the boy in the picture, but they didn't look anything alike to Eric.

He tried to remember life back in that picture—before his mother got sick. He had friends. He never thought about death unless it was a bad guy being killed a movie. In real life, people only died when they were old. He missed thinking that.

He didn't think he could ever smile like that again after what he'd seen today. Even after his mother died, he still clung to the idea that death was for adults. He always knew that kids could die, but it felt like something that only happened on the news.

He put the picture back, turning it facedown. That boy was gone.

He began to pace. He saw the dead boy's face everywhere in the room. On his anime posters. In the soccer ball borders. Even in the crucifix hanging above his bed. He rubbed his eyes and tried to make it go away. But it wouldn't stop.

He heard Susie's dancing in the hallway and then heard her bounce on her bed.

"Eric." His dad knocked on his door. "If you just want to go right to bed tonight without a shower, that's okay. I know after today, you might be a little afraid of the water. I just wanted you to know that it's okay. Just try to get some sleep."

Afraid of water? That was silly. Eric threw his clothes off, leaving them where they fell on the floor. He wasn't afraid.

He walked to the bathroom, slamming the door behind him.

Once in the shower, he hesitated before turning it on. He wasn't sure why but he knew that it wasn't because he was afraid of water. He forced himself to pull the handle. A burst of cold water rained down. He quickly turned it to the left to make it a little warmer.

He stood still a moment as the water dripped from his bangs. He looked down at his feet on the porcelain. They were shaking. He flashed to the ocean again. His feet on the soft chest of that boy, his heels just above the naval.

He moved his hands across his chest to his navel. His skin was just as soft, only he had a pounding heartbeat. He ran his hands down his arms and legs. He tried to remember how tall the dead boy looked and he tried comparing their heights. They had to be close. Everything about that boy seemed so much like himself.

Eric gasped for breath a moment before wailing. Tears spilled from him and mingled with the shower water. He was crying so hard. He never remembered tears like this except for when his mother died.

Eric's legs gave out. He crashed to his knees. He knocked down the metal soap dish, which landed with a loud bang as he fell.

Eric stayed still. He didn't even want to get up. As the water washed over his back, all he thought of was the water washing over the dead body.

Eric's father burst into the bathroom. "Eric! Are you all right? I heard a crash. Did you fall?"

"Go away, Dad." Eric's voice was trembling.

"Eric, you don't have to go through this alone. What happened today was pretty traumatic for you."

Eric stood up. "What do you know?" He punched the wall. "You never found another kid dead. I did. So you can't help. He's dead and there's nothing you can do about it. You can't make him not dead."

His father took a deep breath. "No, I can't. But when your mom died, I tried not to talk about it. It made it hurt more. When I talked to our friends from Church...that did help."

Eric's sobs grew louder. "That boy is dead. He's dead. He's never going to be alive again." Eric took rapid deep breaths. "Yeah, maybe he's in heaven now, but he's still dead. And I still found him. Talking to you, or anybody, ain't gonna change crap."

"No, but neither will letting it get you down. You might not forget what happened, but you can at least make some peace with it. You won't do that by trying to deal with it alone."

Enough of this. Eric had to get away. He shut off the shower and grabbed his towel, wrapping it around his waist and pulling aside the curtain. "Why can't you just leave me alone? Damn it, Dad. Just stop. Nobody can help." Eric stormed into the hall.

His father chased after him. "Eric, I know you're upset. You're right to be. But you can't run from this, Eric." He gently grabbed Eric's shoulder as they entered his room. "You're not going to just get over this on your own. Let me help you."

Eric stopped. He remembered his father holding him the night his mother died. His chest had hurt so much. His father's strong arms made him feel safe. But he was a little kid then. He knew more now. His father couldn't hug away his pain. If only he could...

Eric wanted to run but his legs froze. He missed being little. He missed not knowing about death.

Eric began to sink to the floor, giving up the will to stand. He just wanted to be held again. He let his father's arms catch him.

"Oh Eric." His father gently lifted him from the floor, wrapping his arms around him. "You're okay, Son. I'm here. You're not alone." Eric's father looked him in the eyes. "It's okay, Eric. It's all going to be okay. Daddy's here."

Eric started to wrap his arms around his father. Then he pushed himself away. He walked to his dresser, holding his now-loosened towel up.

Eric glanced at his dad then averted his gaze.

"I love you, Eric. I want to help you. I'm here whenever you're ready to talk." His father walked out.

Eric waited until he heard his father walking downstairs before dressing himself in his checkered summer shorts.

Eric stared at his bed. He remembered his father waking him up that morning—smiling and trying to sing some song about fishing. Eric had laughed before he even opened his eyes. He wanted to laugh again.

Eric felt his chest ache. His dad loved him. He couldn't shake the feelings of guilt for blowing his dad off. He knew that his dad was only trying to help.

He decided to go downstairs. If only to tell his father that he loved him too.

The moment Eric's feet touched the bottom of the stairs, his stomach churned.

His dad was lying on the floor, a narrow, bloody slice across his neck.

Eric ran to his father. "Dad! *Dad*." He touched his father's face—still warm. But his father didn't move. He knelt down. "Dad, we have to talk. Remember? I want to talk now. Daddy! Please." Eric shook his father on the chest. He felt that same stillness he'd felt on the boy's.

His father's shirt grew damp with Eric's tears. "No." He shook harder. "Dad. You can't be gone. You gotta make sure we're okay," he wailed.

Who could do this? He looked around but he saw no one. The front door was still shut.

The killer might still be in the house.

Eric listened for movement. All he heard was the distant hum of the air conditioner. Susie was still upstairs asleep. Eric knew he had to be brave. He had to get her to safety.

Eric took a few deep breaths to get his nerves in order, then darted up the stairs. His foot caught a step, falling forward. He shielded his face with his hands. They stung upon meeting the carpeted steps.

He pushed himself to his feet. There was no time to rest.

When he was upstairs, he ran down the hallway, which seemed ten times longer than he remembered.

He barged into Susie's room. "Susie, we gotta go. Now. Someone bad's here."

There was no reply. She always was a deep sleeper.

"Susie, wake up already." He charged to her bed and shook her.

There was still no response.

He felt something sticky on his hands. He pulled his hands back and saw from the hallway light that they were covered in blood—her blood.

"Susie." He felt his eyes burning again. His chest hurt. He reached down and picked up her dainty little hands. He remembered the proper way she always held her toy teacups that she forced him to play with. He remembered how he broke one of them by throwing it down too hard. He'd bought her a new one last Christmas. It was probably still in this room somewhere.

He kissed her hand. It was still warm. He squeezed it, hoping that somehow she'd wake up, but she didn't.

Afraid to open his eyes but unable to keep them closed, he looked at her and pulled back the covers. A large, bloody gash ran down her chest. A crimson halo stained the sheets around her body, yet her face still appeared peacefully asleep.

Eric grabbed his head as the room began to spin.

He lifted her gently, but her limbs sank like pieces of a broken doll. She was gone.

He sobbed. "Please come back. You can't be dead, too." He brushed aside her auburn curls. "I'm sorry."

His screams echoed in the silence of the house. He'd never heard it so devoid of noise. He could hear every breath he took as if it were blasted through a stereo.

There was an overwhelming metallic iron smell that was almost tangy. Eric realized it was Susie's blood. He never knew blood had a smell before. Her hand still clutched her stuffed kitten, now stained with red splatters. He laid her back down and turned away. It was too much.

Thoughts rushed through Eric's mind. Had she slept through the butchering or woken up? How could he not have heard her screaming?

Then he remembered why he had rushed to get to her in the first place. He was in danger and he knew he had to get out. Susie's windows had been bolted shut for her safety after a series of sleepwalking episodes.

Eric rushed to the hallway. He saw a man hooded in black, holding a bloody knife, blocking the stairway.

"Why hello there." The man took a step towards him.

Eric dashed to his room. He went for the window. A hand pulled him to the ground.

He made another run for the window. Maybe he'd break his leg, but he'd be alive. He wouldn't wind up in that cold place where dead people go. Like that boy. If he could just get outside, he could run to Mr. Nelson's house. Mr. Nelson had a gun.

He was slammed onto his bed. His mattress absorbed the brunt of the fall. Eric stared up into the eyes of his attacker and was greeted with cold, hard glee.

He realized that it was over. All his thoughts about death were about to apply to him.

He watched as the bloodstained blade plunged into his flesh. Agony erupted in his shoulder and shot throughout his entire body. He opened his mouth to scream. The stench of his blood rose to his nose. The cry of a gasp for air echoed in his ears, but his body's plea was denied.

The killer stabbed him again. Eric couldn't tell where this time. The pain just consumed him.

The killer watched in awe as blood poured like a fountain.

Eric coughed up mouthfuls of blood. He couldn't breathe. When would it be over? One minute ago, he'd do anything to live. Now, he prayed for his body to die so he could stop feeling this unbearable torment. He tried a 'Hail Mary' but the prayer escaped his lips as barely a whisper.

The killer plunged the dagger down into Eric's chest, piercing through his still beating heart. In a single second, it all stopped. He felt nothing. His green eyes gazed upon the light from the fixture under the ceiling fan.

Eric saw a light more beautiful than any he had ever seen. He realized that he was no longer in his body. Looking down he saw his own eyes staring back at him, slowly fading away, until everything was consumed by light.

The killer took pleasure in feeling Eric's body go limp. He continued to hack away at Eric's boyish flesh another twelve times.

He turned and looked at the blood splattered on the blue walls and then at the red smear on Eric's Batman sheets. The blood was stained all around the chest and splattered across the hero's face.

The killer ran his gloved hands reverently down Eric's chest. He slid the body off the bed. It landed with a thud. He set it against the bed, hands folded in the lap, a trail of blood leading from the sheets to where the boy now sat. He left the boy's horrified eyes open and stepped back to admire his work.

"It's everything I envisioned."

He gazed at the boy, as if his body was little more than clay and his life's blood mere red paint. He turned to the dresser and set the picture frame upright again. He took a mental snapshot of the entire room and casually walked out, leaving the family to decompose in their pools of red.

CHAPTER 2

Caroline Beasley walked down the steps of her local Catholic Church. As if in defiance of the summer temperatures, she wore a long skirt with a pattern of red flowers and a green short-sleeve shirt. Reverence came before comfort. Her long, curly brown hair rested on her shoulders. She knew the traditional manner in which she presented herself at age eighteen drew both praise and contempt. She didn't care.

The intense heat of the summer had coated her skin in a layer of sweat. She had a slight skip in her step as she made her way towards the corner traffic light.

She saw the worn faces of passing drivers. It seemed she was alone in her upbeat mood. She enjoyed air-conditioning as much as anyone, but she could adapt. Still, she was eager to get indoors. She was adaptive, not inhuman.

As she walked, sweat rolled down her neck and onto her back. She reached into her purse for a handkerchief and a DVD fell out. She caught it before it hit the pavement.

It was a DVD on the life of St. Maria Goretti. Caroline realized that she had forgotten to return it to Burke Holden. Caroline tutored his son Eric.

She had borrowed it for a project the week before. It was his late wife's. Burke liked to watch it on occasion to feel close to her. She had planned to return it the day before but nobody was home when she stopped by. The day was still young so she decided to try again.

She walked the four blocks to the Holden residence, a charming little split level that seemed perfect for the small family.

She walked up to the door and rang the bell. She could hear the ring from outside. The car was in the driveway.

After three minutes of no answer, she rang again. There was none of the usual commotion of "answer the door," "no, you answer it."

She tried knocking. When nobody answered, she peeked in through the side glass but didn't see any sign of the family. The Holdens never walked anywhere. If the car was in the driveway, they must be home. She knocked again.

"That's weird."

Out of mere curiosity, she tried the door. To her surprise, the knob turned.

She gently pushed the door in and stepped inside. "Hello? Is anybody home?"

She took another step. "Hello? Mr. Holden? Eric? Susie? It's Caroline...Eric's Religion tutor." She'd never heard the house quieter.

As she entered the living room, she saw Burke on the ground.

She rushed to him. "Oh my gosh!" She suddenly felt it hard to breathe. "Who? How could...what happened?" She saw the red slice on Burke's neck.

She touched his arm. It was cold.

"Susie? Eric?" She spun around but didn't see any sign of them. What if they saw this? What if they were hurt too? She had to find them.

Caroline pushed herself to her feet. She raced to the kitchen. She looked underneath the table. Then in the cabinet under the sink where Susie liked to hide. Nothing was out of place.

Upstairs. Maybe they were there. They had to be.

She headed for Susie's room.

The sunlight shone through the shades onto Susie's bed. Caroline fell to her knees. Her chest beat with a stabbing pain. She crawled to the bed. She reached for Susie's arm. "Susie..." She flinched. The smell of blood and early decomposition rose to her nose.

She crawled back into the hallway. She took rapid, deep breaths.

She turned to Eric's room. She prayed to find him hiding under his bed. Or in his closet. Alive. As long as he was alive.

She opened the door.

"Oh God!" Blood was everywhere. On the walls. And the carpet. The bed sheets. Even Eric's stuffed frog.

She collapsed.

She gasped for air.

There was a hand sticking out from behind the bed. Dried blood was splattered on it.

A voice inside screamed for her to run. She crawled over anyway.

Eric's butchered corpse sat against the bed. It was

shirtless. She could see all of the wounds throughout his chest and stomach.

She reached out. Her hand was shaking. She placed it against his cheek. Beneath those big green eyes. She caressed his face with her thumb. "Why?"

She shut her eyes and looked away.

She heaved as she tried to inhale air. But she couldn't breathe.

She rocked herself back and forth. Her arms twitched. A sharp chill shot up her spine. She just saw those eyes. Eric's eyes always spoke what he was feeling. Today was no different.

She screamed. Her throat burned with each breath.

Caroline tried to stand.

Where were the police? Somebody must've heard something. She needed to call them. There wasn't a phone in Eric's room.

She stumbled into the hallway. Maybe Mr. Holden had one in his room.

There. On the lower shelf of a night table. She yanked it off the hook and dialed.

Julie walked into the medical examiner's office. It was always gloomy, but the dusk amplified the feeling. She could see the body, already five shades whiter than she remembered, on a steel table as the autopsy on his corpse was being completed. A female medical examiner was standing over the body.

"Cora, how do you do this job?" Julie shivered. The awkwardness she always felt in such a place intensified her heart rate. "Have you found anything?"

Cora scanned the corpse. "It's pretty basic. Somebody placed a pistol on the kid's forehead and pulled the trigger. There's no DNA of any kind on the body. If there was any, the ocean washed it away. Bullet went straight through so there's no bullet to run through ballistics. The size of the wound tells me it was a relatively small caliber gun but I can't tell much of anything beyond that just yet."

"Is there anything else? Can you determine where the murder happened? We're thinking maybe he was dumped from a boat. We're checking with the harbor to see if we can find a lead."

Cora shook her head. "The boat thing's a reasonable theory but the water washed away any possible evidence of where he was killed. So I won't be any help in determining that."

Julie looked at the boy's face, feeling an all-too-familiar knot in the pit of her stomach. "How long has the body been in the water?"

She returned her gaze to the body. "For the time of death, the water does blur things a bit, but I'd place the time of death at about yesterday morning sometime. I'll need a little longer to narrow the window further. The condition of the body also leads me to believe the body was placed in the water hours after death."

Julie rubbed her face. "Why wait so long? The blood from his wound would definitely leave a DNA trail."

"Well, I suppose if it did, you'll find it."

"Were there any signs of sexual abuse?"

Cora again shook her head. "Not a one. There are no other bruises or any signs of abuse on this kid. It was a straight up execution, no games or tortures involved."

The police chief walked into the morgue with a folder in his hand. He scratched his full, gray hair as he entered.

"Hello, Kevin," said Cora. "Maybe you can give her

some of the answers I couldn't."

He looked at the documents in his hand. "Well, I do think I got quite a break on the kid here, so it is something."

Julie approached him. "You find out who did it?"

He shifted his gaze around the room. "Maybe." He opened the file and showed the contents to her. "While we still don't have an official DNA connection, we think we found the kid's only living relative—his father—only he ain't living anymore."

"What? Was he in the ocean too?"

Kevin shook his head. "Nope. They found him in his car on the side of the road near the bay. The boy's clothes were still in the back, drenched in blood. Seems dear old dad put a gun to his head and blew his brains out." He took out a picture of the boy, smiling in a tent with his dad.

Cora looked at the photo and over at the body. "There's still swelling from the time the body was in the water. We'll need DNA to make it official, but it does look like the same kid to me."

Julie stared at the photos of the two. "They look so normal. They always do." Then she remembered Eric's question. "If you know the father, you must know the boy's name. What is it?"

"Well if it's really the same kid, his name's Billy," Kevin said.

"Billy." She set the photo down. "The boy who found him. He wanted to know his name. I saw this look in his eyes. I remember that look in Patrick's eyes after the accident...I'll stop by their place today and tell him. He at least deserves that answer. After something like this, even little things can help."

Kevin nodded. "I'll make sure to look up their address for you."

She smiled "Thanks, Dad."

Returning her thoughts to the case, she bit her lower lip and thought a moment. "So did the father have something going on that could push him to do all of this?"

Kevin's face grew uncertain. "Maybe."

"Well, something had to make him snap enough to shoot his own son."

"If he did it."

She studied his face. "You look unconvinced."

He returned his gaze to the file. "The idea that this guy whacked his own kid is just too damn farfetched for me to buy. Think about it for a second. Why go out of your way to dump your kid's corpse in the ocean only to kill yourself right after? If you're going for the whole murder-suicide thing, the kid's body could stay in the back. It makes no sense to hide the body if you aren't planning to try and get away with it."

Julie nodded. "So you're thinking both of them were murdered by somebody else? Maybe the dad had some outstanding debts or some enemies?"

Kevin closed the file. "I suppose that's possible." He hesitated. "But when I was running his name through the system, I did find a curious police report that makes me think that there could be something else to this. But it's freaking crazy and even I think I could just be seeing things."

Julie held her ground. "I'm standing over a child who was executed. Crazy or not, anything that helps me get the person responsible for it is a lead. We at least need to rule it out. You know as well I do that sometimes the crazy theories wind up being true."

"Well, I found a report for a case from just last week that is still open. It was to a multiple murder and this kid and his father were the ones who discovered the bodies. They found a teenage boy, hanging in his skivvies from a tree in the woods on a camping trip about two weeks ago. There were no signs of sexual assault but the kid's hands were bound, so it was definitely murder. The rest of the family was found dead at the campsite just a few feet away. The remnants of their sandwiches tested positive for cyanide."

"I wasn't on that case but I heard about it. No suspects or anything."

"None. But the fact that the ones who found the body were killed just a week later? It could've been a coincidence, but it was just too freaky. So I looked deeper into it."

"Don't tell me that family found a body too." Julie held her head in her hands.

Kevin scanned through another file. "Afraid so. Well, one of them did anyway. The father of that family killed in the woods found a man beheaded in a canoe during a fishing trip the week before the camping trip."

Julie shook her head. "But this is totally random in terms of MO. Hanging, poison, shooting. Why be so versatile? Why not just stick to one method?"

"Hell if I know. But this does make predicting what he'll do next a lot harder. But his victim pattern is very predictable. I went back as far as I could with this 'chain' of victims, so to speak. At least one of the victims from each murder found a dead body no more than two weeks before they were killed. So it seems like it's not just those who actually find the body but anybody who lives with them that seems to turn up dead. And this pattern goes back about three months. All of the cases appeared to be isolated incidents. But maybe that's what the killer wanted. I think they're all connected."

Kevin handed Julie a few more reports and she rummaged through them. "So the man from the boat found an elderly man, one Frederick Perkins, dead in his bed at a nursing home, from an apparent heart attack."

Kevin nodded. "And that would've been normal had his visiting daughter not also been dead right next to him. She was suffocated. They found strange fibers in her nostrils during autopsy but they didn't match any of the fabrics in the entire facility."

Julie shook her head. "So he brought something of his own. How did he not get caught in a nursing home? During visiting hours?"

"It's probably easier to do during visiting hours. Creep probably blended right in."

"He probably blends in everywhere. He kills flawlessly and leaves his kills in public places. He's confident and comfortable doing this. Even if he's lugging around weapons, it seems he doesn't stand out at all."

She looked through the folder more. "So Frederick Perkins discovered another man in his twenties murdered in the church bathrooms during a carnival. His neck had been snapped while he was...peeing at a urinal." Her eyes widened. "Seriously?"

Kevin shrugged. "I told you this was gonna get crazy."

Julie returned her gaze to the files. "And the urinal guy discovered his coworker dead in a closet at their pizza shop a week before that. Apparent strangulation. And that's as far back as we can trace it."

"I looked that first victim up. Artie Falcon. There's no indication that he ever found a body. So from what I can tell, he's definitely victim number one. Maybe that's where we should start."

Cora raised her hand. "How the hell has nobody noticed all of these connections?"

"None of it seemed connected." Kevin began to pace. "Falcon broke into half the stores at a local shopping center. Apparently destroyed a lot of goods but nobody could ever prove anything to press charges. Cops figured a pissed off storeowner finally did him in. Everything else, the causes of death were so different...there wasn't ever any apparent connection. And I guess nobody thought to look closer." He swallowed hard. "Somebody should have."

Julie set the folder down. "Now I guess we gotta figure out why this killer started where he did. Unless it was just because the target was easy." Julie groaned as she massaged her temples. She pulled out a bottle of aspirin from her pocket, but it was empty. She cursed herself for forgetting to refill it. "So we got some sort of chain serial killer. He chooses whoever finds the body first, and their entire family, as the next targets?"

She froze. She felt a sinking feeling in the pit of stomach.

"But that would mean that Eric's in danger. Why the hell have we been standing around theorizing? We gotta get them all somewhere safe right now."

"We haven't even verified that there's any connection."

"Crazy theory or not. If there's even a chance you're right about this pattern, we can't waste any time."

She turned to Cora. "Call me if you find anything else."

Cora nodded. "Good luck."

Julie bolted out. Her car keys were in her hand by the time she was halfway down the hall.

Kevin rushed after her. "Julie. Hang on. I can send somebody else to pick them up."

"I'm gonna go look up his address right now. Then I'm going to the house myself to get them. Eric knows me. He'll trust me more. Clark should be in any minute. Send him too. We'll need to move fast."

"Julie."

She turned to face him. "I'm not waiting, Dad. When you said that they could be in danger, something inside of me clicked." She thrust her finger out. "I'd rather that father scream at me for upsetting his family than risk them being killed. I have to make sure they're all right."

Kevin and Julie's phones rang. They both stopped in place. Julie's heart beat faster. She fought to breathe. She didn't even have to answer. She knew. She was already too late.

⚬⚬○⚬○⚬○⚬○⚬⚬

Detective Blaine Clark kept a slow pace towards the front door of the police station. "God, I hope I don't run into a Martel."

As he approached the entrance, Kevin burst through. He seemed nervous.

"Crap."

"Detective Clark. Perfect timing." Kevin waved him on. "Follow me."

"Follow you where?"

"There's been another murder. Julie left for it like a cat out of a cannon."

"Why didn't you just have me meet you there?" Clark threw his hands in the air.

"I needed to talk to you."

"Look. If this is about being out of line yesterday..."

"It's not about that, Detective." Kevin opened his car door. "Get in and I'll fill you in along the way."

Clark got in the passenger's side. "Okay, I'm listening. What's going on? I can't remember the last time you went to a crime scene yourself."

Kevin handed Clark a folder and started the car. "There are special circumstances this time. This is one for the books, Clark."

"Okay?" Clark opened the folded and rummaged through the files.

"I don't understand." He shook his head. "What's all this got to do with a new murder?"

Kevin gripped the steering wheel tighter. "They're the links in the chain so far. And we gotta make sure we cut this bastard off now."

As Kevin pulled up to the Holden house, it was already an identifiable crime scene. Police overcrowded the front lawn and walkway. A small mob of curious neighbors had formed as close to the yellow tape as they could get.

Kevin and Clark went inside. Cora was crouched next to the body.

"How'd you get here before us?" Kevin raised an eyebrow.

Cora stood up. "I didn't have to bring anybody." She shot Clark a sly sneer. "Julie's here already. You might want to talk with her. I think she's putting off going upstairs." She pointed to Julie pacing around the kitchen. She then signaled for a body bag for Burke.

Clark looked around at the room. "Doesn't appear there was much of a struggle. He must've been caught off guard. Was probably dead before he knew what hit him."

Julie walked into the room. "The children aren't with him. They might've already been put to bed."

"Cora says you haven't been upstairs yet," Kevin said.

"I'll get there. I was just trying to determine an entrance point for the killer." She pointed to a kitchen window. "That window is low enough to the ground. They're dusting for prints. The windows were unlocked and left open just a hair. Seeing as the air conditioner was on, the windows would've been closed. We know he brought a knife so we'll check the other casing for marks that could indicate a break-in."

Kevin folded his arms. "That's all very good. But since when do you spend so much time looking at a window first thing at a crime scene? Wouldn't the bodies tell us just as much about the kind of killer we have?"

"I looked at the body. Cora couldn't tell me anything more than the obvious yet." She pocketed her hands and twitched a bit. "Are you accusing me of something?"

Kevin shook his head. "No. But you do know what you will find upstairs. And I wouldn't blame you if you didn't want to go up there."

Julie flared her nostrils. "I've seen dead bodies before, Dad. Yes, even little kids. I can stomach it."

"Yeah but you didn't speak to most of those kids when they were alive. There's a difference. Believe me."

Julie stormed to the stairs. "Feeling for the victims is why I'm so good at what I do, Dad."

"I'm not saying you're not."

Clark got between the two of them. "Excuse me, but if Detective Martel can't..."

Julie stormed to the stairs. "I'm fine. I wasn't putting off anything. Now are you two coming?" She charged up the stairs.

Kevin and Clark followed close behind.

⊶◦⟨⟩◦⟨⟩◦⟨⟩◦⊷

Julie squeezed through the officers in the hallway. She could overhear them talking about the bodies. She knew she had to brace herself.

She went to Susie's room and saw the girl's bloody form on the bed. She turned away and covered her mouth.

Clark looked past her into the room. He froze. "What kind of monster could do that to her?"

Kevin said, "Never underestimate how much of a monster humans are capable of becoming."

Julie turned to the light coming from the room painted blue—Eric's room. "He seemed like such a good kid. I hoped he would work through what happened yesterday. Lead a normal life again...there's just no sense to this." She noticed that she'd made a fist with her right hand. It was shaking. She held it close to her to avoid punching a wall.

Kevin put his hand on her shoulder. "Something like this is never sensible."

She moved his hand off of her. "I know that. It doesn't make it easier."

"Look, Julie. If you can't handle this."

"I told you, dad. I'm fine. I just care that a family's dead. The more I care, the more likely it is that I catch whoever did this." Julie walked into the room.

She saw Eric's body against the bed. She knelt down before it. She stared into the empty green eyes, which had sparkled with fear and innocence the day before. In a voice barely above a whisper, she said, "If I had known... If I had any idea, I would've stopped this from happening to you." She wiped aside a tear. "I can't imagine how scared you must've been, and it's my fault. I should've been able to prevent this. I'm sorry, Eric." She cried.

Clark looked at the boy's blood-drenched body and the stained surroundings. "I've been a cop for almost ten years. And this is still worse than anything I've ever seen."

Kevin turned away. "Then consider yourself lucky."

Clark fought tears. "I don't get it. Why go to such an extreme? How many stab wounds are there? There's gotta be at least ten."

Julie took hard, rapid breaths. "I guess the killer decided that this time he'd knife the family, and make each subsequent death more horrific than the one before it."

Kevin asked, "What makes you think the boy was killed last?"

Julie looked up at him. "Judging by how the gruesomeness escalated from Burke to Susie and from Susie to Eric, I'd say it's a viable theory. Burke and Susie seemed to have been caught off guard. Burke was flat on the ground and Susie was in her bed. But this shows signs of a struggle. There's a lot of blood collected on the bed." She stood up and took a closer look. "And the blood's on the lower side of the bed. The sheets are a mess. Like the killer threw him onto the bed to kill him. That tells me that Eric likely wasn't in bed when the killer came. He probably knew the killer was coming and tried to get away, but couldn't."

She turned to the doorway. "Plus, struggling with him and then stabbing him this many times would have made a lot of noise. If the others were alive, they'd have heard Eric being murdered and they wouldn't have been found where they were."

Clark motioned with his hand. "He could've moved

them from where he originally killed them."

Julie shook her head. "There's too much blood collected around the bodies and none anywhere else. He didn't move any of them this time."

Clark nodded. "Okay. But if they would've heard Eric being murdered, why wouldn't he have heard them being murdered?"

"Well, if the killer came up behind Burke with the knife already in hand." She walked behind Clark and put her arm around him and pretended to slash his throat. "Then he would've been dead almost instantly. If the killer made sure the body didn't hit the ground hard, it wouldn't have made much noise."

She walked to the doorway. "Susie was probably asleep. If he did it quickly, it wouldn't have made much noise. Eric's is the only one that would've made significant noise because it was the most violent and it seems like Eric was the only one who saw the killer before he died."

Kevin nodded. "I can agree with that."

Julie went to the window. "This is just big enough for Eric to fit through..." She turned back to the body. "I think maybe Eric might've seen what happened to one or both of them. He was trying to get away. If the killer couldn't let him get downstairs, he might've been trying to go out the window. The killer pulled him away before he could. That's probably when he threw him onto the bed." She felt chills shoot through her body. "He was just a kid. He never had a chance."

She walked over to the body and again crouched down in front of it. "Poor thing. All the fear and pain he must've felt. He probably died quickly but he didn't die instantly. He felt at least some of these." Tears rolled down her face.

Kevin kneeled down beside her. "Hey, we're going to get whoever did this."

She nodded. "I know. I just wish we figured out this connection sooner. We could've saved them. I failed them." She buried her head on his shoulder.

Clark threw his hands into the air "Hey, we're not supposed to get emotional like this. We're police. We're supposed to be professional. We got killers to catch. We ain't going to bring these people justice by standing around crying."

Kevin stood up and faced Clark. "These victims aren't just cases. They were people. They had lives too. I know that we gotta try to be as impartial about this as we can, but sometimes you gotta feel."

Julie wiped her eyes. "He's right. I have to get it together."

Clark shook his head. "You do that. I'll be waiting in the hall."

Kevin turned to her. "The girl who found them is in the master bedroom. We should question her. So we can take her somewhere safe."

Julie nodded and took deep breaths. She felt her hair on her face and brushed it back. "I know. It looks like your theory was right. She's going to be in serious danger. I just have one thing I need to do."

She leaned over to Eric's body and placed her hands over his eyelids and gently slid them closed. "His name's Billy. I hope you get to meet him now."

With his soulless stare covered, he looked at least a bit more at peace.

Julie caressed his hair and face with her gloved hand. "He deserves at least some dignity." She got up and followed Kevin out of the room.

She could hear the violent sobs of Caroline from the opposite end of the hallway. Judging by the frantic voices of other officers in the room, there wasn't much luck in getting coherent answers from her—just half sentences and crying.

Julie walked into the room. "I can take it from here. Could everyone give us some space? We don't want to crowd her."

Aside from Clark, all of the officers obeyed without hesitation.

Julie turned to Clark. "You too. I think she'll be more comfortable with just me here."

Clark shook his head. "I'm staying right here. You're a mess. We need someone on this case who can remain stable on the job."

She turned to Kevin. "Dad, a little help?"

He groaned. "Sure thing."

Kevin placed his arms around Clark and picked the tall man up a few inches off the ground. "Sorry about this buddy." He winced.

Clark unsuccessfully fought Kevin's grip. "What the hell?"

Kevin said, "Julie asked me to remove you. She doesn't need you distracting her or the witness."

Clark struggled to withhold a holler. "This is highly unprofessional."

"I'm a man of results." Kevin set Clark down outside the room. "Professionalism is overrated." Kevin quietly shut the bedroom door behind him.

Relieved at the silence, Julie sat down on the bed next to the trembling girl. "I'm Detective Julie Martel. If you're able, I just need to ask you a few things. Is that okay?"

She waited for the subtle nod before proceeding. "How well did you know them?"

Caroline tried to control her tears and shaking. She sniffled and pulled away from Julie. "We went to church together. I was Eric's religion tutor. Mr. Holden wanted to make sure his son got properly educated in the faith. He promised Mrs. Holden that before she died. He didn't think the parish school was really good in that department."

She sniffled and more tears spilled down. "I knew those kids since they were babies. I remember when Mrs. Holden died. It was so sad, but they had their dad, so I knew they'd be all right." She gazed up at a picture of them on the dresser. "Susie, she had such personality... and dreams too. I just knew she was going to do a lot with her life. Maybe she wouldn't be a dancer like she said, but you just knew her attitude would take her far." She and Julie shared a laugh. "And Eric? Well, he was a boy so of course he had the things that come with that." She smiled as she shook her head. "But he was a good boy. He would've been a good man. I remember after my dad died last year, he came over to my house with a flower and told me that he was sorry for my loss. He told me that he knew how I felt, and that he was going to pray for me."

Julie smiled. "That sounds so nice. I didn't realize he was such a gentleman. But I should've known. When I spoke to him yesterday, he was very lovable."

"He was great. They all were." Caroline sobbed and held her face. "Mr. Holden worked so hard to support them but he always found time to play with them too." She turned Julie. "How could somebody do this to them? How could somebody just murder them like that? Somebody sliced Susie open like she was some animal. And poor Eric... there was so much blood. How could they do that to a little boy? Somebody just butchered him."

"I don't know why anybody would do this." Julie eyed another photograph of Eric and Susie on a dresser. "But I need you to help us find them. Anything you can tell us would be helpful."

"Like what?"

"Can you describe the scene as you found it?"

Caroline tried to recall. "I was just coming to return a movie. I rung the bell and knocked several times, but they didn't answer. The car was in the driveway so I knew they were home. The door was unlocked, so I let myself in. I saw Mr. Holden first. I thought maybe the kids could still be alive. Hiding in a closet or something?" She shivered as she folded her arms. "But then I found them like that. There was so much blood. Their bodies are so small, but they had so much blood around them. So much blood. I didn't know such small bodies had so much blood." She buried her head in her hands.

Julie patted Caroline on the back. "I know that must've been horrible."

Caroline stared ahead at the dresser. "I remember Eric's First Holy Communion last year. He looked so handsome in his white suit. I just can't believe that he's dead now."

"Do you know anybody at all who would want to do this to them? Any enemies?"

Caroline shook her head. "Nobody. Nobody would want to hurt them. Everybody who knew them liked them. They didn't have enemies."

Julie sighed.

Caroline turned to her and gasped. "Why, were you hoping they had enemies?"

"In a way, yes." Julie realized how this must've sounded. She paused a moment and tried to choose the right words. "If they had enemies of some kind, it would give us some suspects. Plus, if enemies did this, it would've also discredited something else I feared."

Caroline lowered her eyebrows. "What are you talking about? Do you know something?"

Now Julie avoided eye contact. "Caroline, we're going to have to take you into protective custody."

Caroline's eyes widened. "What? Why?"

Julie returned eye contact. "We believe there's a serial killer on the loose, and in all likelihood, you will be his next target. Any family you live with too."

"I don't understand."

"We think that the killer is choosing his next targets by seeing who finds his last victims. Whoever that is, he goes after them and their families." Julie took a breath. "Yesterday, Eric found the body of a boy in the ocean who had been murdered. We didn't see the connection until it was too late. But after this, we believe that you are definitely in danger. And I'd like to make sure we keep you safe."

Caroline scrubbed her fingers over her face. "This can't be happening."

"It is. But I promise you, we're going to do everything in our power to keep you and your family safe." Julie placed her hand on Caroline's shoulder.

Caroline shoved Julie's hand away and shot up from the bed. "I don't have a family. My dad's dead and I haven't...It's just me now."

"Well, then in a way, that's good. We only have to worry about keeping you safe."

"So what, I gotta change my name and leave town?"

Julie shook her head. "Not right now. We hope to

catch this guy quickly and hopefully once we do, you'll be okay."

Caroline exhaled a deep breath. "Okay then, when do we leave?"

Julie stood up from the bed. "I'd like to get you into hiding as soon as possible. It only took a few hours for the killer to attack the Holdens after they found the boy's body. I want you in a secure location by this evening."

"Then I guess we'd better get to my place now to get my things." Her eyes widened. "I can take some of my things right?"

Julie nodded. "Yes, you can. But let's make it quick. I don't know what this guy's planning and I want to be prepared for it."

Caroline nodded and took a few deep breaths. "Then I'm ready."

Julie opened the door and escorted Caroline into the hallway. They could see the bodies of the Holden children both being zipped up into the grim black bags. Julie couldn't help but feel the irony of Eric being carried away in the same way he had seen Billy carried away just a day before.

Julie said the 'Requiem Æternam' under her breath. She'd known it since her mother taught it to her as a girl. She couldn't help but remember all the times she'd said it since. "Requiéscant in pace."

Julie watched the bags until they were out of sight.

Caroline asked, "What will happen to them?" She swallowed hard. "I think they bought a family plot after Mrs. Holden died but I don't think they have any near family. Who's going to claim their bodies and make sure they get buried where they're supposed to?" She struggled to hold in tears.

Julie sighed. "I don't know. But I will look into it. But right now, they gotta go to the morgue. They'll do autopsies. Maybe they'll find some kind of clue on the bodies." Julie had grown scornfully accustomed to such phrases yet the words still stabbed her soul each time she said them.

Caroline turned to Julie. "Will I be able to go to the funeral?"

Julie put her arm around the girl. "I'll see what I can do."

Julie led Caroline down the stairs. Caroline attracted the eyes of all the cops in the place. Julie could feel them seeing the girl as the possible next victim. She saw Caroline's face and knew that she must've felt it too.

Kevin met them at the bottom of the stairs. "You ladies ready to go?"

Julie nodded. "We are."

Caroline didn't say anything. She looked back at the house.

Julie looked back as well. Just a day before, it was a warm and loving home. Now the Holdens would never live there again. Their lives there would be erased piece by piece.

<hr/>

With Julie by her side and two armed guards posted in the hallway, Caroline took out her apartment key from her purse. She fumbled as she tried to get it into the lock. "Darn..."

Julie held out her hand. "I can get that if you like."

"Thanks." She handed Julie the key.

Julie unlocked the door and let Caroline in first.

Julie looked around the living room. "It's small."

"And I can barely even afford this." Caroline set her

key down on a ledge.

Julie sniffed. "Do you smoke?"

Caroline turned to her. "No..." She took a whiff of the air and twitched at the foul stench. It was the smell of her childhood—the childhood she'd lived to escape from.

Caroline looked around until she saw the source. She was standing by the window, holding the offending cancer stick. She cracked a smile and exhaled a puff of smoke.

"Mom?" Caroline gasped.

The woman turned around, revealing her frazzled, blonde hair and a wrinkled face. "So what's with all the cops Cari? You finally take after me and get involved with the wrong guy?" She chuckled. "I knew you would. Eventually. Despite your naïve protests to the contrary." She exhaled another puff of smoke.

Caroline scowled at her. "No, Mom. I don't have a boyfriend. I live here alone."

"So the cops are for *you*?" Her mom smiled. "What law did you break?" She scratched her chin. "Did you bomb an abortion clinic?" She widened her eyes with glee.

Julie stepped forward. "Caroline did not break any law. These cops are here for her protection."

"And who the hell are you?" The woman turned to Julie with contempt.

"I'm detective Julie Martel." She flashed her badge. "This morning, your daughter found the bodies of a family who was murdered. We believe she's in danger as a result and are preparing to move her to a secure location."

"A secure location? You mean like witness protection?" The woman seemed truly stunned.

"Witness protection is long-term. We hope to have her return home as soon as we apprehend the suspect."

The woman rolled her eyes. She clicked her tongue and shook her head.

"But we need to get her there as soon as possible." Julie took a step towards her.

The woman turned to her daughter. "Oh good. Then I can stay here."

Caroline looked at her mother like she was crazy. "What do you mean stay here? Don't you still have your own place?"

The woman blew out a ring of smoke. "Naw, Ricky got that in the divorce. I've been living in a motel for about a month but..." She shrugged. "Money's tight. And the hardass landlord decided that he didn't want to give me another two weeks to come up with the rent." She pointed her bags on the floor. "I sorta got thrown out. So I figured that I'd come here and stay with you."

Caroline rolled her eyes. "Because we've been so close since I left?"

"I thought you might turn me down 'cause of that spat we had a few months back. But if you won't be living here for a while, I don't see why I can't crash here."

Caroline froze in speechless disgust.

"You're supposed to be this good and holy Christian. Would a Christian throw her mother on the street?"

Julie stood between Caroline and the woman. "Excuse me ma'am. I apologize if I'm out of line. But you just found out that a murderer could be after your daughter. Is your only concern whether or not you can have her apartment while she's in protective custody?" Julie inched closer to her. "Your daughter is in grave danger. You should be concerned for her well-being, not whether or not you can freeload off of her."

The woman gasped. She thrust her cigarette in Julie's

face. "Excuse me but I clothed and fed her for sixteen years. I think I am entitled to get a little in return."

"She's being targeted by a murderer. Don't you care about that?"

The woman laughed. "Oh please. She'll be fine. I've been engaged to more dangerous men than whoever you think is after her."

Julie leaned in so that her face and the woman's nearly touched. "You know, I really can't stand to be in the same room with you anymore. You're totally indifferent to your daughter's life. As a mother, your attitude is really starting to piss me off."

The woman pulled back. "Then have a glass of wine, lady."

She turned to her daughter, faking a grin. "So honey, can I stay here or what?"

Caroline's wiped a tear from her eye. "You know what? If you want to stay here...where a killer is probably going to be looking for me, then go ahead."

Her mother gasped. "The nerve..."

Caroline marched off to her room.

<hr />

Julie followed Caroline into her room.

Caroline sat on her bed, tears dripping onto her sheets. She stuffed clothes, a small Blessed Mother statue, and a framed photograph into a small suitcase. She tried to zip it shut but the zipper caught. She groaned loudly and punched the suitcase.

Julie walked over. "Allow me." She smiled and pushed the clothes in flatter until she could close the suitcase. "You did a good thing. Standing up to her like that."

Caroline folded her arms. "Doesn't feel like it." She shut her eyes. "All my life, I just wanted her to give a damn. About me." She shook her head. "But now I see that even if a killer's after me, she's most concerned about what she can get out of it."

Julie was moved with pity for the girl. She sat down next to Caroline. "You're a great young woman. I can tell. Any mother should be proud to have you for a daughter. She's a fool for not wanting to nurture a relationship with you."

She grunted. "I doubt she sees it that way."

Julie knew she was right. "Then it's her loss." She took a deep breath. "I know I'd do anything to make sure I have a good relationship with my son. And if..." She stopped herself. Caroline didn't need to hear her baggage. "My mother. She died when I was just a little bit older than you. But she was great. She once told me that when she was twelve, her mother walked out on her. Never gave much reason. She just said she needed to 'find herself.' Whatever that means. My mother never was close with her mother but she said it still hurt like hell. She still felt abandoned. So she resolved to be better. No matter what. And 'til her dying breath, she kept that promise."

"What's your point?"

"My point is that we can't choose our parents. We're given what we're given." She put her hand on Caroline's. "But we can choose to be better. When you're a mother, always remember how your mother made you feel. And make sure you do better."

Caroline shrugged. "You don't think she's already ruined me?"

Julie shook her head. "Not from what I see."

She saw Caroline give a tiny smile in agreement. She looked at the clock. Almost four. "We'd better get going in a minute." She stood up. "Is this all you're packing?"

She looked around at various photographs, religious articles, and trinkets. "You can take more than this. We don't know how long this is for yet. If you want to pack another bag, I can help."

Caroline gave a tearful smile and nodded in agreement.

⊶◠◡◠◡◠⊷

Julie escorted Caroline to a secluded apartment. Kevin and Clark were waiting there when they arrived at a secret suite on the top floor. Patrol guards were posted in the halls.

Caroline looked at it a bit unimpressed. "Another apartment..."

"We're hoping this will be a safe place where we can make sure this guy can't get to you. We have you checked in under an alias and will have armed guards posted at all times. And with any luck, you can go home very soon." She held out her hand to the kitchen. "It's fully stocked, and it won't cost you a cent."

Caroline didn't look at her. She walked around the living room to a window and back again. She sighed and shook her head.

"Look, I know this isn't ideal, but we couldn't leave you at your place."

"It's not that. This is fine." Caroline took a seat on the sofa. "It's just...I can't stop thinking about them."

Julie sat down next to her. "Neither can I. If you need to talk, ever, about anything, don't hesitate to call me." She handed Caroline her number. "Sometimes talking about something can help us get through it a lot easier."

"Thank you." She pocketed the card.

"And remember, there are going to be officers posted outside your room and throughout the halls at all times.

We're doing everything we can to keep you safe."

Caroline got up and began to pace. "I appreciate it."

Kevin approached them. "Well, we'd better get out of here and let her get settled."

Julie stood up. "I agree. We need to start figuring out ways to find this guy."

She turned to Caroline and waved with a smile as she followed the rest of her team out of the apartment.

Caroline walked to the window and watched as Julie got into her car and pulled away. Caroline liked her.

But could Julie find out who did it in time? Caroline wasn't sure.

She turned to investigate the quarters and took a deep breath. They were small but actually larger and nicer than what she was used to. She took a seat in a large rocking chair.

She began rocking back and forth. She thought of Susie dancing with her and Eric sending remote controlled vehicles after her. She remembered seeing them at Church carnivals and bazaars. She'd even had dinner at their house once. They were a family. They were happy. Now they were gone. All of them. It was wrong. Her chest hurt as she thought about it, but they deserved to be remembered—to be mourned.

Caroline's thoughts turned to her own situation. She could hear the guards outside the hall whispering. She didn't know how one day could change her life so much. Not only was that beautiful family gone, but she couldn't shake the feeling of being hunted. And the hunter was closing in.

CHAPTER 3

All quiet on the front of the serial killer. The press had already nicknamed him the Blood Chain Killer, much to Julie's chagrin. Naming him would only stroke his ego. Caroline's officers reported no suspicious activity. She spent the rest of her day, bored, confined to the apartment, with mindless television and predictable novels as the only viable sources of entertainment.

Julie looked at the wall clock above her father's desk. Six o'clock. "Darn. It's getting late. I should be getting home to Patrick."

Kevin slid his chair back from his desk. "Why don't I drive you?" He grabbed the case files from his desk. "It's been a hard day and I'd like to see Patrick. After all this crap with dead kids, I kind of need a hug."

"Thank you," she said. "I think that's a great idea. Patrick will love to see his grandfather." Julie hid the fact that she knew his kindness wasn't totally gratuitous; he expected her to invite him to stay for dinner—he hated eating alone.

It was just after six thirty when the duo finally arrived at Julie's quaint little two-story in a family-friendly development. Comfortable, but cozy, plenty big enough for a small family.

Julie felt more eager to get inside than usual. After the things she had seen, she wanted so badly to take her son in her arms and never let him go.

She walked through the front door and immediately caught sight of her thin, eleven-year-old son writing down something on a tablet at the dining room table. He was wearing an innocent and heartwarming smile. "Hey honey. I'm home!" The sunlight from the window highlighted his light brown hair, which also contained trace hints of blonde and red.

"Hey Mom. Glad you're home." He set aside his homework without a thought and strolled into the living room.

Julie ran to him. "Hey there kiddo. It's good to see you when I come home at night." She gently placed her hand on the back of his head and gently stroked his soft hair. "I missed you." She kissed him and then pulled him into a tight hug. It was so good to feel him in her arms. She never wanted to let him go. To let him leave the place he'd always be safe.

"Mom," he whined. "Come on. Mercy! Mercy!" He chuckled. "I'm too old for this kind of hug."

She laughed and forced herself to let him break free. "Deal with it."

She locked eyes with his bright and gentle baby blues. "I love you so much Patrick."

His eyes narrowed as he focused on hers. His smile

faded. "Did you have a hard day, Mom?"

She chuckled to shelter him from what she knew. "And what would make you ask a thing like that?"

Patrick looked at her compassionately. "It's kind of obvious, Mom. I'm not a little kid anymore. You don't have to worry about making me upset."

"Guess I can't argue with that." She rose to her feet. "I did have a hard day, but it got a lot better now that I'm back home with you."

He smiled. "Good to see you too." He then saw Kevin standing by the door. He signaled to him to come further in. "You just going to stand there or say 'Hello' to me?"

Kevin approached Patrick and ruffled his hair. "I gotta say 'Hello'? Isn't my presence here enough?" He gave him a fist bump and the two laughed. "You know I like having an excuse to come and see my favorite Grandson. How you doing Patrick?"

Patrick pulled back. "Okay, I guess. I've been writing a lot of stuff for camp. Journals..." He shot Julie a shifty glare. "But I'm just about done."

Patrick's nanny came into the living room. She had been his nanny since he was three. Her long black hair complemented her olive complexion. "Oh good, you're home." She took Julie's things from her and set them down beside the sofa. "Welcome home Julie," she said with a smile. "Did Patrick tell you the surprise he had?"

Julie's eyes widened. "Surprise? No, Patrick didn't tell me a word about a surprise." She turned her gaze interrogatingly to Patrick. One look from her peering eyes convinced him that he had to fess up.

He hid his hands behind his back. "Well, the reason I am still writing in my journal is cause I kind of helped Karen make dinner. It's in the oven now."

"Help?" Karen spoke with a tone of astonishment. "He practically made the whole thing by himself. If anyone was helping, it was *me* who helped *him*. And I'd say it was more like supervising, since he really did all of the work."

Julie sniffed the air. A wonderful aroma was swirling around and greeting her nostrils in a warm burst. "Oh, it smells divine in here. It smells like chicken, very good chicken." She closed her eyes a moment to fully appreciate the inviting scent.

Patrick's face lit up at hearing the praise. "It is, and I also have special potatoes as a side. I hope you like it."

"Well if it tastes half as good as it smells, I am sure I will love it."

Karen said, "It's done now. It's ready whenever you are. However, I have to be going."

Julie went to stop her. "No, stay, we'd love to have you."

Karen picked up her purse and swung it over her shoulder. "Sorry, I got other plans. I do hope that you enjoy your dinner." She flashed Patrick a wink. "I know Patrick worked very hard on it."

Julie felt proud of her son, who looked pleased as he watched her reaction to his work. "Okay, thank you." She turned to Patrick. "And thanks for helping Patrick make this. I'm sure he was glad to have some help to surprise me."

"No problem Jules. Hope you three have a good night. The table's already set." She headed for the front door. "See you, Patrick." She waved as she walked outside.

Julie and Kevin walked Patrick to the couch and sat him down. She placed her arm around him. "So, where did you learn to cook this, Patrick?"

He tensed up a bit and blushed. "Well, they had a cooking class at camp teaching us to work with easy recipes. They said we should try to make it at home and record it in our journals. We broke into groups of five and each group got a different recipe to make." He pointed to a recipe card on the coffee table. "This is the one I got. I think it was the best one there. Milo got something with butter and squash and it looked gross. He said he liked it but I know he was lying. But mine really did look good. So I wanted to surprise you and make dinner."

She kissed the top of his head. "Well you did." She gave him a high-five. "I can't wait to try it." She pulled him tighter into a hug, prompting a giggling squirm from him.

She tickled him and caused him to laugh. "Okay, Mom, I get it. No need to squeeze me to death."

She looked him in the eyes. "I haven't squeezed you to death yet, have I?" She smiled.

Kevin hopped up from the sofa. "Well, *I* definitely worked up an appetite today. I hope you made enough for seconds."

"Of course I did. I like being prepared. Plus, they told us to make the whole thing. And it's for five people."

Kevin laughed and patted his stomach. "Well then, let's eat."

Julie and Kevin felt growing anticipation to see what Patrick's first-cooked meal would be like. The places were properly set and the plates perfectly arranged with the meal. Light trails of steam shot up from the dishes.

"I'm already impressed Patrick. Heck, I'm *more* than impressed." Julie took in the steaming chicken and potatoes. "I think my son has a gift." Julie gave Patrick a pat on the back.

Patrick smiled.

The three ate supper together after a prayer.

The only thing Julie loved more than Patrick's dinner—which tasted even better than it looked—was seeing his joy when she and Kevin gave it the thumbs-up.

After the satisfying supper was completed, Kevin bid the two farewell. Patrick finished his homework, showered, and changed into his green summer pajamas, and joined Julie for an evening in front of the television. They sat on the sofa with all of the lights turned off—their favorite way to watch television.

When it was nine-thirty, Julie looked at the clock. "Well, I hate to break it to you but it's time for bed."

Patrick pouted. "Can't I stay up a little late tonight?"

Julie shook her head. "Not tonight, Patrick."

"Alright..." Patrick sulked as he trotted up the stairs. After an extended seven minutes in the bathroom, he finally dragged himself to bed.

Julie quietly walked into his room to tuck him in. "Alright, kiddo. I want to see you asleep by ten."

Patrick stared at her a moment. "Mom, how come you don't ever tell me what's bothering you? I can handle it, you know."

Julie nervously fiddled with her hair. "Did I say something was bothering me? It was just a hard day. I'm fine."

"Something *is* bothering you, Mom. I can see it." He gently took her hand. "You always tell me that I gotta talk about my problems. Don't you have to do the same thing? I won't freak. No matter what. I promise."

She sighed. She looked into his eyes and couldn't brush off the earnest look he gave her. "I interviewed a boy yesterday. He had found a dead body. Today, I found out that he was murdered and I had to go investigate at the crime scene."

Julie tried to hide her pain but she could tell Patrick saw it.

"That must've sucked."

Julie felt herself fighting tears. "It did."

He looked into her eyes. "It was bad wasn't it?"

"Very."

Patrick was silent a moment. "How old was he?"

Julie wiped aside a tear. "Nine."

"No wonder you're upset." He placed his hand on her arm. "I'm sorry Mom. I know you really hate when kids are killed. Especially after Petey."

Julie nervously fidgeted on the bed. "Patrick, I really don't want to talk about that tonight. I just want to go to sleep and get a break from all of that."

"Okay, I understand. Sorry I made you tell me."

She stroked his cheek. "You have nothing to be sorry about." She leaned down and planted a kiss on his forehead. "I love you." She smiled.

"I love you too, Mom." He reached his head up and kissed her on the cheek before turning over on his side.

Julie sat and watched him a moment. For a boy who protested going to bed so much, he always seemed to fall asleep quickly. She could hear the sounds of his faint snores within minutes. She kissed him again.

He looked so peaceful. She savored it a moment. He'd be outgrowing things like this soon. Most kids his age probably already had. She prayed that whether he did or not, that she'd always have him. He was her joy. She had to always make sure he was safe. Even if one day, he wasn't as receptive of her.

"Goodnight, Patrick." She slowly got up and quietly

closed his door as she left.

∞◦⟨◦⟩◦◦◦⟨◦⟩◦◦◦

Caroline awoke to find herself on the floor. She was breathing heavily and sweating. The nightmare of reliving the events of the day was still fresh in her mind. She looked back at the bed and grabbed the sheets, pulling herself to her feet.

She looked at the clock. "Eleven twenty-three." She sighed. It was going to be a long night.

There was a knock on her bedroom door. A female cop walked in. "Are you all right? I heard a bang."

"I'm fine." She brushed her hair off of her face. "Just a little uneasy, I guess."

"Well, just be careful."

"I will."

"By the way, there's a new officer coming on duty in a few. I'll see you tomorrow. You try to get some sleep hon, okay?"

Caroline nodded. "Have a good night."

The woman left and Caroline moved to the window and glanced out. She could see the lights from a plaza not too far away. They almost appeared to flicker. "I don't think I'm going to sleep much tonight."

She left her bedroom and walked into the kitchenette. She picked up a glass and filled it with water from a pitcher in the fridge. She took a sip. Swallowing hurt.

There was a knock on the door.

Caroline jumped before remembering that the guards were about to change shifts.

She took a deep breath before approaching the door, opening it a crack and said, "Yes, can I help you?"

A handsome young officer stood in the hall. His bright blue eyes and light brown hair made her feel somewhat more comfortable. She cracked the door a little wider.

The man said, "I just wanted to let you know that we just changed shifts. I'm Tony, and I'll be your new guard. There's another out here in the hall. If you need anything, don't hesitate to holler, okay?"

Charmed with, but suspicious of, the good-looking protector, she said, "It's pretty late. How'd you know I'd still be awake?"

He laughed. "Because the other officer just left and told me?"

"Right." She chuckled, feeling a bit embarrassed for having forgotten. "Do you want to come in?"

"Just for a minute. To make sure you're all right." He quietly stepped over the threshold. "I know you're probably not in any condition to sleep but you really should try. You've had a hard day and are going to wear yourself out if you try to stay up all night."

"Well excuse me if I don't like seeing dead children in pools of blood every time I close my eyes." She accidentally knocked a vase off a mantle as she threw her arms into the air. It landed on the coffee table and shattered upon impact. The sound of the collision echoed in the empty room. She held her hands to her face.

He quickly gathered the pieces of the broken vase and tossed them in the trash.

"I'm so sorry," she said with a tremble. She was ready to cry.

He smiled. "You got a killer after you. You don't need angry old ladies on your case too. It's understandable to be upset given what you've been through. But still. You might wanna keep the noise down." He handed her a tissue. "Anyway, remember what I said. I'm here if you need anything. I could make you warm milk or something."

She forced out a smile. "Well thank you very much. But really, I'm fine."

"You *should* try to get some sleep. You're going to see their faces either way. Might as well refresh your strength so you can deal with it better."

"I guess you're right." She motioned for him to sit down. "Feel free to watch some TV or something. I don't know what's on this late, but they must have something. I think there's some kind of coffee in the pantry if you need something to keep you awake."

"I think I'll be all right. I'll be just outside if you need me." He smiled. "Have a good night."

"You too." She subtly waved before returning to her room.

◦◦◦◦◦◦◦◦◦◦

Kevin stayed up late, hunting through the case files thus far on all of the victims. He looked for some possible connection or motive, but it became clear that they were looking for a disturbed individual. "Why can't people just kill for unpaid debts anymore?"

He'd know a bit more in the morning when the autopsies of the Holdens were completed. Maybe there would be DNA this time.

Kevin decided to revisit the files of the initial victims.

"First victim, Artie Falcon. Typical thirty-year-old bum. Went to college to party. Majored in Art instead of anything worthwhile." Kevin rolled his eyes. "A real quality human being." He continued looking through the file. "Got his jollies from petty crime. Once broke into an office and painted the walls with a car wreck." Kevin held his hand in the air. "The guy was a freak. No wonder that when he turned up dead, nobody cared. People probably just thought he finally rubbed the wrong person the wrong way. Perfect first victim to keep the cops off your trail, I guess."

Kevin took a sip of the cold coffee that had been sitting in his mug for hours now. He stuck out his tongue in disgust after he swallowed. "Why do I insist on torturing myself?" He angrily set the mug back down and looked at the next file. "So Artie's death didn't leave much suspicion but why didn't we connect to the co-worker? It seems some people were suspicious but we actually thought this was a mugging gone wrong? I so gotta have a talk with some of the people around here." Kevin lamented that so many murders had to occur before he noticed a connection. "None of the scenes were ever really the same. Is this guy trying to be a different killer with each subsequent murder? He's definitely lacking any discernable pattern in how he kills."

Kevin rubbed his head and moaned. "There's gotta be an easier way to figure this out." He laid his head back to catch some shuteye for just a minute. He dozed off and didn't wake until dawn the next morning.

<hr />

While the unknowing players in the psycho killer's game slept, he quietly moved about unnoticed. The perfect state in which to carry out his next crime.

As he sat on his bed, he took a sip of cranberry juice. He smacked his lips and placed the glass back on the table. He reached into a jar on the night table and dipped his finger into it. When he pulled it out, a red liquid substance stained it. "This will be the best yet. I can't wait." He rubbed his finger against the wall and smeared a long, red trail.

CHAPTER 4

Julie awoke to the shout of "Mom."

She opened her eyes. Almost seven.

"I'm coming." She groaned and turned over. She was not ready to face another difficult day just yet.

Patrick rushed into her room and shook her. "Mom. Time to get up. Detective Clark already called and asked where you are."

Julie yawned and sat up. "Of course he did." She hadn't fallen asleep until almost four o'clock. That was usually when she started to wake up.

She groaned as she got out of bed. She realized she was still in yesterday's clothes. "Give me a few minutes to freshen up and I'll be right down."

Patrick nodded. "Sure. What do you want me to say if he calls again?"

"Tell him that his time would be better spent doing his job. I'll be right down."

"Cool. I already made breakfast. That'll save you some time."

She fiddled with her hair a moment. "You made breakfast?"

Patrick leaned against the wall. "Well I poured the cereal and the orange juice. I don't know how to make omelets...yet."

She smiled. "I don't need an omelet, honey. But thank you for getting everything ready."

"No problem. But you'd better get moving. I don't want you to get in trouble."

"Don't you worry. Detective Clark cannot get me in trouble. Even though he thinks he can."

She sent Patrick downstairs so she could shower and change into fresh clothes.

She then went to the kitchen to a simply set breakfast table. "Looks nice, Patrick."

"Thanks" He took a seat and began eating. "I waited for you."

She took a few bites for Patrick's sake and sent the rest down the garbage disposal.

Patrick downed what was left of his glass of orange juice. "You'd have a lot more energy if you ate breakfast, Mom." He set the glass down.

Julie took his glass and quickly washed it in the sink. "I'll grab some coffee on the way to work. That's all I need to get going." She set the glass to dry on the rack. "Plus, with everything that's been going on, breakfast just doesn't agree with me anymore."

"Yo Patrick! Let's go." A boyish shout sent an echo through the neighborhood.

Julie said, "That's Milo. You'd better go. Before he wakes up the entire neighborhood." She stuck her tongue out.

Patrick grabbed his backpack full of things he'd need for the day and swung it on his back. "Have a good day Mom." They exchanged cheek kisses.

He then darted out the front door to a black-haired boy waiting outside with an almost identical backpack. The boy's brown eyes looked eager and impatient.

Julie waved to the two as they walked off for camp.

As they disappeared down the block, she wondered just how much they knew about the murders. A part of her felt uneasy letting them walk to camp alone, but it was only a few blocks to the youth center. She knew she shouldn't worry. The mothers around town always made sure they looked out on the children who passed their homes on the way to camp or school. She told herself that they were safe.

As she turned to go inside, she noticed a flyer on her front door. It was for a local amateur art gallery. She half-glanced at it. Two pictures were on the cover. One was a half toddler, half zebra. The other a shirtless young man with his hands bound behind him.

"No thank you." She stuffed it in her back pocket and went inside to finish getting ready.

Patrick followed Milo down the driveway. "You're early today."

Milo shook his head. "Damien is in one of his moods today. He's got a Calculus test for his summer school. And he's being a real jerk about it. Mom wasn't telling him to stop being mean to his only little brother, so I got out. And we can get to camp early and hang out."

"Good thinking."

He turned to Patrick. "You okay?"

"Yeah." Patrick let out a sigh.

Milo chuckled. "Doesn't sound like it, dude. What's up?"

Patrick shrugged. "Nothing. I just think my mom's having a hard time at work."

"Is it that blood chain killer?" Milo got Patrick's attention. "He's all over the news. Nobody knows who he is and he never leaves any evidence behind so the police can't catch him. Everybody's talking about him. It's like one of those crime shows come to life."

"I guess that's it." Patrick sulkily looked at the ground. "My mom's good at her job." He returned his gaze ahead. "If anybody can catch this guy, she can."

"I hope you're right. This guy sounds really nuts. Wouldn't want him attacking the camp. Then I wouldn't get to throw a water balloon at Sheila Hess. And she has it comin'." He kicked a pebble in his path.

Patrick didn't offer his usual laugh.

Milo tapped his arm. "Cheer up. Maybe he'll make a mistake and leave some evidence behind next time? It's possible right?"

Patrick was unsure. "Well if he does, my mom will find it."

Their conversation then transitioned from real killers to anime villains as they completed their walk to camp at the local playground.

⊷⟨⟩⊶⊷⟨⟩⊶

When she got to work, Julie saw Kevin and Clark waiting for her in Kevin's office. "Any updates on the Holden case?"

Clark showed her the files on Kevin's desk. "Well, the autopsies are done. Cora said she wants to see you, but we decided to wait for you. Thanks for keeping us waiting."

Kevin shook his head in playful disgust. "We just got the news literally one minute ago. Don't let this guy try to fool you."

She mockingly patted Clark on the shoulder. "Don't worry. I know when ole Clarkey is pulling his act a mile away. Now let's not keep Cora waiting."

Kevin sat back and stretched his arms back, bringing them to a rest behind his head. "She asked to see you, not us. You're the one she's tight with. We're going to stay here and try to figure out who did all of this."

"Any leads?"

He flipped mindlessly through the case files. "So far nothing. Aside from the first victim, a crook who everybody and their mother had reason to pop, nobody had any real motive for whacking these people. They were all living normal low-profile lives. No real evidence left behind. Nobody ever saw crap. Frankly, whoever killed might as well just pressing a button from miles away. Do people really not pay attention or is he just this good?"

Clark said, "No killer is this good. He had to leave some kind of clue."

Julie approached Kevin's desk. "Let me see some of the previous crime scene photos. Maybe there's something we missed."

Kevin rolled his chair back. "If you can see something in there that we missed, by all means, give it a whirl."

Clark folded his arms in frustration. He said to Julie, "Didn't you want to go pay Cora a visit?"

"She can wait a minute." Julie examined the files.

Julie gazed over each photo carefully. The first one seemed like a basic murder by strangulation. Nothing at all off. The body was left amidst brooms and cleaning supplies. The second crime scene showed the victim lay-ing on his back on the floor, a stream of urine flowing from his body to the urinal.

Julie held up the picture somewhat disgusted. "Kind of messy this one. Unnecessarily so. A few more seconds and there'd be a lot less mess, and risk of DNA trails."

Kevin rolled the chair forward. "Maybe he wanted to make sure the element of surprise was on his side."

Clark nodded in agreement. "Yeah, killers aren't usu-ally concerned about leaving a mess behind."

Julie stared at the photo shaking her head. "It just seems strange to wait until the guy was actually in the process of urinating to kill him. He could've killed him before or after with just as much surprise. Why kill him while he's peeing?" She took a look at the third one. "And this one!" She held it up. "The old man in the bed is dead and his daughter is slumped over with her head on his chest. They almost look like they're sleeping, but they're dead." She set it down and picked up another. "And the fourth guy has his head cut off, but the killer left the oar and the fishing rods on the boat between the head and the body."

Clark took a seat. "Yeah? I don't get it. What's your point?"

Julie continued with the next picture. "This next one. The campsite shows everybody dead in their sleeping bags, except the one sleeping bag of the boy the killer decided to hang. He's mostly undressed, which could symbolize rebellion of some sort, as his parents are right there. No kid would really take such a risk, but what if the killer decided to do it as some sort of artistic fantasy. 'I'm goofing off right in front of you and there's nothing you can do about it.'"

Clark looked at Julie with a confused stare. "A boy is hung in his underwear, a way millions of people sleep, and you somehow think the killer was going for some deeper meaning?"

Julie rolled her eyes. "Why not?" She showed him the picture. "He went through the trouble of stripping the boy to his underwear but didn't sexually molest him in any way? There was no sign that the boy had bathed within the hours before his death. If he was doing anything else in the woods, he wouldn't be totally undressed because nobody else was. Somebody his age isn't going to take any unnecessary risks only a few feet away from his parents. He might want to have the guts but he wouldn't. His parents are sleeping just a few feet away. He's going to be extra careful to not get caught doing anything, and yet this picture screams the opposite. It doesn't make sense unless the killer had a hand in it. It also has the added moral of his reckless attitude getting him killed."

Clark tapped the desk a minute. "Maybe the killer just wanted to throw us off the scent."

Julie shook her head. "No, if you look at every scene from the second murder on, they all have some sort of pose to them. They aren't just typical shoot and run murders. The killer went out of his way to not only make each one entirely different from the other, but he made them into some sort of twisted scene. If you look at the boy found in the ocean and the Holdens, that pattern remains true, especially for Eric Holden." She picked up the photos from the Holdens' crime scene. "His body was sat against the bed with blood smeared from the sheets where he was killed to where the killer situated his body. His corpse was arranged so that he was sitting against the bed. The intensity of the kills escalated with each kill. In his mind, maybe that means something. I think our killer might actually have a calling card after all."

Kevin took Julie gently by the hand. "Jules, that's a good theory, but it's also a really big stretch."

Clark laughed. "A stretch? It's ridiculous. Nothing in any of these is beyond explanation. And the first guy was a pretty straightforward kill, which breaks your theory."

Julie took a look at the photos. "A dirty crook being stuffed in a cleaning closet isn't exactly devoid of symbolism." She froze a moment. She remembered the flyer on her door that morning. She yanked it out of her back pocket, thankful that she'd been in too much of a rush to toss it. "And I think I know a good way to test this theory out. I found this on my front door this morning. I remember thinking how insane it looked but I had seen paintings as crazy as it many times before. Especially at that art fair that rolled into town last year."

Clark rolled his eyes. "Yeah. Art's crazy. We all know that. What does art have to do with this case?"

Julie handed him the flyer. "Take a look at this. The painting on the cover of the hanging guy looks almost exactly like the crime scene. It looked so gross that I didn't even make the connection until I saw crime photos again. But if you look closely, it's eerily similar to the crime scene from the murdered people on the ground to the young man hanging from a tree with his hands bound just a few feet away." She took a deep breath. "Maybe the killer painted that scene before or after committing the crime. Or maybe some other sicko painted it and the killer is a fan copying the poses. Either way, this is not only a huge lead but it gives us a possible signature. The killer is posing his victims to create some sort of twisted art scene."

Kevin and Clark were left speechless.

"Maybe the first guy is the key." She examined the photos of his murder closely. "He was an art student right? Maybe he knew others into art, and maybe if we find out why they killed him, we can find out why the rest of these murders happened. For some reason, somebody's started this killing chain. And he shows no signs of stopping until we catch him. His victimology is the pattern in which he kills. So it's extremely specific. Yet at the same time, random."

She again pointed to the crime scene photos. "What if this guy is an artist and he sees killing as a form of art? Look at what he did to those bodies. He went out of his way and took a lot of risks just to pose some of them." She closed her eyes. "What if the bodies are like his sculptures and their blood is like his paint? It's crazy. I know that. But if it's true, it does explain a lot. It's worth looking into, isn't it?"

Kevin sat with his hand on his chin and began tapping. "Well, I can't deny, it's a possibility." He sat back in his chair. "It explains some of the weird ways of discovering the body. Since he chooses his next targets by picking the household of the first person to stumble upon his work of art, he might view them as his audience."

Clark gasped. "You gotta be kidding me. You believe her theory?"

Kevin exhaled a deep breath. "Doesn't matter what I believe. Right now it's the closest thing we have to a lead or a workable theory. At least it gives us an angle to investigate that we didn't have before. Why don't you let me look into this dead art student's murder and see what I can dig up?" He turned to Julie. "Jules, you'd better get to Cora before she gets pissed and cremates the bodies."

Julie shook her head. "I think she's gotten used to being kept waiting." She allowed herself the faintest of smiles. "But you're right. I'd better go. Hopefully I'll come back with something. And then we need to investigate that art gallery. There's no address on it. There's probably some game to find out where it is. But we'll find it."

Caroline opened her eyes to a bright sunlight. "It's morning already? Night went faster than I thought." She stretched her arms in the air. For a moment, she forgot about the grim events of yesterday. And her current predicament. After a moment she remembered the blood, the lifeless stare in Eric's eyes, the wounds. She remembered that she was the next target of the monster who did it all. "Damn it." She sulked as the dreams faded from her mind.

She got herself together and changed into casual clothes. She felt her stomach growl. "Guess I forgot to eat yesterday."

She walked out of her bedroom. Tony wasn't there. She didn't know why but was disappointed.

Caroline checked the fridge and pantry to see what could serve as breakfast. Before she could finish, she heard a knock on the door. "Guess that's the next shift."

She headed to the door, checking her hair in a mirror before opening it. Just in case.

She found Tony standing in the doorway with a handsome smile showing his pearly white teeth and a covered platter in his hands.

"My shift ended half an hour ago, but I saw the food in the fridge and it was pretty bad. So, I picked you up some real breakfast. I told the officer on shift in the hall to grab a coffee on the corner. I figured as long as I'm here, you'll be safe. No need for him to suffer through another hour for nothing." He chuckled. "Now, I know you're upset but you gotta eat." He took the lid off of the platter to reveal the meal. "I didn't know how much you like to eat so I got the largest portion size they offered."

Caroline's eyes widened as she gazed upon the sumptuous cuisine greeting her with it's fresh scents. Romantic gestures were completely foreign to her, but if this is what they all felt like, she immediately considered herself a fan.

She tried to regain her composure. The very fact that she felt happy swamped her with guilt as she recalled the Holdens. She tried to act neutral to control herself. "Thank you so much." She opened the door to him. "I was hungry. Come on in."

"Thank you Miss Beasley." He carried the platter in and set it down on the kitchen table, lifting the top off to reveal the small smorgasbord of food choices. Three fluffy buttermilk pancakes with a slowly melting square of butter and dripping syrup, golden scrambled eggs with cut-up breakfast sausage links baked in, three sizzling strips of bacon, and a hefty serving of steaming well-seasoned fried potato cubes. "I even got some ketchup if you wanted it." He held out a few packets.

She placed her hand over her chest and slowly gazed at the meal. "Nobody's ever done something like this for me before." She felt afraid to let go of the grief she had been carrying for the past day but this young officer seemed to make her feel like it was okay. "This is too much. You really shouldn't have done this."

He pulled out a chair for her. "It's not your fault for what happened to that family. You shouldn't be weighed down by grief and guilt. You need something to help relieve the tension. What relieves tension better than a good, hot meal?"

She took a whiff of the breakfast. "It does smell really good, and I'd hate for you to have wasted your money for nothing." She looked closer at the food. "But I actually cannot eat all of this by myself. Not enough room." She ran her hands up and down her flat stomach in a rather unconvincing manner.

Tony saw right through her tactic. "Look, I don't care if you eat it or not. You can just taste a little of everything and we can toss the rest. It's not that much money. I just wanted to give you some nourishment. What you've been through can take a lot out of you. So, just eat what you can. You can always save any leftovers for later."

She walked closer to him. "Actually, I was thinking that maybe you could join me? I don't really want to eat alone today."

Tony smiled. "I was hoping you'd offer that." He again pulled out a chair for her at the kitchen table. "Donuts for breakfast get old after awhile, and yes, cops do eat a lot of donuts. It's a stereotype for a reason."

Impressed with how much of a gentleman and comic the young cop was, she gladly took her seat. "I don't really pay attention to stereotypes. I doubt you really fit one anyway."

"If you say so." He took the seat opposite her. "Let's eat up."

She took a bite of the potatoes. The taste brought back memories of pancake breakfasts at her childhood church. "Wow, you really know how to pick 'em don't you?"

Tony smiled. "Yeah, I like to think so." He took a bite of a sausage patty. "Boston crème hasn't ruined my palate yet."

She smiled as they shared another bite of the elegantly presented breakfast. They enjoyed every bite until only a few remnants of ketchup and grease remained on the plates.

He wiped his face with a napkin and gently pushed the plate forward. "Did you like it?"

She set her napkin down on her plate. "I really did. I'm not used to being pampered. But even more than the good food, I enjoyed the company." She became silent for a moment. "It's kind of hard to appreciate food when you always eat alone. And after yesterday, I almost feel guilty enjoying anything."

"I understand. I enjoyed it as well." He reached for her hand but pulled it back before she had the chance to react. "And don't feel guilty. You're alive. There's no reason why you should pretend otherwise."

⚬━⚬━⚬━⚬

Julie made her way to the morgue where the Holdens were all laid out on separate tables. She could see Cora impatiently tapping her foot as she waited for her.

Cora caught sight of her and unfolded her arms. "You know, I work hard to get you quick answers on this case. The least you could do is not keep me waiting."

"Sorry." Julie walked further in. "We stumbled onto a possible lead. What do you find?"

"Well, I can tell you that the dad was likely killed first, then the sister, then the boy. The killer used the same knife—a dagger—so some traces of blood carried over into the later victims. Also, some traces of both of their blood were found on the boy's hands so he likely discovered both bodies before he was killed. The causes of death for the first two are obvious." She showed Julie the slice in Burke's throat. "The father's throat was slit. A simple and quick kill." She then moved to Susie's body and hovered her finger over her wound. "The girl died instantly when the dagger was plunged into her heart. The rest of the injury is just overkill."

Julie asked, "What about Eric?"

"The boy? He's a bit more interesting." She pointed to the knife wounds on his shoulder and pubic region. "These stabs were delivered while he was alive. He was most likely killed with the next thrust, and that was this one right here." She pointed to the wound from where the knife had pierced Eric's heart. "This one went straight through. He was dead instantly after that."

Julie winced as she saw the deep cuts in his flesh. "Why make the boy suffer? Why not make it quick like the others?"

Cora sighed. "You're the one who gets into their heads, not me. But if you're going to stab someone ten times, I doubt you care much if they suffer."

Julie shook her head in disgust. "What about the rest of the wounds? If Eric was already dead, why make over eight more?"

Cora gazed over the body. "My guess would be to make blood leave the body faster." She thought for a moment. "Or he wanted to make the scene more gruesome."

"That would go with my theory." Julie thought of the crime scene photos as she visually examined the wounds.

Cora became interested. "You got a theory? Do tell."

"It's not proven yet." Julie looked at her. "But I have a hunch that our killer might like art, and these murders are a way for him to make some twisted kind of lifelike art."

"I'd buy that." She shifted her gaze to Eric. "That explains why this kid has more holes than Swiss cheese when it would've only taken the one in the heart to finish him."

Julie gazed over the boy's pale body. "It's so sad that

somebody could do this to a child."

Cora followed her. "It is. But that's people for you. Sick and depraved."

"Is there anything else interesting about the bodies?"

"Well, I am not sure. There was something."

Julie's curiosity was piqued. "What is it?"

Cora showed her a sheet with a small particle of something. "That was on the kid's shoulder. I'm going to have it sent to the lab, but from what I can tell, it's some kind of paint."

Julie gazed intensely at it. "Paint? As in, an artist's paint?"

"Yep, and it's not water colors either. Unless the boy liked to paint, I'd guess the killer must've left it there when he was handling the body."

Julie pulled back. "Well, it looks like my artist theory might be right after all."

"Your theories usually are. Anyway, that's about all there is to tell with these three."

"No DNA? Anything? A hair? A print?"

Cora shook her head. "Guess he was careful." She looked compassionately at their lifeless forms. "Poor family, two days ago they had the rest of their lives ahead of them. Now they're just gone."

Julie focused on them for a moment and thought. She turned to Cora. "Are there any funeral arrangements yet?"

Cora shook her head. "We've tried to contact next of kin. But can't get a hold of any. They didn't exactly have any close relatives. So right now, no funeral arrangements. The three will just have to stay here until somebody shows up to claim them."

Julie tensed up. "What if nobody shows up to claim

them?"

"You know the answer to that question full well Jules." She struggled to hold back some tears. "At least they'd be together."

Julie looked at the lifeless family. She felt for them. Their lives mattered. They deserved better. She imagined Eric and Patrick becoming good friends if they had they been introduced. They were the kind of people she became a cop to protect. Now this is where they were. It didn't seem right. "People shouldn't be thrown in a Potter's Field or cremated and forgotten. They deserve to be mourned and remembered, especially children."

"I agree." Cora clutched her twitching wrist.

Julie gave Cora a serious stare. "If nobody claims them, call me." She turned to the pale forms of the Holdens. "This family deserves a proper burial."

"Indeed." Cora covered the bodies with a sheet. She laid them in drawers and shut them away.

As Julie left the morgue, the images of the family's wounded bodies flashed in her mind. She resolved even harder to find whoever did it and make him pay.

<hr />

After only a little bit of conversation, Caroline really felt herself drawn to the handsome young officer. He was everything she'd ever imagined in a guy. Even his very eyes captivated her. She found her mind finally finding a break from the endless barrage of grief that had overwhelmed it the previous day. She almost felt happy again.

Caroline became a bit flustered from the abrupt change. Not only was this man a relative stranger, but after what had happened yesterday, it was entirely inappropriate. "Would you excuse me a moment? Be right back."

Tony smiled. "I'll be waiting."

Caroline darted off into the bathroom. She took a series of deep breaths after she closed the door. "Get it together Caroline. This is not time to start something like this." She turned the water on and splashed the cold liquid on her face. "I'm too old for this." She grabbed a towel from the rack to dry her face.

After a few more deep breaths, she straightened her hair and went back to the kitchen. "Sorry about that, sometimes I just need to rush off..."

She melted into horror.

Tony was sitting at the table with a bullet hole in his head.

She screamed and ran over to the body. "What happened?" She shook him for a moment, knowing he was gone.

Then it hit her. The killer must still be in the apartment. "He found me." The thought had barely had a chance to register in her mind when a gloved hand covered her mouth. She squirmed to break free but was too weak to overcome the strength of her foe. She was helplessly dragged away.

<hr/>

"What do you mean she's missing?" Julie shouted into her phone as she got the call about Caroline's disappearance. "How does somebody in police protection just go missing?"

Julie rushed to the scene. Clark and Kevin were already there. She saw the bloody corpse of Tony still seated at the table as pictures were taken.

"What happened?" she shouted as she stormed into the room.

"Police protection failed. That's what happened," said

Clark.

"Do not joke with me. I am not in a mood to be joked with." She wiped sweat from her brow. "And why is there a dead cop in the room?"

Kevin said, "From the looks of things, he was having breakfast with Caroline. I guess our killer decided it was good enough to make him part of the household. Or he was just in the way."

Julie looked around. "Any sign of Caroline at all?"

Kevin looked at the kitchen. "Not a one. No signs of a major struggle. And no body."

Julie tried to keep herself together. "So that means she could still be alive?"

"You know better than to think that Jules." Kevin gently placed his hand on her shoulder. "This guy hasn't ever left a victim alive."

Trying to get past the grim likelihood of Caroline's fate, she promptly shifted topics. "What about the dead cop?"

Kevin said, "What about him? He tried to score a date with the lady of the not-so-protected apartment and he wound up in the wrong place at the wrong time. I guess the killer thought that killing him at the kitchen table was artful."

"I have a feeling this was just a murder of convenience. Caroline is his artwork; this cop is just an afterthought." Julie turned to walk out and grabbed her phone.

Kevin asked, "Where are you going?"

Julie turned to him. "I'm going to find this creep. And Caroline. I'm not going to sit by and wait for another body to drop in some twisted pose." She rushed out of the apartment and into a quiet stairwell of the building. It was the only place on the entire level not crawling with cops. Leaning against the rail, she began to cry, restraining herself to keep herself from losing total control.

Trying to smother her weeping, she opened her phone and prepared to dial a number, but decided she required was a personal visit. She dialed the number and left a brief message on the voicemail. "I need to see you. You know where." Then she closed the phone and exited down the stairs.

The church bells rung loudly, signaling noon. However, the inside of St. Claire's Catholic Church was quite quiet and desolate. The bells were only muffled sounds mixed with the shouts of children playing in the soccer fields behind the church.

Julie humbly approached the altar and genuflected towards the tabernacle before getting into the first pew. She sat down on the edge of the smooth, wooden bench. She whispered as many memorized prayers as she could remember off the top of her head. She felt her heart aching and struggled to keep from lashing out in anguish.

"It's rare to see you here in the middle of a work day."

Julie opened her eyes. "It's rare I have a case that upsets me this much." She turned to see a nun, wearing a habit, skirt, and vest all powder blue, with a white top underneath the vest. The nun took a seat next to her.

"So I guess this is why you wanted to talk to me?" The nun took Julie's hand.

"Well Sister," she said almost sarcastically, "I guess living in a convent all these years hasn't ruined your perception abilities." She laughed through her tears. "Remind me again why I'm the one who became a cop and you're the one who became a nun?"

"Because you wanted to shoot crooks and start a family and I wanted to enter the consecrated life?" The nun raised her eyebrow.

Julie nodded. "That might have something to do with it."

"What's wrong Julie?" She stroked Julie's hair.

She tearfully shook her head. "Oh Olivia, everything."

Sister Olivia wrapped her arm around Julie. "I'm not just a nun you know. I'm your sister. You can talk to me. That is why you called isn't it?"

"There's this killer on the loose." Julie sniffled. "I think he's just claimed another victim, a beautiful young woman. She goes to this Church, I think. We had her in protective custody cause we knew he'd be going after her next, and I thought she'd be safe." Julie turned to Sister Olivia. "But she's missing now, and it's very unlikely we're going to find her alive." She looked towards the altar. "Today I visited a family in the morgue I had met two days ago. An entire family. Father, a son, and a daughter, all murdered by this deranged killer. They can't seem to contact relatives to claim their bodies yet. So until somebody does, they're going to lie naked and undignified on a cold slab."

Sister Olivia looked ahead as well. "Well, remember that, as much respect as we owe the bodies of the deceased, when somebody dies, their soul goes into eternity. We should bury our dead, certainly. But the souls of that family aren't in that morgue."

Julie wiped some tears from her eyes. "I know. I guess I just feel that they were good people. They didn't deserve what happened to them, and they don't deserve to be neglected like this. And now somebody else is missing? Not to mention all the other victims." She took a few breaths. "I guess I'm just a little angry. I believe in free will. I don't blame God for this. I'm just angry that a person could make a choice like that."

Sister Olivia said, "It's understandable. In difficult times, it seems so hard to keep the faith." She clutched her rosary. "But we have to do it anyway, as hard as it is. I think it's easy to walk away from faith when bad things happen. If you say that there's no meaning to life, then you don't have to look for answers. We'll never find answers if we lose faith. All losing faith gets you is confusion and resentment. I've seen that firsthand." She took Julie's hand. "Remembering what we know to be true, about our purpose here on earth, and our ultimate home, that helps us carry our cross, however heavy."

Julie let out a smile. "I know this. I believe it. It's just not easy to live sometimes."

"It's not supposed to be easy." Her grip on her rosary tightened. "But if we always look for the easy way to deal with things, we'll be searching for the rest of our lives."

"You're right. I've been taught this all my life. So why am I questioning it now? I've had this job for years, and I've had tough moments, but this killer is different. I don't know, I just feel more lost on this case than I ever have before. It's just so brutal. It's making me question so much of what I should already know."

"Right now, I don't think you're quite as lost as you seem to think."

After a moment of silence, she asked Julie, "By the way how's Dad?"

"Dad? He's being Dad." Julie shrugged.

"I'm sorry to hear that." She grinned and shook her head.

Julie chuckled. "He'll come back eventually, Livy. When Mom got sick, I think it took a toll on him. And the accident? That only made things worse. He lost more than his faith after that."

"I know," she sighed. "It's just hard waiting."

"Well, I guess we both have crosses we can offer up, huh?"

She smiled and patted Julie on the back. "Now there's the girl I grew up with."

The two embraced a moment before Julie got up. "Well, I'd better get back to finding this guy."

Sister Olivia rose to her feet and walked into the center aisle. "I'll be praying for you, Jules."

"Thanks. I need all the prayers I can get."

<hr />

Julie pulled up to a bridal shop located on a main street of the town. She got out of the car and went inside. The midday lull left it silent inside. There were no customers, only one single worker. She was wearing casual clothes at odds with shop's surroundings. She had her back to Julie—up a stepladder arranging things on a shelf.

The woman glared at Julie. "So ma'am, could I interest you in a wedding dress?" She raised her eyebrow.

Julie pretended to think. "Nah that's okay. I think my uniform would suit me better." She flashed a sly smile.

The woman laughed and stepped down from the ladder. "Aww come on. You know you would look great in a meringue." She pretended to swoon.

Julie laughed.

The woman leaned against the counter. "What brings you by, Julie?"

"Well Nina, I was wondering if maybe you could look after Patrick tonight. He and Milo could have a sleepover." She ran her hand across one of the dresses on display.

"Sure thing." She kicked the ladder away. "We love

having Patrick over. He's such a polite child and sometimes I think it rubs off on Milo." She paused. "Sometimes."

Julie touched her chest in relief. "Thank you so much." She looked around. "I just have this case I'm working on. It's really taking it out of me and now we just had another setback and I just want to do everything I can to wrap it up. So I'm going to pull an all-nighter."

"Well, good luck with that." She touched Julie's arm. "But yeah, we'd love to have Patrick sleep over. I doubt the boys will have any objection."

"Tell Patrick that I'm all right. He was worried about me last night and he'll probably be suspicious of this. So make sure he knows that I'm not hurt. I'm just cracking the case."

"Will do." Nina nodded. "And remember Jules, I'm your friend. If you ever need anything, just ask. Even if you just need to talk."

"I might take you up on that one of these days. We can have a girls' lunch out and shopping spree." Julie winked at her.

She turned to go. "But anyway, that's the only reason I stopped by. I need to go. It's going to be a long night. I'll leave you to your indecisive brides."

"Good luck. Take him down."

Julie turned back and looked straight at her. "You know I will."

⸺◦◦◦◦⸺

Caroline opened her eyes after passing out. She was tied to a chair and gagged. She tried to make a sound but only a muffled scream came out.

She looked around at her surroundings but it was almost pitch black. Only a small crack of dim light provided any light. She wasn't sure where the light was coming from. She was able to make out what she believed were empty bookshelves. It was dark but it still felt cramped.

She heard the creak of a door and the sound of footsteps inching closer and closer. She squirmed about but couldn't loosen her restraints.

As the footsteps grew closer, she saw what she believed to be the dark silhouette of a man. He stood before her a moment before touching her cheek and then gently caressing her chin.

"Almost ready." He giggled. He then proceeded to hum a tune she half recognized.

She began to cry, hoping to play on any human sympathies he had.

He leaned in closer so she could see him better and smiled. He seemed to enjoy her pain.

"You're going to look so beautiful." His words sent chills to every inch of her quivering body.

CHAPTER 5

Kevin and Clark were waiting for Julie in her office when she returned. "Good news. We might've gotten another lead in this case." Kevin signaled for her to take a seat.

Julie pulled up a chair. "I'm listening."

Kevin took out a picture of a man and set it before her on the desk. "Professor Harold Kiger, the art professor that taught Artie Falcon at a local university. He recently resigned from the university, following complaints from students that he was way too into what he taught. Almost to an obsession. He made his entire classroom one gigantic work of art and it began to creep out the students. When his classes didn't fill, he became too big a liability for the college and they cut him loose."

Clark sat on Julie's desk. "Maybe our first victim decided that the teacher was way too into the subject and ignited the teacher's fury. After all, he used his artistic talents for criminal purposes. Perhaps this guy felt that this kid should be taught a lesson."

Julie studied the man in the photo. "So what are we waiting for? Let's go have a talk with Professor Kiger."

Clark's expression turned gleeful. "We did one better. We brought him to us. We found the bum drinking at a bar. So Julie, care to channel some of your infamous crime fighting interrogation skills and give this guy a talking to?"

Kevin pointed out the door. "Professor Picasso is in the interrogation room. Let's not keep the man waiting."

Julie had already started for the interrogation room before Kevin had even finished speaking. The two followed close behind.

Julie found the professor impatiently seated in his chair. His obese stature and thin glasses echoed less than fond memories of Julie's own past teachers.

"You folks better start telling me what all of this is about." He fidgeted nervously with his glasses. "I have rights you know."

Julie took out a picture of the Holdens' crime scene and set it before Kiger.

Kiger recoiled in disgust. "What the hell? Who are these people?" He pushed his chair farther away from the table.

"Don't you know?" She gave him a stern glare.

He moved around in his chair some. "How the hell would I know?"

"Maybe you'll recognize this guy." She took out an autopsy photo of his former student, Artie Falcon. "The first victim."

Kiger examined the picture. "That's Artie Falcon. He's been dead for months. I thought the police closed that case."

Julie slammed her hand down before him. "You thought wrong."

Kiger looked up at her. "Are you suggesting that I killed him?"

"What if I am?"

"I'd ask for a motive."

She pulled back and let him see her going through his file. "There are a lot of reports that you are very passionate about art, and this boy disrespected your vision. So you made him pay. Then you decided to have a little fun and make some art come to life by killing people and leaving their bodies in some sick artistic poses."

Kiger laughed. "Interesting theory. With no proof."

"No, not yet." She leaned in close to him. "But we'll get some."

Kiger smiled. "Whoever your real killer is, he has my respect. That's a clever signature he's developed. I, unfortunately, cannot take credit for it." He folded his hands. "Your case against me is non-existent. You don't even have your facts straight. You think that Artie hated my passion for art? I swear on my late mother's grave that this boy shared in it." He paused. "He was troubled, no doubt, and that is probably what got him killed. But he had as much passion for art as I did, maybe more. Perhaps instead of investigating me, you should be looking into his friends. Maybe one of them killed him and then started whatever killing spree you believe I'm responsible for."

"Or you could just be lying to take suspicion off of yourself." She took out one of Eric's autopsy photos and laid it on the table. She then pointed to the many knife wounds scattered across Eric's body. "After all." She slid it closer to him. "It's not like you'd admit to being responsible for this. Juries don't like child killers. You wouldn't stand a chance of any kind of life if you were found guilty. So of course you will try to shine the blame on somebody else if you can."

Kiger laughed. "You will do anything you can to try to make me out to be the killer. Lock me up if you want. When the next victim still turns up dead, you'll know you have the wrong guy and just wasted a lot of precious time harassing an innocent man."

"I don't harass." She gathered the photos from the table. "I get to the bottom of things."

Kiger took off his glasses and stared at her. "Look, I don't know that kid, and I didn't kill him." He sat back in his seat. "But waving pictures of his corpse in front of me isn't going to make me sad. He was a kid. It's not like his death robbed the world of anybody important. You need to worry more about keeping the living happy than worrying about who eliminated a bunch of nobodies."

Julie felt sick as she looked into the man's eyes. He seemed totally indifferent the brutal sights displayed in the pictures. If he wasn't the killer, he still lacked a heart.

Kiger replaced his glasses on his face. "If you're going to arrest me detective, do it. I'll call my lawyer and have your badge." He got up out of his seat. "But if not, get out of my way and let me salvage what's left of the afternoon. It's been fun seeing your vain attempt to pin a series of crimes on me that you have no real leads on. But alas, I grow bored with your foolish attempts to explain why I am guilty. Good luck, though. I always do enjoy a good crime drama." He winked at her, straightened out his suit jacket, and walked out of the room.

Clark swiftly left the observation room and approached Julie. "You aren't just going to let this guy walk are you?"

Julie leaned against the table. "As long as we don't have evidence, we don't have a choice. He may be a creep but we can't arrest him for not crying when he sees a dead boy in a picture."

"Can't we just hold him without charging him?"

"Last thing we need is this guy lawyering up."

Clark angrily punched the wall. "So, what do we do now?"

Julie caught his arm. "We get evidence."

Clark rolled his head in frustration. "And how do you propose we do that?"

Julie smiled. "Very easily."

Outside, Kiger took out his phone as he left the building and got into a taxi waiting at the curb.

"Driver, take me to the mall, I'm in the mood for some Asian food. And let's try to get there quickly." He handed the driver a ten for motivation. The taxi started up and took off. Kiger waited until they were a safe distance from the police station before dialing a number. He made sure the glass between the front and back seats was closed before his fingers punched in the final digits of the phone number.

He heard a calm, masculine voice answer. Kiger took a deep breath before speaking. "You were right. They came after me. But of course their attempts to prove that I did it were weak. They have no clue it's you. Just be careful that you don't get overconfident and mess up. Even blind squirrels like these can find a nut if you leave it lying around."

He smiled at hearing the response of the person on the other end. "I'll make sure to catch the news tonight to see that one. Good luck."

Without another word, he hung up and put his phone

away. As he looked out the window, he noticed that the route they were taking looked like the way away from the mall, not to it.

He opened the glass and shouted at the driver, "Hey, the mall is the other way. Don't you know direction?"

The driver said, "Of course I do. I just thought we'd take a bit of a scenic route." He turned around with a glare at Kiger. Chief Kevin Martel.

Kiger looked back in horror. "What the hell are you doing driving a cab?"

Kevin glared at him in the rearview mirror. "I figured I could use the extra paycheck. Besides, some people are so chatty in a cab. You never know what you might over-hear." He pointed to a microphone over Kiger's seat.

Kiger became frantic. "This has to be illegal. Any-thing you overheard won't be admissible in court."

"Probably not. But that's not why we did this. And I'm still throwing you in the slammer." Kevin made sure his eyes conveyed his excitement to Kiger. "Now we know you aren't the killer, but you know who is. So we're will-ing to bend a few rules to get you to talk so more people don't end up dead. Surely you understand."

Kevin pulled up in front of the police station again. "Well," he said with a smile, "we're here."

Kiger sank into his seat, realizing that he had just made a critical mistake.

<hr />

Patrick stared down the wide span of the camp's in-ground pool as he took a series of deep breaths. The cold water caressed his body in small, almost unnotice-able waves, and his flame-styled swim shorts clung to his body, but not tight enough to make him uncomfortable. He was as ready as he was going to be now. There was no excuse for failure.

He inhaled a deep breath and shot off into the water. He made circles in the air and water with alternating arms, turning his head to take breaths as he needed. His heart raced as he propelled across the water. The other side of the pool inched closer with every stroke. "I can do it." His mind repeated the phrase to him over and over again.

At last, he touched the wall and came to a stop.

The lifeguard in charge of the camp's swimming class clapped. "All right, Patrick. That was a nice improvement over last time. You're learning well."

Patrick tried to catch his breath. "Well, I've been practicing."

"It shows." The lifeguard gave him a thumbs-up.

Patrick stepped out of the pool and looked back across where Milo was standing in the water. Patrick could see Milo shivering from across the pool and he knew it wasn't from being cold. Milo was clearly trying to pretend to not be intimidated by the task before him, but Patrick saw through his charade.

Milo was whispering to himself. His eyes were closed and his fists were clenched.

The lifeguard waved to Milo. "Are you ready?"

"Yeah..." Milo sounded uncertain but he still put on his best confident smile.

Milo took a deep breath and shot himself off into the pool. His arm strokes started off strong but gradually sank into weak paddles. About halfway through the pool, he jumped up, coughing heavily.

The lifeguard jumped into the pool and rushed to Milo's side. He supported Milo as he coughed. "Are you all right?"

Milo gasped for air for a moment before settling down. "I'm fine. I just couldn't stay under anymore."

He patted Milo on the back. "That's okay. You went a bit further than last time. You're making good progress. You won't be able to master everything overnight. Keep working at it."

Milo grumbled under his breath as he was helped out of the pool.

The lifeguard cleared his throat. "Well, that's all for today. You guys were great. You're all making very good progress and I'm proud of all of you. See you all back here next time and keep up the good work."

Milo somberly walked towards the towels and wrapped one around himself. Patrick quickly ran after him and joined him.

Patrick patted him on the shoulder. "You did great. We both did better than last time."

"Cut the crap, Patrick. I suck." Milo pulled the towel over his head. "I can't take water getting in my nose so I can't swim good. I know I suck. I'm not that upset about it."

Patrick noticed Milo hiding his face. "Well you look upset to me."

Milo pulled the towel off. "Look Patrick, I ain't no baby. I don't get upset in front of people. Got it?"

"Sorry." Patrick took a step away from him.

Nina made her way into the fenced-off pool area. "Milo, I'm so proud of you."

Milo turned around in shock. "Mom?" He dropped his towel on the ground. "You're early!"

She picked up his towel and handed it to him. "I know. I had Wendy cover for me at the store so I could get you early. I saw you and Patrick swimming and decided to stay out of sight so I wouldn't make you nervous."

"Sorry you had to see that." Milo sullenly looked down. "I'm not really that good. Patrick's better."

"You did fine." She patted him on the head. "You both did. I think you both should be very proud of yourselves."

Patrick gave Milo a light punch on the arm. "Listen to your mother. She knows what she's talking about."

"Let's not talk about swimming anymore." Milo punched Patrick back. "We gotta get back inside to get our things before everyone is killing each other to get home."

Patrick pulled his towel off. "Yeah, it can be crazier than school at the end of the day."

Nina smiled. "It's okay boys. Just try not to be too long. I know how boys can get in changing rooms. No horsing around." She then flashed them a wink.

Milo feigned offense. "The fact that you even suggest that is hurtful."

Patrick joined in. "Very hurtful."

Returning winks of their own, they took off for the changing rooms.

⋇⊂⊃⋇⊂⊃⋇⊂⊃⋇

Julie had the prison guard let her into Kiger's cell. Kiger was sitting on his bed, shutting out the gray world around him.

Julie brought in a take-out container of Asian food. She slipped it through the bars on the floor, and slid it over to Kiger.

Kiger starred at it a moment and then looked up at her. "What's this?"

Julie pulled up a chair and took a seat. "Dinner. Unlike the Blood Chain killer, we don't get off on people suffering."

Kiger picked up the container and examined it. "If you think he gets off on people suffering, than you're even more clueless about him than I thought."

Julie leaned forward a little. "Why don't you explain while you're eating and maybe I'll sneak in dessert?"

"Like I told your lawbreaking boss, I ain't talking." He sat back on the bed more. "And don't try showing me the picture of the dead kid again. It won't move me, just like it won't move the real killer."

He opened the food container and the smells of Asian cuisine floated out. "You picked a good dish. Maybe you should consider changing careers."

Julie allowed herself to look flattered. "I think I like law enforcement just fine."

He gazed lovingly at the entrée. "Well, you are better at choosing foods than solving crime."

"I don't know about that." She pretended to be considering the matter. "I think I have ways of cracking cases wide open."

He twirled the plastic fork in the lo mein and gently placed it in his mouth, letting out an exaggerated moan as he swallowed. "You have ways? Well, I'd love to see them." He wiped his lip with his sleeve. "I'm sure you checked out my phone by now and saw that it only leads to an untraceable burner."

Julie felt a slight flinch in her brow.

He smiled. "So there's another dead end. You'll have to excuse me if I'm not very impressed with your investigative abilities."

Julie tapped her foot. "You'll see soon enough."

He took a bite of the chicken. "I guess I'll be prepared for a surprise."

"Oh you will definitely be surprised." She folded her hands in anticipation.

He took another bite. "We shall see."

Julie asked, "So you know who the killer is and won't tell us?"

Kiger nodded as he slurped a noodle. "That's right. Why would I tell you so you can go and break up his beautiful art displays?"

"You think what he does is artful?"

"Obviously you do as well, hence how you came up with the theory in the first place."

"I saw the signs of a twisted man who takes innocent lives for sick pleasure."

He set his meal aside. "This man doesn't get off on suffering like you seem to think. He just feels that human beings are beautiful creatures weighed down by themselves."

Julie's interest was piqued. "What the heck is that supposed to mean?"

Kiger smiled. "Like I'd tell you. You can't threaten me officer. I have nothing to lose. You wanna lock me up? Go ahead. The killer will still be on the loose. People will still die. Whether I am locked up or not, your investigation won't progress, because I won't say anything. But since you know that I know, you'll spend all of your time trying to get me to break, while my acquaintance makes more and more art scenes pile up."

Julie said, "And you say I don't know you. I say you don't know me. I'll break you before the night is out."

Kiger laughed as he took another bite. "And how will you do that?"

Julie merely smiled and kept her mouth closed, keeping her eyes locked with the prisoner's.

A few moments later, Kiger held his stomach as a sharp cramp shot through his intestines.

"Is something wrong?" she asked in a faux concerned tone.

Kiger gasped. He scowled at her. "You little bitch! You put something in my food."

"I don't know why you think that. You probably are just having indigestion. It happens when you're stressed out."

Kiger looked around and saw that there was no toilet. He said, "You monster. You had this planned."

Julie said, "I don't know what you're talking about. Sometimes things just, happen."

He banged against the bars. "Get me to a toilet. Now! Or you'll have a big mess to clean up."

She polished her nail with her sleeve. "Actually, since it's your cell, you'll have to clean it up."

Kiger collapsed to his knees. "Unlock this cell."

Julie tapped her chin. "I would, if only I could remember where I put the key."

"Stop screwing around! I need to use the toilet *now*!"

She could see the sweat quickly forming on his head and dripping down his neck.

She smiled sweetly at him. "Maybe you will have to jog my memory about where the keys are."

She locked eyes with Kiger again. She could see the anxiety in his eyes and smiled.

He gulped, realizing that he was trapped. He now was beginning to understand that the rumors about Julie might've been true after all.

<hr/>

Patrick and Milo ran out the front door of the camp building freshened up and changed into t-shirts and shorts. They carried a backpack with their wet clothes and other items used that day.

Nina waited by her car. She waved them over.

Milo leaped the final yard to the car and then stood with his legs together. "Were we fast enough for you?"

Nina pretended to be unsure for a moment. "You two were fine."

"Of course we were." Milo tucked his arms behind his back and put on a proud grin.

Nina turned to Patrick. "Oh I forgot to tell you, Patrick. Your mom stopped by the store today and asked me to let you stay with us tonight. I told her I would. Hope that's okay."

Patrick was silent a moment. "She's working late, huh?"

"Yeah, she's working hard on that case." She took Patrick by the shoulder. "She told me to tell you that she's fine. She just wants to solve this case and she'll do that better if she knows you're being cared for. So what do you say?"

Patrick said, "Well, I always love sleeping over. So of course I'll come."

"Excellent. We can order pizza and watch a movie." She opened the car door. "I'll stop you home so you can pack a bag."

Milo said, "That's okay Mom. If he needs any clothes, he can borrow mine. We're still the same size." He cracked a sly grin. "Besides, we'll probably be dancing around in our boxers all night anyway, with really loud music."

Patrick rolled his eyes. "We won't do that Aunt Nina, I promise." He gave Milo a light shove before heading to his seat. "But he's right about one thing; I don't need to go home. I'm fine in these clothes."

She got into the driver's seat. "Well if you're sure, then I guess we can get going." She loaded the boys into the back seat and then started off for home.

∞⚬∞⚬∞

After the effects of the meal wore off on Kiger, he was transported back to the interrogation room and given medicine to help bind him. He was still breathing heavily and sweating when Julie and Kevin came in to question him.

Kiger said, "You realize you could get in trouble for what you did?" He angrily stared up at them.

Kevin chuckled. "In trouble for what? How were we supposed to know your digestive system didn't get along with Asian food?" He reached out and touched Kiger's hand. "Maybe it was the chef of the day, or maybe it's the summer heat. I know the heat can really do a number on the ol' digestive system. Happened to me all the time back in the day."

"So you deny any part in this?" Kiger raised his eyebrow.

Julie leaned down on the table. "I wonder where we learned that." She could see she was getting to him. "So Kiger, you remember our little deal. It's time to pay up, and don't try to back out now because the results will not be pretty." She reached suggestively into her pocket.

Kiger sighed. "Look, I am not a monster."

Julie slammed the table. "You're covering up several murders, including that of several children. These weren't mercy kills; these people died horrible deaths. I think a jury just might disagree with that assumption, unless of course you prove them wrong and give us some info. Come on Kiger. If you really aren't a monster, show us."

Kiger twiddled his thumbs a moment. "I won't betray

a friend. He was good to me. He gave me something I didn't think possible—hope that all people weren't out to isolate me. I don't approve exactly of what he does. But he's not a bad person, and I don't want to see him in jail. Or worse. So I look the other way."

Julie clenched her fists to maintain control of herself. "You aren't helping him, Kiger. The more he kills, the more he'll feel the sting of what being a killer is. You don't kill people without it messing with your brain. Just cut the games and tell us what we want to know."

"There's an art gallery on Conan Street. Royal's Art Gallery. It's run by Jason Royal, a former student of mine." He scribbled down the address on a notepad. "He was a classmate of Artie's. He's not the killer. That I can assure you. But he'll be able to point you to who is."

Julie looked at the address. She took out the flyer from before and slid it to Kiger. "Is this his gallery?"

Kiger looked over the flyer. "Yes. He keeps information on the flyer scarce because he doesn't want protestors. He's in a discreet office strip. The sign will read 'Royal's Place' outside. He figures the people who want his products will be able to find it and these measures will keep unwanted opposition away."

Julie read the address. "You better not be lying."

Kiger stared down at the table in shame. "Go there yourself in the morning and see for sure."

Julie leaned in close to him. "Why in the morning?"

Kiger pulled back. "It's closed today. Even if you could get a warrant by tonight, you won't get your answers if Jason Royal isn't there to give them. He's out of town. He'll be back in the morning. That's about twelve hours. Think you can wait?"

Julie clenched a fist. "We don't have time to wait. But

if this is the only way, I suppose we don't have much choice."

Kevin approached the table and sternly rested his hand on Kiger's neck. "You'd better be telling us the truth, or a little indigestion will seem like a bubble bath."

Kiger shivered. "That a threat?"

Kevin leaned in to whisper in Kiger's ear. "It's a warning."

Julie asked, "Any chance you know the killer's hideout? Maybe where he has his latest victim?"

"That I honestly wouldn't know. He isn't dumb enough to give me such information. No amount of secret torture will make me able to give you an accurate location. You're on your own."

Julie and Kevin shared a glance, realizing that despite the lead they had, Caroline was running out of time, if she hadn't already.

◦◦◦◦◦◦◦◦

The doorbell rang. Nina quickly ran to answer it with money in hand. Outside on the porch, a delivery boy in uniform held two boxes of pizza.

"Two medium meatball pizzas?" He held the boxes out.

"That's us." She took the pizzas from him. "Thanks for getting here so quickly. How much do I owe you?"

"With delivery, that's nineteen ninety-nine."

She took out a twenty-dollar bill and a five and handed it to the boy. "Keep it. You got it here quickly. You deserve a little something extra."

He took the money and smiled. "Thanks ma'am. Have a good evening."

"You too." She closed the door and took a whiff of the heavenly aromas rising out of the cardboard box. "Boys, dinner's ready!"

Those words acted like lightning to the thunder that followed as three sets of footsteps stampeded down the stairs to the kitchen table. By the time Nina got to the kitchen, the faces of Milo and Patrick, along with her seventeen-year-old son Damien, were all aglow with eager anticipation of the cheesy supper leaking grease in the boxes she held.

"Bon appetite." She placed the boxes on the counter and served a slice to each of them on pizza slice-shaped plates. She then poured them each a foamy class of cola and took her seat at the table. They said grace and then eagerly dug in.

Milo tore off a piece of cheese with his teeth. "I love this pizza. These guys know how to do it."

Damien sneered at him. "You say that all the time."

"Only when we eat pizza at *this* place." Milo took another bite.

Nina asked Patrick, "What's your take?"

Patrick tapped his chin a moment as he chewed. "It's pretty good. Of course my favorite is the pizza my Uncle Tony used to make at his place. I haven't seen him a lot since...Since Dad died."

Seeing an inner sadness in Patrick's eyes, she placed her hand on his. "You know Patrick, we're still here for you if you ever need to talk about anything. I'm your Godmother and that means more than just having you over for dinner."

"I know." He put on a smile. "But tonight's supposed to be a fun night. Let's not ruin it with gloomy talk."

Damien said, "No gloomy talk? I guess that leaves school out of the topic pool. Awesome."

Milo put down his slice and took a sip of soda. "How

about we talk about the awesome action movie I borrowed from the library."

Damien allowed himself a moment of glee. "You borrowed an action movie? Sweet!"

Nina grew worried and nervously picked her nail. "Is this one of those movies I am going to regret showing you like I did the last one?"

Patrick recalled what she meant a moment and his eyes widened when he realized. "I remember that. I still haven't told my mom. She'd never let me out of the house again if she knew."

Milo made a funny face at Patrick. "Don't worry, I looked online and this movie doesn't have a single nude scene in it. It's clean...er" He took another bite of pizza. He turned to his mom. "The only nudity you'll have to worry about is me and Patrick watching it in our boxers."

Damien nearly choked on the pizza. "We are eating. We don't need that visual."

Milo stuck his tongue out at Damien prompting a middle finger in response.

Nina slapped both of their hands. "That'll be enough of that, you two."

Patrick took a sip of soda. "You two still fight like me and Petey did. It must be a brother thing."

Damien slapped Milo's pestering hand away. "I fight with Milo cause he's annoying. That's why. You and Petey were twins, so you were equals. Milo is inferior to me."

Milo fired back. "Well at least I don't spend all day looking at myself in the mirror. Naked!"

"No, you just do it under your covers."

"Do not!"

"Do too. I've seen you."

"Do not. You're just making it up!"

Nina shouted, "Enough you two."

Patrick laughed. "I don't think they hear you. They'll cool off in a few."

Milo said, "It's true. Fighting with this guy gets boring after awhile." He placed his arm around Damien.

Damien scarfed down the last piece of his pizza. "You're so full of crap." He removed Milo's arm. He then reached across the table, cutting in front of Milo's plate, to grab another piece of pizza from the box. He immediately went to work on it.

Patrick loosened up at the often-humorous skirmishes of the Greene brothers. Their antics kept him smiling throughout the rest of the meal. And through the movie that followed as well. As Milo predicted, he and Patrick enjoyed in nothing but their green-colored matching skivvies. Milo always had a way of making Patrick go against his better judgment.

◦⟨⟩∘⟨⟩∘⟨⟩∘⟨⟩∘

The movie ended at nine-thirty, way too early for Milo to think of going to sleep. As they lay on his uncovered bed, Milo thought a moment. "So, what do we do now?"

Patrick turned on his side. "Well, tomorrow's a Saturday. No camp. We could just go to sleep and hang out in the morning."

"No way." Milo bounced himself up. "It's way too early to go to bed for a Friday night."

"We did a lot tonight." Patrick rested his head on his hand. "We even saw stuff blow up on TV. I think we got a lot done."

"We can do more." He tapped his chin a moment. "Hey!" He smiled gleefully. "How about we see what Damien is up to?" He began to snicker.

Patrick groaned and buried his head in his hands.

"He's a teenager. Alone in his bedroom. Do you really wanna bug him?"

Milo rubbed his hands together. "Heck Yeah. I'm his little brother. It's my job to bother him."

Patrick turned onto his back. "Well I am sitting this one out. You're bothering Damien on your own."

Milo shrugged. "Suit yourself. You'll be involved soon enough whether you like it or not."

Patrick shook his head. The brothers Greene were about to go at it again.

Milo quietly snuck across the hallway to Damien's room, which was guarded by a locked door.

Milo smiled as he tried the locked door. "He thinks that's gonna stop me?" Milo chuckled and turned towards the closet. He searched through the towels until he found a hidden key that unlocked all of the bedroom doors. "You don't mess with Milo Greene." He smirked.

He slipped the key into the lock and turned the knob, quickly opening the door and then hiding the key.

Damien shot up from his bed and tossed the magazine he was reading before Milo could see it. "What the hell are you doing here?"

Milo folded his arms and walked in. "I live here. That's what."

"No, this is *my* room. It's like another house altogether." He signaled for Milo to leave.

Milo walked closer to him. "What are you afraid I'm going to walk in on something?"

"You wish you freak." He smacked his fist against his palm.

Milo dashed to where the magazine landed. "Let's see, what kind of reading material do we have here?"

Damien freaked and grabbed Milo, trying to keep him

from seeing the magazine. "You can't see it. It's mine. Go back to your boyfriend."

"What are you scared I'm going to show Mom?" He struggled to break free. "Are there boobies in those pages?"

"No! Now get out." He threw Milo from the bed.

"No boobies? You mean it's boy parts? So that's your secret."

"It's neither of those things now get the hell out!" He pointed to the door.

Milo shot past Damien's block, and picked up the magazine and gave it a quick glance before Damien tore it out of his hands.

"Comic books? You're seventeen and you still read comic books?"

Damien pointed his finger in Milo's face. "If you tell anybody, I will make you regret it like you wouldn't believe."

"Fine, I won't tell anybody." He paused. "If you come play with me and Patrick." He cracked a smile.

Damien took a seat on the bed. "No. You two play by yourselves."

"Come on, you should be flattered that we think you're cool enough to hang out with."

"I'm not, now get out, you fungus."

Milo pouted when he realized he wasn't getting anywhere. "All right, fine." He walked out of the room and into the hall. He saw Patrick lying on the bed tossing a baseball into the air and catching it. He looked bored. Milo then looked back at Damien, who had resumed reading his comic book.

He turned and thought a minute, and then smiled. "Hey Damien! I got something to show you."

He then yanked his boxers down and turned his back Damien, who had fallen for Milo's trap and looked. Upon seeing his brother shaking his bony butt, he became enraged. He shot up like a canon and darted towards his brother.

Milo laughed at getting the reaction he wanted and made a dash for the bed. By now, Patrick had braced himself for the impact of the two brothers landing, only narrowly resisting being knocked out of the bed.

Milo tried to pull his pants but up but Damien stopped him. "If you're going to start flashing yourself around, you're gonna get the punishment."

Damien then yanked the boxers off of Milo, leaving him totally naked. Milo didn't care though, and merely laughed and initiated a wrestling match with Damien.

Milo matched Damien's grabs. "I bet I'm stronger than you."

Damien kept up the barrage. "You wish, pipsqueak. Look at yourself. You're still a little boy. I'm a man. I can trash you."

"Yeah right." Milo pushed back. "Show me what you got."

Damien easily overwhelmed the thin and bony arms that Milo fought back with, but Milo flashed Patrick a look that made it impossible for him to not aid him. He came behind Damien and held his arms back, giving Milo some room to fight back. However, Damien still managed to flip Milo and pin him.

"Say 'uncle' or else."

"Never!" Milo concentrated a moment and then pushed out a fart on Damien.

Damien freaked. "You pig! You farted on me with your naked ass."

Milo laughed. "I know!" He turned around and caught Damien off guard. Together with Patrick, the two boys were able to overpower Damien and pinned him.

Unable to resist the feeling of the moment, Patrick joined Milo in doing a 'victory dance.' Milo continually flashed Damien in the process.

Patrick began to feel weird. He stopped dancing, "Okay, you dancing naked is starting to gross me out. I know you think it's fun, but please put something on."

Milo looked down and smiled. "Oh yeah I forgot."

He went to get his boxers but Damien quickly came to and snatched them away. He dangled them in front of Milo's face. "You want these?"

Milo went to grab them. "Hey, give them back, Damien!"

Damien tossed them across the room and snatched Milo up. "I'll show you what I do to people who moon me."

Milo kicked and thrashed into the air to try and get out of his brother's grip, but it was too tight.

Damien walked to the bathtub and turned the water on. He held Milo while the water filled up.

Patrick chased after them. "Damien, stop it."

Damien replied, "Sorry Patrick. Milo wanted to play games and now he's paying the consequences."

Patrick tried to pull him away. "You're going to hurt him, Damien."

Not wanting to seem like a victim, Milo said, "No he ain't. I can take whatever he can dish out!" He flailed around to break free but he was trapped.

Damien chuckled. "We'll see about that."

He dunked Milo into the water and stuck his head under the falling water. Milo struggled to overcome his weakness of water entering his nose but he failed and it resulted in his face burning.

Damien pulled him. "Had enough yet, twerp?"

Milo struggled for a breath but his ego kept him from surrendering to the likes of his big brother. "Is that all you got?"

Damien shook his head. "I guess not."

He then thrust Milo back into the running water again.

"Aunt Nina. We need help." Patrick tried again to pull Damien off.

Milo thrashed around some more to break free of Damien's grip. He accidentally banged his head on the faucet. Damien could feel him collapse. He quickly shut off the water in response.

"Milo, are you okay?" He checked for a pulse.

Milo placed his hand against his head. "I'm fine, doofus. Its just a bump." He tried not to cry. He knew he was bad at hiding his pain.

Nina rushed to the bathroom and saw them gathered around Milo, who was sitting on the edge of the tub.

She ran to Milo. "What the heck happened?"

Damien and Patrick looked at her with fear.

Not wanting them to get in trouble, Milo said, "I was being a jerk to Damien. I got hurt doing it."

Convinced by the unusual honest tone in Milo's voice, she said, "Be careful you guys. You could get really hurt. Dry off and come downstairs and I'll put ice on it. Oh and Milo, put your underwear back on. Nobody wants to see your business."

Milo chuckled proudly. "I know. It's fine. I'll just keep Milo Jr. all to myself."

Damien looked at him in disgust. "You're eleven years old and you've named your privates? You're such a weirdo."

Milo said, "Actually, Milo Jr. is my butt. My privates are named Boy."

Damien's mouth drooped. "Boy?"

Milo looked down and then up at Damien again. "You got a better name for it?"

Damien walked away. "You're sick you know that?

"Well I learned it from the best big brother. You know, you and Boy kind of look alike."

Patrick grabbed Milo by the shoulders. "Enough! Will you guys stop arguing about stupid things? Just get along."

Nina patted him on the back. "Listen to Patrick boys. He knows what he's talking about. I'll have the ice waiting."

She walked downstairs leaving the boys alone.

Milo took a seat and held his head to stop the dizziness. He tried to stand but he was unsteady. Damien and Patrick helped him dry off and put his boxers back on before heading downstairs for Milo to nurse his newly acquired bump with an ice bag. They sat with him while the ice combated the swelling.

Damien wrapped his arm around Milo. "Hey, I'm sorry about everything I did and said earlier."

Milo hesitated a moment to reply. "Yeah, same here. I was being annoying. I just wanted you to hang with me and I figured messing with you was the only way to do that."

He brushed a lock of hair down over Milo's forehead. "You know I am not against hanging out with you. It's when you're a pain about it that I get pissed. Pulling down your pants is like the worst way to get me to hang out with you."

Milo chuckled. "Yeah, that was pretty dumb wasn't

it?"

"Tell me about it. But I guess it's karma. I thought I looked great naked when I was young and immature. Well, I still think that. But I don't go flashing people. 'Cause they usually think that's gross."

Milo frantically turned to Damien. "You telling me I'm turning out like you?"

Damien smiled in satisfaction. "Yep."

"Well, there could be worse people to turn out like I guess. And I guess you can blame seeing my rear end tonight on your poor example setting skills."

Damien shook his head and smiled. "Touché little bro. Touché."

The two laughed and fist-pumped each other.

Patrick smiled. "I am so glad you two stopped fighting. I was seriously getting a headache."

Damien said, "Well don't get used to it. I plan on letting this little guy have it the next time I feel in the mood to."

Milo took the ice bag off of his head. "Yeah, same here."

Patrick rolled his eyes. "You two are hopeless. But you're both okay in my book anyway."

Milo put his arm around Patrick. "Same here. You're an honorary Greene brother. You can fight with us or prank flash us whenever you want. You're like family, dude. We can all go naked together." He raised his eyebrows to encourage Patrick.

Patrick recoiled. "No way. That's your thing, not mine."

Damien gave Patrick a thumbs-up "Thank you. No offense but I've already seen enough of that crap. I'll already be having nightmares for weeks."

Milo muttered something to himself just loud enough to be heard but just quiet enough to make questioning him on it a futile effort.

Patrick laid back on the couch. "You should do something about Milo, Damien. I think he's got problems if he wants to see everyone naked." He flashed Milo a smirk as the three of them laughed.

Hearing them laugh, Nina came in. "Let's just take a look at that head."

Milo showed her his head. She poked around with her finger to feel for a bump but she could barely feel one. Milo didn't flinch when she touched the area either.

She asked, "You honestly don't feel that?"

Milo shook his head. "Nope. Not at all."

"You're lucky then. I don't think you bumped it that hard. But we could still go to the hospital just in case."

Milo jumped up. "I'm fine. I didn't bump it that hard."

"Are you sure? You couldn't stand well at first."

Milo rolled his eyes. "Give me a break. I never have balance. I am fine. I've banged my head harder at school."

"Wait, what?"

Milo shifted his glance away. "Nevermind."

Nina patted him on the shoulder. "Be more careful for next time. It could be worse then."

Milo sighed. "Yeah, yeah, I understand. I'll be careful."

"It's nothing to joke about. Horsing around can get you really hurt."

"I know, Mom." He hopped up from the couch. "Goodnight."

"Goodnight, Aunt Nina." Patrick waved as he followed Milo up to bed.

Nina shook her head. "What am I going to do with

that boy?"

Damien smiled. "I know a good military school that could use new students."

She smacked him with the towel in her hands before flashing him a smile and heading into the kitchen.

"Yeah, that kid would just drag the rest of the students down."

"I heard that." Milo looked down the stairs at him.

Damien walked up the stairs and shoved him aside. "Mom said to go to bed." He walked back to his room and shut the door. "And if you come in again, a bump on the head will be the least of your problems. Got it?"

"Roger." Milo stuck his tongue out and returned to his room.

⊶⊙⊷⊙⊶⊙⊷

It took nearly an hour to finally turn the lights out. Milo and Patrick's bony forms both fit comfortably in the bed. Both of them stared at the ceiling for a few minutes before realizing that the other was just as much awake.

Patrick said, "All that fighting and you're still not asleep?" He shook his head. Milo was like a machine.

Milo looked at him. "You're not asleep either you know."

"That's 'cause I'm thinking about my mom." He shifted a little and folded his arms. "I wonder if she's any closer to finding out who did all of those crimes."

Milo turned on his back. "She'll get the guy. She always does."

"I know she's good." Patrick looked out the window. He could see stars. He remembered looking at them with his brother. He missed doing that. "I don't know. Yesterday, she felt really different. It's almost like she was after Dad and Petey died."

"Yeah. That really sucked for you."

Patrick turned back to Milo. "He was your friend too."

"Of course he was. Where do you think I got most of my cool ideas? But he was your twin brother." He patted Patrick's shoulder. "You two were as close as a person and his shadow. And I saw how sad it made you. I know I'd go crazy if Damien died and he's not even my twin."

"Other than Petey, you were my best friend." Patrick remembered the games the three of them played. "Sill are. You always were. Everyone liked you and Petey. They just ignored me. I guess Petey did it 'cause I was his brother but you didn't have to hang with me. You could've played with anyone. But you and Petey played with me."

"Well, you've been a damn good friend to me too. You were cooler than you think. You were really smart. I always thought that was really cool."

Patrick looked at him and they said together, "Friends forever!"

Milo smiled. "I know it's been awhile since we did that. I know it's kind of lame. It's for kids. But I just wanted to see if you still remembered. Glad you do."

Patrick laughed. "How could I ever forget? It was our special handshake." Patrick chuckled. "I miss Petey so bad sometimes."

"Yeah, so do I. But at least I still got you, right? And you got me, so it's all cool."

"Yeah, I guess you're right."

"Of course I'm right. Now, we'd better get to sleep."

Milo turned on his side to try and get more comfortable. Patrick went to say something else, but he could hear Milo's faint snoring. "Guess he was tired after all." He turned on his other side and stared at the wall until he fell asleep too.

⋅◦◯◦◦◯◦◦◯◦◦◯◦◦◯◦◦

After a hearty breakfast the next morning, Nina drove Patrick home. She pulled up to the house and then reached back and patted Patrick on his folded hands. "Well, it was nice having you over again Patrick. You can come back any time. We love having you."

Patrick unbuckled his seatbelt. "Thanks. Maybe in a few more weeks. I still kind of like my own bed." He hopped out of the car and shut the door.

She turned back around and lowered the window. "Well, just give us a buzz whenever you wanna arrange something."

Milo rolled down the window. "And remember, you can always invite *me* over for a sleepover too."

Patrick chuckled and waved to Milo as he walked to his porch. "Maybe. If my mom lets me. But we gotta wear pajamas. It's a rule."

"D'oh!" He smacked his forehead.

Patrick waved. "See you later, Milo."

"See ya later, dude!" Milo waved out the window as Nina drove away.

Patrick watched until the car turned a corner. He then turned and went inside. Karen was already doing the morning cleaning.

"Hey Karen. How's it going?" He set his backpack down on the floor.

She dusted off a lampshade. "It's going good. I missed you yesterday."

"Yeah, I slept over at a friend's house. I guess Mom knew she'd be working late and didn't want to keep you."

"Well, she never came home last night, so I guess it's probably for the best."

Patrick took a seat on the sofa. "She didn't come home. At all?"

Karen shook her head. "Nope. She called me and told me she'd be pulling an all-nighter. I guess she really wants to put the case she's working on to rest. But you and I can still have a lot of fun today."

"Guess so." Patrick looked around at the home. He caught a glimpse of the picture of him and his brother on the mantle. The two looked like mirror images of each other. Even their freckles seemed to be perfectly matched. As he looked at the picture, he felt like he was looking into a window to the past, before he lost a part of himself.

Nina dropped Milo home to stay with Damien for the morning while she ran to the bridal shop for a few hours. She parked her car on the street and got out. "I need to hire a manager one of these days."

She walked up to the door and unlocked it before going inside. After seeing the piles of bills and papers she'd left on her desk the previous afternoon, she immediately missed the antics of her sons from the night before.

She whimpered to herself. "Why did I start this business again?"

"Because you love wedding gowns." Her assistant, Janice, walked into the store.

"Ah, that was it." She chuckled.

"Sorry I'm late. The light's broken on Hinkle Street and you know what that means—gridlock."

"It's fine." Nina sorted through bills. "You're still more than early enough to help me sort through all of this."

"Oh joy!" The girl sighed as she set her handbag down. "By the way, love the new window display.'

Nina stopped what she was doing and looked at Janice. "What new window display?" she asked.

Janice pointed to the front display window. "You got a new mannequin. It looks perfect. So life-like. It's bound to draw in new customers."

Nina approached the window. "I never ordered a new mannequin."

Janice went behind the desk. "Well, one was delivered."

Nina hastened her pace to the window to see what Janice was talking about.

⚬⚭⚬⚭⚬⚭⚬

Julie and Clark rode towards the art gallery Kiger had directed them to.

"I hate traffic. Did I ever tell you that?" Clark nervously tapped his hand against the armrest. "You know, when there's an emergency, the person in trouble is in *really* big trouble."

Julie turned a corner. "You don't call looking for a serial killer an emergency?"

"Well." He paused. "It's not like he's expecting us. We made sure Kiger had no way to call and alert this guy that we were coming."

Julie said, "He probably knows anyway."

Just then, her cell phone rang. She answered it with a dignified, "Martel."

Nina was on the other end, frantic. "Jules, you have to get over to my store. Now."

Julie became greatly concerned. "Why? Has something happened? Is it Patrick?"

"No, I dropped him home. Just get over here. I've already called the police but I need you to be here. It's not good, Jules."

"I'll be right there." She hung up the phone and

stepped on the pedal.

Clark was thrust back a bit. He grabbed tighter to the armrest. "What is it? What happened?"

Julie kept her eyes focused on the road. "We'll be taking a brief detour." With tires screeching she turned, jumped the median strip into the other lane, and started rushing towards the bridal shop.

Clark struggled to keep from being thrown. "What the hell are you doing?"

"I'm going to Nina's bridal shop."

"Why the hell are you going there?"

"Because she needs me."

"If there was a break-in, other cops can handle it."

Julie shook her head. "I don't think it's just a break-in."

"How the hell do you know? From the sound of things, she didn't seem to tell you much."

She pulled onto the street of the shop. "Let's just say I have a hunch about these things, Clark. Trust me, we need to do this."

Julie saw a swarm of cops already on the scene in front of the bridal shop. This definitely wasn't just a break-in.

She pulled over and she and Clark got out and ran towards the store. Nina was waiting outside and immediately ran to Julie in tears.

Julie took Nina in her arms. "What's wrong, Nina? What happened?"

Nina tried to get herself together enough to speak coherently. "I touched her hand. It was so cold. It was so cold, Julie. She must've been here all night."

She gently took Nina by the shoulders. "Who's been here all night?"

Nina pointed to the display window. Julie and Clark

approached the window and both felt their limbs quiver when they saw what was behind it.

Caroline, dressed in a beautiful and full white wedding dress, dead.

Her full sleeve dress appeared silky in the light and glittered from the high neckline to the lace base at her feet. Whiter still than the dress was her complexion, which would've made even snow seem almond by comparison. Her eyes were beautifully closed, sparkling with eye shadow and shining brightly, and her hands folded at her waist, the picture of a perfect bride mannequin.

Her cause of death was unknown from a single glance, but there didn't seem to be any blood this time around.

Clark grabbed onto a pole to keep from crashing to his knees. "I thought I'd seen it all."

Julie asked, "Still don't believe our killer is into an artsy crime scene?"

Clark gazed at the display window. "I knew we'd likely find her dead. But this is ridiculous."

"This wasn't supposed to happen again. We should've been able to stop this." She shed a tear over her failure to save Caroline, even thought she knew that finding Caroline alive at this stage would've been extreme unlikely.

Clark turned away from the window. "Your friend owns this shop. While a lot of people probably saw the display, she's technically the one who discovered that her new mannequin was really a corpse. In other words, she's the one who found the body. We know what that means."

Julie rested her head in her hand a moment. "It means she and her family are all this guy's next targets." She looked at her trembling friend who was giving yet another statement to a police officer and then returned her gaze to the corpse bride in the window.

Her mind rushed to figure out a way she could save her dear friends. Nina and her children had been so good to her and her family, and she refused to let the same fate that befell the killer's previous victims befall them as well. The blood chain had to end here.

CHAPTER 6

"She was just a girl..." Nina clung to Julie tightly as they watched the beautiful bride zipped into a body bag. She tearfully turned to Julie. "I know her from Church. Why would somebody hurt her? Why?"

Julie stroked Nina's head. "Because, I guess some people are just bent on being evil."

"Julie, was she the one that you were looking for?" Nina looked up at her. "The girl from the Blood Chain killings thing?"

Julie reluctantly nodded. "I'm afraid so."

Nina backed away with wide eyes. "So that means, me and the boys...we're next?"

"Not if I have anything to say about it." Julie gently grabbed Nina by her arm. "I don't care if I have to personally guard you all every minute of every day until this guy is captured. I am not going to let him kill you."

"You can't promise that." She looked at the body bag

being loaded into an ambulance. "He got to her. He can get to me. Oh God, the boys are home alone! What if he already has them?"

"Calm down." Julie reached out her hand to comfort her. "We've already sent officers to the house to get them. They're going to bring them down to the station. We'll bring you there too. We'll find a safe location for all of you."

Nina grabbed her head in frustration. "Like where? Outer space?"

"This guy isn't omnipotent." Julie looked around the street. "There are places he can't get to."

"Until you know who he is..." Nina wiped aside her tears. "How the heck can you be sure as to where those places are?"

"We'll make sure he can't get to you."

"Julie, I'm scared." Nina took some deep breaths. "Not just for me, but for the boys. I don't want them hurt. And no matter how much you try, you cannot guarantee that you won't find us just like that next time. And you know it."

Julie was silent, realizing the truth of Nina's words. Her resolve too strong to allow them to come true. She refused to give them further consideration.

⁂

"Where are we going?" Milo gazed out the side window as Kevin drove them to the station. "First Mom calls and tells me to go with you and now you say we have to leave our home?"

"You shouldn't worry about it right now." Kevin glanced at him reassuringly. "We'll tell you what the plan is once you and your mom are together at the station."

"What happened?" Damien tensed a bit. "You

wouldn't be doing this and being so secretive about everything if something really bad wasn't going on."

Kevin chuckled. "You're too good at reading people kid. Why don't you keep your brother from asking me too many questions? He's making me nervous with his questions."

"No offense, Mr. Martel, but you've never struck me as the nervous type." Damien looked at Kevin unwavering. "Patrick always tells us how tough his grandfather is and the times we've met you seem to have backed that up."

"Well I guess this time, the stakes are a little higher so I'm a little more nervous." He came to a stop at a red light. "So you'll have to cut me just a little bit of slack and not expect so many answers. You'll get them all in due time."

Milo asked Damien, "What do you think's going on?"

Damien replied, "I don't know, but it can't be good."

As the light turned green, Milo moved closer to Damien and took his hand. Damien could tell by this gesture that Milo was unnerved. He never sought comfort unless he was truly afraid.

⚬━⚬━⚬━⚬━⚬

Nina ran to Milo and Damien the moment she saw them at the station. She planted kisses and hugs on them, and didn't care how much they were embarrassed. She was surprised to find them happily returning her gestures.

Julie sat them down. "I can have officers get some of your things later. Right now, our primary concern is getting all of you to a safe location. We feel the best option right now is out of town. We're arranging a plane right now. We hope to have you leave within the hour."

Milo rose to his feet. "What's going on? Nobody's telling us a thing."

Damien joined him. "Aunt Julie, if we're being forced from our home, I think we have a right to know why."

Julie was left speechless a moment. Their faces looked so frightened. She could only imagine what they were thinking. She nodded reassuringly to try and calm them. "You're absolutely right. You do have a right to know, and I'm not going to sugarcoat it for you because I know both of you well and I trust that you're mature enough to handle this. You've heard about the recent string of killings we've tied together, which the media has dubbed the Blood Chain Killings, right?"

Damien said, "Yeah, so what does that have to do with us?"

Julie took a deep breath. "This morning, the girl who had been missing in that case was found dead by your mother. That means that all three of you are likely the next targets. We tried hiding Caroline in town and he still found her. We realize now that we have to get as aggressive as possible in keeping you safe. Our goal is to get you out of town before he can find you. We'll provide you with money and new names. And whatever else you may need."

Damien threw his hand in the air. "So we're just supposed to leave our hometown with just the clothes on our backs without even saying goodbye to anyone we know?"

Julie nervously gripped her wrist. "I'm afraid we don't have another choice right now. We can't risk leaving you nearby for him to find."

Milo pouted. "But what about Patrick? He's my best friend. We've been best friends since we were little kids. I can't just move away without at least telling him goodbye."

Julie kneeled down to eye level with Milo. "I'll make sure he knows, Milo. And remember, it isn't like this is forever; it's just until we're sure that we have this guy off the streets for good. You guys could be back here within a week. So it's just kind of like a vacation."

A tear rolled down Milo's face. "Well, if it's just for a little bit, I guess it's okay."

Julie smiled and patted Milo on the shoulder. "You're tough kids. You'll be able to make it through this."

She hugged Milo. "Remember, I'm your Godmother. I love you, Milo. I don't want anything bad to ever happen to you. I want to do whatever I can to keep you safe. And once I catch this bad guy, I'll make sure I do whatever I can to make it up to you. Okay?"

Milo nodded. "Okay. Thank you, Aunt Julie."

Clark approached them. "A car is waiting outside for you. Officers will take you to a private plane. Are you guys ready?"

Nina took a deep breath and wiped a tear from her eye. "We're as ready as we're ever going to be."

Milo put on a brave front. "I'm ready."

Damien couldn't hide his expression of disapproval. "Let's go."

Clark led them to the secured car outside. A smiling and gentle-looking officer was waiting for them outside.

He asked, "Are they ready?"

Clark said, "Yes, they're ready."

"Then let's go." The officer opened the door of the back seat to them, and ushered them in, making sure Milo sat in between his mother and Damien, before shutting the door. He then got into the driver's seat. "Buckle up you guys. It's time to go."

After hearing the clicks of their car seatbelts, he took

off for the airport.

Clark watched as the car drove out of sight, praying that they were getting them away in time.

Julie joined him. She could see the three of them turning back and waving. They looked so scared. She waved back. "I pray this isn't the last time I see them alive."

Seeing the fear in her eyes, Clark took her hand. "We're going to fight for them, Julie. This guy won't know what hit him."

She turned to him with her head down. "I really hope you're right. I don't think I could take losing anybody else."

∞⌾∞⌾∞⌾∞

Julie, Kevin, and Clark finally were able to make their way to the art gallery that Kiger had directed them to. They were surprised at how small and unassuming it was. Despite being on a main road, it was a small building with a small parking lot, easily overshadowed by surrounding office buildings and shopping centers. Kiger was right. It seemed a fitting place for an art gallery that wasn't dealing in typical art.

As Julie got out of the car, she looked at the humble building. "To think the answers to crack a case of serial killing could be here."

Kevin joined her in examining in the building. "I know, ironic. The only thing this place seems to hold is code violations. But I guess you can't judge a book by its cover."

"Just like you, Jules." Clark smugly whispered over her shoulder.

"We don't have time for wit, Clark." She walked towards the gallery.

"I know that," he said in a whisper.

Kevin said to Julie, "The crook put the girl's body in Nina's store window. That couldn't be a coincidence, you know. He targeted her." He seemed to study her facial expressions.

Julie stopped a moment. "I know." She turned to her father. "It means he probably knows we're almost on to him and now he's making it personal." She swallowed hard. "All the more reason we gotta figure out who and where he is so we can stop him." She continued towards the art gallery.

She ripped open the front door and stormed inside.

The gallery was simpler than expected. The pictures hung on the walls in neat orderly rows spanning the perimeter of the room. The place looked scarcely bigger than Kevin's office at the station.

A man stood behind the counter dressed in a meeting point of casual and formal. They assumed him to be, Royal, the owner of the gallery, and he quickly confirmed that with a greeting.

They gazed intently at some of the pictures. They were all quite unnerving. Each seemed to play to a certain fetish, frequently nudity, and some form of deviancy.

Kevin glanced over the assortment of paintings. "My God, people actually buy this stuff?"

Royal heard the question and came out from behind the desk. "Indeed they do sir. It's perfectly legal as well, detectives."

Julie turned to him and held out her badge. "We aren't here to bust you for having deviant images in your art."

Kevin held out his as well. "But we may be here to bust you for something else."

Royal put up his hands defensively. "I don't know

what kind of joke you think you're playing, but I haven't done anything illegal."

Julie took out a picture of Kiger and showed it to Royal. "Do you know this man?" she asked.

Royal examined it. "He was my old art professor. Professor Kiger. Why? Is he dead?"

"Not that I am aware of." Julie took out a picture of Artie Falcon. "What about this guy?"

Royal gave it a quick look. "That's Artie Falcon, he's a great artist. What do you want with him?"

"Well, how about to find out who killed him?"

"Wait, Artie's dead?" Royal recoiled in shock. "When did that happen?"

"A few months back."

"A few months back?" Royal became genuinely confused. "That's impossible. I just saw him yesterday."

Julie froze. "Yesterday? Are you sure?"

"Definitely," he took a few steps back. "I don't know where you got the idea that Artie's been dead for months. As of yesterday, he was alive."

Julie shot a nervous glance at Clark and Kevin.

Kevin asked, "How did you see Artie yesterday?" He got closer to Royal to intimidate him. "Regardless of what you know, the world thinks he is dead. So how is he doing business with you?"

Royal smiled proudly. "He's a talented artist and he is kind enough to donate his works of art to my gallery for free." He walked over to the wall of paintings. "I've sold a few already. Got quite a bit of cash for them too. I've offered him royalties but he always declines." Royal smiled and folded his arms. "He says money is no compensation compared to somebody seeing the artistic value in his work."

Nervous looks were shared among the detectives before they returned their gazes to Royal, who seemed to have no clue how severe Artie's actions had become.

Julie asked, "Can I see some of these paintings?"

Royal was pleased, "Sure thing. I have all of them over here." He stopped at one in the middle of the room. "This is one he just brought in yesterday. He seems to come in with at least three a week. I honestly don't know how he does it."

The three of them stood in silent horror staring at the painting before them. It depicted a young woman in a wedding dress, dead in a bridal shop display window. The woman looked disturbingly similar to Caroline and the scene was exactly as they had found her that morning. Even down to the most miniscule details.

Next to it was a painting of a boy leaning against a bed. Dead. With many bloody knife wounds and pools of blood all around him. Paintings of a man and a little red headed girl, also murdered, served as a border, although their murders were regressively less gruesome. The Holden family.

Next to that was a young boy in the ocean with a hole in his forehead. As they studied the rest of the paintings, each matched one of the murder scenes. Only a few were missing. Those, they assumed, were the ones that had been sold.

Royal gazed gleefully at the artwork. "It's beautiful isn't it?"

Clark got in his face. "Beautiful? It's disgusting. He's painting pictures of people who're dead."

"They are just paintings," Royal shrugged. "Plus, I find them all very thrilling. Like this one, of the bride in the window. She's still pure, so her dress is white, and she is on display for the world to see. But she is so beautiful, they don't even realize she is already dead. It's so poetic. It gives me chills"

Julie became annoyed. "What if I told you a girl was found exactly like that this morning?"

"I'd say you were nuts." He laughed.

When they weren't joining in the laughter, his mood grew serious. "Oh, my God, you're serious?"

"Dead serious." Clark shot him a glare.

Kevin said, "In each of these paintings Artie brought you almost exact details of murder scenes we believe to all be connected. However, we thought that Artie was the first death in this chain. Now seems like he might be our killer."

Royal shook his head in disbelief. "No, Artie isn't a killer. He paints grim pictures but it's only art. He would never actually hurt anybody. He has no hate in his heart. If what you say is true, somebody is framing Artie."

Julie gazed back at the bride painting. "Tell me, when did Artie bring in the bride painting?"

Royal thought a moment. "Late last night, just before closing, why?"

Julie looked at him. "We found her this morning. We believe her to have been there for several hours. If somebody is framing Artie, how could they see that painting in time to copy it, exactly?" She could see that she was beginning to get through to him. "He makes his paintings real crime scenes. It's what he does, Royal. And he's going to do it again unless we stop him."

Royal raised his voice. "You can't prove he did these things. It's all circumstantial evidence and it'll never hold up!"

"That's not for you to judge." She moved closer to

him. She grabbed his arm until she could see that he was uncomfortable. "If you see him, you have to tell us. His next targets are already selected. If we can't stop him, more innocent people will die. Royal, can you live with yourself if you could've stopped them from being murdered and you didn't?"

Royal froze. "He said he'd be back with another painting today. But if you guys are here, and if he is as guilty as you say, he probably won't show. You guys should go and I can call you after he leaves."

"How do we know we can trust you?" She pulled him closer.

Kevin inched closer as well. "Yeah, we can't be sure you won't sell us out."

Royal considered for a moment. "One of you stays here." He faked a smile. "In the back. You can bust him if you want."

Julie and Kevin looked at each other.

Clark stepped forward. "I'll do it. I'll stay here."

Kevin shook his head. "No. This could be dangerous. You shouldn't do this without backup."

"Backup could blow our cover." Clark pointed to the room in the back. "I'll stay hidden back there by myself. I'll be quiet until this guy comes in. Then we got him."

Julie was quiet a moment. "We have to do it. This is our only lead. We can't just investigate Artie because everybody thinks he's dead. We'd have to prove he's alive and this is the only way we can do that."

Kevin said, "I don't feel good about it."

"It's our best chance to catch him."

Royal folded his arms. "I still think Artie's clean. So I know nothing will happen. I'm just doing this to clear his name."

Clark took him by the arm. "Well, in a few hours, I guess we'll see who's right."

∞◦◦◦∞

While Clark stayed behind at the art gallery, Julie and Kevin made a stop at the coroner's office. When they got there, they found Caroline's body already covered and in a drawer, her autopsy having been completed.

Julie looked at the closed drawer. "I expected you to still have her open."

"Yeah, I did too, but there wasn't much to look at with her. He snapped her neck about midnight and that's all she wrote. Aside from a few post-mortem contusions I believe she got when he was setting her up in that window, there's absolutely nothing interesting about her body. No signs of sexual assault, or any clue as to who this guy may be."

Julie leaned forward onto an empty slab. "We may not need any clues from her body. I think we might have our man. And it's the last person we would've expected."

Cora folded her arms. "Well, I guess that is good. I'm getting tired of cutting murdered people open so much."

Julie stood up straight again. "Well hopefully Caroline will be the last one from this killer."

The crash of metal was followed by Caroline's mother storming in. "Where is she? Where is my daughter?"

Cora approached her. "Excuse me ma'am, you'll have to calm down and tell me your name."

Julie said, "She's Caroline's mother."

The woman angrily swung her purse over her shoulder. "Where is my daughter? What did you do with her? I want to see her."

Cora opened the drawer and pulled out the slab on which Caroline's body lay. She removed the sheet from the top of the body up to the top of her chest.

Caroline's mother looked at her daughter's pale, life-less form in horror. "My baby, my baby's really dead." She broke into tears. She stepped towards the body and began to sob as she leaned down over her daughter's limp flesh. She looked up and screamed. "She was good to you. She went to church every week and this is what you let happen to her?" She lifted the body up slightly and wrapped her arms around it.

Julie said, "I don't think you can blame this on God."

She set the body down and turned to Julie with a stare of vitriol. "Don't you dare talk back to me, you little bitch. You did this to her. You were supposed to keep her safe and now she's dead. If you had done your job, my daughter would still be alive, not rotting away on some cold cot."

Julie restrained herself to keep from belting the woman. "Excuse me, but you don't exactly have room to act like you gave a damn about her when she was alive. When you heard she was in danger, the only thing you cared about was whether or not you could use her apartment. Well, guess what? As her next of kin, you can have it. Are you happy now?"

"Don't you dare act like I didn't love my daughter." She charged at Julie but Cora held her back. "I did everything in my power to make sure that girl lived a happy life."

Julie looked at her in disgust. "If you're so convinced you did a good job, why is it you didn't show an ounce of concern when you learned of the threat to Caroline's life? I don't doubt you loved her. Maybe you know how much you neglected your relationship with her when she was alive, and maybe that's why you're so angry right now."

Caroline's mother turned an angry shade of red. "How dare *you* speak that way to *me*!"

"How dare you speak that way to me!" Julie stepped closer until their noses were nearly touching, "I actually cared what happened to Caroline in the end, which is more than I can say for you."

The woman was left stunned from Julie's words.

"I'll leave you alone with your daughter." She walked out of the room.

Kevin chased after her. "You realize cops are not supposed to fight with the victim's family, right?"

Julie folded her arms and leaned against a wall. "Well, mothers are supposed to give a damn about their child being in danger before they wind up in the morgue." Without another word, she stormed off to wait for news from Clark on Artie.

⚬⚬⚬⚬⚬

Hanging out in the back of the store, Clark watched as a few customers, none of them Artie, came in to purchase paintings. One of them purchased a painting of a naked toddler without genitals, and another purchased one of a pit of vipers devouring a man. It seemed like Artie may not have been the only disturbed person this shop catered to. Not one piece of art seemed to be anything less than chilling and disturbing.

At a few minutes before noon, a man walked into the store carrying two paintings. The man did not look anything like Artie from the photos Clark had seen, but it was possible that Artie had changed his appearance. After all, if he really had faked his death, keeping a low profile was a logical next step.

Royal approached the man. "What can I do for you, sir?"

The man said, "Yes, I was instructed to deliver these to you by an Artie Falcon." He handed Royal the paintings. "He said he had planned to do it himself but he got kind of pre-occupied with something else. He said to send his sincere apologies."

Royal became nervous. "Thank you." He accepted the paintings from the man, who promptly left. It seemed the messenger wasn't into this style of art either.

Clark came out from the back. "I thought you said Artie delivers the paintings himself."

Royal said, "He does. This isn't like him."

"Well let's see the paintings. They might tell us what he's up to."

Royal removed the sheets from the two paintings and the men stared at them with wide eyes.

Royal gazed at them with admiration. "Wow, these are as good as anything else he's done. From an artistic point-of-view anyway. But if what you say is true..."

"Then we know what this guy's preoccupied with, and we'd better find him before he gets a chance to do this." Clark grabbed his phone and rushed out of the store.

◦◦◯◦◦◯◦◦◦◯◦◦

Nina, Damien, and Milo were waiting in a small lobby for the private plane to be ready. The young officer was one of many standing guard by them. The three felt almost like they were the criminals since they couldn't even use the bathroom without an officer following them.

As the early afternoon dawned, the private plane was finally ready. An officer came in to alert the others and to escort the three of them to the plane. His dark eyes and longish brown hair gave him an appearance slightly more youthful than his authority led them to believe was an accurate assessment of his age.

He said to the young officer, "I can take them from here."

The young officer put his hands on his hips. "You sure? I can come with you."

He turned to hide his face. "No, that will not be necessary."

"Well, okay then. What's your name again? I don't believe I've seen you around before."

He turned around, "Name's Officer Artie Falcon, I'm new to the force, pleased to meet you."

He shook Artie's hand. "Well, welcome to the force, and thank you Officer Falcon. Hope to see you around."

Artie smiled. "No, thank you."

He pulled out a gun, turned, and fired a bullet into the officer's head. The officer fell to the ground, instantly dead.

Having the element of surprise, he did the same to every other officer, prompting screams from every member of the Greene family.

They froze in fear as he approached them with the gun.

"All right you three." He held the gun out with a smile. "There's been a little change of plans. We'll be missing our plane this afternoon. I have a different destination in mind."

Nina held her boys close, trembling at the sight of their assailant. His appearance seemed to be gentle enough on the surface, making the gun he held in their face, and the smile he wore while doing it all the more surreal.

He led them outside through a side door. Nina wasn't sure what troubled her more, the fact that he was kidnapping them or the fact that he'd had every chance to kill them and hadn't. Yet.

He loaded them into the back of a small, unmarked car parked a few feet away. He drove away unnoticed.

He took off his police hat. "Don't worry folks. Where we're going is not far at all. I think you'll feel right at home." He locked all the doors of the car.

Nina saw that there was no way to unlock them from where they sat.

"And don't try anything. Please." He pointed the gun back at them. "We wouldn't want any of you getting shot."

The three clung close together in fear as they saw their abductor's sneer in the mirror.

Milo nervously clung to his mother. "What's he going to do with us?"

Nina stared ahead. "I don't know honey. I really don't know."

"We're his next targets." Damien stared out the window as the airport faded into the distance. "Whatever he's going to do with us, it's nothing good."

"Don't scare your brother. Julie can still find us. She has to." She kissed Milo's head and pulled him closer. She could feel him breathing on her. He was still breathing. There was still a chance.

She felt her heartbeat. It was pounding against her chest. Like a countdown.

Clark rushed back to the station. "Artie had somebody else deliver the paintings, and they're not good. He's definitely after the Greenes. Did their plane take off yet?"

Kevin shook his head. "We got bad news. Somebody kidnapped them from the airport. Reportedly disguised as a cop. There's no sign of them anywhere."

"Did you check their home? Maybe the killer went

back there."

"Yeah, no sign of them."

Julie stormed into the office geared for a confrontation with a bulletproof vest and her gun fully loaded. "I am not going to sit around and wait for a call that my best friend and her family are dead. I'm going to find them if it costs me my badge."

Kevin rose to his feet. "Count me in on that mission."

Clark rubbed his chin nervously. "But where do we look? If there's no sign of Artie Falcon or the Greenes, how are we going to find them?"

Julie took out a picture of her family and the Greenes together. "When you have motivation, you find a way. I've already assembled a team. Now let's go find them before it's too late."

With her resolution firm, Julie set out to find Artie and the Greenes, but with no leads as to where he had taken them, trying to find them was a task much more difficult than she had anticipated.

CHAPTER 7

Dark clouds gathered over the course of the afternoon, making what was usually still a sunny time of day during the summer look scarcely brighter than the dead of night.

As five o'clock neared, Nina asked Artie, "Where are you taking us?"

Artie smiled at her in the rearview mirror. "You'll see soon enough."

"Why are you stopping so much? Are you afraid of being caught?" She nervously stroked Milo's hair.

"Well, it's not like my taking you is totally catching the cops off guard after all the previous stunts I've pulled." He turned around to look at her, "But don't worry. We will get there soon. I am just waiting for the coast to be clear."

Milo decided to ask about the elephant in the room instead of pretending it wasn't there. "Are you going to kill us?" He kept his tone soft.

Artie turned and looked him in the eyes. He smiled lovingly. "Now why would you ask a question like that?" He flashed him a wink before returning his eyes to the road.

Milo burrowed closer to Nina. She gently wrapped her arms around him.

Damien looked out the window. "Hey, this is our neighborhood."

Artie chuckled. "You noticed that, huh? I told you that you would feel right at home."

Despite seeing the familiar houses and buildings that had brought feelings of safety for years, the three of them felt even more uncomfortable seeing their neighborhood through the lens of their captivity. It brought the reality of their situation even closer to home, and it was not a welcome feeling.

"What if somebody sees us?" Milo asked.

Artie shrugged. "So what if somebody sees us? I'm just an old friend dropping in for a visit. Isn't that right Nina?" He said, as he gazed into the rear-view mirror with a grin.

Artie carefully turned the corner onto their street. Looking from a distance, he made sure there weren't any cops at the house. To his pleasure, there were none in sight. He parked a few houses away.

"It never ceases to amaze me how law enforcement can be so clueless sometimes." He sighed happily. "Well, it's time for everybody to get out."

Nina held tight to her boys. "Why should we go any-where with you?"

Artie smiled as he waved a knife around. "Because you're good people." He took out a gun and pointed at her. "And good people do what they're told." He signaled for them to get out with the gun. "And don't even think about trying to make a scene. I hate it when people make a scene and then they get hurt. It's just no fun."

Nina realized that they had no choice but to comply. As hopeless as their situation was if they followed him, they would have no hope at all if they didn't cooperate.

They quietly got out of the car. Artie put his arms around the boys as if he was their friend.

He looked admiringly around at the houses. "This is really a beautiful neighborhood. It must be fun growing up here. If I had kids, I'd definitely want them to grow up here. It's such a picturesque neighborhood. Not that I'd ever start a family "

Nina felt chills up her spine. They grew sharper with every syllable that left the smirking lips of their captor.

She looked at her sons.

They occasionally flinched as she did. They were just as scared.

They came to the charming Greene house. "Well it looks like we've reached our destination. It's so hot out here. Why don't we go inside where it's cooler? Sweat's no fun at all."

He forced them up the stairs. He turned to Nina. "Why don't you get out your key and let us in?"

Nina reached into her pocket and nervously grabbed her keys. She thought of running. They had hope out here. If he tried to shoot them, somebody would see. But if her shot her children, would it matter?

She looked down at the gun in his hand. She'd never seen one up close before.

He pressed it against her back. "Something wrong?"

She shook her head. "No." She unlocked the door and opened it.

He escorted all of them inside.

"Ah, suburbia!" He gazed around the house. "Where anything can happen in broad daylight and nobody sees a thing."

He shut the door behind him and locked the dead-bolt. He looked around.

He inhaled and exhaled with a sigh of relief. "It smells so good in here. I love the smell of fresh home air."

The three of them stiffly followed his lead.

Nina felt like a prisoner in her own home.

Artie leaned in close to their ears. "Why don't we all go upstairs? I am sure it is nice up there too."

Damien said, "I'd much rather we stayed down here. It's brighter and there's more to do."

Artie turned to him. "Excuse me. I wasn't aware the matter was up for a vote."

"It's hotter upstairs." Damien tried to steady his voice. "You came in to get out of the heat. If you want to get out of the heat, you'll stay down here—where it's cooler."

"And where the front door is conveniently a lot closer to get to?" He held out his hand to the front door.

"Well, if somebody knocks, it's good to be able to get to it quickly. It's rude to keep people waiting." Damien forced a smile.

"Oh, is it really?" Artie pretended to care. "And who would be knocking on your door? You were leaving town, were you not? Nobody knows you are here. So who would be knocking? Are you expecting company that I am unaware of?"

"Nobody knew we were leaving town."

"News spreads quickly in this town. I imagine everyone knows by now."

Damien was silent, but kept a focused stare into Artie's eyes. His stern green eyes clearly unnerved Artie a bit.

"*Are* you expecting anybody?" Artie smiled.

Damien was silent.

"Not expecting anybody? I didn't think so. Now let's all be good little boys..." He turned to Nina. "And girl." He grinned. "And go upstairs. There's a lot of fun that can only be had upstairs."

He flashed them a sadistic smile before signaling for them to ascend the carpeted staircase.

Milo led.

Followed by Damien.

Then Nina.

Artie followed behind them.

As they reached the upper level of the house, Artie looked around. "Nice, I could so live here." He poked his head in the master bedroom. "Simple. Not too busy. I like it." He then looked into the bathroom and smiled without making a comment. He looked into Milo's room. "Looks like the picture perfect boy's room. Reminds me of the room I wanted as a boy but never got."

He looked into Damien's room. "A perfectly neutral room. Anybody could sleep comfortably in this room. Why don't you all hang out in here awhile? I got a few errands to run."

They all looked on in silent protest.

He looked at the window and said, "Ah, yes, I knew I was forgetting something. We can't have any of you trying to escape out the window. That's dangerous. You could fall and seriously hurt yourselves. Good thing I swung by after the cops got you. Before I went to the airport. I bolted them shut. A blackbelt couldn't get out those windows. And if you try to break them...glass is dangerous when it breaks. No way you'd reach the ground. Not alive anyway. Plus, I'd hear you breaking the glass." He smiled and chuckled at their gloomy faces.

Damien held himself back from attacking Artie. "You're a sick man."

"I'm going to go take care of a few things." Artie pretended not to hear Damien. "Why don't you stay here? And if you get hungry, I think Damien left a few cans of nuts and some licorice in his dresser. That should hold you over until I get back."

With a smile, he walked out of the room and shut the door.

After he left, Nina could hear the click of a lock.

Damien quickly ran to the door.

It was locked from the outside. He looked down and noticed that his doorknob had been replaced. This one had no inside lock. They were trapped.

"Damn it! We're locked in. He changed everything."

Nina nestled Milo close to her. "There's gotta be some way out of this. I will not just sit by and let him kill you. I won't." She rushed to the windows and tried them. Nothing. "Find something that can break this. I'm getting us out of here."

"But Mom." Milo shot her a teary glance.

"Just do it. I'll get us out of here. In the meantime, you boys shove the dresser against the door. He might've taken away the inside lock but we can still barricade ourselves in."

Damien tried the dresser. It wouldn't budge. "It's not moving, Mom."

She slammed her fists against the window. "Damn it." She looked around for a blunt object. Nothing. Damien's basketball trophies were gone. Anything hard enough to smash the window—removed. "How could he have done all of this so fast? He couldn't have planned for so much. There's no way." She grabbed her head and wiped sweat from her brow. "It's just a freaking bedroom. I'm not going to be a prisoner in my own house."

She pounded on the glass as hard as she could, praying it would smash. Not a crack. She took a step back and noticed that a large sheet of plexiglass was over the window. There was no way she could break it. "No." She cried harder and sank to her knees.

Damien looked out. An occasional car drove by. A neighbor pulled into her driveway. "There's gotta be a way out. This is our home. We gotta think of something."

Milo quivered as he took a seat on the bed. "What if we can't get out? Are we really all gonna die?"

The silence to his question was more piercing than any answer ever would've been. They could only watch and wait until Artie returned. Or rescue came. They were still breathing. There was hope.

Artie had said the cops had already looked at the house. They must've moved on to other possible hiding places. Maybe they would come back.

Nina had to hope. There was a way out. There had to be.

But as the minutes dragged, the possibility of rescue seemed but a bleak dream compared to the likely doom that was waiting just a few rooms away.

It was almost seven o'clock now and there was still no sign of the Greenes. Julie became increasingly worried that she had lost them. She had sent out teams all over town but had found nothing. A team even returned to check the house again but there was no sign of them. It seemed exactly as it had been when they checked it the first time.

Julie returned to the police station, exhausted and frustrated at making no progress. She prayed hard for any clue. Something to help her find them. Alive.

She went to her desk and tore through the files of the previous victims. She wasn't even sure what she was looking for. She just wanted answers. There had to be some clue.

She screamed as she threw them onto the floor. She held her head and cried.

Clark came over to her. "We are going to find them." He picked up the papers from the floor and set them down on her desk.

Julie took a deep breath. "I know we're going to find them. It's a matter of whether we'll find them in time."

"We will."

Julie fought tears. "You saw those paintings. He's targeting them."

Clark reached out to comfort her. "Well, according to those paintings, he wants to kill the boys by putting them in a trunk and lighting the car on fire. Then he wants to burn the mother at the stake. So far, nothing like that has been reported. So they are still alive. There's still time."

Worried tears began to spill out. "But time is running out. I feel like any minute, I'm going to get a call that they found them. Dead."

"We're going to do everything that we can Julie. Where's that cop that gave that art professor tainted food to make him talk?" He smiled at her. He reached over and touched her shoulder.

Julie took a deep breath. "She's suffering from too little sleep and too much stress."

"Well tell her to snap out of it." He pulled back. "We aren't going to find them by acting like we're not."

"Maybe I should go to the house. To check again."

"Jules, the cops went there."

"Maybe he brought them there later." She bit her lower lip. "He has them somewhere. They're right under our noses. I can feel it."

Kevin rushed over to them. "We got some news guys."

"News? What kind of news?" Julie eagerly rose to her feet.

Kevin held out some papers. "They just exhumed Artie Falcon's grave. Not surprisingly, he wasn't in it. Just a bunch of rocks."

"So how did he fake his death? There were autopsy photos."

Kevin shrugged. "I don't know. Maybe that professor threw money at someone." He thrust his finger into the air. "But I can tell you that he's been living in an abandoned apartment building for awhile. Using cash to get by."

Clark asked, "Who told you this?"

"Street sources."

"Street sources?" Clark looked surprised. "You have street sources?"

Kevin set the papers down on a desk. "When you're a cop as long as I've been one, you learn to have a few more tricks up your sleeve than the book offers."

"Well why don't you get one of your sources to tell us where this guy took the Greenes?"

Kevin sighed. "Unfortunately my sources aren't *that* good."

Julie said, "Well, we'll just have to do it on our own."

Kevin scratched his head. "We can look until the cows

come home, but until we get a better idea of where they are, we're not going to get anywhere."

Clark said, "Well, at least we got one good thing. We know how he plans to kill them. So it narrows things down for us." He glanced at the papers on the desk.

Julie couldn't help but feel that relying so heavily on the paintings was going to end up being a mistake, but since it was all they had, it was what they had to use.

The darkness outside was growing thicker, seeming a fitting parallel to the growing danger in the Greene family home.

Milo paced back and forth. "Maybe he's not going to kill us after all. Maybe he's going to leave us here."

Damien clicked his tongue. "Fat chance of that happening. He wouldn't go through all of this just to scare us. This guy means business."

Nina embraced Milo. "Damien, you shouldn't crush your brother's hopes. If he believes we can get out of this alive, let him believe that."

"I don't want him having false hope." He leaned back against the wall. "If we're going to die, it's better that we accept it and prepare than act like we're going to be okay and then not be ready when he kills us."

"Damien!" She rushed up and grabbed him by the shoulders. "Please."

Milo got between the two. "Don't fight. If he's going to kill us, I don't want to spend our last minutes together fighting." He began to cry. "I'm a big boy, you don't have to pretend somebody's going to come kicking through the front door to save us like on TV. I am old enough to handle dying."

Nina gently held his arm. "Milo, I never said we're

going to die."

"Mom, I love you. So much. But you don't have to lie to protect me anymore." He sniffled. "When Dad left, I was too little to understand how he could just walk out on his family for another woman. But I do now. He didn't care enough to be with us. I am not a little baby anymore." Tears streamed down his face. "I'm a big boy."

The two embraced. She kissed his forehead. "Milo, I just don't want to accept it. When you were born, and the doctor put you in my arms, I had so many dreams for you. I just can't accept them ending today. Like this. I can't."

He began to cry and they sank back down to the floor. Nina still held him close.

"You might have to Mom." Milo leaned against her chest.

Damien sat down on the other side of Nina. "You gave us both a good life when Dad left. You were the best Mom ever. If we die today, we don't have to have any regrets. We were never hungry or cold. We always had a roof over our heads to sleep under. Unless we went camping." He chuckled. He took a deep breath to fight his tears. "You gave us love. You gave us our faith. Because of you, we know that death isn't the end. We can be strong in our death, and we can pray to God to face it as bravely as we can. You gave us that. Because you are a great mom."

"The best." Milo kissed her cheek.

Nina tearfully hugged them close. "And you two are wonderful sons. The best children a mom could ask for. You might have acted out sometimes, but you are good kids. You would've been good men. You would've been really good men."

They all smiled through their tears, enjoying being together.

Nina could feel her sons' hearts beating with the same furor as hers. How many did they each have left?

The click of a lock.

The knob slowly turned.

Artie walked in with a smile. "Sorry to keep you waiting. I got a lot more held up than I expected. But I'm here now. And ready for our quality time together."

Nina pulled her boys closer to her, trying to calm their trembling bodies.

"Well, you know what they say, ladies first." Artie signaled with his knife for Nina to come to him. "Please, let's not make this difficult."

Nina turned to her boys and planted a kiss on the forehead of each of them. She whispered to them to be strong and uttered a final "I love you," before slowly rising to her feet.

He smiled and put his arm around her. "Let's go."

Nina turned around and saw Damien and Milo tearfully watching. She could see it in their eyes - they knew what she knew. They'd never lay eyes on each other again in this life.

Artie was calm as he led her out of the room and returned the door to its locked state.

<hr />

Artie forced Nina down the hall. Then down the stairs.

"You know they've been looking for you all around town." He chuckled. "They even came back here to look for you. That's what that whole 'keep quiet or I cut the boy's throat' thing was about earlier if you hadn't guessed. But I guess, fortunately for us, they sent lazy cops to the house 'cause they never thought to check upstairs. Dumbasses." He chuckled.

"They could still come back you know." She clenched her fists to decrease her trembling.

"Yeah, I expect them to." He rubbed his deceptively warm cheek against hers, "But I'll be done with you all and long gone by that time, I'm sure. I sent them on a wild goose chase to help ensure they don't interrupt us."

"And what do you mean by that?"

He smiled. "Those are details you really don't need to know."

He walked her into the kitchen. "We're here."

She stared at him. "You're bringing me to the kitchen?" She gazed at a picture of Milo and Damien on the fridge. They looked so happy. Annoyed to have their Christmas morning interrupted by posing for a picture, but still happy. Their last Christmas. If she'd only known...

"What's in here?"

He slammed her against the wall. "I'm going to be straight with you because that's how I am. I am going to kill you, and then I am going to kill both of your sons. One by one."

She broke into tears. "Please." She winced. "Don't hurt them. They're just children. They haven't done anything wrong."

"I am sure that they haven't. I'm not killing them because they were bad. Or even because I hate them." He ran his hands up and down her arms. "In fact, I think they are both very beautiful boys. Just like you are a beautiful woman."

She tried to break free. "Then why are you going to kill them?"

He tightened his grip on her, "Precisely because they are beautiful. Too beautiful to not be made into an even more beautiful work of art." He ran his hands across her neck. "But here's the thing. I haven't settled on exactly how I will kill them yet. How I kill them is up to you."

"Up to me?"

He nodded, a terribly handsome smile splitting his face. "I'm going to do something to you, Nina. If you scream or fight me in any way, I will kill both of your precious baby boys very slowly. That knife I've been waving around?" He pulled it out and ran it down her pants. "I will use it to cut off their body parts one by one. First I'll start with their genitals. And then their toes, one by one. Then their feet."

He picked up her hand. "Next, I'll move on to their fingers." He squeezed her fingers. "And hands." He leaned in closer. "Then their arms and legs."

He kissed her cheek. "Finally, I'll cut off their heads. They'll be like pieces of a beautiful puzzle." He twitched with a smile.

"At some point during the dismemberment, they will die. And they will be in completely unbearable agony until that happens. It will be pain greater than they ever imagined. But, if you are a good girl and cooperate, I promise, I will choose a much quicker and less painful method of death for them." He twirled his finger in her long, straight hair. "They will still be dead, but their final moments won't be spent feeling their body parts slowly sliced off by my blade. They won't suffer as much." He took a step back. "So, my lovely Mrs. Greene, my darling Mrs. Greene, how will your children die?"

She gaped back at him with raw terror. "Please. I'll do anything. You can torture me. Beat me. Do whatever you want with me. But please, just let my children go."

He shook his head. "I am sorry, Nina, but that isn't

a possibility. All three of you will become my next art sculptures. All three of you will only leave this house one more time—in body bags. I am going to kill all of you, and there is no way out of that." He gently wiped away one of her tears with his thumb.

"What I am doing is giving you the chance to spare your sons a world of agony. Do you want them to die a very slow and extremely painful death, or do you want them to die quickly so their pain is minimal? Why don't you close your eyes and imagine them screaming as I cut off their limbs one by one? Go ahead, do it."

Her will refused but her mind was plunged into the horror of her boys' blood curdling screams as they slowly inched towards their demise. She could hear them call for her as blood flowed from their wounds. It sent such a sharp shiver up her spine that she violently flinched.

Artie moved his lips close to her ear. "How long do you think they'd last until they died? Milo would probably die by the time I finished with his feet. Damien would hang on longer. Maybe even until I was through with his hands." He yanked her arms behind her back until she wailed. "You think that hurts? Imagine a knife taking that arm off."

Nina turned to him and tried to stop crying. "Okay. Okay. Please. Don't torture them. I'll do what you want. Just don't torture them. Don't make them suffer."

Artie smiled and placed his finger over her soft lips. "I will make it quick."

She pulled her head away. "I want your word. Make it quick. And as painless as possible."

He slipped his hands down her back. "I give you my word. When I kill them, it will be fairly quick." He grabbed her pants and ripped them off in what seemed to be a continuous tear.

Tears streamed down her face. "I'll do whatever you want. I won't fight you."

"I figured you'd see it my way." He leaned in and gently kissed her on the lips then pulled back to stare into her eyes. "You're such a beautiful woman, Nina. It's time we fully explored your artistic potential." He pushed her onto the ground and kneeled down on top of her, loosening his pants. He then leaned in and kissed her again, forcefully bounding her hands to the ground.

⚬───⚬⚬───⚬⚬───⚬

Milo clung close to Damien, knowing their time together was growing briefer by the second.

"What do you think he's going to do to us?" He trembled.

"It doesn't matter." Damien stroked Milo's face. "He can kill us. But he can't make us not a family anymore. We'll be a family no matter what he does."

Milo turned to Damien. "I'm sorry, Damien."

Damien pulled back. "What do you got to be sorry for?"

"I was a jerk to you a lot." Milo sulked. "I always bothered you and messed with you, and yesterday I even mooned you. I was a bratty little brother, always not minding my own business. I'm sorry."

Damien smiled. "You don't got anything to be sorry for. Sure, you were annoying as all heck. But you were always my little brother. I never regretted Mom giving me a little brother." He recalled their skirmishes. "And besides, I pushed you around just as much."

The two laughed.

Damien pulled Milo closer to him.

"What do you think it feels like to die?" Milo stared

straight ahead at the wall.

Damien started to cry. He couldn't let Milo see. "It doesn't matter. It could hurt like hell. Or maybe you don't feel anything at all. It doesn't really matter, I guess. We have the hope of something better after it. So whatever happens, we'll face it."

"I'm scared Damien." Milo buried his face on Damien's chest. "I don't want to be scared, but I am."

Damien lifted Milo's head up. "And it's okay to be scared. It doesn't matter what you feel. The only important thing is what you will."

"I know. I just don't want to die. I don't know what to do." He whimpered.

Damien thought a moment. "I do." He got off of his bed and onto his knees and then signaled for Milo to do the same.

Milo wiped his eyes. "You going to pray for God to rescue us?"

Damien shook his head. "No. Right now, I'm praying for something else."

"What else can you pray for right now?"

Damien's expression became peaceful. "Strength. And courage. The ability to look this killer in the eye, and not be afraid."

Milo joined Damien on his knees. "It would take God for me to do that. He's going to know I'm scared. I don't know how to be brave."

"That's why we're going to Him." He gulped. "If you're dying, I don't think there's anybody better to ask for help than Him."

Milo stared at Damien. "Since when do you like praying anyway?"

Damien chuckled. "I guess I deserve that. I haven't

been that good at it lately. Sucked at it, really. But it's never too late to start. We're still alive. So we can still pray every second until we're not. Even in just a couple of minutes, that's a lot of prayers. I guess maybe I was paying attention in Theology class after all."

He put his hands on Milo's shoulders and Milo did the same. They exchanged a tearful hug and even a cheek kiss.

"I love you, Milo. And I know I didn't say it before because it's cheesy and babyish and stupid to say all the time. But I mean it. And whatever happens, I want you to remember that." Damien struggled to breathe through his sobs.

"I love you too." Milo tightly hugged him.

After separating, they folded their hands as Damien decided what prayer they should say. No personal words seemed to come out.

Their fear choked it all.

They began saying the prayer they knew best at the exact same time, as if they both knew what the other would do. As the words left their lips, they felt more meaning in them than they ever had before in their lives.

"Our Father, who art in heaven, Hallowed be Thy Name. Thy kingdom come, Thy will be done, on Earth as it is in Heaven. Give us this day, our daily bread, and forgive us our trespasses, as we forgive those who trespass against us, and lead us not into temptation, but deliver us from evil," and after a pause, they said, "Amen!"

They felt the words really resonate in their hearts, but especially 'Thy will be done.' These were the hardest to say. Damien had said it so casually before. But it was the biggest surrender he could give at the moment. He knew God didn't put them in this situation. But whatever happened, no matter how much suffering it included, he knew God would be with them at every moment.

Damien heard the sound of footsteps coming closer.

Then the door unlocked and opened.

Artie stood in the doorway with that same smile he perpetually wore.

"Well, you two look like you've been busy." He poked his head in the door. "Praying, huh? I respect that. But prayer time is over. For one of you anyway."

He rushed towards Damien and seized him.

Damien knew a struggle would only make things harder. He resolved to accept whatever was going to happen next.

Artie extended his hand to Milo. "You may continue. Damien is coming with me."

Damien and Milo shared a final look.

He could see everything Milo was thinking in his brother's eyes. He felt sick leaving Milo to die alone. That thought upset him more than his own death.

Couldn't this freak at least let them die together? No. He had to take everything from them first. That was the kind of monster he was.

Damien gave Milo a nod goodbye and was led out.

"He'll get his turn soon enough." Artie relocked the room.

He only dragged Damien a few feet.

To the bathroom.

He forced Damien to his knees.

"So how's it going to be?" Damien looked down to avoid giving his killer the satisfaction of seeing fear in his eyes. "You going to cut me up with that knife? Shoot me in the head? Snap my neck?"

"You'll see." Artie ruffled his hair.

Damien fought tears. He clenched his fist as he felt the cold black of the knife against his neck. "Can I ask how my mom died?"

"You can ask." Artie caressed Damien's cheek. He leaned down and licked it and then exhaled a hot breath in Damien's ear. "But I am not going to tell you. How she died is irrelevant to your fate. But you can take comfort in one thing. Because of her, your death will be considerably less painful than it otherwise would've been. Quicker too. See? Your mother really does love you. Thank her when you get to heaven." He paused. "If that turns out to be true anyway."

"You don't believe in heaven? What a shock." Damien tried to appear to pity Artie.

"I don't believe period. I am not saying it's not real. I just am not saying it is. It's really of no concern to me either way."

"I feel sorry for you. Your life is killing people. Your entire existence is pain."

Artie shook his head. "You see, Damien. I don't see it that way. I see art as beauty, and human beings are a great means to that end."

Damien couldn't think of any words to fit such a twisted worldview. He glared at Artie. "Well, what are you waiting for? Do it!"

Artie smiled as he ran his fingers through Damien's hair, "Oh not yet, Damien. I promised your mother your death would be quick. And it will be. But I am not ready to kill you just yet. First, we have something else to do."

Damien's mind raced with all the possible tortures that could be inflicted on him. He'd heard about what this guy did to people. There was no telling what he had planned now.

He scowled into Artie's dark eyes. Show no fear. Whatever happened, be strong.

Artie kneeled down next to Damien and cut off his shirt.

"What are you doing?" Damien asked fearfully.

"Don't move." Artie caressed Damien's chest. "Just watch." He gently pushed Damien down to the floor and continued to strip him.

Damien tried to throw Artie off of him.

Artie pushed him down harder. "This will go a lot easier if you don't try to be a fool."

"I don't want to make it easy for you."

"Then this is going to really hurt." He grinned and went to work.

Artie took out a syringe and gently shot a small stream of a liquid into the air. "Perfect."

<hr />

Milo couldn't help but think how different this was than the movies. The movies had dramatic or sad music when people were dying. Or the sounds of complete chaos and sirens. This was just painful silence. So quiet that he could hear every creak of the floor and ringing of the ear. And his breath. Every breath was amplified. This was the soundtrack to his death. And it was worse than any movie music. This made it real.

Damien was probably dead by now. Like his mother. They were waiting for him.

Milo returned to his knees to pray. It was all he could do. Why wasn't God going to save him?

It didn't matter. God was still there. Milo could feel it.

His knees ached from the pressure of he floor. But he couldn't stop. He had to pray as long as he could. He'd lose his mind if he didn't

He began praying a rosary. He used his ten fingers in lieu of rosary beads. Through his whimpers and wails, he prayed the prayers his mother had taught him—the *Our Fathers, Hail Marys,* and *Glory Bes*. He prayed that his flawed offering of the only rosary he had ever said by himself would be sufficiently pleasing to God. He realized he never really cared before if he was pleasing God. But maybe he should have. He was almost a teenager now and that means you can't be a kid anymore. As his heart ticked towards its final beat, he wanted to be different.

The footsteps returned. Somehow louder than ever.

The door swung open.

Artie. His unbefitting smile.

"Are you ready Milo? It is your turn to become immortalized as beautiful artwork." He extended his hand in invitation.

Milo rose to his feet, not to run, but to walk. He didn't want to be dragged to this. God was still with him. He almost felt his arms around him, giving him the strength to stand. With all the courage he could fill his voice with, he said, "I'm ready."

Every step he took flashed his life. He met Patrick and Petey on a playground and they would become his best friends. His mother sat him down and told him that Petey was dead. He'd hang out with Patrick almost every day since he'd met him. Every precious moment with his brother that he wanted to relive. He made his First Holy Communion, the only time he ever willingly wore white. Every moment of his life that he could remember seemed to dance in his mind, and it all lead to these final moments.

Artie led him out of the room, turning the light off and closing the door behind him. He didn't lock it this time.

Artie led him to the bathroom.

The first thing that Milo saw was Damien.

He was naked and sitting undignified on the open toilet.

Milo crumpled to his knees. "Why did you put him like that? Why did you do that to him."

"People are so predictable in their reactions."

"This isn't art. This is just sick."

Artie placed his hand on Milo's shoulder.

Milo flinched when he felt the cold, sweaty palm meet his skin.

Artie leaned down and kissed Milo's cheek. "You, my friend, are the second half of the artwork. Only once you are added to the mix can the artwork's picture be realized."

Milo walked towards his brother's lifeless form and planted a kiss on his forehead. He cried. "We'll be together soon Damien. You, me, and Mom. And we can even see Petey and his dad again. It'll be great."

He took Damien's hand. "I'm sorry for last night. And all the times I was a brat. I know I called you a lot of mean names so many times and I annoyed you. I take it back. I take all of it back. I didn't mean it. I promise I didn't mean it. Oh Damien, I just want you to be alive again."

He wailed and placed his brother's hand on his cheek. The hand didn't feel like his brother's anymore. It was still warm, but Damien's strength was gone.

Milo let go of the hand and it flopped down to Damien's side.

Why did this monster leave his brother like this? On a toilet? Milo didn't understand how anybody could be so sick as to enjoy seeing this.

"Why are you apologizing to him?" Artie ran his fingers through Milo's curly hair. "He's dead. He can't hear you."

"I think he can hear me. God will let him hear me." He then whispered, "I love you," to Damien.

He could feel Damien saying it back. He was waiting for him.

Artie slipped his hand under Milo's shirt. "It's time."

Milo turned to him, praying silent prayers. "I'm ready. So what do you do? You're going to shoot me, right? Or cut me?"

Artie smiled. "So much like him. It's beautiful."

Milo shot him a confused stare. "What do you mean? I don't get it."

"Well actually, you're not going to die just yet." Artie gently leaned in and breathed into Milo's ear.

Milo's chest hurt.

Warnings from his mother replayed in his head. He never understood what they meant before. But suddenly, it all became so painfully and horribly clear.

He cried and prayed for what seemed like an eternity. Until it was over.

⊶⊙⊶⊙⊶⊙⊶

Julie filled a plastic cup with water from the water fountain. She swallowed hard. It felt like a knife going down her throat. She breathed rapidly.

Kevin approached her. "You're wearing yourself down, Julie. We'll never find them if you get burned out."

"I am not burned out. I just need a little water." She took another chug. "We've been looking all day and we still haven't found them. Now it's dark and they've been missing for hours. What if we're too late?" She whimpered. "Nina's my friend, Dad. And those kids...I've watched them grow up. Milo's my Godson. If I can't save them...I can't even think about it."

He touched her arm. "We're not too late. We haven't had any reported incidents like those paintings describe. And trust me. If a woman was burning at the stake, I'd think we'd have heard about it."

Julie's phone rang. She answered it eagerly. "Hello?" She braced for news about her friends.

"Julie..." It was Clark.

She quickly put him on speakerphone. "Please tell me you have some news for us, Clark."

"Yeah, there's definitely been some news."

She noticed an apprehensive tone in his voice. Her heat beat faster. This didn't sound good.

"About the Greenes?" Julie's hands dripped with sweat.

Clark was silent a moment. "Kind of. I just got a call from Royal. He says we need to get to the gallery. It's urgent. I'm headed there now to check it out. I suggest you two get there quickly too."

Kevin asked, "You think maybe Artie contacted him?"

Clark hesitated again. "It's possible. He wouldn't say anything on the phone. I got a bad feeling about this. But I'm here now. You two should get here as quickly as you can."

"We're on our way!" She hung up the phone.

◦◦◯◦◦◯◦◦◯◦◦

Clark pulled into the lot and rushed in through the front door of the gallery. He saw Royal standing behind the counter, eagerly tapping his hands.

Royal breathed a sigh of relief when he saw Clark. "Thank you for coming."

Clark angrily marched to him. "This better be good."

"It may not be good but it's important. Artie just paid me a visit." He pointed to the two paintings Artie had sent over earlier. "He said that these two paintings he had delivered earlier, they weren't the real paintings he wanted me to sell. He said he'd known you'd find them and that they'd make effective decoys."

"Decoys?" Clark felt a jolt in his heart. "He was on to us?"

"It seems so. He said these two paintings were the real ones." He pointed to two paintings set against the wall. "I looked at them. Objectively, they'd be good artwork. But in light of what I know, they scare me. They truly scare me. Detective, this is darker than anything he's ever done. And if he's done anything like this..."

"Show me." Clark steadied himself.

Royal walked to the covered artwork. "I'm sorry, Detective."

"Do it." Clark cringed.

Royal pulled away the sheets from the two paintings.

Clark resisted the urge to vomit. "Oh my God." He put his hands over his mouth. "What kind of person is this? This is what he was planning. All along." Clark turned away.

He pounded the counter. "Son of a bitch." He hit it again. Tears dripped onto his hand.

"What time was he here?" He turned to Royal.

"Just about half an hour ago."

Clark charged towards the door without another word.

Royal asked, "Hey, where are you going?"

Clark didn't bother responding. He drove off in less than a minute. He was headed for the Greene house.

Clark broke a handful of traffic laws just to get out of the parking lot.

He sped towards the Greene house, praying he wouldn't find what he feared.

⊶⊷

Artie came out from the back with a smile. "Well done, old friend." He patted Royal on the back. "He had no clue. He's playing right into my hand."

Royal turned to him. "That family...did you really do all of that to them? The things in that painting?"

Artie put his arm around Royal. "I did. And if you think that painting is beautiful, imagine the real thing. With real flesh, its beauty is amplified at least tenfold."

He let out a sadistic chuckle.

Royal became greatly unnerved as he stared into Artie's unrepentant eyes.

⊶⊷

Julie and Kevin pulled into the parking lot as Clark was speeding out of it. "I don't like this at all." Julie held her chest.

Julie jumped out before the car stopped moving.

Kevin stopped the car crooked across two spaces.

He stormed out after her. "You trying to get killed? Jumping out of a moving vehicle?"

She didn't answer. She ran to the gallery.

She and Kevin busted through the front door.

Royal was lying on the floor. There was a bloody bullet wound on his chest.

Julie rushed to his side. "What happened?"

Royal coughed up blood. "Artie was here. He dropped off two more paintings. He said that these two were the real ones."

Kevin asked, "You mean the others were decoys?"

Royal nodded.

"Damn it!" Kevin shouted as he punched the wall.

Three pictures crashed to the ground. "He knew we were on to him and used it to his advantage."

Julie held up Royal's head. "How did you get shot?"

Royal clenched his chest. "Clark was just here. He saw these and took off. Artie was hiding in the back. He shot me right after Clark walked out the door and then left. He told me that I wasn't part of the chain. He just needed me out of the way. I thought he was my friend." He swallowed hard. "Somebody who shared my appreciation for art."

"This guy is nobody's friend."

Royal began to cry. "He just wanted to use it for sick things. They were such beautiful paintings. But I'd never want them to become true. I'm not a bad person. I don't want children to die."

His tears caused him to cough up even more blood.

Julie shushed him. "Calm down, you're only going to make it worse."

Royal pointed to the two paintings sitting a few feet over. "Those are the ones he brought in. You're not going to like them."

Julie and Kevin shot a glance over at the paintings. They felt their jaws drop at the images they saw depicted in the paint.

Royal lowered his hand. "He told me that he did that before he left. I'm so sorry. I'm so, so..." He exhaled a final breath. His body went limp.

Julie closed his eyes and set his body down before walking over to the picture to get a closer look.

Kevin eyed the pictures with disgust. "If that's really what he did...my God. He's sicker than I thought."

Julie ran her hands across the canvas, her eyes welling with tears. "It's too late for them. We're too late."

Clark had just arrived at the Greene house. Everything was dark inside.

He still shot up the front steps and kicked in the door.

He rushed to the turn on the lights in the living room. Everything was quiet.

The house seemed totally abandoned. Then he saw a light coming from the kitchen. He slowly walked towards it.

Then he saw the pool of blood.

He knew in his heart what he was about to find but when he finally revealed the grisly image to his eyesight, terror still overcame him. Nina's nude body was lying on the kitchen table with her arms outstretched, a mop impaled through her chest. Her eyes stared towards the ceiling. Her legs were spread apart. Clark could see bruising on her abdomen. He knew what had happened.

At that same moment, Julie and Kevin were looking at the first painting—seeing an almost exact replica of the scene of Nina's murder that Clark was witnessing, down to the setup of the kitchen.

Clark knew he had to check upstairs for the boys. Having seen the painting at the gallery, he knew what he'd find, but he braced himself nonetheless. He slowly ascended the stairs, trying to keep every glimmer of hope that was left alive. He saw the door to the bathroom slightly ajar. It was pitch black inside.

He braced himself as he flipped on the light switch, and he recoiled in terror once the light illuminated the grim scene in the bathroom. He immediately saw Damien's nude body sitting on the toilet; his head slumped against the medicine cabinet behind him.

As he looked ahead a few feet, he saw a child's hand

in the tub. His heart sank. He walked a few feet more into the bathroom and glanced down in the bathtub. There he saw Milo lying on the bottom of the tub, with the water filled up to the rim of the tub, leaving the body totally submerged. He saw blood traces and hair floating in the water. Milo was dead. His eyes were wide open in terror, his arms, neatly at his sides. His color seemed to be completely gone. There was no ambiguity in his fate.

Clark let out a scream and fell to his knees. His mind raced with the final thoughts the family must've had as they were brutally murdered. He looked closer at the tub. "If the cause of death was drowning, where did this bloody water come from?" Clark couldn't let his mind dwell on this question for long. He had to call this in, as hard as it was.

Julie and Kevin gazed in horror at the second of the paintings, which depicted the scene with similar detail to the first, a naked teenage boy dead on the toilet, and his younger brother drowned in the tub. The details of the bodies were extremely vivid. Even the images of the boys looked like Damien and Milo. There was no mistake; he painted these paintings specifically for the Greenes. It was as if he had studied their bodies to make the most accurate painting possible.

Julie put her hand over her mouth. "He did it; he really did it." Her beloved friends, the Greenes, were dead. She'd failed them.

Her cell phone's ring pierced her ears. She didn't need psychic powers to know who was calling, but she answered it anyway, as she would any call.

Clark was on the other end, hyperventilating. His tearful breaths only needed to be suspended for three words to get his grim message across to her. "I found them."

CHAPTER 8

The sight of Nina's bloody corpse was almost enough to make Julie vomit. It took everything she had to steady herself on her feet.

A glance under the table revealed a mop sharpened into a weapon reminiscent of a javelin.

The only good news was that it looked like her heart was pierced upon impact. She was dead before the bladed mop's point had exited the posterior of her body. But she still had to have suffered such unbearable agony, that it seemed little comfort.

Her long hair hung off the edge of the table and dripped blood to the floor.

Julie couldn't hold back the tears as she gazed at the victimized form of her best friend. "I'm so sorry, Nina." She clutched her friend's cold hand. "I wanted to save you. I tried. And I failed. I failed people I loved so much. I'm sorry."

Kevin rested his hand on her shoulder. "You did everything that you could."

"No, I didn't." She released Nina's hand. "I should've known to look here."

"We had men look here twice and they didn't see this." He gazed at Nina's bloody form. "Artie probably was just too far ahead of us. There's nothing we could've done."

Julie turned and walked out of the kitchen. "That doesn't make her being dead any better. And what's worse, I know what's upstairs. And I am terrified to go up there. Damien and Milo...I watched them grow up. I don't think I can take seeing them like he..." She placed her hand over her mouth and cried.

"You'll make it." He took her hand. "You're tough. It won't be easy but you have the strength to get through it."

"Yeah, well, being tough obviously doesn't stop your best friend and her entire family from being massacred in their home." She whipped her hands up to her head and screamed in frustration and grief, slamming her fists on the dining room table. "Damn it!" She felt like she was breaking apart and locked her knees to keep herself upright.

Kevin again tried to comfort her but she broke away and stalked into the living room.

Kevin followed her. "Look Julie, you are a cop and sometimes that means bad things will happen. You can't save everybody. If you try to, you're going to go crazy."

"She's not just some random victim, Dad. I've known her for over ten years. I remember the first time I met her like it was yesterday. And I know I gotta be objective or else I'll be a hindrance to the case. But it's so hard. I don't know if I can."

"I can put someone else on this case. Nobody would think less of you if you step aside now. Heck, maybe it would be for the best."

"No. I started this and I'm going to finish it."

"Julie. He's targeting them to mess with you."

"All the more reason for me to be the one to bring him down."

He threw his hands in the air. "I don't know what you want from me. All I know is this is going to get worse from here on in. This guy's devolving and God only knows what he's capable of doing next. We can't be compromised in approaching this case."

"I know. I have to go up there. I just can't..."

She stumbled to a trashcan and vomited into it. Hyperventilating. Her chest radiated with pain.

Kevin retrieved her a paper towel from the kitchen. "That's it. You have to step outside if you can't handle this. If you cannot deal with this case like a professional, I will kick you off of it."

She took the paper towel and wiped her mouth. "I'm the closest thing this woman has to family in town. Her sister is five states away. I need to be here for her."

"Not as a detective. Look, I know sometimes your emotional investment gives you the drive to get the job done. But I will not compromise this investigation because you are too stubborn to realize when you are in over your head."

She shot up and got in his face. "You know full well I couldn't back off now even if I wanted to. I'm in this case 'til the end. And I get it. I have to pull myself together. And I will. I just need a few minutes to stop my head from spinning. So stop playing chief slash protective father with me and just let me handle this so I can catch this son of a bitch. Okay, Chief?"

"Get yourself together, Julie. You're no use to any-body if you're an emotional mess like you are right now." He looked her straight in the eyes. "Now step outside. That's an order, Detective."

Julie gave her father a rebellious sneer before angrily complying with his demands.

He followed her outside to the front porch. "Look, Jules, I know how you feel. I cared about them too. I al-ways thought that Milo and Damien were great kids. And Nina, I was so glad that she was there for you when Seth and Peter died. And it was good to see you be there for her when her husband walked out on her. I was proud of you for that. They were a great family. I liked being around them. But in this house, while we're still friends, we're also cops, and all three of them are murder vic-tims. Now, we're damn good cops. We can bring them justice, but only if we can keep our cool. We'll have time to grieve for them later. But if bringing them justice is our goal, we'll never be able to do it if we don't maintain control of ourselves. It hurts like hell but we have to put that aside and look at this case as cops so we can nab this crazy artist before he kills again."

"I just can't look at them." She held her mouth a mo-ment. "When I see them lying there, I see people I loved. I believe in eternal life and I have the hope that they are with God. And I'll pray for them every day for the rest of my life. I'm supposed to know how to cope with this but when I'm in that house, I feel like my insides are just going to come spilling out of me. I can't turn off how I feel right now. That people I shared so much with are dead. Brutally murdered by somebody with absolutely no concern for the sanctity of human life. People I shared so much with were put through a literal hell. It's not like it was some tragic accident. Somebody actually came in and killed each one of them. I just can't be all 'business as usual' about that. I can't turn off being human."

"I'm not asking you to." He took her hand. "Your humanity is what makes you able to do this."

Julie walked down the steps and onto the walkway. She took a look at where Milo had left his bicycle. Its matching blue helmet hung from the left handlebar. "Did I ever tell you how I met Nina?"

Kevin took a seat on the bench rest against the rail of the porch. "You can tell me again if you like."

"I had just had the boys. Patrick had been having heart troubles and Petey was having trouble with his lungs. They were weeks premature. Eager to get to the world, as always. Right?"

Kevin nodded with a smile.

"You remember how scared I was that I was going to lose them. I always felt like they were too good for me. That one day, they'd be taken...But that night, for the first time, they were both okay. The doctors said that they were going to make it. They were in the nursery, and I was looking in on them. They were sleeping. So peaceful." She smiled and wiped aside a tear. "I felt like I could watch them sleep forever. My beautiful twin baby boys..." She sat down next to him. "I remember looking over, and seeing another woman. She had that same look in her eyes. She was looking at a baby too. I asked her if this was her first. She told me that it was her second. She had an older son. He was in the cafeteria with his dad having dinner. She pointed out her baby boy to me—Milo. He looked so cute. Even at that age, he had a lot of hair."

Kevin smiled. "I remember. They were three good

looking babies."

Julie nodded. "We got to talking, about our families, our kids. We became such good friends in just that night that we decided to make each other our children's Godmother. Other than Liv, I'd never had a friend like her." She swallowed hard. "Later, I remember talking to Damien in the halls. He was so young then, just five years old. He was adorable—a little button. He was so happy to have a brother. His eyes were so big and bright. You should've seen the way his face lit up when Nina placed Milo in his arms for the very first time. He looked like he'd do anything to protect that baby boy." She choked a moment through the weeping. "As for me, I was so proud. I had my beautiful twins and a beautiful Godchild. All three were such special babies. I was disappointed when they moved away six months later. But three years later, Milo walked up to Petey and Patrick on the playground and I realized that they were back. I got my best friend back." She held her chest. "And I had her for so many years, through so many times. If I didn't have her shoulder to cry on after the accident, I don't think I'd have made it through. She was my best friend, Dad. And the boys...they were like my own nephews. Now they're all lying dead in their own home because some psycho decided they'd look good as some sick sculpture. It's not fair."

Kevin gently consoled Julie as she buried her head on his chest. "No, it's not fair. It's everything but fair. But you have to pull it together so that you can help bring them justice. Don't they deserve us at our best so we can give this case our all?"

Julie pulled back and nodded as she dried her eyes. "You're right. They do. I just hope I can keep it all together. It's so hard."

He gently stroked her face. "They deserve our best. Let's give it to them. There'll be plenty of time to cry later." He smiled at her. "Your mother and I raised you to be a strong woman, Julie. I know you can do this."

Julie took a few deep breaths and headed back inside. She returned to the kitchen. The police were about to zip Nina's body into a body bag.

Julie held out her hand. "Hold on a second." She walked over to Nina's body and closed her eyes. "I'll make sure you all get justice Nina." A tear fell and mingled with the blood on Nina's face. "Mark my words." She then stepped back and allowed them to take her away. She watched as it was taken out of the house.

She turned to Kevin. "I guess we'd better get upstairs."

"From what I hear, they're waiting for us before they do anything. Cora's already done her thing but I guess they want to make sure we investigate the scene."

Julie wiped her eyes. "I'm ready. Just stay close."

Julie and Kevin slowly ascended the stairs, walking past the pictures of the happy family. The smiles they wore on their faces and their twinkling eyes were a cruel contrast to their current states.

She proceeded to the top of the stairs. The commotion was gathered around the bathroom. A few officers were taking pictures, but it was considerably less crowded than downstairs. Apparently, the naked woman with the mop in her chest attracted more attention.

Julie first caught sight of Damien's body.

Kevin looked on in disgust. "I guess this guy thinks putting a teenager on a toilet is art."

Julie examined the entire room. "I think the irony is supposed to be that he's on the toilet while his brother is lying dead in the bathtub." She looked over to Milo's body and cringed. "He was my Godson." Seeing him like this after watching him grow from infancy was worse than any physical torture could be.

Kevin whispered to her. "Remember what I said. Keep it together."

"I'm trying," she ground out through gnashed teeth. She clenched her hands tightly and asked one of the officers on the scene, "Any idea for cause of death for the older boy?"

The officer shook his head. "Not a clue. There is a bit of blood in the toilet but we'll have to wait for the coroner's report before we know anything for sure. Unless the kid takes a crap in the nude, I doubt he was killed on the pot."

"I could've told you that." She examined his body and noticed some bruising on his thighs. "That's something." She could see blood in the toilet under him. She placed her hand over her mouth. "Oh God!"

Kevin said, "I thought I knew just how depraved this guy was. I was wrong." He shook his head.

Julie then moved on to Milo. "What about the boy? Any way to tell if he was dead before he was placed in the water?"

"Again, there is some blood in the bathwater, but no apparent injuries we could see. The coroner will have to confirm it but from the looks of things, he was definitely drowned. There's also some hair in there that we can't explain."

Kevin looked closer. "Do I even want that explained?"

Julie looked into Milo's wide, dead eyes, almost as if she could see his final minute, and feel his body shutting down. "There's blood in the water too but I don't see any obvious injuries." She jumped back and held her mouth in disgust. "The whole family...like it was just some game."

Kevin gasped. "Are we sure about this? That's quite the escalation for somebody who hasn't sexually assaulted any of his victims before. And leaving such a big mess? One test of DNA would tell us he did this."

"He's not concerned about hiding his identity anymore. He's letting us know that it's okay that we know who he is." Julie turned away.

Kevin said, "A part of me hopes you're wrong and that these kids didn't have to suffer like that, but if you're right, we'll know for sure who's behind this. No more guessing."

Julie kneeled down and gazed at Milo's body. She felt tears rolling down her face as she thought about his final moments. It added insult to an already grave injury. She just wanted to hold him and rock away his pain. At least he was with the Lord now. She prayed that God would erase all of the suffering. She felt God crying with her at the crime against humanity perpetrated tonight.

Julie asked, "Can we remove him from the water now?"

The officer consented.

Julie lifted Milo's frail corpse from the water and gently laid it down on a towel on the floor.

Kevin turned to the officer. "Take a sample of that water and send it down to the lab for testing."

Julie leaned down and planted a kiss on Milo's forehead, struggling to keep it together as she gently stroked the chest of her murdered Godson. "You were such a good friend to my Patrick, and you were a great Godson. I'll never forget you Milo."

The red and blue lights of the police cars rose into the night.

Patrick caught a glimpse of them from his bedroom window. "Whoa! What's going on?" He could see that they were coming from Milo's street.

He quickly strapped on sneakers and headed out the front door. He felt a bit uneasy but wasn't sure why. He told himself that everything was okay. Probably just somebody making too much noise this late at night.

He ran the few blocks to Milo's street.

His heart dropped. There were cops and crowds gathered outside Milo's home. What could the police want there? Had Milo called them on his brother?

"I wonder what happened," he said nervously. He squeezed through the crowd and under the barricades. He turned back to the crowds. They didn't seem to notice him at all. They were just staring at the house and whispering to each other. Didn't they have anything better to do? He had to know what was going on. He raced for the door and slipped inside.

There were cops roaming the house.

No signs of Milo or his family.

Now Patrick was worried. Were they kidnapped? Or hurt? He tried to listen to the cops to find out what happened but all the voices seemed to blend into an indiscernible noise.

He then heard more voices upstairs. He rushed to investigate.

At the top of the stairs, he froze.

Damien was being zipped into a black body bag.

His heart crashed into his stomach.

"Damien's dead?" He couldn't believe it. How? Who would hurt him? And why was he naked? None of this made any sense.

Milo! Where was Milo? If he saw this, he must be devastated.

Patrick moved aside as they carried Damien away.

There were still voices coming from the bathroom.

He shuffled over to have a look.

He couldn't breath. There was Milo.

He was on the towel-covered floor. Colorless and naked. Just like Damien. Dead. Milo was dead. His best friend was lying dead just a few feet away from him. Somebody killed Milo.

Tears gushed from his eyes like water from a faucet.

He darted into the room screaming indistinguishable words.

Julie was there.

Patrick ran past her. He knelt beside Milo. "No! No. He can't be dead. Milo. Milo." He screamed and wailed.

Julie tried to pull him away.

He violently broke free of her grips.

"Milo." Tears spilled onto Milo's face. "Please, you can't be dead. Please." He stared into the lifeless eyes of his best friend. He knew Milo wasn't there anymore. He prayed that somehow he'd get a response anyway.

He took Milo's hand and gripped it with his own. "Friends forever, Milo. Remember? Friends forever. You can't die. You gotta be okay."

Julie gently tapped Patrick. "Patrick, what are you doing here?"

Patrick tearfully turned to her. "What are *you* doing here? Why is Damien dead? Why is Milo dead? Who did this to them?"

Julie placed her arms on Patrick's shoulders. "Patrick, you have to calm down."

"I will not calm down." He knocked over the toilet paper rack. "My best friend is dead. Somebody killed my best friend in the whole world. I won't be quiet Goddamnit!"

Patrick couldn't ever remember saying that word before. He didn't curse. And even if he was mad, he knew it was wrong. But what made him even more afraid was the fact that his mother didn't smack him or even reprimand him.

She just stood there. Maybe she got it? She had to see his anguish. His pain. She'd already seen Milo dead. She loved him too. She must be hurting. He didn't want to be selfish. He just wanted his friends to be alive again.

"Patrick, please settle down." She reached out and touched Patrick's shoulder.

"What happened to him Mom?" He looked up at her, crying. "Why is he dead?"

She gently caressed his head. "A very bad man killed him."

"Why? What did he ever do? He was a good boy." He glanced at Milo. "He didn't do anything to deserve this."

"I know." She held him tighter. "Bad men don't kill people because they deserve it."

Patrick stared at Milo's face. "Why are his eyes open? Petey's eyes were closed when he died. So were Dad's. Why are his eyes open?"

Julie shed a few more tears. "Sometimes when people die, their eyes don't close until somebody else closes them. When they die, if their eyes are open, they stay that way. Milo must've not closed his eyes when he died."

"Why is he naked?" Patrick took a deep breath. "I know they take off their clothes later. But he's naked already. Why?"

"We found him like this. He was drowned in the tub."

Patrick shook his head. "Milo doesn't take baths. He always takes showers." He looked out in the hall. "And Damien was naked too. I saw them taking him away. They weren't naked because they were taking baths. I'm not stupid, Mom. Don't lie to me."

"Patrick, please. Let's just go home."

Patrick looked at Milo's body and then back at Julie. "He did something to them. Didn't he?"

Julie avoided eye contact. "Patrick." She whimpered. "I have to take you home. You shouldn't be here. You shouldn't see this."

"Didn't he Mom? He did really bad things to them. It's called rape, right? I know about it. I see the news. I hear people talk. I know what rape means. I'm not a stupid little kid. I know he did bad things to them. That's why you're not telling me. That's why you can't even look at me."

"We don't know that for sure." Julie kissed Patrick's head.

"Did he rape him, Mom?" Patrick calmed himself a moment with deep breathes. "Everyone always tells us not to talk to strangers. 'Cause they could kidnap us and do that. Is that what he did to Milo, Mom? Is it?"

"I'm sorry Patrick." She pulled him into an embrace.

Patrick buried his head on his mother's shoulder and cried harder.

Julie stroked his cheek. "We should go home Patrick. I don't need to be here anymore. We'll let them take care of Milo."

Patrick pulled back. "What will they do with him now?"

Julie said, "They'll take him to the morgue. You remember Cora right?"

Patrick nodded. "She was kind of cool."

"Well, she's going to perform what is called an autopsy on Milo and his family. She'll tell us exactly how they all died. And everything that happened to them. Then she'll keep them from decaying until they can have a funeral like we had for your father and brother. By then, they'll all be dressed up in beautiful clothes."

Patrick sniffled. "Don't let them put Milo in a suit. He hated suits. He'd rather be buried like this than be buried in a suit. He hated how he looked in a suit. He said he looked like some spoiled rich boy. Now, I know you can't bury him like this, but pick normal clothes. Stuff he'd actually wear. Milo would want it that way."

Julie smiled through her tears and placed her hand on Patrick's face. "I'll tell them. I'll tell them all of that."

"One more thing." Patrick gazed back at Milo. "Mom, can I close his eyes? He looks so scared like that."

She smiled at him. "I think that would be a very kind thing to do. Are you sure you want to do it? I can do it for you."

"I need to do it." Patrick crawled next to Milo. "He was my best friend."

"Okay, go ahead."

Patrick leaned over to Milo's body and placed his forefingers on Milo's eyelids and carefully slid them shut. "You look more peaceful now." He laid his head on his friend's chest. "Say Hi to Petey for me, Milo. You were the best friend I could ever have. I loved you so much. You were like another brother. And I'm going to miss you forever." He leaned back and again clutched Milo's hand in his. "Friends forever. I still mean that. Friends forever." Tears streamed out harder than ever.

Julie picked Patrick off the ground and carried his crying form in her arms, cradling him like a newborn. "Let's go home, Patrick."

She gave Kevin a look. He nodded in agreement.

The whole family was gone. How? He'd just slept over last night. How could they all be dead just one day later?

∝⊂⊃∝⊂⊃∝⊂⊃∝

As the cops on the scene started to dissipate, and the crowd outside lost interest after seeing the third and final body carried from the home, the scene at the Greene house quickly quieted down.

With things less chaotic, Kevin had time to wonder where Clark was.

Clark was the one who called in the murders.

Kevin hadn't seen him since he'd arrived at the house. Was he still here?

Kevin checked rooms until he got to Milo's. The room was dark but he could see Clark' silhouette seated on the bed.

He flicked on the lights and took a seat next to Clark. "You've been hanging out here all night?"

Clark kept his gaze straight ahead. "Yeah. I guess finding a family dead took a lot out of me. I needed a place to think. Away from all of the dead bodies."

"You were the first one on the scene. And then you just disappeared."

"I gave my statements. I didn't see what else I was needed for beyond that. I needed time. As you said, I was the first one to find them." Clark turned to Kevin. "I guess we both know what that means."

Kevin was speechless a moment. "Clark, we're not going to let anything happen to you."

He pointed to a picture of the family on Milo's night table. "That's what you said to them. And look how they ended up." He took a series of deep breaths. "I think this guy is targeting people now. He put the girl in their bridal shop. Royal called me specifically about the paintings. He's starting to target his victims without breaking his pattern."

Kevin placed his hand on Clark's shoulder. "We're not going to just sit back and let him kill you."

"We couldn't stop him from doing everything he did here tonight." Clark stared at the ceiling light. "Let's face it. This guy is one step ahead of us." He rested his chin on his hands. "You can't save me any more than you could've saved them. They were a beautiful family and they're on their way to the morgue right now. If he can do that to them, what hope do I have?"

"We know more about this guy now. We can stop him."

Clark shook his head. "We can't stop him. It'd take an act of God to take him down." He sighed and got up to leave.

Kevin grabbed his arm. "Hey, you're not going home alone. We're going to put you somewhere safe."

"Chief."

"That's an order, Detective."

Clark broke free of Kevin's grip. "Can't I just go home and enjoy one more night in my bed?"

Kevin stood up. "If I have anything to say about it, you'll be in that bed a lot longer than one more night. But you gotta get with the program and not just give up. You're a cop. They were just a woman and two children. You can fight back in ways that they couldn't."

"What if he creates a situation that I can't handle? Or

catches me off guard?"

"You'll have back-up."

Clark took a deep breath. "Boss, I'm scared. I've faced down crooks before. But this guy's a whole new level of sick. This could be it for me."

Kevin put his hand on Clark's shoulder. "We're going to get this guy. But we need you to cooperate with us. Can you do this for me, Clark?"

Clark nodded and then followed Kevin downstairs. The second floor of the house was now left dark. The markings of the murders that took place still remained, but now only the moonlight coming through windows made it visible. Once again, all was quiet.

∞◯∞◯∞◯∞

The ride home was brutally silent.

Patrick regained the strength in his legs enough to walk into the door and up to his bedroom. He quickly shed his clothes and changed into pajamas.

"Milo hated pajamas." Patrick laughed.

Julie couldn't imagine that he could turn his mind off enough to get even a little bit of sleep in this condition. But he needed to. She needed to help him.

"If I knew that last night was the last night I'd ever see him..." He lay down and tried to get comfortable. He thrashed about in the bed and punched the pillow. He screamed and threw it across the room.

Julie was scared. She sat down next to him and gently touched his arm.

"Why don't you sleep with me tonight? Like you used to do right after the accident?"

Patrick shook his head. "I'm too big for that now."

"Patrick, you're still my little boy." She held his hand. "I don't want you alone tonight. You've had a very traumatic experience. And I want to be there for you to talk about it with."

"I just saw my best friend dead." Patrick looked at her. "Somebody actually killed him and his mom and his brother. Somebody hated them enough to do that to them. My best friend's gone." His lips tightened. "Is this talking about it enough?"

"Patrick, you know better than that." Julie stroked his cheek. "Remember everything they taught us in counseling after Dad and Petey died? All of that still applies now."

"I know." Patrick struggled to keep back his tears. He clenched the covers. "I know I have to talk about it. But I just can't. Not yet. When Petey died...Milo was there. But now he's the one who's dead."

"*I'm* here for you, Patrick."

"And what if you die next?" He shot his glance to her. "Mom, every day you go to work and you put yourself in danger. You fight the evil people who like to hurt good people like Milo. But they can hurt you too." Tears spilled down his face. "Every day, I'm scared that I'm going to come home and there'll be somebody here... and they'll tell me that you're gone too." He wiped his eyes but more tears fell out. "And I know, what you do is important. You get the bad guys. You keep us safe." He threw his arms around her. "But who keeps you safe? What if one day you get hurt, or worse? Everybody I love dies. Mommy...I don't want you to die too." He buried his head on her chest and cried harder.

Julie wrapped her arms around him. She'd never before realized the toll her job took on Patrick. She lifted his face up. His serious, tear-filled blue eyes radiated with pain. And fear. Such a raw, innocent fear. He'd lost so many people. Why wouldn't he be afraid of losing her too? She knew full well that it'd only take one bullet to take her away from him for good.

"Patrick, I'm so sorry." She felt a knot in her stomach. She was shaking. "I know you're scared of losing me. But I am here right now. Let me help you. Let me make it hurt less, Patrick."

Patrick pulled away from her.

She tried to touch him.

He shot up and darted out of the room.

Seeing Patrick angry was a rare thing. She didn't like it.

She knew she couldn't punish him but she couldn't leave things either. He was clearly emotionally distressed. She was his mother. She had to help him.

"Patrick." She chased after him. "You can't run away from me."

"Leave me alone." He ran into her bedroom and slammed the door.

She stopped the door from closing and entered the room.

He was curled up in a ball in front of her closet, crying.

"Patrick, please, just talk to me." She knelt next to him.

"Why talk?" Patrick scrambled to his feet. "They're all dead. Everyone's dead. They're dead." He tumbled to the floor again. "Why do they all have to die?" He wailed and whimpered as he buried his face on the carpet.

Julie picked him up and cradled him in her arms. She carried him to her bed and set him down softly on its queen-sized surface.

She lay down next to him, keeping her arms lovingly

around him.

"Patrick, I know you're in a lot of pain. I know how much it hurts to lose somebody you care so much about. I lost my best friend tonight too. I've known Nina since you, your brother, and Milo were all little newborns in the hospital." She stroked his arm. "You were all so cute. I knew you'd all grow to be good friends."

"I remember you telling me that." Patrick turned to her. "But I don't remember meeting Milo until I was older."

"Well, they left for a few years. Then they came back. That's when you and your brother really got to meet Milo."

"I remember Petey and I were playing." Patrick smiled. "Milo ran up to me and tagged me and told me I was 'it.' Petey told me I had to chase him. It was the rules. But I tagged him instead and told him to chase the both of us." He laughed through his tears. "He did it too. I think we were only four. But we stayed friends until... until one of us died. First Petey, and now Milo. Maybe..."

"Don't you dare go there." Julie turned Patrick to her. "I am never going to let anything bad happen to you."

"You couldn't protect Petey or Milo." He held himself. He was trembling. "And I'm not mad at you for that. I know you tried. But...if somebody wants to hurt me, maybe nobody can stop it. Just like nobody could stop Petey and Milo from dying."

Julie brushed a lock of hair away from his face. "You can't assume because people you loved have died that you're next. You gotta have faith Patrick."

He sniffled in lieu of a response.

"I love you. So much, Patrick. So much. I will always make darn sure I keep you as safe as I can."

"Do you think you can catch this guy?"

Julie leaned in close to him. "I promise you. I will. He won't go free. Not after killing all of the good people he's killed. He's done a lot of evil things and he will have to answer for every one of them."

"I miss him, Mom." He curled his lips. "I know it's only been a little bit, but I miss him so much. I'm never going to see him again. It's just like when Petey and Daddy died, they're gone forever. Until we die too. It's scary, Mom. We'll never just hang out again."

"I know that pain. Life's so quick, but when somebody you love is gone, it's also so long. You have hope of seeing them again in heaven, but there's still that part of you that's missing. And it hurts. I know it hurts a lot." Julie pulled him closer. "And I can't say that the pain's going to go away any time soon. But if you give it a little time, it will hurt less." Julie pulled him closer. "You'll start to heal again. Just like you started to heal from Petey and Dad."

"I still miss him every day, Mom. A lot of times, something good happens. And for a minute, I go to tell him. But then I remember he isn't there. He's dead. Or sometimes I want to ask Daddy for help and I remember that he's gone too. I believe in heaven. I know it's real. And I hope that they're there waiting...but I want them here."

"I do too, honey. I want them here every day."

"I pray for them every night. I pray for them every day."

"That's good, Patrick. That's very good."

"I pray a lot. I talk to God. And I try to be nice. But sometimes it just hurts so much...and I ask Him why it has to hurt so much. Why it can't stop hurting. Why can't people stop dying? I know it's not 'cause we're bad people. But it hurts so much and I just want it to stop."

She took his hand. "God hears you, Patrick. God always answers prayers. Sometimes we just don't understand the answer yet."

He lowered himself off of her. "Even when I wanted to talk to Dad or Petey and they weren't there, at least I always was able to talk to Milo. He was my friend. I thought that maybe...maybe he was there because God wanted me to have somebody to talk to. My best friend. Now I can't do that anymore either." He buried his head on the pillow and poured out tears some more.

"It's going to be okay Patrick." She wiped away tears from his cheek. She wished she knew what else to say. He was bearing his soul to her, and she felt like all she could do was offer kind words that probably did little to ease his pain. She prayed for guidance. She just wanted to make her little boy stop hurting so much.

"What do you think they're doing to him now?" His eyes met hers. "Do you think they're already cutting him open?"

Julie looked him in the eye. "I don't want you to think about it. I want you to try and get some sleep. Milo's in good hands. His soul and his body."

After a short pause, he said, "Mom, I'm sorry I yelled. I was being a brat."

"No, you were just upset." She smiled and hugged him. "Let's just try to get some sleep. We'll stay right here."

She planted a kiss on his forehead and turned out the light.

She heard his light snoring in a matter of minutes. She was a little surprised. She expected him to be unable to sleep for hours.

But the night had clearly taken a toll. His body needed to rest.

"Goodnight, Patrick."

⊶⊶⊶⊶⊷

Julie and Patrick went to the early Mass the next morning. They couldn't sleep past dawn, and they figured moping around the house all morning would do them no good.

Julie gave Patrick money to light a votive candle in the church for each of the Greenes.

She smiled as she watched him turn the flickering red lights on.

Sister Olivia approached Julie. "I heard about what happened. I am so sorry, Julie. I know how close you were with them."

Julie nodded. "Yeah, and it's really hit Patrick hard. I'm worried about him." She looked at him staring at the statue of The Blessed Mother. "Petey's death is still so fresh in his mind. Now to lose his best friend...it's too much."

Sister Olivia put her hand on Julie's. "How are *you* holding up? Nina was your best friend and Milo was your godson. It can't be easy on you."

With tears in her eyes, she said, "It isn't. But I can't fall apart. Patrick needs somebody he can lean on and that has to be me, cause I'm all he has left."

"He has his grandfather too."

Julie shook her head. "I can't burden Dad with a grieving child. I just have to deal and help Patrick deal too. He's a lot younger than I am and he doesn't look death in the face every day like I do. As horrible as this is for me, it's a lot scarier for him."

"But the Greenes were your friends. You don't get

used to people you love dying. I realize Patrick needs his mother right now, but you need somebody too. I'm here if you need to talk, Jules."

"Don't worry. I'm not Dad. I'm not going to go stop coming to Church or lose my faith because my friends died." She walked towards the altar. "I'm not happy about it. But my faith isn't that weak. I buried a child and didn't lose my faith. So I think I can handle this."

"I know that you won't lose your faith. But you still need healing."

"I just need to catch this guy and make him pay." Julie took a deep breath.

"Revenge, Julie?" She raised her eyebrow.

"Not revenge. Justice." She looked at a picture of the Greenes from her wallet. "Somebody who would do what this guy did to Milo...he can't be allowed to walk the streets."

Sister Olivia smiled. "Well, if you ever need somebody to talk to, I'm here."

"Thank you." She hugged her. "Can I ask you a favor?"

"Sure."

"I know you're busy and you got all sorts of nun things to do."

"You make me out to be some kind of freak." She folded her arms.

"I don't mean it like that. I just know that this will inconvenience you. But I need to ask anyway. Could you watch Patrick for a few hours? I need to go take care of something."

"Of course I can." She smiled. "You know I love spending time with him. And everyone here loves having him around. We need more faithful, young Catholics like

Patrick in the Church."

"Thank you. I'll be by later to pick him up." She walked over to Patrick and wrapped her arms around him in a hug. "Be good for your aunt, Patrick. I love you."

He turned to her and hugged her back. "I love you too, Mom." He kissed her on the cheek.

She kissed back and hugged him again.

After a moment, she slowly backed away from him. She couldn't look away. He looked so fragile standing there in the isle. She just wished she could find a way to help him.

But she knew the first step was to catch this killer.

CHAPTER 9

Julie's stomach tightened as she approached the morgue. The dim gray halls seemed even more dark and uninviting than usual.

"I don't know if I can do this." The fact that she was about to see people she thought of as family on Cora's table gave her a horrible feeling she had known only once before, when Petey and her husband were the ones on those slabs.

She had never before realized how uninviting the door to the room was. "This thing really is hideous." An old and fading paint job, and several stains, marked the humble entrance to the mortuary, where the dead of the town waited until they were claimed and transported to a funeral home. She gently rested her hand against the grimy glass.

She took a deep breath. "You can do this. It's just like any other crime victim. They deserve your best." She repeated this to herself a few more times in a barely audible whisper before opening the door and stepping inside.

Cora was standing over the corpses of the Greene family, each occupying a slab in the morgue. The oldest-to-youngest arrangement made for an eerie sight.

Julie took a deep breath as she approached. "I'm here. Tell me what you found. All of it."

Cora sighed. "You're not going to like any of this. Jules, I'm sorry."

She rubbed her face. "I saw the crime scenes. I know not to expect anything good. Just tell me."

Cora handed her some papers. She couldn't even look at Julie. "We tested the bathwater. You were right. It's that Falcon guy. And the things he did to them...It wouldn't give you peace to know them. I wish I could not know."

"He's my Godson. And this is a detail-oriented killer. I can't chance missing something."

She showed Julie some photos of Milo. There were bite marks all over his body. Most were confined to the abdomen.

Julie recoiled in disgust. "Oh my gosh." She regurgitated a little in her mouth. "That's not what I think it is, is it?"

Cora struggled to fight her own tears. "I told you. It's exactly what it looks like. Poor kid, probably had no clue what was going on. Wish that sick bastard was the one on this table. Anybody who can do that to somebody else...a child...they don't deserve to live."

Julie tearfully placed her hand in front of her mouth. "How is somebody so heartless?"

"What I don't get is this. He never did any of this before. Why is he starting now?"

"He knows we're on to him. What reason does he have to hide his identity anymore?"

"Maybe. I don't know. It just seems like only the sickest of criminals could do this to an innocent family."

"Well we are clearly dealing with the sickest of criminals." Julie took a deep breath. "What about the causes of deaths?"

"Well, not surprisingly, Nina was killed from the force of the mop impaling her chest. But the boys you might be surprised about. Damien was given a serious lethal injection. That drug stopped his heart within a few seconds." She pointed to a small needle prick on his neck. "Luckily for him, he probably had the least painful death of the three of them."

"And Milo?" She wiped away some tears.

"Well, I can definitely tell you he wasn't drowned. There was no water in his lungs. When he went under, he was already dead."

Julie's eyes widened. "What? If he wasn't drowned, then how was he killed?"

"His windpipe was crushed and there was significant bruising on his neck." She pointed out the bruising to Julie. "My best guess right now would be that the killer crushed it with his own two hands."

"...Monster." Julie's control over her emotions slipped and tears spilled out even more. She tried not to imagine those final moments for each of them but her brain did it anyway. If only she found them in time.

Cora said, "Jules, I've been doing this for a few years now. I've seen kids killed from all kinds of things. Accidents, abuse, fires, suicides, and yes, even murders. But I've never seen a body that made me cringe as much as this. I could barely get through the autopsy. Maybe it was because I sort of knew him. I saw him at Patrick's birthday party once. He wasn't just a random corpse anymore. It was just so disgusting to see what that pervert did to him. He was so frail and that seemed to just make the creep do more damage."

Julie asked, "So what now?"

"We've contacted her sister. She'll be flying in to claim them." She leaned against the wall. "That's all that's left to do. We know who did this and how. Next comes the hard part—really saying goodbye."

Julie gazed into the lifeless faces of the Greene family, her friends, people she loved. It sickened her to see their closed eyes and colorless complexions lying on those tables. They should be smiling and enjoying the chaos of family life.

"Thank you for telling me everything." She whimpered for just a moment before she tried to force her emotions down. "At least we now have confirmation as to who our killer is. No more guessing."

"Julie, find this guy. Anybody who can do what he did to these people can't be left on the streets."

"I will. I will definitely find him."

Cora covered the three corpses and closed them back into their drawers. She then walked Julie out into the hall.

Julie turned to her. "This is a change. Usually you stay in there."

Cora shook her head. "Not this time. This time I can barely look at them. Julie, I've always been sort of an agnostic. I never really bought into any big origin of the species idea. It didn't really matter to me how we got here. Big bang, God, it was all the same to me. All the people who thought one way or another just seemed to be wasting their lives. I remember praying from time to time and I guess I had some natural concept of a creator but I never really lived my life like I believed. I guess over the years, I sort of subconsciously convinced myself that there wasn't a heaven. I guess I made room for the hope of one, but when I saw the lifeless remains of people, saw their internal organs not functioning, their limbs limp, and their very faces, the picture of who they are, unmoving...I don't know. I guess I just figured that they didn't exist anymore." She tensed up. "Everything that made them who they were was lying exposed on my table. It was like a machine that couldn't work anymore. I didn't want to believe that their story ended like that. But I did."

Julie reached out and took her arm. "You never told me any of this."

Cora chuckled. "You're Catholic. I didn't want to get into a religion debate."

"You think I would've debated it?"

She gently hit her. "Of course you would've. And you know it."

Julie chuckled. "Why are you telling me this now?"

Cora shed a tear. "Because I want to believe in heaven right now. I want to believe that that family in there is happy somewhere, together. I want to believe that that boy in there didn't spend the last moment's he'd ever exist with some pig violating his body in the worst way imaginable. I want to believe that they still can have peace."

"I'm not going to tell you to believe in something to make you feel better." She clung to a crucifix that hung from her neck. "I'd tell you to believe in it because it makes sense. Or because you believe it's true, even if it doesn't. To me, the very fact that we can ponder such a thing as an afterlife seems to me to indicate something greater for us beyond that white light. If you want to believe, you can."

Cora looked up at the ceiling. "But how can I reconcile those bodies in there with an all-loving God? I don't know how to do that, Julie. How can I reconcile all the evil in the world with Him? How can I reconcile stealing a child's innocence and then his very life? How can I reconcile any of that with God? I can't do it. It just seems to contradict Him so much."

Julie shrugged. "How can I reconcile people like the Greenes without Him?"

Cora became confused. "What?"

"The Greenes were there for me when my husband and son died. They brought food. They comforted me. They held me when I cried." Her face lit up as she recalled their memory. "Milo gave Patrick a reason to get up after losing his brother. He gave him a reason to still enjoy his childhood. And of course, every time I look into my son's eyes, I have no doubt in my mind that there's a God behind it. As for how I reconcile that scene in there with God? It's not easy. How do you make sense of any of it? It looks so grim, so final, so horrible."

Cora pointed inside. "How could God allow that, Julie?"

Julie looked right at her. "Because man has free will. And man has a bad habit of just seriously abusing it. I know it's a clichéd answer but it's the right one. God gave us free will and that means standing aside sometimes while we go and use it to do all the things He told us not to do. Some more obviously horrible than others."

"But isn't there a limit? This isn't just robbing candy from the store. This is just sadistic."

"If God got in the way of choices, that wouldn't really

be free will. Would it? We don't understand God's plans. We always try to make Him conform to how we understand things but He's beyond that. I trust in Him. Even when it hurts and I don't understand, I trust that in the end, He'll make sure there's justice for everyone." She took a deep breath. "Free will goes both ways. Each and every day, at every moment, we can choose to use it the right way. After every major tragedy where people die, we get this brief recommitment to do that. But it always fizzles. Eventually the good deeds stop and we're back to going through the motions until the next time somebody flies planes into buildings or shoots up a school. Or does something like this to a good family in their homes. We're so quick to blame God for everything that goes wrong. As if He's responsible for the damage that comes when people ignore the things He said will keep us whole."

Cora remained silent. She avoided eye contact.

Julie took a step closer to her. "I believe God's given us the grace to make the right choices even when it's hard. And if we truly believe in Him, believe in everything we're taught in the Bible, everything we accept through faith, I think we'll make every effort to use our free will to glorify Him. And for people who use their free will to do God's will, I believe there's a reward for them. For going through all the suffering, the trials, the agony. I believe heaven awaits those who lived for God to the best of their ability. I try to do that every day, and bring justice to those who had their lives stolen from them. I probably don't say nearly enough rosaries, and I tend to get caught up in life and not think about God as often as I should, but I'm trying to do better. I want to be a better example of a follower of Christ than I am. And whenever my time comes, I have the hope that God will be a fair judge."

"Julie, my life's pretty sad. I cut dead people open for a living." She spaced out a moment in thought. She looked back into the morgue. "College boys overdose. Women succumb to the abuse of a boyfriend or husband. Families are torn apart because somebody got behind the wheel after having too much to drink. Children are raped and murdered by some horrible monster of a human being. All of these victims, my job is to cut them open and find out how they died. It's a tough life, Jules. Faith would make it so much easier to deal with. But maybe that's all faith is, a crutch to get people by. Something to help them avoid admitting that this is all there is. That the people who end up on my table don't exist anymore. They're like a deleted computer program. It doesn't matter how much we love. One day, we all die, and then it's all over. Some of us go peacefully in our sleep, some of us die quickly in accidents, and some of the unluckiest of us get such unspeakable violations by another before our life's breath is forced from our lungs. Any way you try to spin it, we still end up that pale, lifeless corpse. And eventually we decompose to unrecognizable matter." She cried. "Maybe that's existence Julie, maybe that is how life goes."

Julie exhaled peacefully. "Or maybe there is something else. Another state of existence. A place where we can be happy with God who made us. And with the loved ones He gave to us. Maybe it's a comforting belief, but to me, it makes the most logical sense." She put her hand on Cora's shoulder. "If what you said were true, it would be a sad existence. Such a sad existence that I don't think love would be capable of existing. We'd be surviving, co-existing at best." She took out a picture of Patrick and looked at it, "But we wouldn't love. We couldn't be moved at the very laughter or hug of a child. We couldn't look into somebody's eyes and see their innermost thoughts. We couldn't look at a dead body and cry at how unfair it is that the person we knew is gone. It wouldn't matter that they were gone. It would just be how it was. We wouldn't be who we are. But we do love. We do feel our hearts skip a beat when we see our children at play. We do cry when we see innocent people killed. We cry when friends and family are taken away. It's not just a side effect of an advanced brain. It's something more. To me, it's proof of immortal souls. It tells me that there's an existence greater than ours. There has to be. Love to me is just something too great to be meaningless in the end. Love doesn't die."

"Those people did."

"Yes, they did. They all died horrible deaths. So did a man in his thirties about two thousand years ago. We hear it so much, maybe we go numb to the thought of it. We romanticize it as some epic movie. Or we only think of the triumph three days later. But we're going to have that triumph too. We just gotta wait a while longer." Her lips tightened. "I know that they're dead. And now, their bodies, they don't have the souls of the people we came to love anymore. But I know those people still exist. And I hope to meet them again one day. I can't make you believe, Cora. I can't give you a thousand reasons why a particular theory is right. All I can do is ask you if this life being all there is really makes any sense. If this is all there is, why find out who killed these people? Why cut them open at all? Why cry over their deaths? Because we know the truth. I think we use difficulties with a particular theory of faith as excuses to ignore what's already in our hearts. We know we're made for more than this. I think we're just afraid to go there sometimes. Because it requires a lot of surrender to go there. And we don't like to surrender."

"You almost have me believing you." Cora sighed. "I'm just not there yet."

"Pray on it. God will help you through any difficulties you have."

Cora smiled. She saw grief on Julie's face, but there was a hint of peace there. And maybe it was just a desire to believe Julie's words, but Cora felt a small sense of peace coming over her as well. She knew it wasn't belief yet, but her doubts finally seemed to have something to keep them in check.

Julie took a breath. "Well, I'd better go. Artie Falcon isn't going to find himself. We gotta make sure we keep Clark safe from him so the Greenes can be your last victims."

Julie went to walk out.

Cora called out to her. "Thank You."

Julie turned and said, "Don't thank me." She smiled back at Cora. "By the way, did anybody ever come to claim the Holdens?"

Cora shook her head.

Julie said, "Then I claim them. Their souls may be in another place, but their bodies are still sacred. They shouldn't be kept in a drawer."

"Jules, you can't just claim them."

"I'm a friend. If no family contests it, there shouldn't be a problem."

"Well, if you put in the petition, I won't have any objections."

Julie tearfully smiled. "Thank you. Oh and give Milo a kiss for me. And I know what you're thinking. But maybe he'll still receive it."

Cora smiled. "I'll do that."

Without another word, Julie exited the mortuary.

Cora watched her steps as she walked. There was even more resolve in them now. She could see that Julie was still hurting, but Cora felt that Julie's own words seemed to help her. Julie had lost her friends, but she'd get them justice. Artie Falcon had made a big mistake when he decided to mess with Julie Martel.

Kevin was waiting for Julie in a police car outside. "Anything interesting about the bodies?"

Julie grunted. "You really do not want to know the answer to that question." She tried to block out the things she had just learned. She couldn't. She stopped herself from crying. Now wasn't the time for that. "But we do have confirmation that Artie Falcon is our killer. He raped all three of them before killing them."

Kevin flinched. "All three? God, I knew he was a pig but that's an atrocity."

"Any sign of him?"

"Not a one. His former lair is pretty much abandoned, and since all records have him considered dead, he isn't exactly easy to find."

She got into the passenger's seat of the car. "He must be using something for money and staying somewhere."

Kevin got into the driver's seat. "Well, whatever he's doing, he's doing a good job at covering it up."

"What about the paintings? He must be buying the paint somewhere."

"I'm sure he is, but paint isn't exactly a gun. Lots of people buy paint. I doubt he's dumb enough to buy it all in one place so I am not really sure pursuing that angle is going to lead us to him."

"What about Clark? How's he holding up?"

"He's a nervous and unstable wreck. The guy is convinced he's going to die tonight and is really not liking the accommodations of police protection."

Julie chuckled. "Clark's always been stubborn." She stared out the window. She understood his frustration. He hated being ordered around. And combined with his life being in danger? It must be making him insane. "He's a good man. We'll do whatever we have to in order to keep him safe."

Kevin started the car. "Well his stubbornness is going to land him on Cora's table if he doesn't watch it."

"We have to be patient with him, Dad. He's a serial killer's next target."

Kevin pulled out of the space. "Well, if he wants to not become the next link in these Blood Chain Killings, he better start cooperating more cause we can only do so much to protect an unwilling target."

Just then, Julie's phone rang. She took it out and answered with a professional "Hello."

There was snickering on the other end.

"Hello, I am speaking to Detective Julie Martel, correct?"

"You are. Who, may I ask, is this?"

"My name is Artie Falcon, and I am the perpetrator of the crimes you have labeled the Blood Chain Killings."

Julie felt a shiver shoot up her spine like a bullet.

Seeing her change of expression, Kevin asked, "What's wrong?"

Julie said to Artie, "This is new for you, calling the police."

He laughed. "Well, I figured since you finally know

who I am, why hide any more?"

"You realize we can trace your call, right?"

He shrugged. "That's fine. I'm calling from a pre-paid cell I'm disposing of when we're done anyway."

"What do you want?"

"I'm just calling to tell you that by tomorrow night, I will no longer be a problem."

"And why is that?"

"Because I have decided that that night will be the night that I die."

Julie's eyes widened. "Why have you decided to die that night?"

"I just will. I know it. I will continue to make a few more final pieces of artwork and then I will let myself become one."

Julie struggled for a counter. "Is that the only reason you called? Just to let us know you're going to die tomorrow?"

Artie chuckled. "No, that would be a bit of a waste of your time. No, I came to offer you a gift, my motives."

"You're going to tell me why you did all of this?"

"Well, yes. I figured it will save you time on speculation." He gave a sadistic laugh. "Plus, I doubt I'll have time to give it come tomorrow night. So I decided to end the mystery and let you know why I did all of this."

She held the phone firmly to her ear. "I'm listening.'"

Kevin became frustrated. "What the hell's he saying?"

Julie began recording the conversation. Just in case he left any clues.

∝⋯∝⋯⋯∝

Artie readied himself. "Well, I was born to an unwed mother named Lisa Gould. My father's name was Arthur Falcon. I was born Arthur Falcon Jr., but Artie was always my nickname. My mother died in childbirth, leaving my father the sole person to raise me. But he was a drunken fool. He never cared for me." Artie clenched his fist. "One time, he got drunk with a lit cigarette in his hand and the house caught fire as a result. I was burned over half my body, third degree. The firefighter found me in my room. In flames. I was supposed to die. They said I wouldn't make it through the night. But I did. Somehow, I survived. And after a lot of therapy, I recuperated and was theoretically able to lead a normal life. But I was left with severe burn scars across my entire torso and abdomen. Even down my legs. Long clothes covered it up. As long as I was dressed, I was just like anybody else. But alas, life doesn't allow one to remain clothed all the time. Eventually, you have to get naked, especially when you live in a foster home and go to public school." He took a deep breath. "Every day, I stripped in front of people with normal bodies, people who weren't deformed. As if the humiliation I felt wasn't enough, they always ridiculed me, made fun of me, made me feel like I wasn't human. I never had a friend until I grew up."

"Is this sob story supposed to make me understand what you did?"

Artie chuckled. "No silly, I am explaining my motives. You didn't even let me get to them."

"You had a sucky childhood and now you think it's all right to murder innocent people in cold blood?"

"No, I don't see it that way. May I continue?"

"Sure, I'm all ears."

"Thank you. Anyway, as I was saying, I was harassed. Nobody liked me. I was ridiculed, and the sad part was, I didn't blame them. Those people had beautiful bodies, well formed, natural, the way they were created to be. The genitals of those boys looked like they should, proud, artful, not all disfigured like mine are. As I entered puberty, I began to become obsessed with the human body. I began to look at pornography, not for erotic stimulation but for my appreciation of the human form. I was even willing to put up with the ridicule in the school showers because I got a chance to see the human body in person. Eventually, I discovered I was sexually drawn to both males and females. But it was more than just about pleasure, I saw a genuine beauty in human flesh. But then I remembered how bad those people had treated me, and I wondered how great it would be if I were able to see their bodies without them being in it. The human soul mars the beauty of the human body. Only once the soul is removed is the human body truly beautiful."

"But once the soul is removed, the body begins to decay and become ugly."

Artie sighed. "And that is one of the great tragedies of our world. But a single day of full, unmarred splendor of the human body is worth it. When I went to college and studied art, I came to a full appreciation of the body and it's magnificence and I saw that clothes could compliment it, as could bodily fluids such as blood and sweat, among others. Statues and paintings are stunning indeed, but they are only blueprints for real flesh."

"Why did you become a petty criminal if art is your thing? Robbery and vandalism aren't exactly beautiful."

"I hung with the wrong crowd. Youthful desires to still 'fit in,' I suppose. I faked my death when I realized what they were doing was merely distracting me from my goal to bring true art to the world. Faking my death..." He laughed. "That was a fun experience. It's amazing what some people will do when you can convince them that somebody's trying to kill you and you're trying to start fresh. And nobody questioned that all the autopsy photos had a normal body in it? The questions people won't ask when they really don't care." He clicked his tongue. "And of course, my faked death gave me a very good launching pad for my artistic endeavors. I could finally do everything I always felt called to do. I tell you, when I turn a person into art, I don't see it as killing them so much as perfecting them."

"Why not just kill them quickly then? On your last victim...You went as far as to...Why?"

Artie said, "I don't consider it a loss. I think it would be distracting to feel bad about what I need to do. Pain is of no consequence to me. Only the art is. Human emotion is used only to make my sculptures cooperate so everything goes according to plan. I've learned about the human mind enough to manipulate it into being turned off so the body's beauty can be fully realized."

"You're sick. Totally depraved."

"I expected such adjectives to be used. They don't bother me. What I did is considered sick and depraved by society. I consider it beautiful. The body reaching its fullest potential is worth the ceasing of its functions."

"So that's it? That's your motive?"

"You don't sound impressed. You expected some sort of lustful pleasure or vengeance-driven motive? I am sorry to disappoint you. None of that describes me. I just value art, art that my body will never become. Sure, my death will have artistic value, but not the value that those I worked on would. I was truly in awe of their beauty as I gazed at them. My eyes have captured the image better than any picture could. It still thrills my mind to think of each one." He giggled.

"Why the pattern of killings?"

"I just figured I'd reward those who first discover my art scene for what it is, and their families as well." His eyes brightened. "Now, this is probably where you tell me that I won't get away with this, and then I say that I don't intend to. I will be dead by the end of tomorrow. And not from natural causes. By then, more art scenes will be made. I don't intend to get away with this, Detective. Your rulebook of typical killers won't help you much in dealing with me. If we're going to play ball, you're going to have to change your game. But I think I have said enough. I don't want to eat up all of your time. I will see you soon. Dearest Julie."

Julie tried to keep him on the line but he hung up the phone without another word.

She stared into the phone as she digested the words she had just heard. She struggled to keep herself from getting sick as she thought of the sight of the lifeless bodies of the Greenes. How casually Artie had justified their murder. She closed the phone and clenched a fist.

"By the look on your face, I'd guess that he didn't have anything good to say."

"I knew this guy was nuts." Julie closed the phone. "But after hearing him talk, I think he's a whole new level of crazy. He says he's going to die tomorrow."

"He's calling to announce his death?"

"Yeah. And that makes me very nervous. A killer like this planning to die is even more unpredictable. He's capable of anything now."

Julie and Kevin tracked the location Artie had called from and rushed to the scene. It was near the docks, but there was no sign of him.

Kevin looked out over the water. "Well, I guess we shouldn't be surprised he didn't wait around for us to show."

Julie looked around. "I doubt he'd have called knowing we could track him if he didn't at least want to leave us a present."

"What do you think he planted a bomb?"

"Bombs aren't his style. He wants to see the corpse, not turn it to ash." Julie focused her attention on the various objects at the docks. "Besides, we're not his targets. Clark is. I hope you have him in a safe place."

"He's resisting it like hell. But we got him secured. Artie ain't going to be getting to him any time soon."

"That's good." Julie walked farther down. Any sign of a clue that Artie could've left for them, even if it was just to further his sick game, would be a helpful puzzle piece. "What did you leave us, Artie?"

She noticed on a pole was a small piece of paper. It could've been nothing but her gut told her to take a look anyway. A single glance at the picture made her very glad that she did. She picked up the paper and glanced over it. "I think I found Artie's message."

She showed it to Kevin. "I think we better get back to Clark as quickly as possible."

The paper was a picture of Clark walking around in the quarters they were keeping him in. Supposedly to keep him safe.

"How the hell is a guy the world thinks is dead so damn resourceful?" Kevin angrily handed her the picture back.

"It doesn't matter. We just need to stop him." She quickly returned to the car. She waved Kevin on to hurry up. "We gotta make sure we get to Clark before Artie does."

Artie stepped out of the shower and walked to a mirror. He wiped it with his towel to clear the steam away from it.

He gazed at his deformed naked body in the reflection. His entire body was severely burned from his neck to his feet. He held himself and tried to drown out the insults he'd gotten as a child. He pictured himself as he used to be. Before the fire. When he was beautiful too.

His burns caused him only a fraction of the pain they had when they first happened when he was seven. But they were still a cosmetic repulsion. He could barely stand to look at his scalded flesh.

"Those people don't know how blessed they are to be provided with radiant flesh." He placed his hand against the mirror. "But they will learn." He picked up his knife and angrily hacked away at the mirror until the shards of glass were all gathered in the sink. "Much better." He smiled and walked out of the bathroom.

He dressed himself in casual clothes that were on the bed, covering his burns and making him look like normal again.

He looked at himself in another mirror, more satisfied. "These will be good clothes to die in." He gave his shirt a dignified tug. "I almost look beautiful."

He walked over to a chair where Kiger was sitting.

He was dead from a bullet wound to the head. His eyes and mouth drooped open. A bottle of scotch, with half of its contents spilled onto the rug below it, was still clasped in his hand.

"Well, thank you, Professor, for giving me a lot of

help. I know you didn't approve of my methods. But you really helped me. I could've never done this without you. You cultivated my appreciation for art." He patted Kiger on the shoulder. "I know you are not part of my beautiful chain of blood, but I figured you deserved to become art for all you did for me. Thank you, my friend."

He carried a few of his paintings from the floor of the hotel room. He grabbed Kiger's keys and shut off the lights as he left. "Farewell."

He tossed the keys in the air with a smile and walked to Kiger's car.

He pressed the button to unlock the car, sounding the double beep.

He opened the trunk and picked up one of the paintings, gazing at it admiringly. "Oh Detective Clark, you wouldn't know it by looking at you, but you have amazing artistic potential." He then set it down in the trunk and picked up another and gazed at it with similar admiration. "You don't even know you're a player in this game yet." Doing the same with that one, he picked up another. He smiled at it, but said nothing as he set it down. Then he picked up the last. "The most beautiful of all." He placed his index and middle fingers together and kissed them. Then he gently touched the painting before setting it down with the others.

The painting was a picture of a boy. He was lying sideways on the ground, a bloody bullet hole in the side of his head. His arm rested in front of his face, a stream of blood dribbling from his mouth and his baby blue eyes widely staring. He had a shirt on but his lower half was exposed. A naked man lay behind him with his arms wrapped around the body, clutching it like a little doll. Blood surrounded his abdomen.

Patrick in Artie's arms. The final work of art. Artie thought it would look more beautiful than anything he'd ever done before. And he'd never get to see it. But everyone else would. And they would never forget it.

"Oh Patrick, we're going to have a lot of fun together." He smiled. "You'll make such a beautiful piece of art. Just as Milo did."

He shut the trunk and got into the driver's seat of the car. He started the engine. "But, first thing's first. We got a cop to visit. We can't have our fun together until some things fall into place." With a smile on his face, he drove off from the motel, in search of his next exquisite scene.

Chapter 10

Clark chugged another mouthful of beer. He stared down into the drink.

Guards stood at all exits.

Clark looked around the bar. There had to be a way he could sneak away. Being guarded by other cops was more frustrating than being a killer's next target.

Kevin walked into the bar and took a seat at the stool next to Clark. "I'll have what he's having."

The bartender quickly filled the order and set the glass down before Kevin

"You know you're not even supposed to be here." Kevin turned to Clark.

"I'd like have some alone time on my last night alive." Clark set his glass down. "And I wanted to get in a last drink here."

"And what makes you think this is your last night alive?" Kevin took a sip of his beer. "You been reading them biased newspaper horoscopes again?"

Clark chuckled. "I heard about Julie's little chat with the killer. You didn't honestly think I wouldn't find out, did you?"

"Look..." Kevin looked away.

"It's okay." Clark held out his hand. "I get it. I wouldn't have told me either. But I know everything he said. He's planning to die but he's planning more murders first. That's plural. I'm not his last target. That means I'm dead by the end of the night."

"You don't know that."

"See that's the thing; I do know it." His lips tightened. "If he's planning to die by tomorrow, then he certainly isn't going to make me his grand finale. I'm just not big enough. I just fear for whoever does find me. They won't have long...It'll probably be you or Julie. He sent me to find the Greenes. He targeted me. He's working his way up to you two. He'll probably kill me tonight and dump me where he knows you'll find me."

"We don't have to let it come to that."

"Have we been able to call any shots this entire case?" Clark shook his head. "He's been one step ahead of us at every turn. He's been ready to make any progress we make irrelevant. He doesn't even care if we catch him anymore. He knows he's done enough damage that if he decides to let us live, we'll never forget it. Or him. He's made himself immortal, in a way."

"I used to come in here all the time after my wife passed." Kevin sipped his beer some more. "I started coming again after Petey and his father were killed." He pushed his glass aside. "I came every night for about a year after that. And it was always the same. I wouldn't get drunk. I'd just order one drink." He held up his finger.

"That's it. Just a single drink. I never even got tipsy."

"Whatever works." Clark shrugged.

"I have no clue why I did it. It never made me feel any better." He looked around at two gloomy-looking men downing shots at the other end of the bar. "I guess I felt at home here...with other people who were miserable. I think maybe that's why I never had more than one drink, because I knew it wouldn't really help. I guess I just needed that little taste of drowning my sorrows."

"Is that what you think I'm doing?" Clark turned to him. "Drowning my sorrows?"

"Well, you're convinced that you're going to die tonight and you're in a bar drinking."

"Can't argue with that, can you?" He took another chug of beer. "Of course." He thrust his hand out. "If I was trying to get hammered, maybe I'd be ordering something stronger."

"You're trying to get a taste, not get hammered out of your mind." He tapped his glass. "As much as you want your fear numbed, you don't want to be high as a kite when this nutjob confronts you. If you die, you want to be able to look him in the eyes first."

"Since when are you a profiler?"

"Since when do you give up and accept defeat so easily? The Clark I know is a go-getter—a stubborn son-of-a-bitch. He doesn't give up until the mission is completed."

"I've failed plenty of times." Clark recalled his career on the force. He thought of the bodies. The vile words uttered by criminals as he led them away in cuffs. The crying loved ones of those he didn't get to in time. He couldn't remember the last time he thought about them. It had all begun to hurt so much that being offended at Julie's tactics seemed an easier burden to bear day to day.

"I'm no credit to law enforcement."

"Bull. You never gave up. Even when you were given good reason to." Kevin swallowed a mouthful of beer. "Do you remember your first case after you made detective?"

"How could I forget? It still keeps me up at night. Especially with this Blood Chain Killer on the loose."

"It was bad." Kevin nodded. "All those kids taken from those playgrounds, turning up dead at the same site just days later. Gives me chills just thinking about it." He twitched. "People were afraid to let their kids out of the house, much less anywhere near a playground. Places where kids were supposed to be free to play and just be kids were turned into dangerous crime scenes."

"Yeah, life's a bitch like that sometimes." Clark shrugged. "What's your point?"

"My point is that because of you, we caught the guy. You're the one who figured out that it was somebody working for the city that was taking the kids. You helped us catch him. And we found that little girl alive because of you. You helped give families in town some security again. And you gave the families of the victims closure."

"I didn't do anything other than my job." Clark stared into his glass.

"And that was enough." Kevin put his hand on Clark's shoulder. "You didn't give up even when all of us thought we'd never catch him. So that's why I can't stand to see you giving up on yourself right now."

"I didn't try to become some psycho's prey. I'm not giving up on myself. I'm just being realistic. I'm accepting my fate."

"So we haven't been able to stop this guy so far. That doesn't mean we write you off yet. Not only are you a damn good cop, but you're my friend."

"And I can't thank you enough for that friendship Kev." He swallowed hard. "But I know in my gut my time is up." Clark felt himself fighting tears. "Just like I knew in my gut that we could find that playground killer. You've always said I got a good gut. Well, my gut tells me that I'm dying tonight." He finished his beer and set the empty glass down at the bar. "You've been a good friend. And a good chief. Despite how immature I get when Julie does her thing, she's been a good friend too. But you're going to have to let me go and focus on saving future victims."

Clark got up to leave.

Kevin grabbed him.

"I'm going." Clark pulled away.

"You don't expect me to sit back and just let this guy kill one of my best men?"

"No, I don't." Clark turned to him. "But, there's nothing you can do to stop it. If he wants to get me, he'll get me. I'm not going to be looking over my shoulder. I have a gun too. The best I can hope is to be prepared to face him head on instead of running. Maybe I can take him down with me. It's better than hiding away waiting to die." He looked to the officers standing guard. "Plus, they'd only get caught in the crossfire. It's better this way." He marched off.

"Where do you think you're going?"

"What?" Clark stopped. "You aren't going to let me use the bathroom now?"

"Clark..." Kevin looked down a moment. He sighed. "Just don't do anything stupid, detective."

Clark smiled as he shed a tear.

"Whatever you say, chief." He turned to head towards

the restroom. When he reached the men's room, he took a look back at Kevin who was still staring back at him.

Kevin nodded at him.

Clark took a deep breath and then snuck out an unguarded back door. He quietly crept to his police car. He looked back to make sure he wasn't being followed before getting inside.

He took a deep breath as he put his key in the ignition and started the vehicle. There was no going back now. He drove away.

He shed a few tears as the bar disappeared into his rear-view mirror. The bar held so many memories for him. Ever since he received his badge, it had been a hangout for him and fellow officers. All the friendships that had been formed over a beer, the conversations shared at those tables, and the dreams confessed under the saloon's dim illuminations. He felt like he was driving away from it all for the last time as he drove down the dark road that led home.

The drive home was a short ten minutes. The parking lot for the apartment complex was almost full. Clark had expected that. After all, it was a Sunday night.

He pulled into the only free space he could find—the one in the corner of the lot next to the dumpster.

As he stepped out of his car and locked it, he felt a wave of sadness sweep over him. He looked at his building. It was cozy and charming, but hardly where he wanted to be in life. He'd once dreamed of moving out of the cramped apartment and into a warm and loving home. With a family. The cliché American dream. He wanted it so badly. When he was young, he used to think he could find it. He'd meet the right woman and they'd get married and settle down.

Like Julie.

Somehow, he had never gotten around to it. Now, it was too late.

A part of him felt it was for the best. He'd seen how shattered Julie was after her husband and son died. He sometimes thought she'd have given up on life altogether if it weren't for Patrick.

Then again, at least she had real memories. All he had were flashes of dreams he'd long since given up on.

He set aside his regrets as he ascended the stairs to the upper level of the apartment building. He was careful to not cause much of a disturbance.

He unlocked the front door of his apartment. It was so dark when he stepped inside. He'd never noticed before just how dark it could get.

He turned on a lamp. Everything was exactly how he had left it.

He looked around at the paltry place he called 'home.' There was hardly anything personal in it. Only a picture of his brother's family and a single childhood photo of him and his brother served as truly personal items.

He set his keys down. Their clang as they hit the furnished wood of the coffee table echoed in the silence.

He went to his bedroom and disrobed. He was surprised how cold he felt. His apartment's AC had never been like this before. He checked the thermostat. It was still at 72 degrees. Nowhere near cold enough for him to feel a draft.

He stepped into the bathroom and caressed his towel. It looked so lonely hanging on the rack alone. He remembered it used to be fluffy. And blue. Now it was tattered and pale. He realized he hadn't bought a new one in well over a decade.

He stepped into the shower and turned the water on. A blast of cold water shot out at him. He quickly turned the nozzle to make it warmer.

The water grew warmer, but he was still shivering. Was he afraid?

He got out of the shower after only seven minutes. He couldn't remember the last time he'd taken such a short one.

He went to his room and dressed himself in boxers and a tee. He left his towel crumpled on his bed.

He walked to the kitchen area and opened the fridge. There was some leftover take-out in there but from the smell of it, he figured he'd best stay away from it. He opened the freezer and it was just as empty. He never realized how rarely he stopped at a grocery store. All that was in the freezer was a packaged chimichanga and a TV dinner of rib-shaped pork patties and rice.

At least Clark liked that entrée. He could do a lot worse for his last meal.

He took it out of its box and popped it in the microwave for the specified amount of time. He stared at the tray as it turned. His mother had always told him not to do that. But he felt like it didn't quite matter anymore. It sounded its shrill beep when it was done.

He took it out and took it into the living room. As he tasted the rib sauce, he flashed back to his youth. He'd eaten this same meal with his parents and younger brother at least once a week. He never saw his older brother eat it. His older brother was a loner and had left home when Clark was only ten.

He and his younger brother were twelve years apart but they were still very close. The fond memories of being a teenager and playing with his kid brother brought a smile to his face. He remembered leaving for the Academy and his younger brother ran out crying to hug him goodbye. He'd still had his "little boy" voice as he begged Clark to stay.

Clark remembered patting him on the head and telling him that he'd still see him every day. No matter what. And he kept that promise. For a while.

Clark hadn't seen his brother in two years.

He turned towards the phone and stared at it for a moment. If he was really going to die tonight, he couldn't do it with regrets. He had to speak to his brother one more time.

He reached over and picked up the phone. He dialed his brother's number, hoping he would pick up.

He felt his hands tense as he heard the ring tone three times before finally hearing "Hello" on the other end.

"Hello? Ricky? It's Blaine."

"Big brother! I was wondering when I'd hear from you again." There was a smile in Ricky's voice. "You haven't called in over a month and you haven't visited in...I don't know how long. But it's been a damn while. I was thinking I'd have to send out a PI to track you down."

"Well, I guess I've just been busy with police crap." Clark laughed. "How've you been?"

"Been busy, but I do have good news—I passed my test. I'm a resident now."

"Alright Ricky!" Clark whistled. He held the phone against his ear so he could clap. "I knew you could do it." He picked up the phone again. It slipped against the sweat of his hand. "You're gonna be a damn good surgeon, kid."

"I'm going to try at least."

"How's that nephew of mine doing?"

"He's great. He's just excellent. He's been talking up a storm. You won't believe the stuff that comes out of this kid's mouth." Laughter. "And he always asks about his 'Uncle Bain.' He still can't manage to say your name right. Maybe if you visited more..."

"He'll learn regardless. He's smart like his dad."

"He misses his uncle. Sure, he sees pictures ever day. And maybe sometimes he talks to you on the phone, but he hasn't seen you since he was two."

"Yeah...I'll have to fix that. Is the little guy awake now?"

"Sorry. He's been asleep for a while now. It *is* almost eleven, you know."

"Yeah..." Clark felt his stomach knot. He'd wanted to hear his nephew's voice one more time too. "What about Cheryl? Is she good?"

"She's been a bit morning sick lately, but other than that, she's just peachy."

"Wait, morning sickness." Blaine sat up in his chair more. "You mean to tell me?"

"Yep, we're having another baby. You're going to be an uncle again. She's due in February. You'll definitely have to fly in now to see us."

Clark was silent a moment.

"Well...yeah. Of course." Clark forced a laugh.

"Blaine, is there something bothering you? You don't seem yourself."

"I'm just stressed." Clark cringed at how phony he sounded. "Been working on a really intense case. Lots of setbacks and there were a lot of really good people we couldn't save...and I guess I've just been feeling like we're not going to be able to stop this guy. He's a bad one."

"You will. I believe in you. You're good at what you do."

"So is he, unfortunately."

"Look, bro. I know you and I know your team. I met the infamous Chief Martel when I came into town a few years back. And I met Julie too. They seemed good and competent. I remember Julie took me aside and said how valuable you were. She said that she didn't know what she'd do without you. I thought she was being sarcastic at first but she seemed really serious."

"She really said that?" Clark's mouth dropped. He knew his assessment of Julie was a bit melodramatic but he never felt that she thought so highly of him.

"She did. You guys make a good team. I have no doubt you guys will nab this creep and the streets will once again be a little bit safer. Thanks to you. And if it helps any, I'll be praying for you."

"It definitely helps a lot." Clark chuckled. "Thank you."

"So, any chance I'll hear from you again before Christmas?"

Clark froze a moment. He knew the answer. His brother couldn't. He'd find out soon enough, but he deserved an extra night to not know. But Clark knew he couldn't let the last thing he said to his brother be a lie. He tried to think of a dodge.

"Blaine? You there?"

"Do you honestly think I'm *that* neglectful? I called you for Easter. And Father's Day. Don't act like I never call."

"Okay, okay. Fair enough, brother." Ricky laughed. "But please, call a little bit more? I get worried about you."

"You don't have to worry about me." Clark paused a moment. "I fell out our bedroom window once and was fine. Remember? It takes a lot to keep me down."

"You were hardly fine. Your arm was in a sling for a month. You were just lucky mom's rosebush broke your fall."

"You're missing the point." A tear rolled down Clark's face. "I'm okay. You don't have to worry about me." He paused. "But I'll make sure to check in more often"

"I'm holding you to that. It's good to hear from you."

"It's good to hear your voice too, bro." He looked at the clock. It was getting late. He didn't want to chance his brother hearing an ambush. "Anyway, I'd better go. Give Cheryl my best. And kiss that nephew for me."

"Will do. You do the same to the team. The giving the best part. Not the kissing."

"Roger that." Clark laughed. "I love you, Ricky."

"Love you too, bro."

He hung up.

Clark sat in silence.

Tears spilled out. He hadn't cried so hard in years. He knew it was likely the last time he'd ever hear his brother's voice.

He slowly finished the rest of his meal remembering some of the fondest memories of his childhood. He remembered sledding down a snowy hill with his brother. He remembered sneaking to a nearby lake and going for an evening swim. He remembered going to elaborate measures to convince his brother that Santa Clause was real. Then sneaking down the stairs early on Christmas morning to find the tree surrounded with all of the presents his brother had wanted. His brother's bright eyes and smile were so beautiful. He still had that same look of joy.

No brothers closer in age could've been closer, or at least he felt that way. He felt that Ricky kept him in line, and forced him to set a good example.

More tears streamed down his face as he thought of his brother receiving that call, wondering what happened and how his brother could've known and not told him.

He heard the sound of footsteps.

He felt his entire body tense as he slowly turned his head to see Artie standing just a few feet away from him. He wore a casual smile unbefitting of the serial killer that he was.

Clark whipped out his gun. He opened fire on the assailant.

He was surprised that Artie didn't even try to return fire.

All four of his bullets missed.

"Hello to you too." Artie chuckled. He looked at the holes in the wall. "I thought cops were better shots than that."

Clark fired again.

It missed and buried itself in a table.

Clark stood confused. "I *am* a better shot. I don't understand." He tensed his grip on the gun. "How'd you get in here?"

Artie pointed with his thumb. "I came through the front door."

"I think I would've seen if you did that."

"Well, you weren't here when I came in." He raised his eyebrows.

"You mean you've been here the entire time?"

"Yeah, been hiding in the closet." He shot a quick glance back at the bedroom. "You got some interesting old things in there. I didn't know you played basketball. Or collected stamps. No pornos though." He frowned. "That was shocking."

"Why'd you wait so long to come out?"

"I was curious as to how you'd spend your final hour alive. Now that I know, I'm pretty impressed." He scratched his chin and nodded.

Clark tried to fire again but he became dizzy. Artie seemed to dance in midair.

He grabbed his head.

"Oh what's the matter?" Artie took a step towards him. He almost looked like he cared. "Got a headache?"

"You did something to me." Clark glared at him. He looked towards the container that had held his dinner and then back at Artie. "You put something in there."

"Wow, even drugged he's very observant." Artie put his foot on the arm of the sofa.

"How'd you know what I'd eat?"

"It's not like you made it hard for me. Nobody in their right mind would go for that science experiment in the fridge, so it was either that or the chimichanga. I took a guess at which one looked more like the 'final meal' type."

"So how are you going to do it?" Clark stumbled about, trying to steady himself. He didn't care about saving himself now. But he had to find a way to at least wound this maniac. "You going to shoot me? Stab me with a kitchen knife? Stick my head in the oven?"

"All good ideas." Artie clapped his hands. "But no. I figured this would work just fine." He took out a cable and gave it a tug.

Clark tried to fire again. He couldn't even keep his finger on the trigger. He dropped the gun.

"You didn't by any chance plan on some suicide mission to take me out, did you? I hope not, cause I would hate for your plans to be dashed like that."

Clark charged at Artie. Maybe he'd knock him out. Any damage was something.

He sent himself straight into Artie's clutches.

Before he knew it, the cord was around his neck, tightly strangling his breath away.

The drugs coursing through his body immobilized him enough to prevent him from effectively struggling or fighting back.

He tried to scratch Artie's hands but he could barely move.

"You're too easy to kill Detective Clark. I knew your pride would undo you. You just had to take me with you."

Clark saw flashes. His childhood. His brother. Every innocent person he'd failed to save.

They all ran before him and disappeared into an imaginary horizon.

He prayed that he would be this monster's last victim. He prayed that Julie and Kevin could stop Artie and save whoever was unfortunate enough to discover his body.

Then he closed his eyes.

And fell dead in his murderer's arms.

Kevin quietly knocked before walking inside Julie's house. He could hear the sounds of the television and see the dark living room illuminated only by the lights of the screen.

As he walked up the stairs, he could see Patrick sitting on the couch clad only in boxers.

"Hey buddy. Your mom here?"

Patrick pointed. "She's in the kitchen paying some bills."

"Thanks. You doing all right?" Kevin walked farther in.

"I'm fine Grandpa." His tone was unconvincing and lacked eye contact. A stark contrast to how he usually was.

Not wanting to start something, Kevin headed to the kitchen and took a seat across from Julie.

"Hey, Dad." She looked up from her checks. "Hope you don't mind. Bills don't wait for people to not be dying."

"No. Not at all."

"I need to be here for Patrick. As much as I want to find this guy, I can't let my son grieve alone."

"I'm handling it. We don't have anything new. Sitting around the police station waiting for a break is just giving him more power over us."

"I've tried to talk to him." She looked over at him. "I thought I got through but he's just been sitting there all day. He hasn't eaten a bite. I'm scared, dad. I don't want him to slip away."

"Give him time. He's been hit with a lot."

"I know..."

"Julie..." Kevin sighed. "Clark escaped our custody."

"What?" She put her pen down.

"He escaped. He left. He's gone." Kevin looked down at the table to avoid her gaze. "We stopped by his apartment, but he isn't there. There were bullet holes in the wall. But no blood."

"How did he get away?"

"You know better than to ask a question like that." He shook his head. "This is Clark we're talking about. He ain't going to stay under armed guard protection."

"Dad, if Artie Falcon finds him..." She rubbed her brow. "He's dead."

"He knows that, Jules." He took a deep breath and exhaled. "He's just accepting it."

"Well he can't just accept it." Julie shot to her feet. "If he dies, then somebody else will be the target. He should know better."

"He didn't want to feel hunted anymore." Kevin got to his feet as well.

"He better still be alive somehow." Julie grabbed her head. "We have to find him."

Kevin was silent. He didn't know what to say.

Julie walked into the living room.

Kevin followed her.

Patrick gave them a passing glance before looking away. The wonder of television, usually reflected in his eyes, was gone. He looked worn.

"This family's lost too many friends already." Julie turned away. "Clark can't just go and get himself killed like that."

"I have people looking for him. There's no use in you worrying." He gently led her back to her seat. "Maybe Clark will find this guy and bring him in. He's a good cop, as you said."

"I hope you're right, Dad. I really hope you're right."

"Why don't I stay the night? You'll need somebody to talk to. And maybe I can get through to Patrick a little bit."

Julie shook her head. "I'm trying to give him space. I have to believe he'll talk when he's ready."

"Are you sure?"

She nodded. "You should go. I think right now, we

both need to try and get some sleep. Not that I can. Tomorrow's the day. If he was telling the truth, he's planning something. That terrifies me. He's holding all the cards. He's closing in on me. If he really has Clark, he probably already knows exactly where he's going to leave him. A part of me just wants to hide away so we can make sure that whoever finds the body...it isn't me or Patrick. Is that selfish?"

"No. That's just wanting to keep your son safe. This guy's running out of options and he knows it. That's why he said he's planning to die, because he knows he can't keep this up. He's planning a showdown tomorrow, and when he does, we'll be ready for him."

<hr />

Artie loaded Clark's body into his trunk. He had dressed Clark in the clothes he'd been wearing before.

"You look good, detective." He smiled and slammed the trunk lid closed.

He got into the car and gleefully drove off to work on his next masterpiece. He knew exactly where he was going to set it up.

CHAPTER 11

"You found his body?" Julie gasped.

"Where?" She felt her heart pounding. Could Clark really be gone?

"I'll be there as soon as I can." She shut her phone.

"Patrick. I have to run out as soon as Karen gets here. Something important's come up in the case."

He walked down the stairs. He was already dressed. "Okay. Good luck, Mom."

He still seemed so sad. She wanted to hold him and embrace away all of his pain. He was too young to hurt so much.

When he reached the bottom of the stairs, she reached out and hugged him. "I love you, Patrick. Please remember that. Always. No matter what. I want you to be able to tell me anything. If you're in pain, tell me. I want to be there for you."

He nodded. "I know. I love you too, Mom." He

looked away. "I know you want to help. Maybe when you get home, we could talk some more?" He sniffled.

She smiled. "Okay then. Tonight." She pulled aside his locks a moment and kissed his forehead. Then she brushed them back down with her hands. "You've really grown into a handsome young man."

"Mom..."

She saw Karen coming up the walkway. "Karen's here."

"It's okay. We can talk later."

"No, you can finish telling me."

"Mom, you have to go catch a bad guy. We'll talk tonight."

"Are you sure?"

He nodded. "Go get 'em." He leaned over and kissed her forehead.

"Okay. Be careful. I'll call you guys in a little bit."

Her chest hurt as she stepped away from Patrick. But she knew that she had no other choice.

<hr />

Julie walked over to the parking lot of the local department store. It hadn't opened yet and so it was almost entirely empty aside from a few scattered cars. And the spectacle gathered around a stop sign.

She squeezed her way through the scene, keeping her badge visible.

Kevin was waiting by the pole.

Julie froze when she got there. A charred corpse was tied to a pole. While the body appeared to be of Clark's build and height, it was beyond recognition.

Kevin approached her. "Well, he did use that decoy of somebody burning at the stake to throw us off about Nina. Maybe he decided to use the idea after all."

Julie folded her arms. "I suppose." She circled the body. "Are we sure this is Clark?"

Kevin handed her an item in a plastic bag. "That was laying a few feet in front of the body."

It was Clark's I.D.

"Awfully convenient place to leave it."

"Well, this guy does want us knowing who his victim is. It makes sense to leave some identification. Plus, this is his style."

"I don't deny that this is Artie's work." She scanned the body head to toe. "Who found the body?"

"The manager of a clothes store saw the body when he came into work."

Julie felt her heart skip a beat. Then she felt horrible for thinking what she had been. Somebody else found the body. Somebody else was the target. Not her.

She shook off the thought. It wasn't right.

"Where is this person?" She looked around.

"I don't know. Nobody seems to know." He looked around. "An officer who arrived on the scene early said he took the guy's statement but hasn't seen him in a few."

A chill shot up Julie's spine. She twitched.

"What is it?" His eyes narrowed.

"Something about all of this doesn't feel right." She looked around the parking lot. "It's a regression in his escalation. We might want to accept such an idea because it'd buy us more time. But it doesn't make sense. He targeted Nina and her family and he targeted Clark. Why just leave a body randomly again for anybody to find? If he's supposed to die today, why go out with the final target being some random employee of a store in the mall? It doesn't make sense. It's not Artie's style."

"You don't think this is connected?"

"Oh, this is his work." She looked again at the I.D. "I just don't think it's Clark." She handed Clark's identification back. "I think it's a decoy. He left that here on purpose to make us think it was Clark. That means he probably does have his body..." Her stomach sank. "He's just going to leave him somewhere else."

Her phone rang.

Her heart dropped.

She reached into her pocket and pulled it out.

Her hand was shaking. She didn't want to be right. But she had to know.

⌖⌖⌖⌖⌖

Patrick walked around a local convenience store as Karen picked up a few things that were needed for the house.

She stuffed some toilet paper and detergent into a shopping cart.

Patrick walked to the trading card rack. He remembered how both Petey and Milo used to love them. He'd never really cared, but he liked looking at the shiny ones. Petey called them "foils." Milo called "holograms." They were always really good at the games.

As he looked at the starter decks and booster packs on the racks, he remembered how much he wished he had learned to play. Milo and Petey always seemed to be having so much fun as they laid down cards and yelled, "Attack". It looked silly. But he missed out on hours playing with them. He couldn't get that time back. He could've enjoyed it too.

"So, you think thirty-five is strong enough for your skin or do you need to go fifty?" Karen's words from behind him were heard but weren't registered in his mind.

She turned her head to Patrick when he didn't respond.

"Earth to Patrick. You okay, buddy?" She waved the bottle of sunblock in front of his face.

He snapped out of his daze.

"What? Is something wrong?" He shot her a worried glance.

"You were spacing out on me." She put on a smile. She showed him the bottle of sunscreen. "I wanted to know if this sunblock is strong enough. What does your mom usually buy?"

Patrick didn't really pay any attention to the bottle. "Oh, that looks like it's it."

"Are you sure?" She looked at it again.

"Pretty sure." He nodded. "It's no big deal either way. As long as it works."

"You sure you're okay?" She placed her hands on her hips, "You seem distracted."

"Just can't stop thinking about Milo." He sighed and tucked his hands into his pockets. "But I'm all right."

Patrick could see that he wasn't convincing her. He really didn't want to talk about this here.

"All right." She smiled and walked towards the cashier. "I'll pay for these things and then we'll go home."

"Sounds good." He pretended to be happy but his voice betrayed him.

She paid for the items quickly and carried them in a small plastic bag on her wrist.

"All right, I'm ready." She waved him on.

She pushed the door open with her arm and stepped out.

Patrick somberly followed her to the car. He hopped into the back passenger seat and buckled himself in.

Karen got in and started the car. They headed for

home.

Patrick gazed at the floor. He didn't want to chance seeing all of the things they passed that reminded him of Milo.

He looked up to see Karen eyeing him in the rear-view.

"Patrick, you know...I lost a friend in high school. She wasn't murdered but it didn't make it hurt any less."

"How did she die?"

"She overdosed on drugs." Karen exhaled slowly. "It felt like there was a piece of *me* missing, when her father called to tell me. But I did eventually move on. I remember it helped me a lot to talk about it."

"Let's just go home." Patrick looked away. He regretted it when he caught sight of camp. He saw the other kids arriving. Did anybody even tell the camp that Milo was never coming back?

"It gets better Patrick." She paused. "We could stop for a treat on the way if you want. It'd be our little secret."

"I'm not really hungry."

"Oh come on. How often do we ever have enough time together to go out and get something to eat? I know a place that makes really great Italian Ice. Best around. What do you say?"

"Maybe some other time?"

"I'll hold you to that Patrick."

Patrick watched as they passed the Italian Ice shop. He'd never tried it before but Milo had. He'd said it was better than ice cream. Patrick was sure he was right. He did want to go and get some. Just not yet. Not until his chest hurt a little bit less.

The rest of the ride home was silent.

Patrick closed his eyes when he passed Milo's street.

He tried not to cry. He knew that crying in front of Karen would mean she'd force him to talk about it even more.

He took deep breaths until they turned onto his street.

Karen pulled into the driveway.

Patrick was way too tense to be crammed into a space as tight as a car. He quickly hopped out as soon as she put the brakes on.

"Patrick, I know you're sad." She got out of the car carrying the bags from the store. "But please don't give me the silent treatment." She hung her purse on her shoulder. "We know each other better than to be unable to talk."

"You're right. I'm sorry." Patrick walked to the front door. "Maybe we can watch a movie or something when we go inside." He forced a smile, hoping she'd buy it.

"Now there's an idea." She took out the key to the house. "I think that's exactly what we should do." She opened the door and they went inside.

When the pair reached the living room, any thoughts of pleasant recreation were thrust out of their mind faster than blood from a fresh bullet wound.

The bag in Karen's hand hit the ground with a thump. The smell of lemon wafted through the air from the now broken detergent bottle.

Clark sat motionless on the sofa, a spilled beer bottle in one hand, and a half-eaten donut in the other. There was no blood but both Karen and Patrick still had a sick feeling in their stomach.

"Is he dead?" Patrick stepped back and knocked into Karen.

Karen steadied Patrick and walked over to Clark.

She felt Clark's carotid artery. "Yes, I think so, Patrick." She took a nervous step back.

Patrick remembered that he had overheard Julie saying that Clark had found the bodies of Milo and his family. He also remembered the Blood Chain Killings he had heard about on the news.

"Oh gosh!" He began to breathe heavily. He scrubbed his hands down his face. "No, no. This isn't good." He repeatedly shook his head.

"What is it Patrick?" Karen kneeled down to eye level with him.

"*We* found him." His eyes welled with unshed tears. "That means *we're* next."

"What? What are you talking about?" She took another step back.

"We're going to die." He collapsed to the ground, hugging himself with his arms. "Oh my gosh, we're gonna die." He cried.

Patrick's grim words hung in the air.

Karen scrambled for her phone to dial Julie.

"Karen? Is everything all right?" Karen rarely, if ever, called during the day unless something was wrong. Julie felt a sick feeling when she heard Karen's voice when she answered her phone.

"I don't know how to say this to make it sound better than it is so I'm just going to spit it out. There's a guy on your couch. And he's dead. I think it's that guy Clark that you work with."

Julie froze upon hearing the words. All hope of finding her friend alive drained from her. Not only that, she knew what this meant. "Are you sure it's Clark?" She shut her eyes.

"Pretty sure. He's got a beer bottle and a bitten donut in his hand. There's no blood on anything."

"I'll be right there."

"There's something else." Karen huffed. "Patrick said that because we found him, it means we're next."

"He's right." Julie cried. "You're both in danger. The fact that he left the body in my house means he targeted Patrick and me. Now what he said makes more sense. And I was right. This was a decoy. He probably just wanted to get me away..." The thought that she'd allowed Artie an opportunity to get to Patrick echoed in her brain. She couldn't bear the thought of Patrick being hurt. She had to get to him.

∘⊂⨯∘⨯⊂⨯∘⨯⊂⨯∘

"What are you talking about?" Karen's voice grew more frantic. "Julie, I'm scared now."

Suddenly, she heard a creek upstairs. Patrick heard it too. They both looked up.

Another creak. They screamed.

Somebody else was there.

"Karen! Karen is everything all right?" Julie's voice sounded frantic.

"I think somebody's here." Karen's whispered voice trembled.

The sound of footsteps.

"Karen, I need you to take Patrick and get out of there as fast as you can." Julie was gasping. "Don't ask where to go. It doesn't matter. As long as he can't find you. Don't wait. Hang up the phone now and go."

She hesitated a second but quickly closed the phone and dragged Patrick by the arm. "Your mom says we have to get out of here now."

Karen rushed for the door.

"I wouldn't do that if I were you." Artie began descending the stairs. He held a gun in his hand.

He fired the gun.

The bullet lodged in a wall.

Karen and Patrick screamed.

They quickly dashed for the door.

Artie fired again.

The sound of glass shattering echoed in the house.

They practically jumped down the stairs and to the car.

"Buckle up, Patrick."

Karen frantically started the car and quickly rushed out of the driveway and down the street.

Patrick did as he was told as Karen rapidly turned a corner.

Karen could see in her rear-view mirror that a car was behind her.

Artie's slick face smiled back at her from the driver's seat.

Patrick braced himself as Karen made another sharp turn.

"Where are you going to drive to?" Patrick shot a quick glance behind them. "He's right behind us!"

"Just sit tight." Karen nervously gripped the wheel. "You might not know this by looking at me but I actually did a lot of crazy driving stunts as a teenager. Just make sure you don't get hurt."

She did a u-turn and started speeding in the other direction.

Artie quickly matched her maneuver.

Karen tried an abrupt left turn and then an abrupt right turn.

Artie remained on her tail.

Karen glanced at the speedometer and prayed that she could maintain control of the car. She was speeding faster than she had in years and had violated at least a dozen other rules of the road as well.

"God, if you can't spare me, at least protect Patrick." She had come to care deeply for Patrick during her time as his nanny and she didn't want to see him hurt. She felt her heart beating faster out of concern for him much more than for herself.

As she drove, she heard the honking of an oncoming truck.

She and Patrick let out a harmonized scream as she whipped the wheel to narrowly avoid it. '

Artie's car disappeared behind the mammoth truck as it crossed the intersection.

She continued her pace on the other side and hoped to increase the distance between her and Artie. But as soon as the truck had passed, she could see the car speeding towards her again.

Patrick turned around and saw the approaching vehicle. "He's going to catch up to us and kill us."

"No, I won't let that happen." Karen shook her head. "I don't want you to give up either. Even if you have to run away from him on foot, don't give up."

"I can't outrun a car." Patrick was out of breath.

"Well, let's hope you don't have to." She glanced in her rearview mirror and was horrified to see Artie right behind her. "When did he get so close?"

She tried speeding up but couldn't increase the gap between the two cars.

She then noticed the small, rarely traveled bridge spanning the river up ahead. It was desolate. Karen hadn't realized how far off the main road Artie's chase had led her.

She thought she was escaping him. What if she was playing right into his hand?

She then noticed the bridge was open.

"Damn it!" There wasn't a boat in sight. "Why is this thing opening?" Was the world out to stop her from escaping this madman? "It's eleven o'clock." She remembered that this bridge opened this time daily, regardless of whether or not there was a boat that needed to pass.

By the time she realized what was going on, both she and Artie had crossed the onto the bridge. Karen felt her breathing increase. Her way was blocked.

Patrick gazed out at the open bridge and then back at Artie. "We're trapped."

The distance between their bumpers was only inches.

Karen quickly tried to maneuver the car to make a u-turn, but Artie was quick and slammed into the side of her car.

Then he pulled back and slammed them again.

Karen heard Patrick scream. He sounded so afraid. She had to be brave

Then she heard a creaking sound.

The bridge rail was caving in and the car was sliding off the side.

Now she screamed.

"We're falling." Patrick shouted and grabbed onto a handle.

Karen tried to stop the car from going over. None of the controls did anything. She was helpless.

Artie slammed into them again.

There was a loud rumble as the car tipped over the side.

Karen and Patrick screamed in terror as the car fell to the large watery grave below.

It crashed with a large splash and quickly sank to the river's depths.

Carrying the two terrified passengers with it.

∘⚬◌⚬◌⚬◌⚬◌

Water was everywhere.

The door opposite Patrick was crumpled and immovable.

Patrick felt raw fear that the car would become his grave.

Thoughts of another time in a car went through his mind. As the water picked away at his consciousness, it was like he was living this memory again.

It was dark—late at night—well beyond his bedtime. He was almost eight years old, but just far enough to still be considered "only seven" by adults. The lights of the cars passing were pretty. It felt good to be on the road again.

He looked ahead and saw his dad's warm face in the mirror.

He then looked over at his own flesh and blood mirror image—his twin brother Petey. They were the pictures of identical twins.

"Was that game great or what?" Petey smiled over at Patrick. "I was like so seriously thinking that ball was going to come flying right at us." He clapped a fist against the palm of his other hand. "And then Dad would have to catch it. I mean that ball was going, going, gone. It was like super cool. It's never that fast on TV."

Petey turned to Patrick. "How much fun was that game?"

"Lots of fun." Patrick smiled back. "But it never would've been as much fun without you."

"Oh yeah, you being there definitely makes everything more fun. It's no fun cheering alone you know. You gotta have your bestest friend slash coolest twin brother ever with you." Petey initiated a fist-pump with Patrick.

"What's that for?" Patrick laughed harder.

"Brothers forever. Like always. Well, that and also just 'cause you're cool!" Petey cracked a proud grin.

"Yeah. Brothers forever. And you're cool too."

"I know that silly. We're twins. If you're cool, I'm cool. And if I'm cool, you're cool. It's how it works." He pointed back and forth between the two of them. "Life's just awesome like that." He took Patrick's hands and they shook.

A loud crash ceased their conversation.

A large van smashed into the left side of the vehicle as they turned the corner onto their street.

Blood splattered throughout the car.

The force pulled the boys' hands apart.

∞◦◯◦◯◦◯◦◯◦◦

The smoking engine and flashing lights awoke Patrick out of his momentary unconscious state.

He felt aches all over his body. Pain was everywhere. He looked down and saw blood. It wasn't so much that he figured that he couldn't possibly be alive, but enough to tell him that he was really hurt.

He felt a sharp pain in his head. He reached up to touch it, aggravating his arm.

He saw oozy blood on his hand after pulling it back from his head. "Oh no!" His breathing grew heavy.

He then looked ahead and saw his father slumped over on the steering wheel.

"Dad?" There was no response. He shouted "Dad" again and met the same silence.

He then looked over to Petey.

His eyes widened in horror.

His brother's bloody form lay against the crushed in

door.

Petey's eyes were closed and his mouth was drooping and bloody. There were lots of cuts across his face.

The window next to his head was smashed.

"Petey!" Patrick felt his the strain from the high decibels his voice achieved.

He reached over and touched Petey, trying to wake him. His brother had to be okay. He was going to wake up.

Petey didn't respond.

The color in his face was gone.

"No. Petey! Petey wake up. Please, Petey. Petey!"

He shook Petey again.

There was so much blood.

The door next to Petey was wrecked. Petey almost seemed stuck to it.

Patrick's anxiety added to his difficulty in breathing.

He tried to unbuckle his seatbelt.

It was stuck.

His door was jammed too.

"Somebody help. Help me. Help." He was crying. Wailing. Choking. Gasping for breath.

"Don't worry honey. It's going to be all right!"

He looked outside the car window to see his mother. She was trying to get the door open.

He could see red and blue flashing lights also coming onto the scene. Help.

Julie pried off the door. She reached in with a knife and cut Patrick free of his seatbelt.

"Mom, you're here." He reached out his hands for her. "I'm scared. That car just came so fast. And Daddy and Petey..."

"Are you all right?" She caressed his face. Her hands

slid on the blood.

"I don't know. It hurts, Mom. It hurts real bad." He cried harder.

"What hurts?"

"All of it."

"You're going to be okay. I promise, Patrick." She kissed his forehead.

"What about Daddy? And Petey?"

Her face turned grim.

She reached in and touched Petey's neck. "Oh God..." He wasn't moving. Patrick wondered why she was touching his neck and then crying. "My Petey."

"Is he all right, Mom?"

Julie was silent. She tried to wipe tears from her eyes. "Don't worry about him. We just have to worry about getting you help."

Patrick tearfully nodded. "What about Daddy?"

Julie looked at her husband's slumped over body. She felt his neck too.

She twitched and thrust herself back.

She buried her head on the headrest of the empty passenger's seat—the seat she usually sat in.

"Mom. Is Petey going to be okay? And Daddy?" Patrick began to breathe heavier.

She gently caressed his arm. She looked away.

"Mom, are they dead? Daddy? And Petey?" Patrick began crying. "They're not okay, are they?" His eyes welled with tears. They streamed down his face.

Julie wiped them aside. She didn't have to answer.

He looked over again at his brother. Petey was his twin. And now he was dead. Gone. Forever. Patrick felt it inside.

He looked over at his father. His daddy was gone too.

"Petey's in heaven now with Nana. But he'd want you to get out of this okay." She wrapped her arms around Patrick. "So you have to be strong. Okay, Patrick?"

Patrick nodded. He wrapped his arms around his mother and she gently carried him out of the car.

At least he had his mommy. And Petey had their daddy. He wasn't alone either.

"You're going to be okay, Patrick. The ambulance is here and it's going to take you to the hospital. And the doctors are going to make you all better."

"What happens to Petey and Daddy?"

"They'll be taken care of. I promise."

Julie carried Patrick to a stretcher and laid him down. She kissed his head again. She brushed his locks of hair over his forehead.

They quickly wheeled him towards the ambulance.

"Mommy, Mommy! Don't leave me." He stretched out his arms.

They stopped.

Julie turned to the lifeless forms in the car. Half of her family. Then back towards her injured child. Pleading with her not to leave him with teary wide eyes.

Patrick's grandfather was there. He put his hand on Julie's shoulder. "Go with him. He still needs you."

"But what about Seth? And Petey?" She whimpered and tried to muffle her cries. "My husband. And my little boy...I can't just leave them here."

"They're gone, Julie. Patrick's not." He gazed at the car. "I'll stay here with them to make sure they're treated with respect."

She looked towards the car. "I can't even process this. I know it's true, but I..."

"You're still in shock. Right now, Patrick needs you.

Go with him."

"Mommy." Patrick cried harder. He stretched out his hand to her. "Mommy. I'm scared. I don't wanna go in there with them."

Julie looked over to him.

She was at his side in an instant.

She comforted him with gentle strokes against his cheek. "I'm here honey. I'm not going anywhere."

She followed him onto the ambulance.

Patrick heard the ambulance doors shut and felt the vehicle moving. The flashes of the accident scene that had halved the happy family disappeared into the distance.

"Mommy, what's gonna happen to us now?" He wailed.

"I told you; the doctors are going to make you all better." She stroked his head.

"No, I mean what's gonna happen to *us*? Without Dad and Petey."

"I don't know Patrick, but you'll always have me. I won't leave you." She took Patrick's hand.

"And you'll always have me, Mommy."

The pain of losing their family hurt so much in that instant. And it would only get worse when the grim reality set in when they went home to their silent, empty house. Their family would never be the same again.

But they had each other.

∞◦◯◦∞◦◯◦∞

Water drowned out any vision.

Patrick felt himself floating. Somehow he had gotten out of his seatbelt. He couldn't remember how. He was holding his breath but he couldn't do it much longer. He was sure he'd drown if he didn't get air within a few seconds.

For a brief moment, he was tempted to stay there.

To let himself die.

He could see his father, Petey, and Milo again. He missed them so much. Maybe he should just close his eyes and inhale his doom.

Then he heard something. It sounded liked the very voices of those people telling him to get out. They wanted him to live. Giving up wasn't the right decision. He felt it in his heart.

God wanted him to fight. His mother wanted him to fight. He'd always felt that God wanted him to do something special after he survived the accident. He couldn't die now. His mother needed him. He was all she had left.

"Patrick." Petey's voice. "Get out, Patrick."

He had to find a way to the surface before he drowned.

He looked around and saw no sign of Karen. She had gotten out somehow.

He looked for a way out of the car.

He tried the door.

It wouldn't open.

He panicked. He didn't want to die now.

He looked around for an opening. Anything.

But this car was looking more and more like a watery grave—*his* watery grave.

<hr />

Karen took a deep breath as she burst through the surface. She looked around in the murky water. She couldn't see any sign of Patrick anywhere. Or rescue.

"Patrick? Can you hear me, Patrick?"

All she could hear was the river water.

She considered diving back down to look for him. She didn't have the stamina to make it to the car and back to the surface again.

Could Patrick really be gone? He couldn't be dead.

"Patrick?" She screamed as loud as she could but only piercing silence replied.

The shore wasn't too far off. Maybe Patrick was there. Unconscious or out of breath.

She prayed for that. It was the only chance of seeing him alive again. She swam to the shoreline and took deep breaths as her feet set foot upon the shore.

"Patrick?" Her cry met the same results as before. She was surprised nobody had seen her go over the rail. Even for a desolate road, she felt like rescue should've been there by now.

She looked around for signs of Patrick—anything—but there was nothing. No footprints. No clothes. No body.

He must've still been in the water.

She looked back towards the river. Patrick was lost somewhere in there. He was still just a little boy. He would've turned twelve soon. He wouldn't have needed her for long, but she knew he'd still make sure to see her. That's the kind of kid Patrick was.

"No, he can't be dead." She tearfully placed her hand over her mouth. "But there's no way he could've survived that." She'd failed to keep him safe.

At least he was at peace now. With his brother. He didn't hurt anymore.

She looked around the shore. She needed to find help.

She saw a man walking down the hill, but she couldn't see his face.

Not even considering for a moment the identity of the stranger, she ran to him shouting and waving.

"Hey, sir. I need help."

She froze in horror upon locking eyes with the man.

It was Artie.

Before she could even turn to run, she saw an arrow flying towards her from a crossbow in his hands.

It pierced her chest.

She coughed up blood and collapsed to the ground, hemorrhaging from her wound.

Her body convulsed as her organs struggled to hang onto their fading life.

They lost.

A final breath exhaled her body.

∞◯∞◯∞◯∞

Artie walked over to her impaled flesh and gazed into her lifeless eyes staring back at him. "Well, you went down even easier than I thought you would."

He looked around the shore and out at the water.

"Now to find Little Boy Patrick. I hope the tyke didn't drown in the river. I have such big plans for him."

Artie sulked a moment. Patrick drowning in the river wasn't what he'd had in mind. Nobody would see Patrick's beautiful body until it was fished out. That wasn't right. A boy like Patrick deserved to be seen by everyone.

"He's tough. He's alive." Artie smiled. He thought of everything he wanted to do to Patrick. His limbs shook in his excitement.

Then he turned his attention to Karen. "First thing's first. We cannot forget about you."

∞◯∞◯∞◯∞

Air felt so good in Patrick's lungs.

His head burst through the surface of the river and he inhaled as deep a breath as he could. He exhaled slowly and repeated the cycle. Getting out of the car had taken a lot out of him. He was grateful for his swimming lessons now. They really were useful to him after all.

He looked ahead. He could see the shore not too far

in the distance, but it would take a lot out of him to get there. He wasn't sure he had the energy.

Still, he had swam out of the broken window of the car and made it to the surface. He had come too far to drown anyway. He needed to get to that shore.

He took a deep breath and recalled his swimming lessons as he darted off for the shore.

Circular strokes. Remember to breathe.

The distance to the shore was many times that of one end of the pool to another. Milo would never have been able to do it.

Patrick took each stroke one at a time. He fought the urge to rest. He'd never get there if he did.

With each stroke closer to the shore, he became more and more determined. Heavy breaths nearly sank him but his heart felt relief as his drenched sandals set foot on the grassy shore.

He wanted to shout for help. But the swim to shore had left him breathless and weak.

He lay down on his back a minute to catch his breath. He felt his eyes drawn up to the clouds. He flashed back to when he used to do the same thing with Petey and Milo. He could almost hear them trying to figure out what it was the clouds looked like. Dogs or cars? Cats or dragons? Flowers or gargoyles? Petey and Milo always saw something, even if they didn't always agree what.

He never saw many shapes in them. They were always just cotton-like fluffs in the sky to him. But as he looked now, he could swear he saw their silhouettes in them. His, Petey's, Milo's...

Maybe it was the water that had drenched him from head to toe or the shock of crashing off a bridge, but he could see something in the clouds for the first time ever.

As he watched the clouds, his eyes were drawn to a tree. Something was leaning against it.

Patrick shot to his feet to take a closer look at it.

With every step closer to the tree, the image became clearer until he could distinguish exactly what it was—Karen.

Patrick screamed.

He jolted back.

The bloody corpse of his nanny was pinned to the tree by an arrow through her chest. A note that read "Sale" was pinned against her chest. Her wallet was in her hand.

Patrick cried as he gazed upon her bloody form.

"No. He killed you too." He took the wallet out of her hands and saw her bloodstained fingerprints on it. "Why is he doing this? Why is he doing this to us?"

"Because you are beautiful!" Artie's voice. Behind him.

Patrick shot around to face him.

The psychopath wore his signature smile and stared back at Patrick with a sadistic glare, as if he was already picturing him as a corpse.

Patrick backed away from him. "Why are you killing everybody? Milo and his family?" He shed a tear. "Detective Clark, Karen? Why did you kill them all?"

Artie shook his head. "I told you, because they needed to become art. The human body is imperfect until somebody turns it into a work of art. Every person should be so lucky as to become art when they are young and their flesh is not marred by age. Don't worry. You will join them soon."

"No, I won't." Patrick shook his head. "I didn't get out of that car to die some other way."

"I'd say you did. You weren't meant to drown. I already have your cause of death selected. Death is not something to fear, Patrick. Look at it as being made whole as your body becomes even more beautiful without your soul to inhibit it."

"What if I don't want to be art?" Patrick clenched a fist. "What if I am happy with keeping my body the way it is now?" He angrily glared at Artie. "I don't want to become art. I want to stay like this. Leave me alone!"

"You're just acting in your ignorance." Artie took a step towards him. "People have lied to you that living is better. Only in death can your body truly exist as it was meant to. Likes and preferences matter nothing. Your body suffers because of your soul. That needs to be removed as soon as possible so that your body can reach its full potential. You need to die so your beauty can be perfected, Patrick." Artie gleefully rubbed his hip.

Patrick took a step back. "That makes no sense. You're crazy."

"I've been called a lot of things." He chuckled. "I am not fazed by insults. I am fazed by results."

He approached Patrick.

Patrick shot off towards the road, running as quickly as he could in the slippery wet sandals on his feet.

He turned to see Artie easily keeping a short distance behind him without even breaking a sweat. He seemed inhuman.

Patrick felt his chest. His heart was pounding like he'd never felt it pound before.

"God, I'm scared. Help me." He ran a little quicker but still felt like Artie was too close. The man wouldn't stop until Patrick was just like the rest of them.

Patrick darted out in the street.

A large truck honked its horn as it quickly sped in his

direction.

Patrick screamed and made a jump for the other side of the road.

He narrowly avoided certain death.

Patrick quickly got to his feet. He saw a mall in the distance.

"Maybe I can hide there."

He then noticed that Karen's wallet was still in his hands. He hadn't intended to take it but considering that he had it now, he had no choice but to try to use the money inside to get away from the madman closing in on him.

Patrick ran towards the mall, hoping the crowds would give him some protection. If he couldn't find anybody to help him, maybe he could at least blend into the crowd enough to lose Artie until he could get home.

Visions of his dead body looking like Karen's and Milo's flashed into his mind. It scared him greatly to think of what it must feel like to die. He wasn't ready and he had to escape.

After running for what felt like ages, he finally arrived in the mall parking lot. The entrance was in sight, but Artie still walked a close pace behind him. Patrick was amazed at how fast Artie walked. He wondered if the madman was intentionally not running, just to toy with him. With the threat to his life looming, he thrust those thoughts away and darted towards the mall's closest entrance, hoping to find security inside.

CHAPTER 12

Patrick's waterlogged sandals made sloshing sounds as he stumbled his way through the doors of the mall. He remembered now that he had been in this mall before, and he didn't like it. It twisted and turned, had several sections, and was considerably darker than most malls. It was definitely not the choice he would be ideally making for a shelter, but he wasn't in a position to be picky.

He ran further into the building, hoping to find a place to hide and escape his pursuer. No store seemed safe because each had a large display window that would give him away if Artie passed by.

As he ran, his slippery sandals skidded against the floor. He fell forward but extended his hands to break his fall. He attracted attention from passersby, but none of them tried to help him up.

"Ouch." He whimpered.

He struggled to his feet. His clothes were still heavy

and wet. When he looked back behind him, he was alarmed to see a water trail. That would surely lead Artie straight to him. He needed to get out of these wet clothes right away. But how?

He remembered the wallet still in his hands.

He checked inside. He found at least fifty dollars. It wouldn't buy him a fancy suit but it could buy a change of clothes. The new clothes could also serve as a disguise. Artie wouldn't be expecting him to change clothes. But if he waited in line to buy them, he'd be a sitting duck. He had to think of a way to not be seen.

Stealing clothes seemed risky. If he got caught, Artie would certainly find him. If he didn't get caught, he could get away. But stealing was wrong, even in these circumstances. But he might not have a choice.

He saw a clothes store that sold clothes for all ages. He darted inside.

The lines at the cash register were long. There was a sale going on that attracted a large number of the town's local women. If he waited in that line, he'd be dead before he reached the cash register. He might not have a choice but to steal.

Seeing Artie pass by outside, he quickly hid behind a shelf.

Artie walked right by.

He wanted to believe that he was home free but Artie would definitely be back. He had to get out of his dripping wet clothes and fast.

He quickly scanned the store for clothes. He saw a tan pair of shorts and a short-sleeve hoodie in his size. He'd never seen a short-sleeve hoodie before—it looked neat. Not only that, but a hoodie also seemed perfect to hide from Artie in. He also grabbed a pair of red boxers in his size.

The store didn't sell any footwear. But he couldn't wear his sandals anymore. He'd have to go barefooted.

He walked into the dressing room area, preparing to try on the clothes. He checked under the doors for feet. The first was occupied. A second looked empty and the door to it appeared to be unlocked. Patrick opened it. There was a half-dressed boy on the other side.

"Care to knock first?" The boy inside kicked his feet together and leaned back against the wall. His dark brown eyes peered at Patrick with a bit too much suspicion to seem genuine. He made some maneuver to his brown hair to seem tough.

Patrick backed away, embarrassed. "Sorry, I thought this was empty."

"Ah, it's okay." His demeanor had completely changed. "I'm waiting for my mom to come back with my clothes. She wants me to try on new stuff for Church. I swear, if she doesn't come back soon, I am going to embarrass her and run out there naked. Your mom making you try on clothes too?"

"Something like that." He chuckled in what he hoped was a believable mimic of the brown eyed boy's nonchalance to avoid suspicion.

"Well, the stall next to me is free." He pointed with his thumb. "You can go in there to change."

"Thanks..." Patrick shut the boy's door.

Patrick had been hoping to not have to interact with anybody. While the boy seemed nice enough, now wasn't the time to make new friends.

He hopped into the next one and set the clothes down. He quickly disrobed. The stall door might've given him security but his bare skin still caught the presence of a light draft.

"Man, I hate doing this." He was surprised that despite the clothes being drenched, his body was more soggy than wet.

"Wow, I didn't know other people got naked in here too."

He looked up to see the boy looking down at him from the stall next to him. How he got to the top, Patrick didn't know since the boy didn't seem nearly tall enough to stand that high.

Patrick draped the boxers below his waist. "Um, why are you spying on me?"

"Relax, dude. I ain't spying." He swung his hand dismissively. He jumped down and shouted across the stall, "I think it's cool that you got the guts to do it here. You ain't afraid of nobody. I'm like that. We're so much alike." He banged against the wall of the stall. "Stop by when you're done. I wanna see if those clothes look cool on you. I might try to get my mom to buy me something I actually wanna wear to make up for making me wait all day while she talks."

"Good luck with that." This boy's personality seemed so familiar. He felt rude dismissing him. But he didn't have a choice.

He quickly stepped into the boxers and shorts. They fit comfortably. He then slipped into the shirt and it too fit nicely. Patrick looked at himself in the mirror. He looked quite good. These weren't just throwaway bargain clothes.

He then looked over each of them and yanked off the price tags so he wouldn't set off the alarms when he left.

He saw the boy looking over the top again.

"Wow, you look so cool. I should get one of those shirts in blue and we can go around the mall and get respect from everyone."

Patrick twitched a bit. "Thanks."

"Why were your clothes so wet anyway?"

"They were wet?" Patrick pretended to be ignorant. He didn't have time to explain.

"Dude, your clothes are soaked." He pointed to them clumped on the bench, "And when you got undressed, let's just say I've gotten out of the shower dryer than that."

Patrick was surprised; he thought he was surprisingly dry.

The boy's eyes narrowed. "Did you like jump in a pool or something?"

"Look, dude, I can't really talk long." He looked around nervously. "It was nice to meet you but I really need to go." Patrick peeked out the door. The lines were still long.

Patrick looked at the price tags on the floor. He knew he couldn't in good conscious steal these. But he couldn't leave money for somebody to find. Especially with Mr. Meddlesome still peering over the stall.

"I see you ripped off those price tags from those clothes. You ain't here with your mom, are you? You're going to walk out without paying for them."

"No, I'm not going to steal them." He checked to make sure nobody was listening. "I just can't pay for them in line. I gotta leave the money somewhere."

"Why don't you leave it in the stall with those wet clothes?"

Patrick rolled his eyes. "Why? So you can steal it?"

"I don't steal." The boy straightened proudly. "I may like getting into trouble but I don't take anything that isn't mine. I had that happen to me once and it sucked. You can trust me. I can even tell somebody who works here when you're gone."

"I don't know." He tapped his foot nervously. "How do I know you ain't lying?"

The boy thought. "Come here." He signaled Patrick to come over with his index finger.

Patrick reluctantly snuck over to the boy's stall and shut the door behind him.

The boy said, "Hold out your hand."

"What? Why?"

"Just do it!"

Patrick obeyed.

The boy held out his own hand.

He placed his hands on top of Patrick. "Are we friends?"

"If you want to be, I guess we could be." Patrick felt nervous. "But I really have to go." He could feel his heart racing as he imagined Artie coming closer and closer to him.

"I say we're friends, and if we're friends, we gotta trust each other. I promise I won't let anyone take it." He flashed Patrick an earnest and wide-eyed smile. "I'm Jacob by the way, in case you care. What's your name?"

"I'm Patrick. Now, dude, I really need to go."

"What's the rush, Patrick?"

"Look, I just really need to go."

"Okay then, go."

Patrick poked his head out of the stall door and saw Artie in the store looking around.

Patrick pushed Jacob further into the stall. "Get up on the stall and stay hidden." He locked the door.

"What is it, dude?"

He placed his hand on Jacob's mouth. "Just do it."

Jacob tensed up and quickly obeyed. The two got up

on the seat and curled up into as small a ball as possible.

Patrick watched as he saw Artie's feet outside the stall. His heart was racing.

Artie stopped in front of the stall. He seemed to linger way too long. Was this it? Would he fire through the door and kill both of them? Patrick couldn't bear the thought of getting this kid killed. Jacob was trying to be nice. He didn't deserve to die because of it.

Artie walked away.

Patrick breathed a sigh of relief.

Jacob peeked over the stall and saw Artie walk out of the store. "He's gone. Who was that guy?"

"A very bad man." Patrick hopped off of the bench.

"Is he like one of those pedophiles who touches our boy parts?" He looked down at Patrick. "My mom's always telling me to never talk to any strangers cause they might be one of those. She's had Dad give me all of these talks so I know never to let anybody do that. I don't know why anyone would want to anyway. That's weird."

"Well, he's weird and he's dangerous." Patrick felt the urge to leave quickly. "Dude, he's trying to kill me. For real. That's why I was all wet. I was in the river."

"What?" He jumped down. "That's crazy."

"Well it's true. If I don't get out of here, I'm going to die. So seriously, I'm sure you're really cool and maybe we can hang out one day if I don't die. But I seriously gotta get outta here."

"Okay then. Sure thing." He looked down at Patrick's bare feet. "What about your feet? You gonna run barefoot?"

Patrick shot a glance at them. He shrugged. "I don't have a choice."

"Bull. Take mine." He picked his up from the floor. "I

don't need them." He handed Patrick his.

Patrick's eyes widened. "What? You'll get in trouble."

"So what. Mine are old anyway." He smiled. "We're actually going to be getting new ones at the mall today. I'll just tell Mom somebody stole them while she was wasting all day picking out a shirt."

"Are you sure?"

"Damn straight, dude. I hated them anyway." He placed them in Patrick's hands. "You need these. What if you needed to go outside? I walked on a hot parking lot once. Not fun."

Patrick quickly slipped into them.

Patrick then opened the wallet and took out forty dollars. "This should be enough." He snuck over to his stall and tucked it under his shoe. He then snuck back to Jacob's stall. "Thank you for everything. I'm sorry I doubted you."

"Ah, it's fine." He giggled. "Try not to get killed cause I'd like to hang out with you."

"Same here."

Jacob shot a look at the crowded store. "How are you going to escape if you get noticed?"

"I'll find a way."

Jacob thought a second and then snapped his fingers. "No, I will."

He pulled down his underwear, his only clothes, and tossed them on the bench. He then stood proudly before Patrick. "How do I look?" He winked.

Patrick gasped. "What are you doing?"

Jacob replied, "Creating a distraction."

"Naked?"

"Hey, I told you I wanted to do this." He leaned back against the wall. "Besides, you flashed me. Now I flash you. Enjoy the show." He winked as he opened the stall door and walked out of the fitting area.

Patrick laughed at Jacob considering spying on him while he was naked to be the equivalent of 'flashing.'

Jacob ran up to the front of the store where his mother immediately freaked about seeing him without a stitch of clothing on.

She smacked both sides of her face. "Jacob! What are you doing?"

He spun around to let her see him at all angles. "I was hot and tired of waiting. Hi Mrs. Hinkle." He waved with a grin to horrified eyes.

Patrick chuckled as he snuck by.

Jacob gave him a wink.

His horrified mother dangled clothes in front and behind him to shield him from view from the other customers in the store who had already begun to gawk.

Jacob slipped away. He stuck his tongue out at her. "Go on. Try and catch me."

She chased him, shouting punishments awaiting him when he got caught.

He danced away unfazed. He laughed louder.

With everyone was focused on Jacob, Patrick slipped out unnoticed.

⋄⋄⋄⋄⋄

Patrick wandered back into the mall.

He looked both ways for Artie. There was no sign of him. Maybe he was free of him. He could somehow get home to his mother, and she'd be able to protect him herself from this lunatic.

He ran from the store, his new clothes comfortably fitting and making running a lot easier. He pulled the hood over his head, aiding in his new disguise.

Patrick then realized that he was near the mall security station. "Maybe they can help me." He quickly dashed towards the security station, which was just coming into sight.

A woman with pitch-black hair stood behind the desk. She was sorting through some files. Patrick could see her nametag. 'Chelsea.'

Chelsea happened to look up as Patrick was running towards her. Her face grew concerned.

"What the hell?" She leaned forward on the desk when it became apparent that Patrick was headed straight for her.

Patrick caught his breath a moment. "Please. Help me." His eyes watered up.

"Young man, are you all right?" She perked up. "Are you here all by yourself?" She poked her head out and looked around the mall. She instinctively placed her hand on the phone.

"No, I'm not all right. There's a man chasing me. And he's trying to kill me." Patrick looked around for any sign of Artie before returning his gaze to Chelsea. "Please, you have to help me. He's going to kill me if he finds me." Patrick gulped. "And he might kill a lot of other people too. Please, you have to call the cops or something. So they can stop him. My mom's a cop. She'll make sure somebody comes. But please, you have to hurry!"

Chelsea scanned Patrick a moment. Like she was unsure of whether or not to believe his story.

"I know it sounds crazy. But you gotta believe me."

She exhaled a moment.

Her eyes told Patrick that she was coming around.

"All right, sit tight." She held up her finger. "I'll get somebody."

Patrick watched her dial a number and then step back to deliver a message. He couldn't hear what she was saying.

He nervously tapped his hand against the desk. He was grateful for help. But she was too calm. Somebody was trying to kill him and she was acting like he was just a little lost. He began to think that stopping to ask her for help was a mistake.

Patrick then looked over to see Artie casually approaching him.

He walked a calm pace.

He was still a number of yards away, but Patrick felt like the man was already in front of him.

"He found me."

Patrick saw Chelsea still on the phone. He couldn't wait anymore. He had to run. He saw an exit just around the corner. He went towards it.

Chelsea shouted, "Hey, come back. Kid."

Patrick had to ignore her.

"I hope I can find somewhere to hide out there." He made a dash for the door.

He didn't look where he was going.

He almost knocked into a lady and her young son.

He did a quick turn and almost fell. He grabbed onto a bench to prevent his body from crashing to the ground.

The woman went into mother mode. She seemed totally oblivious to the fact that Patrick had almost knocked her down.

"Oh my gosh! Young man, are you all right?" She ran to his side.

Her little boy ran next to Patrick and pulled him up from the bench. "You okay?"

"I'm fine." He waved. "I was just running too fast. I'm

sorry for almost running into you."

"Oh it's fine." She took her son's hand again. "Just be careful. You don't wanna fall and get hurt."

"No I don't." He chuckled. Beaming with an acted smile, he waved goodbye. "Have a nice day."

"You do the same, hon." She walked away with her son.

The young boy turned and waved back. "Bye-Bye."

Patrick turned to go out the exit that was just a few yards away.

He heard a scream. It sounded like that lady.

He whirled around.

He saw the lady fall to the ground with a bloody wound in her chest. She was dead before she hit in the ground.

Two security guards fell to the ground dead as well.

People screamed and scurried in all directions.

Patrick met Artie's cold eyes. The monster smiled as he waved casually to him.

Patrick felt every muscle in his body tense up. He'd been caught. He shot a glance to the door. Could he make it out to the parking lot?

"Patrick, Patrick." Artie walked a few steps closer. "We already have enough of a scene here. Why don't you come quietly and spare everyone else the trouble?"

Patrick backed away. "No, I didn't run away from you to just let you kill me."

Artie grabbed a woman who was hiding in a merchandise booth.

He slashed her throat with a knife he pulled from his pocket.

Her violent scream tapered almost instantly to a sad, pitiful gurgle.

He held onto her for a few seconds. Then he released her lifeless corpse to the ground. He didn't even bat an eye.

"I'll repeat. Come quietly. Or somebody else dies."

Patrick then saw the tiny son of the lady who had been shot standing frozen in fear. He was looking down at his dead mother. Tears welled in the child's eyes.

"Mommy. Wake up, Mommy." He threw himself onto her.

The madman walked closer to him.

He pointed the gun at the boy.

"Come with me quietly, Patrick." Artie smiled. "Or this boy will become art too."

"I thought you said being turned into art was a good thing." Patrick tightened his fists. "Why are you blackmailing me with it?"

Artie shrugged. "You don't share my views. Hence they make effective blackmail."

Patrick looked at the innocent face on the toddler. His big, jade green eyes looked back and forth between him and the killer holding the weapon that had taken his mommy away. He looked so confused and scared. He wasn't crying anymore. He seemed terrified beyond that. He couldn't understand what was going on, but Patrick thought like he knew that Artie was a very bad man who was trying to hurt him.

Artie clicked the gun and rested his finger on the trigger. "What'll it be, Patrick?"

Patrick gulped. He hesitated a moment.

The boy stared at him with such charming eyes.

Patrick couldn't bear to see this innocent child killed. He didn't deserve to die. Patrick couldn't be selfish.

"Okay, I'll come quietly."

"You won't regret your decision." Artie sneered at him.

He pointed his gun at the little boy.

He fired a single shot into the boy's forehead.

Patrick heard the boy's skull crack.

The bullet burst through his brains and exited out the back of his head.

The little boy crumpled to the ground. The grisly event never had a chance to register.

Patrick felt like he had been punched in the gut.

He couldn't look away from the suddenly vacant, staring eyes and blood flowing like a river down the lifeless form of the toddler.

He had to fight to control the bile that rose in his throat.

"Why did you do that?" His voice was almost breathless. "I was going with you." His eyes welled with tears. Now five people were dead because of him. This little boy paid the price for his cowardice.

"The boy's mother was dead. Maybe I was being compassionate." Artie pointed the gun at Patrick. "Plus, he was a very good boy. He deserved the chance to be made into such magnificent art. I think he looks beautiful."

"But you're supposed to only kill me." Patrick looked again at the small bloody body. He shut his eyes and wailed louder. "I'm the one in the chain. You're only supposed to kill *me*."

"Says who?" Artie pretended to be stumped. "I created my pattern of killings. I can change them whenever I want. Since today is my last day alive, and you're among my last chained targets, I decided to shake things up a little."

Patrick had been willing to go if it spared the boy. But

he saw the massive amount of blood spilling out of the head of that tiny body, already pooling around the boy's petite frame. Artie couldn't be trusted to keep his word. He was a liar.

Patrick knew he had to get away now. No matter what.

He darted off for the exit.

A bullet flew by his head.

It shattered the pane of the glass door.

Artie skipped in front of Patrick.

"Going somewhere?"

Patrick made an abrupt turn back into the mall.

Another crack.

A security guard fell dead.

Patrick didn't even realize he had started running the same way he had come. He just wanted to get away from this creep.

Patrick's legs felt sore and tired. He felt like they were dragging behind him. He tasted a weird chemical taste with every breath. His chest was tight. He couldn't run much longer. He could barely move.

His pace had to be slowing. He felt like he'd collapse to the ground at any moment.

"Help me, God!" He forced his body through each subsequent step.

Artie was easily closing in on him. Without even walking briskly.

The multi-yard distance between the predator and his prey began to close until only a few short steps separated the two of them.

<hr />

Julie was frozen. Her home was a crime scene.

She stood over Clark's dead body as it was taken away. This time there was no doubt that it was him. She struggled to fight tears as she watched him carried out.

"I'm sorry. I never treated you with the respect you deserved."

"I'm sorry, Jules." Kevin placed his hand on her shoulder. "We did everything we could."

"We didn't try hard enough." Tears tracked down her cheeks. "If we did, he wouldn't be dead right now. And my son wouldn't be this creep's next target. I can't lose him, Dad. He's all I have left."

She looked at a picture of Patrick on the mantle. His vibrant blue eyes were the center of the happy picture.

Kevin's tearful gaze found its way to the picture of Patrick as well. "We're doing everything we can to find this guy but he isn't making himself easy to find. And if he's convinced he's dying tonight, there's no way we'll be able to take him alive."

"Any sign of Karen and Patrick? Any at all?"

"Not a one." He somberly shook his head. "If Karen's goal was to make her and Patrick disappear, she succeeded."

"What if he already has them?" She buried her face in her hands. "What if they're already dead?"

"You'd feel it if Patrick was dead. You knew Petey was gone before you even reached that car."

"That's just it. I feel it that he's in grave danger." She took a few aimless steps. "So if he isn't dead, he's in trouble."

"What about you? This guy is going to be coming after you too, you know. He kills entire households, remember?"

"Patrick's the one he came after first. God...if he's hurt him. I'll...I can't let that happen."

Kevin's phone rang.

He answered it.

Julie couldn't get what was going on where the one word replies of Kevin, but she could tell by his expressions that it wasn't good. After uttering a barely audible, "Thank you. We'll be right there," he hung up the phone.

"Who was that? Is it about Patrick?"

"Well, they found Karen." Kevin looked at her with a serious stare. "She's dead. Her car went off a bridge. Landed in the river."

Julie's hand flew over her mouth and she burst into tears. "Oh God, please no. He's not dead. He can't be dead."

"We have no proof either way. Karen's body was found arrowed to a tree with a note on it. Not in the car. So if she got out, maybe Patrick did too."

"If he's not at the scene, then where is he?" She froze. "What if my baby is on the bottom of that river?" She cried harder.

"You can't think like that. We have divers looking. But you'd feel it if he was already gone. Now let's get to that river. Maybe we can get some answers."

"What if Patrick did escape and comes back here?"

"We'll have people here who will alert us if that happens. But odds are if he crashed into that river, he probably wouldn't be getting back here on his own."

Convinced enough for the moment, Julie agreed to leave the house and the two rushed to the accident site.

Kevin raced the twelve yards from his car to the scene in just a few seconds. "What do we have?"

An officer said to him, "You gotta see it to believe it."

Kevin and Julie then caught site of Karen's bloody 'art scene' and struggled to keep from sinking to their knees in horror.

"My God, this guy's nuts." Kevin steadied himself.

"He thinks he's going to die tonight." Julie turned away. "Do you honestly expect him to mellow out?"

Kevin approached an officer. "Any sign of the boy?"

The officer shook his head. "There's no sign of him anywhere near this site and he's not anywhere in the river. His body isn't in the car. We suspect he got out somehow based on the shoreline trails."

Just then, Kevin's phone rang and he answered it. Julie could tell by his expression that the news on the other end wasn't good. He hung up. "We got a problem."

Julie prepared for the worst. "And what is that?"

He put his phone away and clenched his gun. "Somebody's opened fire at the mall down the street. He's said to be armed with a gun *and* a knife."

"Oh just great, that's all we needed; some screwball to give Artie Falcon a cover to escape."

"There have also been reports that there was a boy matching Patrick's description present during the initial shooting."

Julie suddenly realized what Kevin was trying to tell her. "No, it can't be. It's not his MO. Killing a whole mall of people isn't part of this guy's pattern."

"You said it yourself that any limits he had are gone. As long as he gets the last victims in his chain killed, what are a few extra bodies?"

Julie digested what he said for a moment; he was right. "Then let's get to that mall before this creep kills anybody else."

Julie quickly made a dash for the car.

Kevin followed close behind.

He got in the driver's seat. "I hope you're prepared

for whatever we're going to find there."

"You don't prepare to see what this guy does." Julie loudly exhaled. "You just gotta be ready to take him down without hesitation."

Patrick felt Artie just inches away from him. He couldn't let this monster get his way.

"Somebody help me." He turned a corner.

Just then, a man and his young son came out of the restroom. They looked unaware of the chaos that had been going on.

Artie grabbed the man and quickly slit his throat.

Then grabbed the young boy and pressed him against the wall.

The five-year-old screamed and clung to a worn-out, one eyed teddy bear.

"What are you doing?" He looked up at his attacker with sad and terrorized eyes.

Artie called out to Patrick. "So Patrick, you don't care if this boy dies?"

Patrick froze and turned around.

He was almost close enough for Artie to grab. This second go at blackmail was unnecessary.

"I don't want him hurt." He wiped aside tears. "But you still killed that last kid. Even when I said I'd go with you."

"Oh, you're right." Artie returned his gaze to the boy. "So I guess I'll just kill this one too." He then plunged the knife twice into the boy's chest.

The boy couched up blood and struggled weakly for a few seconds.

Then he was dead.

Artie dropped the bloody body to the ground. It landed with a crash.

The boy's lifeless left arm landed around his stuffed animal. The well-worn bear's one eye stared as sightlessly at the ceiling as did its now dead owner's.

Patrick screamed. "Why are you doing this? These people are innocent. You want me, not them. Stop hurting them!"

Artie laughed cruelly. "I don't think I'm hurting them. Your perception of what death is lacks much." He held out his hand to the body. "I am making them beautiful. And as for wanting you, *I* am the killer. Who says I can't change my pattern whenever I want? You're going to die today either way. There's no rule saying you have to be the only one."

Patrick didn't know what else to do. So he ran.

After a moment, a man stood in front of Artie and grabbed his hands.

Patrick turned around as the two struggled for the knife. He noticed the man's strong stature when compared to Artie's. The man looked like he was a health nut, a body-builder, a military man, or a self-absorbed player.

Patrick didn't waste much time watching. He took off into the mall. This was his chance to widen the gap between them.

The man said to Artie, "I don't know who you are or why you're doing this to innocent people. But this ends now."

"For you it does." Artie giggled.

He had pressed his gun against the man's chest.

He fired.

The man fell to the ground dead.

"Carrying two weapons comes in handy sometimes."

Artie kicked the body.

He chased after Patrick at a slightly accelerated speed now. Over the next few feet, he slashed a teenage couple dead when they came out of a store and into his path.

As Patrick came back to the clothes store where he had gotten the clothes at, he saw Jacob and his mother standing inside. The woman was frantically explaining something to the manager, who looked quite pissed.

Jacob was standing in the archway between the store and the mall with a proud smile on his face. He was fully dressed now.

"Hey man." Jacob caught sight of Patrick. He smiled and went further into the mall. "How's it going? Didn't think I'd see you again so soon. You get away from that guy yet?"

"You gotta get out of here." Patrick waved his arms to stop him.

"What? Why? Is he still here?" Jacob scratched his head.

An arm suddenly thrust Jacob against the wall.

Jacob looked up to see the smiling face of Artie peering down at him with a sadistic glee.

Artie placed his bloodstained blade against Jacob's throat.

Just a little pressure could draw blood. A single swipe could end his life in a second.

"No, let him go!" Patrick felt his eyes tearing up.

Artie said, "We've been down this road before, haven't we?"

"Don't kill him." Patrick took a step towards him. "Let him go and when he's safe, I'll go with you. I promise."

The mother and the manager of the store ran out in panic.

"Jacob!" The woman fell to her knees. "Somebody help. Somebody has to help my son."

The manager was completely frozen in his fear as he watched the psychopath holding a child hostage with such a threatening weapon.

Jacob struggled to break free. "Darn, you weren't kidding when you talked about this guy." He tried to hide his fear but his body trembled uncontrollably.

"I'm sorry, Jacob." Patrick whimpered. He imagined Artie killing his new friend. He couldn't let somebody else die because he was scared. "I didn't want anybody else dragged into this."

"But you had to run." Artie shook his head at Patrick. "So poor little Jacob here is going to have an extra hole in his body. Or rather, a large slit."

Jacob's mother rushed Artie.

He knocked her to the ground with a single kick.

"No ... please." She pounded the floor. She tried to get up but collapsed again. "I won't let you kill my son."

Artie waved his hand in the air. "Could somebody please put a towel in her mouth? Her voice is annoying."

"If you keep killing all of these people, the cops will come and then you'll never be able to complete your chain." Patrick took another step towards Artie. "They're probably already on their way. If you want me, I'm right here. I won't run anymore, but only if you let Jacob go free."

"I'm not afraid of this guy, Patrick." Jacob flailed around. "I can take whatever he dishes out."

Patrick almost thought that Petey and Milo were speaking through this boy. They'd have said the same thing. He now understood exactly who Jacob reminded him of.

He prayed he could help his new friend avoid the fate that those two had met. Even if it cost him his own life.

"It's not about whether or not you're afraid." Patrick shifted his glance.

"Why do you care so much about a boy you just met?" Artie studied Patrick. "You're more concerned for a stranger than yourself? You didn't know this kid from crap an hour ago. Now, all of a sudden, you're willing to die to save him?"

Patrick looked Artie straight in the eyes. "You don't have to know someone to know the right thing to do for them."

Artie smiled and lowered the knife from Jacob's shaking neck. He threw him to the ground.

Jacob quickly ran to his mom. The two embraced in a tight and tearful hug.

Patrick stood and watched with a slight smile on his face.

Artie walked over to him.

"Goodbye, Jacob." Patrick kept his voice confined to a whisper. He could've run but he had to keep his end of the deal. Or risk Artie going back on his.

So he stayed. And allowed Artie to grab him by the neck.

"You realize you just sealed your fate?" Artie rubbed his face against Patrick's. "You will become my final piece of art."

"Do what you want." Patrick trembled. "I'm not going to let you try to make me sorry that I helped Jacob."

Jacob turned to the two of them. "Hey you, put him down." He put his fists up.

"You don't want this boy's sacrifice to be in vain by doing something stupid do you?" Artie turned to him and pointed a gun. "I'd get out of here if I were you."

"No, I'm not letting you take him away." Jacob inched closer.

Before Jacob could do anything, his mother swooped him up and carried him away.

"Hey, put me down." He flailed about in her arms.

She held him tighter and disappeared around a corner.

"Well, that was amusing." He laughed. He smiled and carried Patrick to the nearest exit.

Artie stopped a few feet from the door.

"Do you want me to shoot this boy?" He smiled.

"Are you confident you can shoot faster than me?" Chelsea's voice. She was here. She was going to help him after all.

"Do you want this boy's blood on your hands? You're not a cop. You're a mall security guard. Your job is to stop shoplifters and hooligans. You're not trained to stop killers. Like me." He chuckled. "I didn't even know they gave you guns. What are they for? To shoot kids who steal clothes?" He rubbed Patrick's shoulder suggestively. "I'll bet you don't even know how to use one of them."

Artie tightened his grip on Patrick.

Patrick winced in pain.

"You wanna play rough, do you?" Artie snickered. "I will kill him."

"I have the barrel of a gun pressed against your skull." She took a deep breath. "It doesn't take much to know how to end you from here. So let the boy go, or you die."

She called out to Patrick. "Hey, kid, are you okay?"

Patrick nodded. "I'm fine. I'm sorry I got you into this."

"No, I'm the one who's sorry. I should've taken

quicker action when you told me what was going on. I should've believed you."

"I just don't want you to get hurt." His knees were shaking.

"I'm going to get you out of this. Don't worry." She returned her focus to Artie. "So what'll it be?"

"Very well. I'll let Patrick go. Killing him isn't exactly worth my life." Artie loosened his grip on Patrick just enough.

"Good, now turn around, slowly."

"Whatever you say." He quickly grabbed his blade and spun around.

He sliced Chelsea's neck with the blade.

"Was that slow enough for you?" He stuck out his tongue.

Chelsea held her neck as blood squirted out. Her limbs gave out and she fell to her knees.

"No!" Patrick ran to her in horror. He cried and knelt down beside her.

"I'm sorry." He took her free hand. "I'm so sorry."

She tried to reply but blood choked her. She closed her eyes and exhaled. Then she was gone.

"She was just trying to help me." Patrick released her hand. "It's not fair that she had to die. It's all my fault."

"Then you should be proud." Artie yanked Patrick to his feet. "But we can't hang around here too long. We have work to do."

Patrick broke free of Artie's grip and made a run for the door.

There was nobody else around for Artie to grab. This was his last chance to live.

If he were shot dead, at least he'd die quickly.

Patrick didn't get a yard before Artie grabbed him

again.

He slammed Patrick against the wall.

Patrick screamed as pain surged through his body. "That hurts." He wailed harder.

"That was your punishment for going back on your word. Now let's go." Artie dragged Patrick out the doors into the parking lot.

The slam had removed any of Patrick's remaining strength to fight Artie.

Artie dragged him to the car.

"Don't be sad about death." Artie opened the trunk with one hand and brushed against Patrick's face with the other. "Embrace it and bask in the knowledge that you're body will be turned into something truly beautiful." He threw Patrick into the trunk.

He landed with a thump.

"I can already picture it. It'll be the most beautiful work of art I've ever created. Truly worthy of a grand finale." He slammed the trunk shut.

In the distance, Patrick could hear the sounds of sirens. Police cars.

"They're coming already?" Artie acted surprised.

Artie got behind the wheel and quickly drove out of the lot.

As he tried to get as comfortable as possible in the cramped trunk, Patrick noticed the paintings standing next to him.

"Go ahead Patrick. Look at them. You'll see a preview of what awaits you."

Patrick looked at the one in the back first. It was the scene of Clark's death to almost the exact detail.

The second painting. It was Karen, mounted to a tree with an arrow, a 'sale' sign on her chest. Exactly as Patrick had found her. How was this possible?

Patrick's heart pounded. He wanted to wake up now. This had to be a nightmare.

He looked at the third painting. He was horrified to see a mall just like the one he had been in, scattered with bloody dead bodies, many of who were young children. He'd planned to chase him through the mall.

"How? How did you know?"

"People aren't as unpredictable as they think. Art is shocking, yet it is quite predictable at the same time."

"Aren't you at least a little sorry about what you do? You killed all of these people and you don't seem to be sorry at all."

"Sorrow leads to nothing fruitful, Patrick. Art leads to beauty and brilliance. The human body is so exquisite, from the haunting colors of the eyes, to the elegantly curved lips of the mouth, and the infinitely refined designs of the face and head. The generous wonder and softness of the torsos and the powerful composition of the back .The incredible artistic details and the sculpted wonder of every single inch. It's so unmatched in beauty. But people's spirits bring it down. Worry, fear, desire, greed, selfishness, and all of the emotions that plague humanity. It's a paradoxical wonder that the body begins to decay only when it reaches the peak of its beauty. But it's how it is. I am an artist. It's my mission to make art the best I can. You will be the last piece I shall ever make. You should be honored. Take a look at that last picture. It will give you an idea of what your art scene will look like, since you will not be able to see it."

Patrick turned to the final painting. He was horrified at the painted image of his lifeless, half naked form. This was how his mother would find him. This is what she'd always remember.

"You're going to do to me what you did to Milo. Aren't you?"

Artie chuckled. "You're perceptive... for a child."

The horrifying image of his painted corpse sent shivers up Patrick's spine that radiated throughout his body. He vomited.

His empty wide-eyed expression.

The bloody hole in the side of his head that would end his life.

His violated body.

This was real. This is what Artie was going to do to him. He couldn't run anymore. He was really going to die and it was going to be slow and painful.

Patrick began to cry as reality set in.

"God, please help me!"

He silently prayed through his tears as Artie drove on.

"Please God. I don't wanna die like this. Please..."

CHAPTER 13

Kevin and Julie entered the mall from the exit where the shooting had begun. The first things that they saw were the sheet-covered bodies of the first victims of the massacre.

Seeing the littlest one, Julie kneeled down next to it and pulled the cover down. She viewed the bloody body of the toddler, still left untouched in the position that he had fallen. She could see the ragged hole in his forehead and cringed at imagining his exact moment of death.

She gently extended her hand to the toddler's tiny face and shut his unseeing eyes before recovering the body.

"A toddler. A little boy. He barely had the chance to be alive and this guy just kills him like he's nothing. I can't accept that a human being can be this heartless. I've dealt with killers who kill for revenge, money, hatred, convenience. Even lust. But this guy...he just kills because he likes it. It's like he's some demon in a human body."

"Sometimes humans invite demons in." Kevin shook his head at the bloody sight.

His mother was just a few feet away. Julie looked under the sheet. There was so much blood. This woman had no idea that she'd go to the mall on a Monday morning with her little boy and neither of them would be going back home.

"Even if it's not relevant, the mother in me wonders what each of these people were doing here today. What normal thing did they expect when they wound up in this maniac's path?"

An officer approached her and handed her a large envelope in an evidence bag. "These were found on her."

Julie opened the envelope and slid out a sheet of wallet-sized photographs. It was the woman with her husband and the little boy. They looked so happy together. Julie took a slight consolation in knowing that this mother wouldn't have to suffer through losing her child. But that almost seemed overshadowed by knowing that a man was about to learn he'd lost both his spouse and his child. Julie knew that pain all too well.

She slid the pictures back into the envelope. "Make sure the husband gets these. He'll need them to get through this."

The officer nodded and took the envelope back.

Julie stood up and tried to gather herself together.

She looked around. The mall was empty aside from the covered bodies and police. She didn't expect people to be there, but the emptiness amplified the eerie feeling she felt. "Where are the others?"

An officer pointed. "Down the way a bit." He led Julie and Kevin down a portion of the mall where Artie had done the most killing.

The clothes outlets and other stores were all closed now. A few workers who were witnesses remained in their respective stores. They were petrified as they stared at the pale white sheets over the bodies.

Julie passed the bodies of the father and son. She saw a tiny hand sticking out of the sheet, resting on the stuffed one-eyed bear below. She covered her mouth to contain her sorrow and pressed on.

She passed the guards killed. The man who had reportedly died trying to stop Artie. The young couple killed in each other's arms were together under one sheet.

A few feet ahead, she could see a young boy about Patrick's age and his mother talking to police. The boy obviously had no interest in conversing with anybody. The scene was eerily similar to when she first came to the case to question Eric. Only this boy seemed a lot more physically agitated. He smacked away attempts to comfort him and nervously paced back and forth with his arms folded. The boy shouted something to one of the officers trying to question him and stormed over to a wall. He leaned against it and tried to hide his tears.

Julie knew she had to try to minimize the influence of her personal stake in this case. She had to treat it like any other to get the best results possible.

She approached the mother. "If you don't mind, I'd like to question your son."

The woman shook her head. "Can't you see he's upset? He doesn't want to answer questions. He almost died today. I can bring him by in the morning but he needs to go home."

"Ma'am, lives are at stake. If we wait until morning, it'll be too late. Please, anything he can give us on this guy can help. Maybe he heard something about where he took my..." She stopped herself and took a deep breath. "The boy he took."

"I didn't hear anything." The boy approached her. "He didn't say anything. He just held a knife to my neck and threatened to cut it if Patrick didn't do what he wanted."

Julie smiled. "But Patrick wouldn't let that happen, would he?"

"He said he'd go only if he let me go free." The boy looked down. "He wanted to make sure I'd get away. It's my fault he's gone." The boy began to cry.

Julie looked at the young man in front of her and saw her son. Her heart ached for this boy who had come so close to losing his life, and who now blamed himself for her Patrick being taken by Artie.

"What's your name, honey?" She asked as kindly as she could. She could feel his mother resisting the urge to hit her for making him cry.

He looked up at her with the biggest brown eyes she had ever seen, tears coursing down his cheeks. Though she wouldn't have believed it could, her heart broke just a little bit more.

"My name's Jacob, Ma'am. Nice to meet you." He held out his little hand just like a man. Julie stared in shock. Even as upset as he was it seemed it was ingrained in him to be well mannered.

"I'm Julie Martel. And though I wish the circumstances were different, it's nice to meet you too." She wrapped her hand around his and then leaned down to be on his level.

"It's not your fault, Jacob. This guy is twisted and he was after Patrick. He would've gotten him sooner or later no matter what you did." She looked into the boy's despondent face. "May I ask how you met Patrick?"

"He was changing clothes in the dressing room 'cause his were all wet. I didn't know what he was doing at first but he told me everything after the guy came into the store. We hid and the guy went away. I decided I wanted to help this kid so I helped him get away unnoticed by causing a distraction. I thought he'd get out of the mall and go to the police. And they would help him. I had no idea how dangerous that guy was."

She gently held Jacob's face. "I'm sorry you got dragged into all of this. You didn't deserve that. But thank you for helping Patrick."

"Patrick's a cool kid. He seems so nice. Why would somebody want to hurt him?"

She stroked his head. "Because some people are just very bad."

Jacob shed a few tears, which Julie gently wiped away.

She looked him right in the eyes. "I'm going to catch this guy. I will."

"How can you be sure?" He looked down a moment. "He got away with Patrick. What if he's already killed him?"

She shook her head. "I don't think so. From what I've learned of this guy, he'll drag it out. That'll give us some time to find him." She saw that her words didn't ease the boy's worries. "Plus, I have extra motivation to solve this case."

"What do you mean?" He looked at her with a puzzled stare.

"Patrick's not just another boy to me." She smiled. She wasn't sure if she should volunteer this information, but she suspected that the boy needed to hear it. "He's my little boy."

"What?" Jacob's eyes widened. "You're Patrick's mom?"

"Yes, I am. So I am going to make sure I bring him home safely. Patrick's been through a lot these past few years. He's lost a lot. I think he's lost enough."

Jacob thought a moment. "I'll bet he could really use a friend then."

She smiled. "I'm sure he could."

"Would it be okay if I was his friend when you bring him home?"

Julie rose to her feet. "I'm sure he'd like that a lot."

"I'm sorry I can't help you. I really wish I knew something that could help." Jacob wiped more tears from his eyes. "But I don't. If I did, I would tell you."

"I know." She turned to walk away. "Thank you anyway, especially for helping Patrick." She walked away.

Jacob's mother walked after her. "The guy who did this...he won't come back for Jacob, will he?" She asked, wringing her hands rhythmically.

"I don't think so..." Julie thought a moment. "I think this is his last stand. He's not planning to get away with any of this. He's going to be taken down. And he knows it." A chill shot up her spine "He won't live to go after Jacob again."

"I'm sorry about your son. As a mother, I don't know what I'd do if he had Jacob. I wanted to smack Jacob so hard when he streaked the store. But when I saw that guy with a knife to his throat, I..." She paused. He lips tensed and she swallowed hard. "I felt like I'd let him streak the entire town. If it would keep him alive. In that moment, I didn't care about impressing people with how good my child was or making him act mature and grown-up. I just wanted my little boy to be safe."

"I understand, ma'am."

"Jacob was sick as a toddler. Really sick. We almost lost him. There was a night I held him and I...I truly thought he'd slip away in my arms that very night. I was afraid to sleep because I didn't want to wake up and he'd be..." She cried harder. "But he pulled through. And now he's a happy and healthy boy. But today proved that I could still lose him so easily."

"Human life is fragile at any age." Images of her dead husband flashed into her mind. "But especially during childhood." She remembered finding Petey. Finding Milo. She flinched. "Your son is okay ma'am. He's alive. And I hope he never has to deal with anything like this again."

"I'll say a prayer for your son's safe return."

"Thank you." Julie took her hand. "We'll need it. But you should get Jacob home right now. I'll have them take you two out a back door. That way you won't have to have him walk past the bodies. He shouldn't see them. They'll only traumatize him more than he already is. Those images stay with you. Take it from me."

She smiled gratefully. "Thanks. I'll do that." The woman then put her arm around Jacob and walked him towards the exit.

Julie watched them until they were out of sight.

"We're going to find him." Kevin walked up behind her

"I'm sure we'll find him." Julie sighed. "Falcon wouldn't have it any other way. I just hope we find him before Falcon kills him."

<hr />

Kevin's phone rang. He ripped it out of his pocket. It nearly slipped out of his sweaty hands.

"I gotta take this in case it's one of my guys."

Julie nodded. "Go ahead."

He walked away to hear better and answered with an agitated "Hello."

Artie's sick laughter boomed through the receiver. "Kevin Martel. I don't believe we've ever been formally introduced."

"How'd you get this number?" Kevin froze.

"Is that really the question you want answers to? Or is there something a little more pressing that should take precedent in this conversation? Yes, I am referring to your surviving grandson. As you've probably surmised by now, I have him. And he's still alive. Whether or not that remains to be true hinges on what you do next."

"Don't lie to me, Falcon. You plan to kill him and Julie regardless of what I do. It's how you operate."

"Aren't you the professional profiler? Has the FBI contacted you with a job offer yet? Maybe you could move to Quantico and travel the country chasing down people like me." He chuckled.

"Cut the crap, Falcon." Kevin forced himself to control the rush of anger that flooded through him. "Just tell me what you want."

"Come to the back parking lot of St. Claire's. And come alone. If you're not alone, you'll find Patrick dead. I'll be waiting there with the boy and we can talk trades."

"Trades? Since when do you do trades?" Kevin clenched his fist in suspicion.

Artie became agitated. "Do you want the boy's corpse shipped back to your house? 'Cause I am not above doing that." He paused. "It sounds like a fun trick to try now that I think about it. But I suspect you want to at least try to save his pathetic life. Correct?"

"I'll be there. And yes, I'll come alone." He angrily hung up the phone and immediately started for the nearest exit.

Julie went to follow him. "Was that him? He wants to meet, right? Sick bastard loves to torment us. Well, if you're going to meet this guy, I'm coming with you."

"No, you stay here." Kevin turned to her. "He said to come alone. Plus I can't risk him pulling something and hurting you."

"He has my son. I'm willing to risk it."

"If something happens to me, Patrick's only chance is you."

"How am I going to know where to find him if you don't tell me?"

"You'll figure it out. Maybe you could even go meet your sister to pray about it. That always seems to work."

Julie threw her hands in the air. "Why are you mocking my faith at a time like this?"

"I ain't mocking anything. I'm just trying to get to your son before this guy kills him. Now if you don't mind, I got a meeting to keep." He stormed out the exit without another word, leaving Julie behind on the bloodstained floors of the mall.

<hr />

Patrick began to feel his legs cramp from being locked in the trunk of Artie's car. He couldn't see much through the darkness, but from the sound of it, they were stopped in a low-traffic location.

After what seemed like endless hours of silence, Artie spoke to Patrick. "So, have you read any good books lately?"

The casual tone in which he said the question seemed to be a complete turnaround from the man who heartlessly put a bullet in a toddler's head earlier in the day.

"Why do you care what I read?" Patrick sat up a little to hear him better. "I thought you just wanted to kill me."

"You may think I am a monster, Patrick. And maybe I am by your definition. But that doesn't mean I can't relate to being a human. You may not believe it, but I am one too. I have experiences just like anyone. Just like you." He took a breath. "Human souls may corrupt the beauty of the body but they still exist. And I do feel that those who die artfully do find some existence beyond ours where they can reach contentment. That's what I want for you."

"Well I don't want to die." He sniffled. "Why can't you just let me go? You've killed so many people already. Isn't that enough?"

"No, you're the last link in my chain. You have to die for it to be completed. But since it isn't time yet, I figured I might as well know a little more about the boy I am killing."

"You don't know anything about me." Patrick felt himself growing angry.

"I know that your mother's maiden name is Martel, and she married a guy with the last name Martel. People teased them about being incestuous, but they were no more related than you or I. I know that your father and twin brother both died in a car accident a few years ago. I know that you can't see yourself in the mirror without seeing your dead brother looking back."

Patrick squirmed about, wondering how Artie knew such personal information.

Artie continued, "But what I don't know is the most inner workings of your mind, Patrick. I'd like to know if you'll tell me. So again, let's start. Read any good books lately?"

Patrick was silent a moment. He wasn't sure whether he should play or not. What if he lied and Artie saw through him? He figured there was no reason not to answer. Maybe there was a small chance he could humanize himself enough to not be killed. It was worth a try. "No. I don't read much. I usually just watch TV."

"You don't have to be afraid to tell me that. I am not going to stone you for anything you like. Sometimes I feel books are overrated myself. What about foods? What kinds of foods do you like to eat?"

"I like sandwiches. And turkey. I like turkey a lot. Especially turkey sandwiches. Turkey sandwiches are really good."

"Is that a fact? Interesting. I was always more of a roast beef guy myself but I liked turkey too. What about cheese? What kinds of cheeses did you like?"

Patrick trembled. "Provolone. I like provolone." Did this guy really care about cheese? There had to be another trick to this.

Artie grew cheerful. "That's awesome. I like Provolone too. Nothing beats provolone. It's like miracle cheese, wouldn't you say?"

Patrick tearfully nodded. "Yeah, it's good." He sniffled. He held himself. He just wanted to go home. He prayed that the trunk would open and his mother would be there. She'd lift him up and bring him home and Artie could never get him again.

"I used to love this chicken cheese steak I got at this one small restaurant. It was a quiet little place but it had really good food." Artie sounded almost human. Like a normal, non-murderous person. "Of course it's gone now, but I still remember how good it used to taste. You ever have a chicken cheese steak?"

"A few times. It was good."

"You got good taste kid."

Patrick gave no response. He merely continued crying in muffled sniffles.

"Now why are you still crying?"

"You're going to kill me." Did he really not get it? Was he playing with Patrick? Or was he really that self-absorbed? "That's why I'm crying."

"You don't realize that being killed is really what's best for you. I'm doing you a favor by turning you into art, kid."

"Stop saying that! You're wrong." Patrick smacked the floor. "You killed my best friend. And all of those other people."

"I was doing them favors. You just have been trained to think negatively of things that are actually very good."

"No they're not. Killing people is not a good thing. It's cruel. It's evil. I don't want to die. Please. Don't kill me."

Artie sighed. "You'll see what I mean soon. You'll see."

Patrick was silent for five minutes. There was no reasoning with this guy. A wave of complete helplessness overcame him. He was going to die and he couldn't fight or run. All he could do was squirm about while Artie did whatever he wanted. Patrick felt weak. Maybe he deserved to die if he couldn't even get away.

No. Milo wasn't weak. Neither was Damien. Or Detective Clark. None of the people Artie had killed were weak. They were strong. They were good people. Sometimes even strong just wasn't enough.

"Will it hurt?" Patrick whimpered.

Artie tapped his fingers against the steering wheel.

"You've seen the painting. You know that I intend to shoot you in the side of the head. The bullet will kill you instantly. You will be dead before you have a chance to feel pain. No suffering. Just art."

"What if you're wrong? What if I don't die right away? What if it hurts a lot?"

"Trust me, Patrick. I know how to end a human life very quickly. For such a tainting thing, the human soul is so easily removed from its shell."

Patrick tried to breathe deeply to get a hold of himself. He hated showing such weakness to his attacker. Such fear. It was only feeding Artie's desire to kill him more. He wished that he could look this monster in the eye and show him no fear. He wished he could be brave.

"Why can't you just kill me? Why do you have to do what you did to Milo to me?"

"It's called sex, Patrick. Using euphemisms for it doesn't change what it is."

"I'm too young. And I'm a boy."

"You've been poisoned to think a certain way. Anything that falls outside your comfort zone, you see as wrong. I just see it as another beautiful expression of art. I hope that you will come see it that way too."

Patrick grabbed his head. "No, I won't." He thrashed around until it hurt. "Please, if you have to kill me, don't do that. Please."

"Kids today know too much. They're taught to live in fear. Don't worry. I'll show you how wrong the outdated values you've been taught are."

Patrick heard a car pulling up outside.

Artie snickered. "Wow, he actually came. And he followed instructions too. I must admit, I did have my doubts."

"Who came? Who's here?" Patrick banged on the trunk. Could this be somebody who could help him?

"You don't have to worry about it Patrick. Just sit tight. This might get just a little bit bumpy."

"What are you doing?" Patrick shouted. His heart dropped when he felt the jolt of the car accelerating. It was a feeling he was all too used to experiencing when his grandfather picked up speed to make it past an inter-section before the light turned red. If Artie was speeding towards something, it couldn't be good.

⊶⊙⊶⊙⊶⊙⊶⊙⊶⊙

Kevin pulled up in his vehicle. He parked in a crook-ed position that took up four parking spaces. He'd have ticketed somebody for such rudeness any other time, but the minor details of the law didn't particularly concern him with his grandson's very life on the line.

He stormed out of the car and ran towards the church. He had his gun in hand, preparing for a possible show-down inside. No way was Artie going to go quietly.

"Where the hell are you, nutcase?"

He heard the screech of another car speeding towards him.

⊶⊙⊶⊙⊶⊙⊶⊙⊶⊙

Kevin jumped out of the path of the speeding car. He fired his gun at the car but it made a sharp turn out of the way. Then it continued to chase him.

Kevin ran as fast as he could but the car kept speeding up. The bumper was just inches away.

Kevin looked behind him and then focused his gaze ahead. He ran as fast as he could.

There was a field behind the parking lot guarded by a fence. If he could just get to the other side, he'd be safe. There was no chance of this car making it through a metal fence.

Just a few more feet.

The car was right behind him.

"Damn these Japanese cars!"

The car slammed right into him.

He went crashing into the windshield. Then he rolled across the vehicle.

He landed hard upon the ground on the other side.

Covered in blood.

∘⌒∘⌒∘⌒∘⌒∘

Patrick screamed at grim sounds of a body impacting with the car and rolling over the top, hitting the ground with a thud.

"Why did you do that?" He tearfully screamed and pounded the vehicle. "You killed somebody else."

Artie glanced out the window at Kevin. He looked dead. Artie was convinced enough. "Just getting a pest out of the way. That's all."

"Who did you hit? Who was that?"

"It's none of your concern. With that out of the way, I'd say we can go inside now."

He drove the car around to the side of the church, away from Kevin's bloody form. Then he opened the trunk.

He locked eyes with Patrick. The boy's baby blues seemed to reflect the last remaining traces of sunlight not squeezed out by oncoming dark gray storm clouds. He could see the fear and dread in the boy's eyes. The glimpse into his soul that they provided seemed to Artie to be almost as pleasurable as imagining Patrick dead.

He picked Patrick up from the car and forced him to carry the painting of his demise.

Patrick looked sick as his eyes held the dead eyes of

his painted reflection.

"Let's go inside." Artie grabbed Patrick's shoulder. His slender shoulder felt so good in his palms. He couldn't wait to explore more.

∞⊂∞⊂∞⊂∞⊂∞∞

The Church building was simple but very beautiful. Patrick always felt safe in it.

Now it would be the place where he'd take his last breath.

Dying in a Church had symbolic meaning, but he didn't want to defile such a sacred place by being murdered within its doors.

He prayed to God for a way out. Even more than dying, Patrick feared what tortures Artie could do to him before that.

Would God save him? Patrick prayed harder than he'd ever prayed. But he resolved himself to not hate God no matter what. God gave every person the choice to do good things or bad things. Artie was choosing to do bad things. All Patrick could do was pray for God to give him the grace to handle it.

"Can't you do it outside?" He stopped. "I don't want to die in there. I don't want to ruin it for everyone."

"What? Are you afraid of bleeding out on the carpet? You people have a statue of a dead guy on a tree and you're afraid of being executed in the same place? You should be glad to die in a Church. It's what every good Christian strives for."

"I know what you want to do to me." Patrick didn't know but he could imagine. "Artie grabbed Patrick's shoulder. "I don't want you to do it in there. Nobody will see us outside. Nobody comes around here this time of day."

Artie shook his head. "You seriously need to stop being stubborn. My plans remain unchanged. Now walk."

He gave Patrick a slight shove on the back and moved him towards the entrance to the Church.

So many times Patrick had walked up those steps, but this time felt like it would truly be his last.

He took one more look at the faint glimmer of sun squeezing through the clouds. It was so beautiful. The light came down in an almost heavenly beam. At least life would go on after he'd die. There would still be beautiful things. There would always be things that were really beautiful. Artie's polluted sense of beauty could never erase that.

Patrick turned away. He tried to accept that he would never see the sun again with his human eyes.

He stopped resisting Artie. There was no use in fighting anymore. He opened the stained-glass front door and stepped inside.

CHAPTER 14

Nathaniel Strauss struggled to put on his altar server robe. The thing seemed like a massive white tent to him. "How do you put this thing on?"

A kind feminine voice said, "I thought Father Gibbs taught you all about this." The woman helped Nathaniel find the hole in the robe for his head.

He popped his red-haired head through the hole and wore a smile. "Thanks, Sister Olivia."

Another boy flicked Nathaniel. "Figures you can't put a robe on. You're bad with clothes. You probably need help from your dad to figure out how to put on your underwear." The boy glared at Nathaniel. His dark brown hair fell over his eyes a little but Nathaniel could still easily see the mocking in the boy's eyes.

Nathaniel stuck his tongue out at him. "Yeah, yeah, yeah, says the guy who got stuck in his Halloween costume."

He wagged his finger at Nathaniel. "Hey, that wasn't my fault. That costume was a piece of junk."

"Whatever you say, Ethan."

Sister Olivia placed her hands on a shoulder of each. "Hey you two; stop fighting. You guys are going to be serving your first Mass this weekend. Is this any way for new altar boys to make a first impression?"

The two white-robed boys shook their heads. "No way." Their voices harmonized defiantly.

"Then why don't you two try to get along a little bit? You don't want to look like hooligans when Father comes."

Nathaniel asked, "How many Masses are we going to have to do every week?"

Ethan said, "Dude, you shouldn't ask that. You do however many you are asked to do. That's what my dad says, anyway. He used to do two Masses every week." He smirked proudly.

Nathaniel's mouth dropped. "Every week? Wow!"

Sister Olivia laughed. "Don't worry, you two. We have plenty of altar servers here. You should only have to do one Mass a week. And some weeks you probably won't have to do any at all." She flashed them a glare. "But of course we still expect you both at Mass. Father will know if you're not." She leaned in closely to reinforce her point.

Ethan turned to Nathaniel. "So there, Red. You got your answer. You can't slack off on coming to Mass anymore."

Nathaniel lunged at him. "I've been coming to Mass every week since I was born. Just like you. So don't act like I don't."

"You missed one week five years ago."

"What? You don't count that. I was in the hospital for a tonsillectomy."

"Excuses, excuses." Ethan playfully shook his head at Nathaniel.

Nathaniel pushed Ethan against the wall. "Valid excuses. You don't have to come to Church if you're sick."

Sister Olivia pulled Nathaniel away. "Sorry, Ethan, Nathaniel is right. But enough fighting or we'll never get anything done."

"Fine." They both pouted.

The three of them exited the sacristy and entered the sanctuary.

⊶⌬⊶⌬⌬⊶⌬⊶

As she led them out, Sister Olivia saw a man forcing Patrick up the center isle.

Artie.

She could see Artie holding a gun to Patrick's back. Patrick fought every step but Artie pushed him until they were at the foot of the altar.

"Somebody's here." Patrick turned to him. "We should go somewhere else."

"Now why would people being here be a problem?" Artie raised his eyebrows.

Patrick's eyes widened at the implications his gun-toting captor gave.

Sister Olivia hid the two boys behind her. She wanted to tell them to run but she feared making any sudden movements.

"What do you want?" Her voice shook. "This is Church. We don't want any trouble here."

Artie snickered.

Ethan whispered to Nathaniel. "Wow, that guy looks creepy. Wonder what a kid's doing with him."

Nathaniel glanced over the two. "They must be cousins. No way would that kid go with that guy if they weren't."

Artie threw Patrick to the ground. "Sorry to bother you, but I'm going to need you three to leave. You see... I'm going to kill this boy. And I'd prefer that nobody see my work until it's done."

"Sister Olivia remembered everything that Julie had told her. This guy lived up to the hype. She could feel evil radiating off of him. And he had her nephew in his clutches. She tried to think of something to do but she was powerless. And she had two other boys to protect. How could she save all of them?

She began a silent prayer for guidance. Any way to keep the children safe from this wretched man.

Ethan became petrified with fear. "What does he mean he's going to kill that kid?"

Sister Olivia tried to subtly signal to Nathaniel and Ethan. They had to run. She just hoped she could shield them.

"Why don't you boys go back in the sacristy?"

Ethan asked, "Is something wrong?"

Nathaniel backed towards the wall. "You're scaring me now.

"Just do it." She tightened her fists.

The boys gazed out at Patrick.

Patrick gave off a vibe of complete terror. His face was soaked from tears and sweat. He was trembling.

Artie held out his gun. "Sorry, you took too long."

Sister Olivia rushed to block it.

She wasn't fast enough.

Artie fired a single bullet into Ethan's head.

Before the boy had any chance to react, he sank to

the ground dead. The force of the bullet thrust his body against the wall. His eyes were left open in a confused stare. His hand gently clutched a miraculous medal. It had been in his pocket. He'd instinctively reached for it. Blood flowed in an unchecked river down the center of his face from the jagged hole in his forehead, staining his pristine white robes a deep, ruby red.

Patrick, Nathaniel, and Sister Olivia screamed simultaneously as they saw the blood splatters on the wall behind where Ethan had stood just seconds before.

There was little time to act before even more bullets were fired in the direction of Sister Olivia and Nathaniel.

Sister Olivia blocked the bullet from hitting Nathaniel. She was hit in the leg.

She screamed and collapsed to the ground.

Artie fired again before Nathaniel could escape.

She couldn't get up to block them this time.

Nathaniel was struck twice in the chest.

He crumpled to the ground. His garments were painted the same color as Ethan's.

Patrick screamed and tried to run to them but Artie restrained him.

"No. No. You didn't have to kill them." He gasped.

"Killing altar boys on an altar, gotta love the art in that." Artie gleefully lowered his arm. "I couldn't have planned it better myself if I painted it."

"Aunt Olivia." Patrick's voice was shaky. "Are you okay? Please. Say something."

"I'm fine, Patrick." She tried to push herself to her feet but her legs were in so much pain. But she had to keep trying. She couldn't let this monster kill Patrick like he'd killed so many others. "Don't worry about me."

"I'd come up there and finish you off but let's just say

I got a superstition against killing nuns." He folded his hands in a fake piety. "One was a bitch to me when I was younger and I guess I don't feel they deserve to be made into art, which is the only reason you're still breathing."

Sister Olivia took a deep breath. "You can't kill a nun, but you can kill two altar boys without flinching?"

"What can I say?" Artie chuckled and shrugged. "Art is twisted sometimes."

Sister Olivia crawled over to Nathaniel.

He was rapidly hemorrhaging blood from his wounds and struggling to breathe.

"It's going to be all right, Nathaniel." She placed her hand on his head. "In just a few moments, you'll be okay. It'll all be over."

Nathaniel struggled to find energy to speak. "T-tell Mom, I'm sorry for b-breaking the glasses last week. T-tell her, I d-do love her. I d-didn't mean what I said when she y-yelled at me."

He was so honest in his plea, so eager to not leave any ill will behind him. That his mind went to such a place at such a time, it revealed to her a level of maturity she'd never seen in him before, but which seemed to dominate his trembling form now.

She smiled and tightened her grip on his hand. "I will."

"Tell Ethan's mom he l-loves h-her t-t-too. We're s-sorry we were s-such p-pains." Every word was a struggle for him. Drowned out by involuntary whimpers. Yet, he managed to put on a smile with his words.

Sister Olivia tried to compress his wounds and slow the blood flow.

It didn't stop it. All it did was paint her hands red.

She pushed harder on his wounds. She felt helpless to

stop the bleeding but was still desperate to try.

"I'll tell them, Nathaniel. Your mom loves you too. And you weren't pains. I'm sure. You were joys to have around."

Nathaniel couldn't take another breath.

He tried. His choked gasps echoed in the open church.

He gazed up at the crucifix hanging from the ceiling.

Sister Olivia remembered Nathan's admiration of the sacramental. He'd always been humbled by the image of the crucified Christ.

Sister Olivia was glad that it was the last thing his eyes would ever look at.

He'd understood Christ's sacrifice long before most of the kids his age. She was not surprised when he applied to become an altar boy as soon as he was old enough.

His exhaled one last breath. Then he was gone.

His eyes remained open, fixated on the large statue.

He didn't have to settle for statues anymore. He was seeing the real Jesus now.

Sister Olivia checked for a pulse. Even though she knew he was already dead.

She began to cry from the pain, both from seeing too vibrant young boys murdered before her eyes, and from the radiating pain of her wound that was beginning to shoot throughout her body.

She set Nathaniel's bloody corpse against the wall. She gently closed his still-upward-gazing eyes, returning his red bangs to their resting place over his forehead. She kissed his forehead.

She then struggled to crawl over to Ethan. When she finally made it to his lifeless body, she closed his eyes and kissed his forehead as well.

"Be at peace, both of you." She collapsed to the

ground, breathing heavily and flinching from the shooting agony.

"I'd stay behind that altar if I were you." Artie sensually ran his hand across Patrick's neck. "You don't want to see this masterpiece until it's done."

She struggled to move. "You think I'm going to just lie here and let you murder my nephew? Think again." She attempted to stand but the pain in her leg left her as good as crippled. She pushed herself an inch off the ground. She screamed in agony as it caved in beneath her. She crashed back down with a thump.

Patrick screamed. "Aunt Olivia, are you okay?"

"Don't worry about me." She winced in pain. "How are you?"

Patrick was silent a moment. "Just stay back there." He cried harder. "I don't want you to see what he's going to do to me."

"Patrick, don't give up. I'll find a way to help you. Don't give up hope."

Patrick sniffled. "It's not giving up hope. It's just accepting that I can't stop him. He's gonna do whatever he wants."

She screamed again. She refused to give up. "Look, you can do what you want to me. If you want to hurt Julie, kill me. I'm her sister."

"This isn't about hurting anybody." Artie pushed Patrick against the front pew. "I've already decided what my final artwork project shall be and I am not changing my mind." He shoved Patrick into the pew. "Now, let's get to work."

∞◦⟩◦⟨◦⟩◦⟨◦∞

Julie left the mall and returned home. It was still taped off but the cops had cleared out. She walked up to Patrick's room. His bed was left made in Patrick's typical fashion—neat enough to show he had heart but not neat enough to be on level with how she'd have done it. But it was a vast improvement over how Petey would've left his bed each morning.

She sat down on the bed, hoping to feel closer to her sons. She could still smell him on his pillow.

She wanted so desperately to help Patrick. The search for him was being conducted as well as it could.

She needed to do more. She didn't know where to look. She felt helpless.

"God, please, don't take Patrick away from me. He's all I have left. He's been through so much pain. Don't let his life be stolen from him now."

Images of Petey's dead body flashed through her mind. She remembered that horrible moment when she'd felt that her little boy was gone. She couldn't let Patrick wind up like that. She couldn't let the final chapter of Patrick's life be written by the hands of a crazed killer.

"What can I do?" She cried. "Where would he take Patrick to kill him?" She asked herself these questions over and over but no answer seemed good.

Why didn't her father tell her where he was being told to go? "I know it was dangerous, Dad, but you had to know that if something happened to you, you would've been signing Patrick's death warrant by keeping the information to yourself."

She was right. He had to have known that. She knew her father well. He wouldn't do anything to put Patrick in danger. There was no way he wouldn't have considered the possibility that he was being set up for a trap. So he had to have a contingency plan. Could he have told her where he was going without her realizing it? She mentally replayed the last things he said to her.

Then it hit her.

"Maybe you could even go meet your sister to pray about it. That always seems to work."

It had been staring her in the face the entire time. The church.

She quickly hopped up from the bed, taking a final look at a picture of the twins smiling together. It had been the last picture of Petey and Patrick together.

She couldn't save Petey. Or her husband. She would save Patrick. No matter what. She couldn't even entertain the possibility of coming back without him.

"I'm going to bring him home, Petey."

She rushed down the stairs and out the front door.

She hopped into her car and quickly accelerated around the block towards the church.

"I'm coming, Patrick. Hold on."

<hr>

Patrick looked back at his attacker with sad eyes and then gazed over to the horrid picture of what he was to look like in just a short amount of time. Seeing Artie's grim arms around him sickened him.

He turned to Artie. "Can you just do this in the halls or something? Or in the bathroom? Anywhere but here. This is Church. It's a place where people go to feel safe. We shouldn't ruin that for them because of something like this happening here. Please, just take me somewhere else."

Artie placed his finger under Patrick's chin. "They should be so lucky to know the beautiful thing that's going to happen here."

He then lifted up Patrick's hand and kissed it. "So soft, young skin. Like mine used to be."

Patrick felt disgust streaming through every inch of his body. He struggled to break free.

Artie was stronger.

Patrick closed his eyes. He tried to pretend that he was somewhere else. He envisioned seeing his father, Petey, and Milo again. That would make all of this worth it.

Artie forced Patrick's hand to his cheek and cuddled it. "Now, isn't this beautiful?"

Patrick didn't answer. It was horrible. Every cell of Artie's body seemed to radiate evil. Every touch brought a sharp pain. Patrick didn't want to lie but he didn't want to enrage his attacker more by telling the truth. He clenched his lips so he wouldn't talk. He just wanted this to be over.

Artie looked deep into Patrick's eyes. "You didn't enjoy it, did you?"

Patrick struggled to talk without whimpering. "You know I didn't."

As Patrick stared into Artie's eyes, he could swear he almost saw a tear form. It was almost invisible but it was there, just a hint of weariness. Maybe even Artie was beginning to not be able to stomach his actions. But he still wasn't stopping. Maybe Patrick just wanted to believe that no human could enjoy this so much.

Artie caressed Patrick's cheek. "It's okay. Don't be afraid to tell the truth. I think by the end, you'll enjoy this plenty."

He gently stroked Patrick's back, through his shirt, with just the tips of his fat fingers. He then worked his hand under Patrick's shirt, making contact with the boy's smooth skin.

Patrick cringed as the man's fingers ran a map-like course up and down his back.

Artie said, "I'll be gentle. I promise."

Patrick's stomach knotted.

"You're too thin, kid, like skin on bones."

Patrick gave only a trembling whimper.

"Don't worry. I still think you're perfectly beautiful."

Artie pushed Patrick down on the pew.

Patrick knew what was coming next.

His shorts.

"Nice clothes you stole. You really did think of everything, kid."

Patrick tried to tune everything out. He stared up at the large crucifix hanging from the ceiling. He had always been taught to carry his cross no matter how heavy it was, but this seemed to be an unusually high burden. He didn't know if he could do it. He prayed for the strength anyway. If this was going to happen, he knew he had to pray for God to carry him through it. And he know God would. Whatever happened, Artie couldn't take away his faith. "God, make me strong enough."

There was a loud crack.

Artie shot up.

The church doors slammed open.

He quickly returned Patrick's clothes to normal and forced him to his feet. He clutched his gun.

Julie burst out of the narthex and into the sanctuary. "Artie Falcon. This ends now." Her voice echoed loudly in the building. Her gun was firmly in her hand, steadily pointed ahead.

Artie knelt down behind Patrick.

He shoved the barrel of the gun against the side of Patrick's head.

Patrick shivered as the cold metal placed pressure against his skull. He could see Artie's finger on the trigger.

It would take just a slight movement—just a tiny

squeeze—to bring an end to his entire life.

As easy as turning off a light.

"Artie Falcon!" Julie shouted with her gun pointed at him. "Let him go. Now."

Patrick locked eyes with his mother.

He could see the fear in her eyes. Even if she was much better at hiding it than he was. He could tell by her expression that she could see how scared he was. His knees shook. He could barely stand.

The gun was so cold against his head.

"Julie Martel, I didn't expect you to get here so soon." Artie exhaled softly. "At least not until I was done working on your beautiful boy here. I guess I underestimated you."

"I guess it's a good thing I'm smarter than you give me credit for. Now, let him go. Or I'll end you."

"I planned to turn this boy into a work of art. And I intend to follow through. I might have to change plans a bit. But the end result will still be beautiful." He grinded his teeth. "I didn't intend to live past today anyway. So you're out of luck. You might've saved your boy's innocence. But you're too late to save his life."

Julie trembled as she clutched the gun. She aimed it firmly at Artie.

Patrick was shaking as his life hung by the thinnest of threads. He was relieved to see his mother. But could she save him? He wasn't sure. He was sweating. His heart hammered in his chest. He'd never been more scared. But what scared him most of all was a disturbing feeling in his gut that he was about to die.

CHAPTER 15

Julie remembered how bright it had been on her first day after making detective. She had so much hope about the good she could do and the people she could help. She'd make a difference.

As she walked to the front door, she couldn't wait to tell her family about her day. She could just see her twin little boys waiting to hear about all of the bad guys she was taking down. And she couldn't wait to tell them.

"I can't believe I really did it." She stared admirably at her badge. It was hers. This was real. And she had really earned it. She could breathe easy knowing her father had given her no special treatment. This was all her.

She started up the front steps. She could hear the sounds of her happy six-year-old boys running to the door.

"They must have supersonic hearing."

The door swung open before she even reached the

top.

"Mom! I can't believe it. We saw you on TV. It was so awesome. You were like so cool talking to that reporter lady." Petey burst through the front door with his hands in the air and his voice already fired up.

"Yeah, it was really sweet." Patrick hopped out of the house.

They both ran into her arms, nearly knocking her down.

"I missed you both." She embraced them tightly.

Patrick kissed her on the cheek. "How could you miss us? You weren't gone any longer than last week."

"Can't I still miss my favorite boys in the whole world?" She kissed him back.

"What about me?" Seth walked out with a smile. The two met with a hug and a kiss.

She looked lovingly at her husband. "You're all my favorite boys." She kissed him. "In fact, I got them because you were really my favorite." She winked.

"Eww! lalalalalalala" Petey and Patrick held their ears and ran inside.

Julie and Seth laughed as they joined them.

The boys were waiting on the couch, flashing Julie eager eyes that her mommy radar could flawlessly read.

They wanted answers. They wanted stories.

She couldn't resist.

She took a seat beside them. "Well, I suppose you boys would be wanting to know how my first day went, huh?"

Patrick kicked his feet together. "Only if you wanna tell us."

"Don't listen to him." Petey hit Patrick. "We wanna hear everything that happened like really, really bad.

Don't leave anything out. Tell us everything."

Seth took a seat on the chair. "You heard the men, tell us."

Julie smiled. "Well, at the start of the day, your grandfather gave me my first task. I had to find a guy who had been selling drugs to teenagers at the local high school."

"That's not good. Drugs are bad." Patrick tensed up.

Petey flailed his arms in the air. "Yeah, they like mess you up inside. People are really stupid if they take drugs, 'cause drugs really suck, like a lot."

Julie patted him on the head. "Well, we followed a lot of clues as to who was doing this. When one of the students took too many drugs, he didn't make it."

"No." Their mouths turned down.

"Turns out, it was one of the teachers in the school." She leaned in closer to excite them more.

The boys gasped. "No way," they shouted in unison.

"Yes way. He was selling drugs to the kids and nobody knew. But we figured it out and busted him. Now he's in jail and he's gonna pay for everything bad that he did. And when we were taking him away, the news people had shown up and they wanted to talk with us."

"That must've been so cool." Patrick was awestruck.

Petey leaned back into the couch. "Of course it was cool. She saved all of those kids from the bad drugs. And the bad teacher. Our mom is like seriously the best."

"Well, I try to be." Julie smiled.

"I gotta go tell Milo this." Petey shot up. "He's going to be so excited." He bolted for the door.

"Hey, hold up mister." Julie held out her hand. "Your father is going with you. You know you're not allowed outside alone."

He turned around and stamped his foot. "Well then

make Dad hurry up."

"I'll have him home before dinner. Don't worry." Seth laughed as he got up.

"You realize that means having him home in less than twenty minutes right?" Julie shot him a suspicious glare.

Seth nervously smiled. "I love a good challenge." He winked.

He quickly followed his energetic son.

Petey was already out the front door, complaining about his father being too slow.

Julie shook her head as Seth chased after him.

Julie turned to Patrick. "Aren't you going to go with them?"

Patrick shook his head. "No, I think I'll stay here with you." He pulled closer to her and rested his head on her chest.

She wrapped her arm around him. "You know, just because I am working a little more now doesn't mean I am going to stop spending as much time as I can with you."

"Oh I know." He looked her in the eye and smiled. "I don't mind. You have an important job. You're the one who gets all the bad guys. There are a lot of bad people out there who want to hurt good people. And that's bad." He shook his head. "But you find those bad people and you stop them. You make them pay for hurting people. You send them to jail so they can't hurt people anymore. You get the bad guys." He nodded. "That's a good job. So I'm happy that my mom gets to do it." He stared up at her with an almost angelic look of innocence.

He looked so precious right now.

Julie began to feel a pain of regret in her chest. She knew the risk she'd been taking every day for years and she'd probably be staring down criminals even more directly in the future. She knew she might not come home one night. Her poor little boy was still so naïve to see her as this superhero. She knew he'd grow to realize the severity of the daily risk to her life one day. She just prayed he'd never have to know the pain of losing her.

"I'm glad you feel that way." She smiled and leaned down to plant a kiss on his forehead. "It makes me even more proud to do this job. I love you, Patrick."

"I love you too, Mommy." He wrapped his arms around her and cuddled closer.

⊶◌⊷◌⊶◌⊷

It had been a long five years since that happy day. The memory flooded Julie's mind and still felt so fresh. She longed for those days. Those simple days.

Now she was staring down one of the baddest 'bad guys' she'd ever seen.

He had a gun pointed at the head of her precious little boy.

She had to live up to Patrick's description of her. She couldn't let him down now.

But staring into the deranged eyes of the Blood Chain Killer, she couldn't think of a way out of this that didn't involve the only baby she had left losing his life.

Julie said to Artie, "This doesn't have to end in death. If you put that gun down and let Patrick go, I can still help you."

Artie laughed. "You will have to excuse me if I don't believe you. I murdered a lot of people. Heck, look up on the altar. You'll see two of them."

Julie looked and felt sick as she saw the corpses of the altar servers and streams of blood flowing from their bodies down the altar.

"Julie, you can't let him get away." Sister Olivia managed to crawl out from behind the altar. "He shot them. In cold blood. Without even flinching. He won't stop killing. Until you stop him." She flinched in pain.

Julie didn't expect to see her sister injured. She felt herself become even unsteadier. "Are you okay, sis?"

"I'll be okay." She took a deep breath and groaned. "You have to help Patrick."

"Mom! He killed people at the mall too, just like he did those boys." Patrick cried. "There were kids there too. And he just killed them. And he didn't care at all. He liked it. He liked making them suffer. And he killed Karen too. And Detective Clark."

"I know Patrick. I know." She cried. "He's killed a lot of people."

"Is Jacob okay? Do you know if he made it out?"

She nodded. "He and his mom are fine. They're worried about you."

"He's a cool kid." Patrick tearfully smiled. "I just wish everybody else there didn't have to die."

Artie tightened his grip on Patrick.

Patrick to winced in pain.

"See what I mean? I've killed a lot of people." Artie pulled Patrick closer to him. "You can't help me. I'm a child killer. I raped a little boy. Then strangled the life out of him. For that alone, I'd be killed in jail. I wouldn't even survive until an arraignment. I've made choices full knowing their consequences." He shrugged. "My life is over either way. I have nothing to gain from listening to you. So cut your lies about being able to help me. I am not biting. I don't intend to exit this church alive. I might not be able to do all I wanted to dear Patrick here..." He kissed Patrick's neck. "But I still intend to put a bullet in his head. There's nothing you can do to stop me. Sure. I'll leave this church in a body bag. But Patrick will be carried out in one right alongside me."

"I'm a quick shot." Sweat ran down her back. He was making too much sense. He really didn't have any reason to listen to her. "Maybe I can kill you before you can pull the trigger." She clenched her gun.

"Or not." Artie inched himself closer to the altar. He kept Patrick in front of him. "If you could kill me, I'd be dead already." He giggled. "Besides, if I die, my finger could tense up, and then little Patrick here would go boom. Or I could survive just long enough to pull the trigger." Artie's eyes lit up. It looked like he'd had epiphany. "But..." He put on a sadistic smile. "I do have a way out of this for you. Sort of."

"What way out?" Julie trembled. What was this sick pervert up to now? She wanted to shoot him right then and there. Patrick couldn't block him completely. But it was too close. She couldn't risk shooting her little boy. "Will you let Patrick go? If you want to kill me instead... fine. Do it. Just let Patrick go, and my sister too."

"No Mom!"

Artie pretended to weigh her offer. "That wasn't really the way out I had in mind."

"Well, I'm listening." She inched closer to him on a slight leftward angle. She had to find a way to get a clear shot.

"Well first, I advise you to take a look at that painting over there." He pointed to the painting set against a podium.

Julie shot a glance over to the painting.

Her little boy, dead and raped.

It was only paints on a canvas, but it looked too real.

Acid rose in her throat. "If you consider that art, Falcon... then you don't even know what art means. You disgrace the word beauty by applying your definition to it."

Artie looked at her unfazed. "Well, since I don't think you'll let me rape your little boy in front of you, I have to forsake my original artistic vision." He pouted. "But that's okay. Because I got a new one. One that I think you might accept."

Sister Olivia cried out to her. "Don't trust him."

"He won't let me go no matter what, Mom." Patrick was breathing heavily. "Don't believe anything he says."

Julie ignored both of them. "What's this deal?"

"Either way, your son is leaving this church in a body bag today." Artie took a deep breath. "There's absolutely no way around that. But, I am giving you a chance to go with him." He met her eyes. "If you shoot at me, I shoot him. But if you don't shoot me, I'll let him run to you."

She froze. Would he really let him go? No. It was too easy.

He continued, "You can both have one final embrace. One final kiss goodbye. A last chance to hold him tight and tell him that you'll be there for him forever. Then I will shoot both of you in the head. You'll die simultaneously in each other's arms. Such a beautiful way for a mother and her child to leave this earth behind."

Patrick gasped for breath. "Mom! No." He began to cry harder.

Julie struggled not to open fire on Artie that instant. She withheld only because Patrick was in the way of a clear shot.

"What the hell kind of deal is that? Patrick's dead both ways. Why would I choose to die too?"

Artie cracked the most evil smile she'd seen yet. "Because your father is dead. Your husband is dead. If I kill Patrick, *both* of your sons will be dead. You won't have anything left to live for."

"What do you mean my father's dead?"

"I killed him in the parking lot."

"You mean that was who you hit?" Patrick breathed heavier. "You killed Grandpa?"

"Did I forget to mention that?" He cocked his head. "My bad."

"Just because you killed him..." Julie struggled to hold back her tears. "Doesn't mean I'll let you kill me."

"Julie, you remember when Petey died right? You were a mess." Artie clenched his gun tighter. "You know if I put a bullet in the head of young Patrick, you'll never have peace. First and foremost, you'll watch him die. You'll see the bullet exit the other side of his skull." He moved the gun to Patrick's temple. "Or maybe the other side of his pretty little face." He stuck his tongue out. "You'll see the brightness in his eyes vanish like a light going out. But they'll remain open. Staring back at you as you watch his bloody corpse crumple to the ground. Then he'll lay there lifeless, staring blankly back at the mother who failed to save him. Until you close them." He caressed Patrick's neck. "You'll want to hold off closing them to see his beautiful baby blues just a little bit longer. But staring into his eyes knowing that he is not really staring back will be a feeling of raw horror that will give you nightmares for the rest of your life. You'll hold him close to you. Until they forcefully remove him from your arms."

She winced. She couldn't believe the words she was hearing.

"Then you'll pull strings with your buddy Cora at the

morgue to stay with him for the days it'll take to arrange funeral arrangements. It'll be well over a week before you can finally let go of his rotting flesh." He was giddy with excitement. "You'll pick out clothes for him and dress him in them yourself. Then you'll watch as they lower him into the cold ground. In a box. Every day you'll come home to silence. An empty house. Haunted with the echoes of the family you used to have. When Petey and your husband died, you were devastated. But you had something to live for. You had Patrick. But now if Patrick dies, you won't have anything. You'll be left totally devastated. You'll have absolutely no reason to breathe another breath. And each one will hurt so much, you won't even want to."

Julie couldn't believe how accurate Artie's vision of how she'd react was. It made her sweat even more. "Then maybe I should just stop you from killing him."

"But you can't." He laughed. "I have the upper hand here. I'm killing Patrick today no matter what. But if you die with him, you won't have to watch him die. You'll both be reunited with your entire family. You'll be at peace." He raised an eyebrow. "Do you want him to die with my arms around him, or yours?"

"No Mom. You can't do it." He struggled in Artie's grip.

"Why are you so set on killing Patrick?" Julie trembled. Her lips tensed. "If you don't plan on getting away, what's his life? I know you targeted him to get to me. But that was just a game, right? You have no reason to have anything personal against us."

"Is there where you try to psychoanalyze my motives in an effort to shock me?' He rocked his head back and forth.

"Maybe I've just figured you out. Why you seem to hate us so much. Why you became the monster you became."

"Well, why don't you tell Patrick this one last bedtime story before I put him to sleep for good?" He grinned and bobbed his head. "We're all ears. Let's hear your theory, Detective."

"You outright told me that your body is burned. And that you were ridiculed because of it." She shot him a stern glare. "You're not 'beautiful' to yourself. You haven't been for a long time. But you thought other people were beautiful. I think target people like Patrick because your jealous of the acceptance they get. You kill them so violently in an attempt to destroy their beauty, not to create it. You say it's just art. Well I don't believe you. I think art is just an excuse to take out your rejection issues on innocent people who have the lives you always wanted but never got."

Artie froze. He curled his lips. "I must say that I'm impressed. It's certainly a viable theory. Perhaps one that might be true if I took the time to honestly ask myself. So congratulations, Detective. That's a theory right out of a climactic crime show showdown. I applaud your insight." His sneer widened. "But do you really think this changes anything? That explaining my motives to me will somehow make me question them? Or shake me off my game and give you an opening? I'm afraid on that front, you've failed. Nothing's changed. My terms remain. And while your little theory was entertaining, I am growing impatient for your decision." He pressed his arm against Patrick's neck. "Clock's not slowing down. Better make your decision."

Julie felt chills shoot up her spine. Her plan didn't

work. Artie was still as determined as ever. What options did she have left?

Visions of her little boy in a casket flashed into her brain. And that quiet, empty, lonely house. He was her life. If she couldn't save him, could she even take another breath?

"Honey, I want to save you, but I don't think I can go on if you die too." Julie started to tremble. She was actually weighing his offer. "It was so hard losing your brother, but I still had you. If he takes you, I won't have anything left."

"You'll have your job."

Julie was horrified by the assertion that he thought her job could replace him. "Patrick, you mean more to me than my job ever could."

"But you are still good at it. You have to catch all the bad guys, Mom." His eyes looked almost the same as they did on that morning when he'd last spoken those words. Only now they were filled with tears. "Even if I die, you have to stay alive so you can catch more bad guys."

"Patrick, there are other people to do that." She sniffled.

"They aren't as good as you." He shook his head vehemently. "You help people. You save people. They count on you to keep bad things from happening to them." He began to hyperventilate and struggled to pull himself together again. "They need you, Mom. They need you to make sure they stay safe. To make the people who hurt them go away." He took a few deep breaths. "You can't stop helping people because of me. You can't."

"Patrick, if you die, I won't be able to catch the bad guys anymore." She was crying just as hard as he was now. "You're my only reason for getting up in the morning."

"What about everybody else's kids?" He cast a meaningful glance towards Nathaniel and Ethan. "There are bad guys out there. And they want to hurt them." His terrified eyes met hers. "Isn't keeping them from getting hurt like those kids, or me, worth getting up for?"

"Patrick." She sobbed. She couldn't stand for this. She had to rescue him.

She fired her gun at Artie.

He yanked Patrick aside.

The bullet buried itself on the marble podium.

He dug the gun into Patrick's skull.

Patrick screamed in agony. His limbs gave way and he almost collapsed.

Only Artie's hold on him kept him upright.

"Patrick." Julie screamed. "I'm sorry. Please. Don't hurt him."

"You see I am not bluffing now?" Artie smiled. "Next time, that will be a bullet."

Julie looked at Patrick. He was shaking. He looked so helpless in Artie's grip.

She couldn't let those murderous arms be the last thing her little boy felt. But she knew she had to stop Artie. She gathered herself back together as well as she could and regarded Artie as steadily as possible.

He stared back with his usual cold stare, a sly smile complimenting his evil.

She felt him reading her every thought.

Artie said, "It looks to me like you've made up your mind."

Sister Olivia shouted, "Shut up you son of a bitch!"

"Now is that any way for a nun to talk?" He giggled.

Julie took a step towards Artie.

He didn't seem to notice.

There had to be a way out.

She prayed to God for a way out. Any way that could save her precious Patrick. He'd survived so much. She refused to let that be for nothing.

But Artie was still using Patrick as a shield.

Any move she made now would give him the chance to pull the trigger. She tried to think of a trick that he wouldn't see through. But her mind was blank. All she could see was Patrick's trembling face and the horrible black pistol aimed at his head.

"Patrick...I don't know what to do."

Through streaming tears and heavy whimpers, he said, "Mom, I love you." Patrick gazed up at her. "Don't die because of me, please." He tried to smile. "I'm a big boy. Remember? I'll be brave."

Julie felt tears blinding her eyes. She took another step forward. "I love you so much Patrick, always remember that. You were such great sons, you and your brother." She struggled to get another breath out. "Say hello to him for me, please? Your father too."

"I will, Mom." Patrick forced out a tearful smile and nodded. "They'll be so excited to see me."

"You wait for me up there." Julie closed her eyes a second. "And pray. Pray hard. Because I don't think I'm going to be able to go on without them."

"You bet I will. I love you, Mom."

"I love you too, baby. More than anything in the world."

Artie grunted. "Well, this is getting a bit too over-the-top sentimental for my taste. So, Julie, my dear, what is your final decision?"

"I'm not playing into your suicide game." Julie firmly

clenched her gun. "You're going down Artie."

"Well, then I guess you made your decision." Artie smiled. "I must say, I thought you'd go with him. I guess it goes to show that there's always a surprise waiting for you. Say goodbye to Patrick. His life is officially over."

The sound of a gunshot firing filled the church with an echo.

Patrick crumpled to the ground.

Almost in slow motion to Julie.

She felt her mouth drop open.

A shrill cry howled, amplified by the large empty building.

"No." She felt paralyzed.

She'd fired her gun. She was sure she'd pulled the trigger. But she didn't hear a second gunshot. How? Did it jam? Did she only imagine shooting it? Was her mind playing games with her?

She tried to squeeze the trigger. She couldn't. It was like the gun was jammed. Or was it her heart?

She couldn't even breathe. Maybe this had been his plan all along. What was to stop him from killing her now? Did she even want to stop him?

Sister Olivia began to weep for her nephew.

She buried her face on the floor to avoid looking up.

Julie saw Patrick's life play over and over in her head. All the holidays. The Birthdays. All the little moments she'd been too busy to appreciate. How could it be over just like that?

Artie was standing there frozen. Blood had splattered on his clothes. He was looking down.

Then she saw it. His gun at his feet. When did he drop it?

"That's for giving me a killer headache you sick son

of a bitch."

Whose voice was that? It sounded like...her father?

She looked up.

Kevin was standing by the foot of the altar.

Clenching a smoking gun.

She saw Artie's hand. The hand that was holding the gun to Patrick's head. It was oozing with blood.

Julie then looked at Patrick lying on the ground.

He was blinking.

His eyes weren't lifelessly fixated ahead. They were actually opening and closing. He looked to be in shock, but there wasn't any blood.

He was alive.

Kevin rushed at Artie and slammed him to the ground. He cuffed him.

"I don't understand." Artie's voice was shaking. "Patrick was supposed to be dead. So were you. How did this happen?"

"I guess the great artist's plans went a bit awry." Kevin twisted his arm. "So much for your twisted vision. I'd say I'm sorry...but I'm not."

Julie ran to Patrick.

She scooped him into her arms and hugged him to her as tightly as her arms would allow.

"Oh Patrick, are you all right? Are you hurt?" She kissed his face repeatedly.

Patrick remained silent. He was clearly alive but he looked almost to be in a trance.

"Patrick, are you all right?" Julie became concerned. She gently stroked his cheek. She turned his face to her. "Patrick?"

"I think I'm fine." He took a few deep breaths. "I don't hurt anywhere. Except maybe you squeezing me a little."

"I'm so sorry." She quickly released her hold on him. "I was just so relieved. You're alive. I thought he...it looked like you..." She pushed a lock of his hair out of his face. She thanked God for keeping her little boy safe. "I was so scared. I thought I'd have to watch you die."

She saw his trance melt away. He cried and wrapped his arms around her. "I'm fine now. I was just so scared, Mom. I really thought I was gonna die." He buried his head on her shoulder.

She gently patted his back. "You're safe now. Don't worry. He can't hurt you now."

She stared Artie down.

He glared back at her.

She pulled Patrick to her. She dried some of his tears.

"Mom, I'm sorry you were so scared." He turned away in shame. "I put you through all of this."

She turned his head to her. "Hey now, I'll have none of that. Only Artie is to blame for this."

He nodded halfheartedly.

She scanned him head to toe a moment. "Patrick, you don't have to answer this if you're uncomfortable or not ready. But I have to at least ask. Did he do anything to you? Did he..." How could she form this question without it sounding as horrible as it was?

Patrick took a deep breath. He closed his eyes and shed a tear, avoiding eye contact.

Julie felt her stomach turn. "Oh Patrick, no." She hugged him tighter.

He pulled back. "No." He shook his head. "He didn't do anything like that. You got here just in time. You saved me, Mom. You're good at that."

Julie wasn't sure if she could believe Patrick, but now wasn't the time to press the issue. She hugged him again, even tighter this time. "I thought I'd lost you forever."

He reciprocated her embrace. "You'd never lose me forever. We may have been apart for a long time. But we'd be together again one day."

"I'm just so glad you're okay." She kissed his cheek. "It's much easier to get the bad guys when I have the best son in the world waiting at home. Coming home at night wouldn't be any kind of relief if you weren't there, Patrick." She tearfully stroked his face. "I'm not as strong as you think, Patrick. I wouldn't make it without you."

"You're stronger than anybody else I know, Mom." Patrick laughed. "Except maybe Grandpa."

"Are you sure you're okay?" She examined him quickly for wounds.

Patrick smiled as he moved her hands away. "Mom." He laughed. "I'm fine now. Really." He took a moment to catch his breath. "Is it really over?"

Julie looked towards Artie, bleeding and cuffed, well under Kevin's control. "Yes, it's finally over."

Kevin approached her with Artie in tow. "Mind telling me what I walked in on when I came in?"

"Just a little mind game." Julie sneered at the culprit. "But he's finally gotten what he deserves. I'm fine." She turned to Kevin. "But what about you? He told me you were dead."

"I feel almost dead with this damned migraine." Kevin rubbed his head. "The bastard ran me down in the parking lot. Guess he didn't bank on this tough old coot being able to handle his little sneak attack car tricks."

Julie looked down at Artie, who was strangely silent. "So what do you have to say for yourself?"

Artie stared up at her. "I'll tell you, but only you."

Julie picked him up and dragged him to the back of

the Church. She threw him to the ground. "Okay. Talk."

∞⟨⟩∞⟨⟩∞⟨⟩∞

Patrick and Kevin ran to Sister Olivia.

Kevin helped her sit up. "How are you? He didn't hurt you, did he?"

She shook her head. "It's just a leg wound. I'm fine. It's them that got the worst of it." She pointed to the bodies of Nathaniel and Ethan.

"My God, how could somebody do that?" Kevin recoiled in disgust. He'd overlooked their bodies before.

"Ethan died instantly I think." She tearfully turned away from them. "Nathaniel lingered a moment. He was in so much pain. It was only a few seconds but it must've been agony for him."

Patrick approached Nathaniel's corpse and took the boy's hand in his. "I'm sorry you and your friend had to be dragged into all of this." A tear dripped onto Nathaniel's hand. "You must've had so many fun things to do and now you're like this." He cried harder. "I'm sorry. If he just killed me, you guys wouldn't be dead." He set Nathaniel's hand down.

"It's all my fault." He buried his head in his hands and wept uncontrollably.

"Don't you dare blame yourself." She reached out and took Patrick by the hand. "He was a heartless killer. He planned this. He would've killed them no matter what."

"Not if I stayed in that car and drowned."

"Stop it. I won't let you relieve Artie of any blame in this. It all goes to him. Every bit of it. Never blame yourself for anything he's done."

Patrick turned away. He knew she was right. Now he just had to convince his heart.

∞⟨⟩∞⟨⟩∞⟨⟩∞

Julie pointed her gun at Artie. "Is this your chance to try one last mind game with me? One last futile attempt to make your failure easier to bear?"

"You realize I won't be kept in a prison cell?" Artie put on a taunting smile.

"Maybe you think that, but you're going away in the deepest, darkest, most well-guarded prison cell we can find." Julie shook her head. She leaned in closer. "Your crimes are so heinous, they might even bring back the death penalty just for you, Artie. Then you'll be the art scene as they strap you down and inject you with drugs to stop your heart. If that happens, Artie? I'll be there to watch, letting one of the final things you'll see be me smiling at you getting exactly what you deserve."

"I faked my death before." He looked up at her with a sneer. "I can do it again."

Julie suddenly felt chills up her spine. "You can't fake your death in prison."

"You willing to take a bet on that?" Artie giggled. "When I get out, I'm coming after Patrick again. I didn't get to finish my original art scene vision this time, but I will. One day I'll find him. I'll strip him naked and then I'll force him to discover every single sexual act I know in the most humiliating way possible. Rape won't even be a good word to describe what I'm going to do to him. He'll be cursing his own body and begging me to kill him by the time I am done. And I will grant his wish." He salivated. "After he is nothing more than a violated shell of a human being, I will kill him, and I will make it very slow. And very painful. Not the quick shot to the head he'd have gotten today. I'll torture him until he wills his body to die to escape the agony. I'll leave his body where you can find it." He licked his lips. "One day you'll come home and you'll find him. Then you will curse the day you saved him. Because the pain and shame he will feel will be so much greater. That will be a beautiful art scene." He turned to her and smiled.

Julie felt sickened as she stared into his eyes. Then she looked down and noticed his cuffed hands going for her gun.

She quickly grabbed the gun as he lunged at her.

She threw him to the ground.

He shot to his feet.

He lunged at her.

She emptied the clip into him.

Bullets flew through his chest, neck, and head.

He crumpled to the ground. Dead. Finally, he was dead. He could never hurt another person. Now he was getting exactly what he deserved.

Julie stared down at his bloodied corpse. Had he really gone for her gun? Or did she just imagine it as an excuse to make sure he could never come after Patrick again? She wasn't sure. All she knew was that he was gone. Maybe this was what he really wanted.

⊶⚬⊶⚬⊶

Julie left the bloody mess of Artie where it fell.

She walked to the front of the church. She was still holding the smoking gun.

Kevin met her midway down the isle. "What happened?"

"He tried to escape." Julie turned back to Artie. "I reacted." She stepped around Kevin and walked over to Patrick and Sister Olivia. "Are you both all right?"

They nodded.

Julie took out her phone. "We'd better get an ambulance here before that leg bleeds out."

"I'm fine." Sister Olivia pulled herself to her feet. "Don't worry about me."

"Please, I'm the big sister." She caught Sister Olivia as she fell. "Let me do the thinking." She helped her to a pew.

The two exchanged a smile as Julie dialed for help.

Julie gazed at her son.

She actually caught him letting out a faint smile through his horror and regret. He wouldn't get over this anytime soon. But he was alive. He'd broken the chain. That was a cause for at least some joy. It was a nice change in the midst of all that had happened those past few days.

They could finally breathe again.

⋅⋅⋅⋅⋅⋅⋅⋅⋅⋅

Statements were made. The dead bodies were removed in body bags. An ambulance came to examine the shaken final victims of the killer. The next hour passed in a blur. But at least now it was just about over.

Sister Olivia was taken to the hospital. She refused Julie and Kevin's offers to come with her. They had been through enough that day. They had to worry about themselves. She'd be fine, and indeed she was. Upon arrival to the hospital, her wound was promptly treated and her prognosis was quite good.

Patrick was given an examination. Luckily, none of Artie's abuse had left any serious physical injuries on him. Psychologically, he was visibly shaken. He didn't speak more than he had to. The medics said he'd need counseling. Maybe even that he should be taken to the hospital that night for psychiatric evaluation.

Julie balked at such a notion. Her son needed his home, not a hospital bed. And certainly not doctors who had no idea who he was or what he'd been through. She wasn't a shrink, but she knew best how to help her son cope. She'd helped him before, and she'd help him again.

Not wanting to argue with a police detective, they cleared Patrick to go home.

After what seemed like hours, the last cop finally let them leave.

Patrick stepped outside of the church into the intense heat waiting outside. Daylight had returned just in time to make a final appearance before the sun had set. Seeing the light of day was a good feeling.

"The sun's so nice." He smiled. "I thought I'd never see it again."

"It'll be even nicer in the morning." Julie placed his hand on her shoulder. "We should get you home. You've had quite a tough day. You must want to get showered and get to bed."

"Can I skip the shower?" A chill ran up his spine as he thought of Artie's hands on his skin. "I just wanna go to bed."

Julie nodded. "Then let's get you home."

Kevin held out his hand. "How about I come with you?"

"You should be joining Olivia at the hospital." She gave him a light shove. "You were freaking hit by a car. You're lucky to be alive. Let alone going home."

He pouted. "You know I've always had a hard head." He winked at her.

"Patrick and I had a long day. We really just need to get home and get some sleep. Artie's dead. You don't have to worry about us."

"Maybe I just came too close to losing everything I loved today. Plus you know I can't stand staying in the hospital." He took her by the hand. "The paramedics told me I'm fine. They stitched me up and gave me some pills. I ain't checking myself into the hospital to wear a paper robe two sizes too small. And I am not going home alone. So unless you want me to crash on one of these pews, I'm coming with you."

"Let him come, Mom." Patrick took Julie by the hand. "You know you'll need somebody to talk to tonight. And I'm tired...I just wanna try to sleep a little bit. You should let Grandpa come. You need *your* dad tonight."

Kevin said, "Well you heard the boy."

"Okay, okay." She put on a smile. "Grandpa can come." She escorted the two of them to her car. Then she drove home.

As they rode, Patrick felt a twinge in his chest. "Mom, will the nightmares start again tonight?"

Julie sighed. "You saw a lot today." She looked back at him in the rearview. "You're probably going to be scared for awhile. But I'm here for you. So you won't be alone."

Patrick stared out the window at the houses going by. He could see Milo's house as they turned a corner. He thought of how greatly his life had changed in the past few days. He knew he was still just a kid. How he could go back to being 'just a kid' after everything that had happened? He'd seen innocent people die horrible deaths before his very eyes. He'd felt the cold barrel of a gun pressed against his temple. And then what Artie almost did to him...he could never look at himself in the mirror again and not remember.

He felt his chest. His heart was beating. It was *still* beating. It had finally slowed down, but it hadn't been stopped. That was more than he could say for all of those poor people at the mall. For those altar boys. For Milo.

For everyone. He was still alive.

God had answered his prayer.

Now he just needed to try and figure out how to live again. How to be a normal boy. How to be happy.

These thoughts troubled him for a minute or two more. Then the stress of the day caught up. He slowly drifted off to sleep. He'd fear nightmares. Maybe they'd still come. But for now, for the first time since before this nightmare had started, he felt a sense of peace.

When Julie got out of the car, she saw that Patrick had fallen asleep. "Poor thing."

"No use waking him." Kevin opened the door. He unbuckled the seatbelt and picked up Patrick from the seat.

The boy instinctively wrapped his arms around him.

Kevin smiled. "This takes me back." He carried him to the front door.

The house was disturbingly quiet given all that had happened that day.

"I can take him from here." Julie held her arms out to her father.

Gently passing Patrick to her, Kevin said, "Give him a kiss from me."

"I will." She began to ascend the stairs with her sleeping child in her arms.

When she arrived at his room, she set his body down on the bed and undressed him to his underwear. The house had gotten hot from nobody being home to turn up the air. She knew he'd be hot in anything else.

She folded the clothes and noticed they were new. Did she even want to know? "You definitely have good taste in clothing." She chuckled and planted a kiss on his forehead. "Sleep well my precious child."

Without waking from his slumber, he turned on his side and made himself comfortable. As he always did when he was peacefully sleeping.

She gently closed the door and left her son to his mental restoration from a long and incredibly difficult day.

She went downstairs.

Kevin was waiting for her on the sofa with a peanut butter and jelly sandwich and some lemonade.

"Thanks, Dad." Julie placed her hand on her chest. "But I'm really not hungry."

"Bull crap you're not hungry. You haven't eaten a thing all day and when you don't eat, you get wiped out." He signaled for her to sit next to him. "The only reason you ain't on the ground now is because you had an adrenaline rush. With that fading, you're going to need your strength."

"I think I'm a little past PB and J."

"Nonsense. This was always your favorite as a girl. And something tells me you're still quite fond of it." He winked. "Now come on. Sit down to a little light supper with your old man. After everything that's happened today, I think you could use it." He patted the cushion next to him.

She sighed and rolled her eyes. "Fine, fine. I'll eat." She walked over to the sofa and took a seat on it next to him, grabbing a half of the carefully made sandwich. Saying a quick prayer, she bit into it and closed her eyes in delight.

"See?" he said proudly. "What did I tell you?"

"Oh stop gloating. I've been so stressed out I'd eat anything short of tofu."

"You're stubborn in admitting when I'm right." He smiled proudly. "Just like your mother."

"I am not like Mom." She smacked his leg. "She'd never allow me to eat in the living room like this."

He laughed. "Touché I guess. Maybe."

"There's no maybe about it."

Kevin chuckled. "So was he still asleep when you got to his room?"

"Yeah. He was still sleeping like a baby." She leaned back and closed her eyes. "It's for the best. I can't imagine what he went through today. He's been through more trauma today alone than most people experience in their entire lives."

"You think he'll need therapy?"

"Maybe...I mean...I'm sure we'll try it again. The problem is that therapy doesn't help Patrick. Not the kind doctors offer anyway. We tried it after Petey died. It just made things harder. Patrick's just not the usual kid. So their usual tactics just don't work for him."

"Maybe it'll be different this time."

She shook her head. "I wouldn't bet on it."

He put his arm around her. "Always the rebel, aren't you Jules?"

She smiled and took his hand. "Just like my dad."

Realizing she was right, he smiled and planted a kiss on her forehead. "Yep, just like your old man."

<hr>

Patrick heard the sounds of a swing creaking as it swung back and forth.

He felt the thin seat under him, making its uncomfortable imprints on his butt, even through his clothes.

He hopped up from the swing and turned around to see the swing sway in the breeze for a moment.

He looked around at the rest of the playground.

It was the playground he had always played at when

he was younger, before he went to school. He had first become friends with Milo here.

The playground look deserted, even though it was a sunny evening.

Then he heard something.

Cheers and joyful shouts. They were other children. The voices were coming from somewhere nearby.

He turned around. And then back again. He didn't see them. Where were they?

They seemed to be coming from the right.

Patrick slowly walked in that direction.

The cheerful sounds quickly led to a large fence. There was an unending, lush green field on the other side. It was almost like a mystical meadow and a striking contrast to the overgrown ball fields that Patrick had remembered being next to the playground. This wasn't the place he knew at all. It was so much better. So much more beautiful.

He pressed his face against the fence.

Kids were playing ball. The game they were playing didn't resemble any he knew, but they seemed to be having fun.

As he looked closer, he was shocked to discover that two of the kids were the two altar boys he had seen murdered in the church. Nathaniel and Ethan.

Two little kids watched from the bench. The same kids from the mall. They were cheering. The one still clung to his stuffed animal. But it looked newer.

A girl came up to them. She put her arms around them and they looked at her. She had long, flowing auburn hair. Susie. That was her name. Patrick remembered her picture from the news. A man and a woman stood behind her, looking lovingly at her. Her parents.

Eric threw a ball to Billy. They looked like best friends. They were happy. He never saw them aside from their happy photos on the news. He'd never heard their voices. Yet, in this moment, it was almost like he knew them. He knew them so well.

He felt his heart pick up more speed. Damien and Milo were there too. They were playing with all the others. They were all like a group of very good friends.

Karen, Clark, and Nina were cheering from the sidelines. A beautiful young lady was there as well. Caroline. They clapped and shouted words of encouragement.

His father was cheering along with them. He looked so different than Patrick remembered. Younger. Thinner. But he still recognized him. He looked like Patrick wanted to look when he grew up.

And then there he was.

Petey.

He was leading the game. Taking charge as he always did. He looked like he was having so much fun. But now he was older. He looked the same age as Patrick. Like he'd have looked if he were still alive.

Something was different about them though. They weren't wearing any kind of clothes. Yet they weren't naked either. But they still had a noticeably human form. And they were free from any kind of injury or imperfection. Patrick couldn't explain it. He didn't understand at all. How was this possible? Was this what their souls looked like?

All of these people were dead. He'd seen many of them dead. How was he seeing them now? Alive and happy? Did he really die too? Did he only imagine being rescued? Was this heaven?

He tried to climb the fence but he didn't get off the

ground.

"Petey!" He heard his voice echo in the fields.

Petey turned to Patrick. He waved and ran over to the fence.

"Hey, Patrick. It's good to see you again. I didn't expect you to visit after you almost came over earlier today. I really thought you were going to come over. Like for real. But it's okay that you didn't. It's not time yet. You still got lots to do. Don't worry, though. You'll be here one day when you're ready. And since you stay here like forever, there's no rush at all."

"Wait, what is this place?" Patrick looked around.

"It's a dream silly." Petey laughed. "Well, sort of. I can't really explain what it is so you can get it. You'll just have to go with this and like not ask too many questions."

"Then why am I here?"

"Well, 'cause I guess we all just wanted to all tell you that you don't have to be upset or afraid about us. Just pray for us. That's all you need to do. We're fine."

"I have prayed for you. Every day since you died."

Petey smiled. "I know." He touched his chest. "I felt every one. And I prayed for you five times as hard. And God gave the ones I didn't need to somebody who did. So keep doing it. He never lets prayers go to waste."

"What do you want me to do, though? I've been praying. That can't be why I'm here."

"You just gotta live. That's all." Petey reached through the fence.

Patrick took his hand. It felt real, but even stronger than ever before. Like his own size now. But it was still Petey's hand. That same soft skin. It was so good to hold it again. For a moment, it felt like they'd never been pulled apart in that accident.

"We saw that you were pretty badly shaken by everything that happened. And we get it. But we want you to get better, Patrick. We want you to be happy again. It might not be for like a hundred years for you, but you'll join the party here soon enough. And while we're super psyched that somebody cares enough to miss us and pray for us like you, we don't want you like letting it make you all mental."

Patrick pouted. "Easy for you all to say. You're all dead. You don't have to deal with missing you every day. I get so sad. And lonely. Sometimes I miss you so much that it hurts. It really, literally hurts, Petey. I want my friends back. I want my brother back."

"Yeah that must suck." Petey shot Patrick a sympathetic smile. He held his hand tighter. "I don't expect you to like just automatically feel better 'cause I told you to. I know it's gonna hurt for long time. And I know you're gonna be sad. You can't help it. I'm just telling you, don't be afraid to be happy again. It's okay. We want you to be able to smile and really make it real." He nodded. "Anyway, I gotta get back. They're waiting."

"Just one more minute." He took a deep breath. "I just need another minute of this. Brothers forever."

"Of course we're brothers forever. And don't you ever forget it either"

Patrick let go of his hand. "Petey, do you think I'll go to heaven? To see you all again?"

"That's up to you." He pointed up. "Keep close to Him, and you know you will."

Patrick smiled. "So is this really just a dream? You guys aren't really here."

Petey shook his head. "Patrick. I think you know in your heart that this isn't just your ordinary dream. Now really, I can't stay. I gotta go. But I'm still looking out for ya. Just like I always did." He winked.

Patrick watched the ball fly through the air. "So they have ball in heaven?"

Petey turned back to Patrick, puzzled. "Is that like all you see? Gosh, they weren't kidding when they said that earth eyes don't see the whole picture. Later bro." Petey waved again. Then he ran off and gave the ball in the game a fierce and forceful kick that sent it flying into the air.

The dream faded away. Then transitioned into other ones.

Patrick would forget those by the time dawn opened his eyes the next morning.

But he remembered this dream. It was a little fuzzy, but it remained a presence in his memory.

He would never go so far as to say that it healed his emotional wounds or prevented future nightmares and emotional fits resulting from the horrors he had seen. But it did renew his sense of hope. It gave him something to cling to during those tough times. He never told anybody else about the dream. Other than a priest. He never needed to. He knew healing would come in time. Until then, he and his mother had all they needed to get to that relief on the other side of the grief.

Epilogue

The very next morning was the first in a long series of funerals that Julie and Patrick were to attend for the rest of the week. There was often even more than one funeral each day.

The week itself was a step above a blur to Patrick. He had never seen so many dead bodies before.

Julie was worried about him not being able to handle it, but he took it in stride. Even if he was quite uncomfortable wearing a suit and tie every day in the steamy summer weather.

The first funeral was Billy's. Hardly anyone was there. This saddened Patrick greatly. Billy was just a little boy. He should be mourned and remembered.

Patrick knew that if it were him up there, lots of people would be grieving him. It wasn't right that this boy was so much forgotten. He and his father were arranged in cheap suits in open coffins next to each other. Aside from an uncle, no family cared enough to come.

Billy's hair was combed over his forehead, hiding the fatal bullet hole.

Patrick said a prayer as he kneeled before the coffin. If nobody else would pray for this boy, he would.

The funeral that Julie had arranged for the Holdens came next.

Julie felt it ironic that Eric was being buried on the same day as the boy he had found dead. In the chaos of the past few days, she felt guilty that she had almost forgotten about him—the one who really made the case personal for her. She couldn't afford fancy clothes for the three of them, but in their semi-casual clothes, they looked cared for.

Susie wore a cute blue dress. Burke and Eric were dressed in fine collar shirts and pants. They all looked dignified. It was better than being left to rot naked on a slab for months on end. Their souls may not have been there to care, but their bodies were still sacred and deserved a proper burial.

Patrick felt sorry for Eric as he gazed at his lifeless form in the open coffin. They could've been friends if they had they known each other. He somehow was able to read everything about Eric's life just by seeing his body. He gave him a prayerful goodbye similar to the one he had given to Billy. He didn't know him. But he could relate.

The funeral crowd was small. Julie understood why. There wasn't any family. The Requiem Mass and burial were simple. There wasn't any pomp that makes funerals memorable. However, given all of that, it was actually larger than Julie had expected. Many parishioners who had known the family came to pay their respects. At least some people were there to mourn the family. Julie couldn't bear it if nobody who knew them cared that they were gone. She even received some money to offset the costs of the burial.

Some of the victims from the mall were buried on Tuesday.

Karen was too. Patrick had never seen her look more beautiful than she did in the white dress her family buried her in. Julie and Patrick couldn't believe that in all their years of knowing her, it took her dying for them to meet any of her family.

The next day, Caroline was buried in a closed casket ceremony. Her funeral was more crowded. Not packed, but the Church was half-full. Julie even connected some with Caroline's mother, who seemed less hard on her and more aware of her role in her lack of a relationship with her daughter.

Thursday, the hardest day of the week–the day on which Greene family was laid to rest. Their funeral was more crowded than all the others combined. Julie knew that the Greenes had been well loved by just about every-body in the community in addition to countless friends and family from out of town. Still, the turnout surprised even her.

The three were arranged next to each other on the altar, each in open caskets. They looked asleep. Had Ju-lie not seen the brutalized, dead bodies of all three, she might've half bought the arrangement. But neither she nor Patrick could be fooled. They knew that their friends were gone. A prettier picture didn't make that reality cut any less deep into their hearts.

A bright spot was that neither Milo nor Damien were dressed in suits. They both wore casual clothes barely a step above a tee shirt and jeans. It was definitely uncanny, but it was better than burying them in the nude, which is what Milo would've chosen over a suit given the choice. Since it was his body, it seemed proper that his wishes were honored, even if they were unconventional.

Nina was dressed beautifully in contrast to her sons. A full and elegant blue dress, fit for the finest of weddings. But they all looked dignified. Nobody would be able to tell their final moments by looking at the peaceful corpses resting in the fine caskets at the foot of the altar. Perhaps that would help ease the pain of those who would miss them who didn't know the full circumstances of their deaths.

The funeral service brought Julie and Patrick much needed closure over the loss of their friends. It felt relieving to have a sense of peace over their deaths for the first time. They still missed them. But they could breathe again.

Surprisingly, despite the heavy turnout, Julie and Patrick were both asked to eulogize their friends. As much as everyone else there loved them, it was determined that Julie and Patrick knew them best.

Clark's body was shipped back to be buried in a family plot. Julie and Patrick were unable to attend his funeral, but they sent their wishes. Julie spoke briefly to his brother on the phone. She could tell that it was hitting him hard. She offered to check in regularly on him. Just to make sure he was okay.

On Friday, the victims from the mall massacre were memorialized in a service. Separate funeral Masses had already been held for most of them. Even those of other faiths were represented. It brought the community together. As much as the individual murders hurt the community, this was a mass killing in a public family place. People didn't feel safe anymore.

Julie felt that maybe this service could help ease that fear just a little. Coming together like this was proof that their community was still good.

Nathaniel and Ethan were buried in a joint funeral Mass on Saturday. That was to be their first official Mass as altar boys.

This time the caskets were closed. Julie understood why. She was surprised there were as many open caskets as there were. Maybe these families realized that a less horrible image wouldn't be enough to make things better.

Since they didn't know any of the families, Julie and Patrick stayed in the back during the entire Mass. They went home when it ended.

Finally, the last of the funerals was behind them. Now they could try to move on. Maybe one day, they could feel that life was normal again.

⊱•⊰•⊱•⊰

After arriving home from the funeral, Patrick practically ripped his clothes off. He swore he felt his body temperature cool considerably the moment the suit was on the ground instead of on him.

He put on a sleeveless t-shirt and shorts that were loose fitting enough to keep him as cool as possible.

He threw himself down on the couch and stared at the ceiling. He let out an audible sigh.

Julie approached him and took a seat on the other side of the couch.

"Well, I have the rest of the day off. What do you say we do something together?" She tickled his toes and smiled when he yanked them back with a giggle. "I can take you out to eat or something. We need something fun to do. After this past week...we need to cool off. Wind down a bit."

"I'd like that a lot." Patrick smiled.

He stepped into his old sandals. He could never bring himself to use the ones Jacob gave him. Even if the blood stains from the floor did come out. These old ones were a little small and his toes nearly touched the tops but they'd make do until they could get new ones.

"Let's go."

Julie put her arm around him. "Patrick, I just want you to know. You can tell me anything."

"I know." He hugged her. "And I will. But it's a nice day. And right now we're going somewhere."

She stroked his head. She wanted him to open up to her. But she had to trust that he'd talk to her when he was ready. He was smiling a little again. And he wanted to do something. That was a good enough start for her.

The two stepped outside. Jacob was waiting by the end of the driveway.

Patrick immediately recognized the boy. He ran down the stairs to greet him.

"I didn't think I'd ever see you again." He avoided eye contact. "I thought you wouldn't want to see me after I almost got you killed."

"You saved me, dude." Jacob approached him. He held his hands behind his back. "That guy had a knife to me." He twitched and moved his hands to his pockets. "I really thought I was going to die. After he took you, I saw other people covered with sheets. I saw one of the bodies when the cops lifted it up. The person was really dead. And that's how I would've been if you didn't let him take you."

"If I wasn't there in the first place, you wouldn't have been in danger at all. Everyone who died there...it's my fault."

"That's crap and you know it. That guy was nuts. You said so yourself. You didn't want to die. But you would've let him kill you if he let me go." He swallowed hard. "Nobody's ever done something like that for me. Even at school. Bullies liked to steal my clothes after gym or dunk my head in the toilet. And nobody does anything. And heck, why should somebody go with somebody who's gonna kill them, just so I wouldn't die? But you did. You helped me. I'm not dead 'cause of you. I know he would've killed me if you hadn't done what he wanted. You could've just ran away. And maybe he wouldn't ever have gotten you." He gave Patrick a pat on the back and looked him in the eyes. "Some kid I don't even know does that for me. Almost anybody else would've left me to die. You didn't have to help me but you did anyway. That makes you a friend."

"Well, you ran around a store naked to let me get out." Patrick chuckled. "It was the least I could do."

"I did that mostly 'cause I wanted to flash Mom. And those old ladies from church who always pinch my cheeks." He giggled deviously. "They'll never be able to look at me again much less pinch my cheeks." He rubbed his hands together. "I love it. I'm finally free."

The two laughed.

"Mom and I are going out to lunch." Patrick pointed to the car with his thumb. "Wanna go with us? Hang out or something?"

"I dunno." Jacob kicked his feet together. "I'd have to run home and ask my mom."

"Why don't you just call her?" Julie came down the driveway. She held out her cell phone to Jacob. "Just let her know where you are. And you can put me on if she wants to verify it.

"That's okay. You don't have to."

She smiled. "Patrick could really use a friend after everything that's happened. You seem to me like you'd be a good friend." She pushed the phone closer to him. "Go on. Just give her a quick call and get her okay."

"Well, I guess it's okay." He smiled and took the phone. "She does sort of owe Patrick, I guess." He winked at him as he dialed his mother's number.

He received his permission in under a minute.

Taking the phone back from him, Julie signaled for them to get into the back seat. "All right boys, into the car."

The two eagerly hopped into the back seat of the car and buckled up.

As they pulled out of the driveway, Julie asked, "Any idea where you boys wanna go?"

Jacob said, "I don't care."

"I'll be happy any place we go. As long as the food's good."

Julie laughed. "Well, then. I think I have a good place in mind." She turned the corner and headed down the road.

Patrick could see Milo's street as they passed. It was bittersweet passing it knowing that he and his family now lay lifeless in boxes under the earth. But he had the hope that their spirits were waiting for him with God. He'd prayed for them every night since they died. And he'd continue doing it. It was his way to do something for them. He felt that they were praying for him.

Jacob noticed Patrick staring at the street. "Is there something special about that street or something? You were looking at it kind of weird."

Patrick didn't know how to answer. Not without sending himself into an emotional spell. And how could he explain everything to Jacob? Not to mention his similarities to Milo. Patrick didn't want Jacob to think he was just trying to replace his friend. He really did want to be Jacob's friend.

Julie stepped into answer for him. "Just a lot of good memories with friends, Jacob."

Patrick smiled. "Yeah, what she said. Good memories with friends. Ones that last even after they're gone." He laid his head back against the headrest and breathed a sigh of relief. He felt a little bit more of his pain ease away.

Jacob asked, "Yo, it's a bit quiet in here. Can we turn on the radio?"

Patrick said, "I don't know. We keep the stationed tuned only to the local Christian rock station. You think you can get into that?"

Jacob shot up. "Does a chicken pot pie taste really good?"

Both Julie and Patrick were silent. They weren't sure of what answer he expected.

Jacob realized how awkward the silence was. "Yeah. It does." He shrugged and shifted his eyes.

Julie and Patrick laughed.

"Christian rock it is!" Julie tuned on the radio.

Orchestrated violins coupled with intense rock beats in the tune that pumped out of the speakers.

"Oh, I love this song." Jacob put his hands up and started dancing.

"It's one of my favorites too." Patrick started mimicking Jacob's moves as the two moved to the beat.

"Careful boys." Julie flashed them a glare. "Don't rock too hard. We *are* in a car."

"Yes, Mom." Patrick slowed down. Just enough to be obedient.

Jacob moved his hands in a circular motion. "Your mom is so cool to let you listen to this and not complain."

Patrick nodded. "Yeah, my mom's the best." He looked up at her. "I always know that she's there. And she'd do anything for me." Anything. He'd seen just how much.

Julie's eyes met Patrick's in the rearview. For a moment, she wanted to say something to him. Then she decided that it was better not to. This simple moment was becoming too precious to her, and she knew better than to push her luck.

ACKNOWLEDGEMENTS

Acknowledgements suck. You can't possibly remember everyone you have to thank but you have to thank them because you couldn't possibly have finished the book without them. If I have forgotten anyone who in any way contributed to my growth as a writer, first and foremost, I thank you from the bottom of my heart.

I'd be ungrateful if I didn't pay due thanks to Jesus Christ, my Lord and my God. He blessed me with many gifts that I'm still struggling to use properly. I can't claim even a fraction of my words are exactly what He had in mind, but I hope one day something I write can bring Him glory. I'm just a transcriber, in the end, aiming to best give back what I have been given. It's a struggle, but I pray God continues to illuminate the way.

I thank my parents for contributing to my character, introducing me to the shows that have inspired me to tell stories of my own, and for passing on their own wild and twisted imaginations to me. I couldn't have done it without them.

I thank Jansina and Rivershore Books for making the publishing process so comprehensive. The process can be a monster that can often devour writers. Jansina has helped dominate this monster and finally make publication sensible again. Not to mention she's brought my book to life through formatting and cover designs that I could've only dreamed of.

I thank Trish: mentor, friend, and the one who gave me several hard kicks to refine this story. Her thoughtful and often rigorous critique helped drive this novel from draft to serious contender for publication. Not to mention all the pep talks.

I thank Gina, my random, kindred spirit of a friend. You helped me give that final refining to the book that helped smooth out all the rough edges. This book wouldn't be what it is without you. From our talks to your insistent revision suggestions, you helped this final product be the best that it could be.

I thank Katie for years of friendship and readership. In particular to this book, I thank her for providing pictures to help make this cover. (Thanks to her family for posing for them too.)

I thank all the readers over the past few years whose input has helped in one way or another. Mallory, Jessica, Erin, Kandle, Bryce, Rhoda D'ettore, Rhoda's mother (don't ask) and all those who've I've overlooked, I thank you for your input. You are all awesome.

I thank every TV show I've watched, every movie I've viewed, and every book I've read. Good or bad, it's the fuel that keeps this storytelling engine running.

I thank anyone who's ever slammed my writing, including an editor, for reminding me early that nothing I write could appeal to everyone.

I thank Julie, Dr. Lee, Prof. Pappas, Prof. Zelitch and Prof. Markovitz—my CCP Writing instructors and advisors. Your direction helped me earn the Creative Writing Certificate and grow as a writer. That experience shaped this novel into what it is now. And my classmates, you were all amazing. I thank each and every one of you for your critique and friendship.

I thank the NRTeam at NewReleaseTuesday for the fellowship, support, teaching, and friendship.

Lastly, I thank you, the reader. Whether mentioned above, friend or family, or one who knows me only through my writing, there'd be little point to this book without you. Writing is communication. You complete the process. In reading this book, you've breathed life into my words. For that, thank you.

Author Bio

For J.J. Francesco, the seeds of writing were planted with entering Reading Rainbow story contests as a young child. In the coming years, his writing often took unique forms—from making up his own Pokemon to imagining soap opera storylines in his head based off of anime characters. As a teenager, the writing moved to the page, starting with fanfiction, then serialized character dramas, and ultimately resulting in his first novels and short stories. "Mirror, Mirror," was his first publication in the award-winning college literary magazine *Limited Editions*, with "Untitled Short Film" following in the next annual issue. Literary magazine *Transient*, published a third short story, "After School." In 2014, J.J. published his debut novel, *Blood Chain*, through Rivershore Books. He also serves on the staff of the hit website, NewReleaseTuesday. J.J. lives in Philadelphia with his family.

RIVERSHORE BOOKS

www.rivershorebooks.com
blog.rivershorebooks. com
forum.rivershorebooks. com
www.facebook.com/rivershore.books
www.twitter.com/rivershorebooks
Info@rivershorebooks.com

www.ingramcontent.com/pod-product-compliance
Lightning Source LLC
Chambersburg PA
CBHW070753280626
47162CB00016B/264